The Darkest Prince

Rochelle McPherson

The Darkest Prince

Olympia Publishers
London

www.olympiapublishers.com
OLYMPIA PAPERBACK EDITION

A CIP catalogue record for this title is
available from the British Library.

ISBN: 978-1-80439-007-8

This is a work of fiction.
Names, characters, places and incidents originate from the writer's
imagination. Any resemblance to actual persons, living or dead, is
purely coincidental.

First Published in 2024

Olympia Publishers
Tallis House
2 Tallis Street
London
EC4Y 0AB

Printed in Great Britain

Dedication

To my darling Isabelle, never stop chasing your dreams, no matter how far out of reach they may seem.

Acknowledgements

My dear readers, what a journey this has been.
A truly wonderful and exciting journey that has enabled me to
share my little world with you. I am so thankful for all of the
incredible love and support that I have received whilst writing
The Darkest Prince.

To my wonderful friends, who always believed in my story, and
encouraged me to keep on writing, even when my dream
seemed so far out of reach—I thank you. I shared my first draft
with you. The very first, unedited, and awfully written first
draft! But your enthusiasm and endless encouragement pushed
me to keep going. You gave me the motivation and
determination to pursue my dreams and bring The Darkest
Prince to life. I thank my lucky stars to have such incredible
friends by my side.

And finally, my readers.
Thank you for choosing my book. From the bottom of my heart,
I am so grateful for you. The Darkest Prince is only the
beginning, and I truly do hope that you will continue to follow
this incredible journey!

CONTENTS

Chapter One

For the first time in thirteen hours, the Grill Steak House was almost quiet.

The noise of the chaotic day had settled, and Evie Gray felt her body relax as the final table waved goodbye. Heaving a sigh of desperate relief that her day was at last coming to an end, Evie followed the family of five to the door, locking it soundlessly behind them.

It had been a ridiculously busy day and her aching feet craved the release of a hot bath, but a quick glance at her watch told her it was already nearing midnight, and with a heavy sigh, her eyes fell onto the gold-plated mirror that hung on the wall beside the main doors.

Evie barely recognised the girl staring back; she was shocked to see how exhausted she looked. She lifted her hand, removing the bobble that held her hair in place, allowing a sea of wavy brown curls to fall loosely past her shoulders. Already, the tension in her head began to dissipate. With a yawn she glanced around the messy restaurant, sighing heavily. The bath would have to wait she thought miserably, and reluctantly she began to clear the tables, conscious that she was being watched.

Turning to face the kitchen doors, Evie smiled.

"Are you planning to help? Or are you just going to stand there gawking?" she asked, raising an eyebrow at the girl stood in the doorway.

Robyn Edwards giggled. With her slender figure leaning

against the wooden frame, she lifted her hand, brushing her black fringe away from her eyes.

"And take all that fun away from you? What kind of best friend would that make me?"

Evie rolled her eyes, smirking.

"I thought that last table would never leave! I'm exhausted!"

"It has been a tiring day," Robyn agreed with a yawn. "At least it's over now."

"Hallelujah! I'm not sure what hurts more; my head, or my feet!" Evie groaned.

The restaurant had been awfully busy for a Tuesday evening, and she couldn't quite understand why so many people had decided to eat out. For one thing, it was British winter. The air was freezing, and the ground covered with a layer of crisp, white frost, leaving her puzzled as to *why* these people would even *want* to leave the warmth of their homes, just to eat at the grill.

Not that the Grill wasn't a great restaurant, of course. In fact, it was one of the best in London, but if Evie had to choose between going out to dinner or staying in the comfort of her cosy apartment, she would have definitely chosen the latter.

Then again, she'd spent most of her life living in North Carolina, where eating out had never really been part of her life growing up.

"Definitely the feet," Robyn said. Then added with a huff, "Plus, it's Christmas next week, so it will only get worse!"

"At least we will have each other for support," Evie said hopefully.

"That, my friend, is very true," she replied. "Hey, are you almost done out here? I could really use some help in the kitchen. Michael has left me in a huge mess."

Evie glanced around the restaurant, looking at the messy

tables behind her, and said, "What do you need?"

"Could you take out the rubbish bags for me?" she asked. "I would do it myself, but I have so much prep to do, and I really just want to get started. Do you mind?"

"Okay, I guess I can do that," Evie said, and the two of them made their way into the large kitchen.

There were only four bags to take out. Thankfully, Michael, the Grill's head chef, had already disposed of the larger ones.

Leaving Robyn to her preparation, Evie grabbed the bags and headed into the cold night. The air was bitter against her bare arms, causing her to shiver as she tossed the bags into the already overflowing bin. Hugging her arms against a sudden, icy breeze, Evie turned on her heel and froze.

She wasn't alone.

The metal gates that acted as the back entrance into the restaurant were bolted shut, yet there he was, a man—tall, muscular, and inhumanly beautiful. He wore clothing from a long, forgotten past, and his impeccable silver hair made his familiar face appear sharper beneath the luminous moon.

His golden eyes were fixed on her, and she noted a muscle ticking in his tense jaw. He stared at her for what felt like eternity; the small yard where they stood filled with a heavy, brimming silence.

Despite the freezing temperature, he wore only a single grey T-shirt, black fighting pants, and a pair of heavy black boots. Around his pale neck, Evie recognised a grey choker necklace, and her eyes rested upon the silver stud that lay in the centre, shining brightly.

The moment Evie had feared for five long years had finally arrived.

They had found her.

"Lucas." Her voice quivered as she spoke his name.

"Evie," he replied, keeping his own voice quiet. "It's good to see you."

"You're...here..." Evie could hear the panic rising in her shaky voice. "How? How did you find me?"

"The *how* doesn't matter. I think the question you should be asking is *why*," Lucas said, and with the blink of an eye, he was stood in front of her, his face barely inches from her own.

Even after all this time, his inhumane speed still startled her. Lucas smiled, revealing a set of perfectly bright white teeth as he gripped her shoulders. He pulled her towards him, crushing her against his solid chest and said, "You have no idea how it feels to see you right now."

Evie pulled away quickly, her mind rushing with the memories she'd worked so hard to forget.

It had been one of the hottest days of the year so far, and she had spent the day alone in her room. Her parents were dead. Murdered without a trace of evidence. Her only brother missing, and her life slowly crumbling away with each passing second.

She was a witch and had spent most of her life practicing spells and enchantments as she trained to fight as a Guardian Warrior.

The Guardians were an ancient people, trained in the magical arts. For a thousand years it had been their duty to protect not only the magical world, but the non-magical world too. But Evie no longer wanted to be a part of that world. Her parents were murdered because of their magic, and she no longer wanted it in her life. She hated magic. She hated her parents for leaving her.

The day after they were buried, Evie ran, leaving the magical world as far behind as she possibly could...

"Why are you here Lucas?" Evie asked, slowly returning her

14

eyes to his.

"You're a part of The Circle, Evie," he said. "Ever since you left, our magic has weakened. We aren't in sync, and we haven't been for a while. We need you to come back to The Academy, back to The Circle. Without you, we can't do the job we were destined to do."

"What are you talking about?" Evie asked, confused by the desperate tone in which he spoke.

His eyes glimmered with an unspoken fear, and Evie felt herself crumble slightly at the intensity of his stare.

Whatever Lucas was about to tell her, she knew it couldn't be good.

"You're our only hope for defeating The Dark Prince," he said quietly. "We need you to come home."

"The Dark Prince?" Evie mouthed. "No, that's impossible. The Guardian's killed The Dark Prince. They told us so."

Evie recalled memories of the man who called himself *The Dark Prince* and frowned.

He was a witch, and a very powerful witch—judging from the stories her father had told her—who had turned his eye to dark magic. The Guardians had captured The Dark Prince, locking him away in the terrifying fortress known as Vanguard. Located far away in the middle of Black Sea, the fortress had been built by The Guardians to house the world's most dangerous magical creatures.

Lucas shook his head roughly as a dark shadow flashed across his face.

"They lied," he said through gritted teeth. "They never captured him. He was too powerful, and The Guardians were too embarrassed to admit defeat. So, they made up a story and have fed us nothing but lies.

"And now, thanks to their lies, he has spent the last few years gaining power. The Dark Prince is after something, but we don't know what it is. We have tried, and failed so many times to fight, but he is too powerful, and he has an army of demons at his beck and call. We took an oath to protect both the magical and non-magical world, Evie. We have to stop him before it's too late."

"Why would The Guardians lie?" Evie asked. "Do you hear how ridiculous that sounds, Lucas?"

Lucas shrugged. "Say whatever you want but it's true. A lot has changed since you left The Academy, Evie. The Guardians aren't what they used to be."

"If what you're saying is true, then I guess I am right in thinking The Guardians *weren't* the ones who sent you here?" she mused, raising an eyebrow.

Evie heard his answer through his silence and folded her arms across her chest.

"I'm sorry, Evie," he said. "Listen, we don't have a lot of time. You need to go home and get your things together. Everything will be explained once we get back to The Academy."

Evie recoiled, stumbling backwards.

"Academy? Lucas, I'm not going back. My life is here, in London, and this is where I am staying. I don't want to be a part of whatever bullshit magical war is coming. Magic is the reason I have no family, Lucas. I don't want anything to do with it. I'm sorry, but you've wasted your time coming here tonight. You should go now, before someone sees you."

"Evie, The Dark Prince is a threat to everyone. He's already killed over a hundred innocents, including normads. I'm sure you have heard about the couple who were brutally murdered last month, not far from where we stand?"

Evie nodded, feeling an icy chill trickle down her spine as she recalled the female news reporter talking about the two bodies that had been found in the park only a few streets from her apartment. The nightmares had haunted her for weeks.

"That was him," Lucas said angrily. "Well, his demons, and

there have been many more since. Every Academy in the world has been put on high alert. Our power stems from our ancestors, Evie. The Circle was chosen to serve and protect. Without you, we are nothing. We have to stop him."

Evie said nothing as she stared at Lucas. Her head throbbed painfully, and as she thought of Robyn her eyes began to sting. Robyn was her best friend. The first person she had met when she arrived in London all those years ago. The thought of leaving her tore at her heart, and she bit back the bile that began to rise in her throat. She didn't want to leave without saying goodbye, but she also didn't know how she would even begin to explain her reasons for leaving.

Robyn was a normad. A human. Who had no idea about the magical world Evie came from. She inhaled a deep breath and reluctantly met Lucas' golden eyes.

Chapter Two

A loud *thump* on the apartment door suddenly pulled Evie out of her thoughts. She had been lying on her bed for almost half an hour, surrounded by a pile of scrunched up clothes and a small empty suitcase.

Evie had left Robyn at the restaurant, claiming that her headache had grown worse, and had rushed back to the apartment they shared. Her mind was reeling with so many questions, both rational and irrational, and in an attempt to make sense of it all, she had thrown herself onto her bed, hoping the silence of her room might offer some peace for her aching head.

She didn't want to go back to North Carolina. That was a fact. Her life was here, in London, and she was happy.

The thought of going back to the life she had escaped terrified her, but the look in Lucas' eyes had told her that she didn't have a choice.

The banging continued, and Evie jumped to her feet, silently cursing Robyn for forgetting her key again. She had played out the conversation that she would have with Robyn over and over in her head, but she still didn't know exactly how she would find the words to say goodbye.

She reached out for the handle, but before her fingers could touch the metal, the door suddenly burst open with a loud, deafening bang.

"By the Gods, Cora was that necessary?"

A deep, familiar voice erupted from the hallway, forcing the hairs on the nape of Evie's neck to stand.

"Give people a chance to answer next time!"

"Unfortunately, time is against us Lucas."

Cora's sweet velvety voice filled the apartment, and as she came into view, Evie became momentarily dazzled by the electric blue eyes that now stared back at her.

Five long years, and Cora Jenkins had barely changed. Tall, beautiful, and bursting with self-confidence, Cora stood in the doorway. Glaring.

"Cora," Evie said quietly, watching as Cora waved her hand towards the door, forcing it to fit soundlessly back into its frame.

"Hello Evie," Cora replied, pushing her wavy, metallic silver hair behind her shoulders. "I hope you're packed and ready to leave."

"No, I'm not!" Evie said with urgency. "Look, I can't just *leave*. I have a life here! I have a job! I can't just disappear!"

"It wouldn't be the first time you *just* disappeared. You had a life in Wilmington too, but I can see you've forgotten all about that since living amongst normads."

Cora's voice was as cold as ice, matching the glare of her eyes as they bore into Evie.

"Unfortunately, you don't really have a choice, Evie. You took an oath and you're bound to stand by that oath. So, I suggest you get over yourself and go pack your things. We are leaving in ten minutes. And as for your *job,* I think your duty as a Guardian Warrior trumps waitress, don't you?"

"What about Robyn? I can't just leave without giving her some kind of explanation!" Evie demanded.

Cora chuckled. "Oh Evie, living in the land without magic has seriously altered you. Can you not tell a witch when you see one anymore? Wake up and smell the magic, girl. Robyn is one of us. She knows we are here...actually, she's on her way up right now."

"What did you just say?"

Her expression switched from shock to anger as she replayed Cora's words in her mind.

"You heard me," Cora replied.

"No. That's impossible. I would have known…she would have told me!"

"She is one of us. You'll find she belongs to the London Guardians. Honestly, you *seriously* didn't know?"

"I don't believe you," Evie snapped, ignoring the angry burn that threatened her eyes.

"Well, why don't you ask her for yourself," Cora crooned just as the apartment door swung open.

Robyn froze at the sight of the four figures in front of her, her eyes widening with fear. She looked at Evie, the colour draining from her face as their eyes met.

Robyn quickly looked away, turning her attention to Cora and the three others who stood behind her.

"You aren't supposed to be here!" she said in a hushed voice. "You said you would be gone by the time I got back!"

"Change of plan, honey," Cora said, admiring her perfectly manicured nails. "You're coming with us."

"I wasn't aware of the plan changing," Robyn said, and added, "When did this happen?"

"It was a last-minute decision," she said, her voice bored. "You're coming with us. That is all you need to know."

"Uh, hello?" Evie seethed. "Would anyone care to explain to me what the hell is going on?"

"I'm sorry Evie," Robyn said hurriedly. "You weren't supposed to find out like this…I'm so sorry."

"Enough of the chit chat," Cora warned. "We don't have time for this. We need to leave."

"I'm not going anywhere until someone explains to me *why* my best friend has been lying to me," Evie cried and turned to glare at Robyn. "You're a *witch*!"

Robyn nodded. "I am. Evie, I really am sorry. I wanted to tell you, really, I did. But Jack made a deal with the London Guardians, and I was sworn to secrecy. I couldn't tell you. I'm so sorry."

"Jack? He *made* a deal?" Evie was furious as she wiped her eyes. "So what, you've been *spying* on me? Giving reports on my life?"

"No! It's nothing like that, Evie. I swear to you!" Robyn pleaded. "Jack just wanted to make sure that you were safe, that's all."

"Bullshit!" Evie growled. "Where is *Jack* anyway? Why isn't *he* here?"

"Jack is a Guardian Leader. He has more important things to do with his time than chase *you* half-way across the world," Cora sneered. "Now can we please get a move on. We really do need to leave."

"All this time." Evie sighed, ignoring Cora as she stared at Robyn. "How did I not know?"

"Because you cuffed your powers sweetie," a soft voice said, forcing Evie's eyes to lift.

Tessa Henley had changed a lot since Evie had last seen her, and as she twisted her head, she was surprised by the woman who stood before her.

Gone was the shy, timid teenager, and in her place stood a young woman filled with the same confidence Evie had always admired in Cora. Her long brown hair was gone, replaced by a short, pixie like bob with luminous pink streaks that hovered above her shoulders. She wore a pair of black framed glasses and a silver stud sparkled in her nose.

Evie glanced down at her arm, noting the thick, black leather bracelet on her left wrist.

"Oh. Right."

"The bracelet doesn't just block out *your* magic, it blocks out the magic of those around you too," Tessa explained. "You would have never known."

"Right, that's enough talking," Cora pressed urgently. "We need to leave. Zac, call Flynn and tell him to have the van ready in five minutes."

Zac looked up from his phone, momentarily confused by Cora's instruction. "Flynn?"

"Yes, Zachary…Flynn. Our driver?" Cora replied. "How many times have we been through this plan today? Now is not the time for a relapse in memory Zac! Pull yourself together, darn it!"

Zachary Mills said nothing as he punched several numbers into his phone. For a moment, his dark eyes fell onto Evie's, and an icy chill trickled down her spine.

His eyes, so dark and empty, resembled a bottomless pit, and it was all she could do not to rush over to him. Zac shook his head, as though in response to her unspoken question, and turned away. Evie watched his thick, muscular figure leave the apartment, wondering what on earth had happened to him to make him look so… *broken*.

"Seriously, why is that guy never on the same page as us?" Cora sneered.

"Give him a break." Tessa sighed. "Jack shouldn't have made him come with us tonight."

"Well *Jack* has made us all do things we don't particularly want to do," she hissed.

"What are you talking about?" Evie asked, ignoring the bitterness in Cora's velvety voice.

"Evie, I'm sure there are a lot of questions that are simply burning inside of you, but now is not the time for them. We have to get the hell out of here and back to Wilmington. You can ask whatever damn questions you want when we are in the safety of The Academy. Now, for the final time, will you *both* go and pack your things."

Chapter Three

The night air was bitterly cold against Evie's face as she stood outside the apartment building.

She twisted her head slightly, staring at the red and brown bricks that had been her home for the last five years, and felt a wave of emotions flood through her.

It wasn't the biggest apartment, nor was it the warmest, but the monthly rent had been cheap, and it had eventually become her home.

She would miss it. Miss the cosiness of her room, and the endless nights sat on the couch watching silly movies with Robyn. She would miss everything about the life she had created here, despite the circumstances that had led her to London in the first place.

Evie forced her eyes away from the apartment and lifted her head towards the inky black sky. The moon, so luminous and bright, was partially covered by thick white clouds, but they did not stop the beams from falling onto the streets below.

She felt someone move beside her and turned her head slightly to see Lucas.

Evie stared at him, unable to peel her eyes away. His own golden eyes were fixed on their surroundings, and she noted the sharpness of his stunningly perfect features. His mouth twitched slightly at the corners, and she quickly forced her eyes away as his mouth curved into a smile.

Lucas had always been handsome, but since becoming a vampire, he had become so much more.

Evie remembered the terrible day when Lucas had been bitten. The day death had torn away his human soul, leaving behind a devastatingly beautiful man, hell bent on fighting against the life he had been cursed to live.

Evie blinked away the memory as a black van pulled up beside the curb. They climbed in, and the van sped away into the night.

"*You* were supposed to be here ten minutes ago Flynn, where the hell were you?" Cora demanded from the front passenger seat.

"Sorry. I got lost," the driver, Flynn, replied in a dull tone.

"Pathetic!" Cora hissed. "You weren't followed, were you?"

"No," he replied.

"How are we getting to Wilmington?" Evie asked.

"We're flying," Lucas answered, with a smirk.

"Okay, but Heathrow isn't this far out," she said, confused by the darkness of the country lanes they were now speeding along.

"We aren't going to Heathrow," Cora said. "We can't risk travelling amongst the normads and giving The Dark Prince an excuse to hurt more innocent people. We are already taking a huge risk just by being here."

"So, if we aren't going to Heathrow, where are we flying from?" Evie wanted to know, and added nervously, "I'm assuming it is a plane we will be flying in, right?"

Cora's heavy sighs were enough to tell Evie that she was annoying her, but she didn't care. She had every right to ask questions.

"You assumed correctly," Cora said. "Can we stop with the questions now, please? You're giving me a headache and I'm trying to focus."

"I'll ask whatever damn *questions* I want, Cora," Evie snapped. "I think I have every right, since you guys have practically just kidnapped me from my own home."

"Actually, no you don't, and for the record, no one has kidnapped you," she said sharply. "You're the one that left Evie. *You* made that decision. Instead of turning to your friends for support, you chose the easy option and ran away from your problems rather than face them. The only reason we are here is because Jack ordered us to come. None of us actually want you to come back."

"Cora!" Tessa declared, staring at Evie apologetically. "She didn't mean that."

"Yes, I did. Every damn word of it," Cora snapped, and as the van came to an abrupt stop, she forced the door open and hurtled out into the darkness.

"Ignore everything she just said," Tessa said, embarrassed by Cora's words. "She's a little ratty lately."

"A little?" Lucas said, rolling his eyes as he followed them out of the van to stand on the snow-covered grass. "I think we can both agree that she's a total bitch. I'm just not afraid to say it."

"I am not afraid of Cora Jenkins!" Tessa mumbled. "She shouldn't have said those things. It was uncalled for and completely untrue!"

"We all know how much of a bitch Cora has been lately," Zac said, as he moved to stand beside Evie. "Don't take it personally. Are you alright?"

"I'm fine," Evie replied, watching as Cora stormed ahead.

An explosion of rippling anxiety surged through Evie's body as she watched numerous golden sparks erupt from Cora's hands.

Magic.

Evie clutched her sides, unable to shake off the cold shiver that seeped over her body.

It was the first time she had seen magic in over five years, and the sight of those magical sparks made her feel nervous. Evie inhaled a deep breath, silently trying to control the emotions that threatened to overwhelm her, but despite how desperately she wanted to look away, she could not remove her eyes from Cora's retreating figure.

"I should talk to her," Evie said quietly.

"I would wait until she's calmed down," Zac advised. "Those sparks she's dishing out *hurt*. We should make our way to the jet. Cora is right about one thing; we do have a tight schedule to keep."

"Where is this jet?" Robyn asked.

She was keeping her distance and walking a few feet behind.

"It's not too far," Lucas answered. "I'm Lucas by the way."

"Yes, I know." Robyn giggled, and Evie could hear the nervousness in her tone.

Evie smiled, keeping her eyes ahead. She still wasn't ready to talk to Robyn, but she knew she wouldn't be able to stay mad at her for long.

The five of them continued to walk on, following Cora further into the dark field. It was difficult to see what was in front of them, and after a few moments Tessa lifted her hand, allowing it to erupt with a bright, white light.

The same nauseating feeling suddenly erupted in Evie's stomach at the sight of more magic, but the sound of Cora's angry voice forced the rising bile in her throat right back into her stomach.

"Where is it?"

The five of them ran towards Cora's frozen body, staring at a large, and very *empty* space.

The jet was nowhere to be seen. Neither was Flynn.

"Something isn't right..." Zac began, his eyes rapidly scanning the field. "Cora? Where is *Flynn*?"

A loud explosion suddenly erupted ahead, closely followed by an illumination of red and green sparks that shot excitedly into

27

the sky. Panic filled Evie's body, and she subconsciously moved closer to Lucas' side.

The light in Tessa's hand vanished quickly, and the field was filled with deep, menacing screeches.

"The Dark Prince?" Cora mouthed.

"*Demons*," Lucas hissed, shaking his head.

His enhanced vampire senses alerted him to the demonic aura that rippled through the air, forcing his body to become rigid beside Evie.

"How many?" Cora asked urgently.

"About a dozen," Lucas said. "Normads too, though I can't tell how many."

"We need The Guardians!" Cora declared. "They can open up a portal!"

"Cora, The Guardians don't know we are here!" Lucas snapped. "Jack is who we need. We can't open a portal without *his* magic!"

"No cell reception," Tessa shouted, shoving her phone into her back pocket. "Damn it!"

"We can try and open a portal ourselves," Zac quipped. "There are enough of us here. It should work!"

"Jack is the only one of us who can open portals," Cora said, shaking her head. "It won't work without him. You know this!"

"We won't know unless we try," he said. "Look, with our magic, as well as Robyn's, it could work. We have to at least try, Cora. Unless you would prefer to fight whatever is coming for us!"

"Okay, fine," Cora seethed. She twisted her head, and her eyes fell onto Evie's hands. "Take that ridiculous bracelet off your wrist. We will need *your* magic too."

"I... I can't..." Evie's voice quivered.

Her chest ached with rippling anxiety. Breathing became difficult as her sweat-licked hands began to tremble.

Evie lowered her head, staring at the snow-covered ground, feeling scorned by the numerous eyes that bore into her. Words failed her, and her mouth grew dryer with each passing second.

Seconds turned to minutes, but Evie did not move. Every inch of her body had frozen.

Evie felt him before she heard him.

Lucas stood in front of her, his hands resting upon hers as he unclenched her fists, holding her hands against his.

"It's okay," he said, and despite the urgency of the situation they were in, his voice remained soft. "I know you're scared, but you have to push past it. If you don't, and this ends in a fight, you will be powerless.

"I know you haven't used magic in a long time," he said. "But it is still within you. You don't have to be scared. You're a witch, and magic is your birth right. I know it destroyed you, but you can't let that consume you, Evie. We need you. Now more than ever, we need you. Take off the bracelet."

Tears filled her eyes as she reached for the bracelet, her fingers caressing the coolness of the leather. She gripped the bracelet, tucking her fingers around it until she was confident with her hold.

Sucking in a deep breath, she ripped the leather with a reluctant tug.

An explosion erupted, forcing her to fly backwards through the air. Evie fell to the ground with a hard thud, her eyes widening with utter panic as she lifted her hands.

They both held a fiery orange glow, illuminating the perplexed faces of her friends.

"What was that?" Tessa gasped, as Lucas and Zac pulled Evie back to her feet.

"I have no idea," Evie said, staring at her hands as though they did not belong to her. The glow had vanished, but her hands were burning. "My hands...they feel as though they are on *fire*!"

Burning. She was burning. Her entire core danced a steady beat as the flames flickered before her eyes. Yet despite the heat that now raged through her body, Evie could not remove her stare from the flames.

"Evie! What are you doing?" Cora demanded. "Stop it! Now!"

"I'm not doing anything," Evie said quietly.

She was mesmerised by the sight before her.

"We're too late!" Tessa cried. *"They're coming!"*

The menacing demonic screeches were louder now. Evie forced her eyes away from the flames, watching as a hunched group of figures moved with a deathly stealth towards them. The fire in her hands grew hotter, and without much conscious notice, Evie found herself slowly moving forwards.

"Evie, stop! What are you doing?" Robyn yelled, gripping her elbow.

"Get behind me!" Evie ordered. "Go…get ready to open the portal…"

"What?" Cora demanded.

"Do it Cora!" Evie yelled. "Trust me! Do it now!"

Magic pulsated within her, rushing through her veins, eager to escape its dormant prison.

Evie paused. Standing motionless as the flames in her palms grew. She no longer felt nauseous. She no longer felt nervous. Her breathing steadied; her heart no longer thumping beneath her chest.

She released the wicked flames, forcing them straight at the demonic creatures. Excited voices quickly turned to agonising, deathly, high-pitched screams as her fire engulfed the creatures. Evie turned, racing back to where the others stood. She squeezed Robyn's hand with her own, and the others followed suit.

Evie closed her eyes, focusing on her old home, and was suddenly gripped with an image of The Academy. She smiled as a shimmering oval shaped hole appeared before them, and without a second thought, Evie twisted her head to Cora, and nodded once.

One by one, The Circle hurtled themselves into the darkness of the portal.

Chapter Four

Evie lay with her face buried against the coldness of hard, wet pebbles. Slowly, she lifted her head and was overcome by a rush of searing pain. She lifted her hand to clutch her head, and was met with a warm, sticky wetness dripping down her cheek.

The smell of fresh blood caused her stomach to churn.

"Evie!"

Robyn ran towards her. Her heavy footsteps louder in the silent night.

"Gods, Evie! Are you alright? What are you doing on the floor?" Robyn helped her stand up, steadying her with her arm. "You're bleeding!"

"What happened?" Evie asked.

"I don't know. We went through the portal, and everything just went… black…" Robyn replied hoarsely. "I didn't know you had *fire magic*! It's really unheard of!"

"I didn't know either," Evie said, confused. She felt drained. "I've never done anything like that before. Where are the others?"

"Right here!"

Zac's voice drifted towards them, and as her eyes adjusted, Evie felt relief wash over her as four figures hurried forwards.

"Are you both okay?" he asked.

"She's bleeding," Robyn answered. "I think she hit her head."

"I'm fine," Evie said, waving her off. "What happened to the demons?"

"*You* had better start talking," Cora demanded. "What the hell was that? Where did that fire come from?"

"I don't know," Evie said. "It just happened. What's the big deal? We're safe, aren't we?"

"*The big deal?*" Cora eyed her up and down. Disbelief flooded her face. "Evie we're witches. We don't have that kind of magic! This is serious, we need to find Jack, now!"

"Oka..."

The pain in her head suddenly became crippling, and her eyes blurred as she stumbled, slipping into an unconsciousness that her body did not want to fight.

The last thing she heard was the sound of her best friend, screaming her name as she fell to the ground.

***

Evie woke to the smell of fresh lavender and honey. She opened her eyes, and a soft yellow glow brightened her surroundings. She pulled herself up into a sitting position, wincing slightly as a dull ache rippled through her head. Though the pain wasn't as severe as before, it did not stop her from clutching the side of her head.

"Evie!" Robyn's voice was a flutter of worry. "Dear Gods, you scared me! Are you alright?"

"What happened?" Evie asked, wiping her eyes on her sleeve.

"You passed out!" Robyn told her as Tessa, Lucas, and Zac edged closer to the bed.

Evie propped herself against the pillows, taking in the room. The infirmary had always reminded her of a Victorian style hospital. It had six, metal framed beds that were separated by tall wooden dividers. The stained-glass windows were high in the walls, and the old brown beams on the ceiling made the room feel slightly enclosed. But it was welcoming, and surprisingly Evie felt herself relax.

"I passed out?" she repeated, frowning.

"Yeah, you did," Robyn said. "We couldn't wake you up. Lucas had to carry you all the way here! How do you feel now?"

"Drained," Evie admitted, casting her eyes around the infirmary. "Where is Cora?"

"She's talking to Jack," Tessa answered. She turned to Zac and Lucas. "He will want to know that Evie's awake. Maybe one of us should go and tell him?"

"I'll go," Zac offered. "Glad you're feeling better Evie."

"Thanks," she said, watching as he left.

"I didn't have *you* down as the passing-out kinda gal," Lucas teased. "Are you sure you're a Guardian?"

"What can I say? My magic is a little bit rusty," she replied, smiling. "What *did* happen in that field?"

"Well, we were hoping you could tell us that," Tessa said. "Honestly, you just changed. One minute you were a nervous wreck, and the next you were this fire-wielding badass! You took care of those demons with one hit, and you opened the portal without so much of a whisper of our magic, Evie."

"I did?" Evie said, biting her lip. Her entire body ached, and she could feel the exhaustion slowly creeping in. "Witches can't wield fire magic. Fire abilities belong to...dark magic...to demons..."

"Yes, you're right," Tessa said. "I'm sure there is an explanation to all this. Try not to worry too much. You need rest. You whacked your head pretty hard when you passed out."

Evie sank back into the pillows, her mind filling with hundreds of questions, but before she could start asking them, the old oak door to the infirmary swung open.

She twisted her head and was stunned by the figure that stood in the open doorway.

Jack Saunders was *hot*.

Gone was the skinny, boyish teen she had last seen five years ago. In his place, stood a man, tall and muscular, with chestnut brown hair, and eyes so blue it was difficult *not* to drown in them. He wore black clothing, and his sleeveless T-shirt revealed two very strong, toned arms, one of which—his left—was covered with tattoos that stretched up to his shoulder.

Jack smiled as he strode towards her bed, his entire body oozing with a confidence that caused her stomach to flutter.

She found it difficult *not* to stare.

"Evie," he said. "It's good to see you."

"Jack," Evie said his name, and suddenly felt nervous.

Jack smiled and twisted his head towards the others.

"Would you guys mind giving us a minute? Cora's in the common room getting pizza."

"Sure," Lucas said, before turning to Evie. "We'll save you some pizza, just try not to pass out again, will you?"

"I'll try my best." She smiled.

Once they left, Jack waved his hand towards the door, closing it behind them and turned back to Evie, seating himself in the chair beside her bed.

"You look like hell, Gray." He smirked.

"So would you, if you'd just been kidnapped," she snapped at him. "You made them bring me here. Why?"

"Still as dramatic as ever," Jack teased. "You already know why Evie, and after tonight, I would have thought you would understand the seriousness of the situation."

Evie sucked in a deep breath, ignoring the ache in her head. "How did you know where I was? And more importantly, *why did you order Robyn to spy on me*?"

Jack sighed, rolling his eyes. It seemed clear to Evie that he had been expecting this. She had always been known for her hot temper.

"Firstly, I did not order Robyn to spy on you. I only wanted to make sure you were safe. You left without talking to anyone. What was I supposed to do? You were sixteen years old. Your parents had just been murdered. I couldn't just let you wonder off by yourself. I reached out to Robyn because I knew you would become friends, and I was right.

"Secondly, in the nicest way possible, you're not the best at *hiding*."

Evie grimaced, annoyed, but said nothing.

"I'm sorry you had to find out about Robyn the way you did," he said, keeping his voice soft.

"You made a deal with the London Guardians," she seethed. "You used her spy on me."

"I did not use her to spy on you," Jack retorted. "I made a deal with The Guardians so that Robyn could look out for you. What else was I supposed to do? Just leave you to fend for yourself. You were a young witch living amongst normads with no friends or family around you."

"I would have been fine," she said coldly.

He gave a flat stare and said, "So you and Robyn aren't friends? Because if I *had* left you to it, she certainly would not be in your life right now."

"Shut up," she snapped, unable to find the words to argue against his statement, "you shouldn't have made her do it."

36

"I didn't make her do anything," he said crisply. "Look, we can sit here and argue all night about this, but I think we can both agree that we have more important things to discuss."

"You're an *ass,* Saunders," she said, ignoring the corner of his mouth as it stretched into a smirk. "You know what happened in London?"

Jack nodded.

"I don't know why you created that magic, or how you were able to do it, but it is something we will need to look into."

"Do you think I have demonic blood inside me?" Evie asked, horrified by the thought.

"I highly doubt it," Jack said, rolling his eyes. "I'm sure there is a simple explanation behind all this."

"A simple explanation?" she mouthed. "You know as well as I do, witches don't have this kind of magic, because it is dark magic, Jack."

"We will look into it," he said softly, and rose from the chair. "I'll let you get some rest. We can talk more tomorrow."

"No!" Evie said and jumped to her feet.

The movement made her feel nauseous again, and she wobbled on her feet as a wave of dizziness surged through her body. Jack reached out his hand, grasping her shoulder.

"The magic you used in that field was powerful, Evie. It drained you of your energy and caused you to burnout, and eventually *pass* out," he said softy. "You really should lie down and rest."

"I don't want to lie down!" Evie protested. "My clothes are damp, and I'm hungry."

Jack grinned. "Fine. But I'll walk with you. You're like Bambi on ice right now."

"I'm not that fragile. I can walk by myself," she said moodily, pushing past him.

"I didn't say you were," Jack muttered.

Chapter Five

Evie was surprised by how much The Academy still looked the same. The infirmary was located in the basement of the old manor, and as she climbed the stone steps to the ground floor, her mind was filled with memories of her life here, before she'd left five years ago.

The Academy was centuries old and had been built by the original Guardians. The manor resided on a sprawling estate, complete with its own stables, numerous gardens, and outer buildings that housed the Guard's training rooms. It was used as a school for witches who had shown the talent and ability to become a Guardian Warrior.

The manor itself was set over three stories and ran purely on magic. From the outside, the normads, or *non-magical* people, would see an old, derelict manor, signposted with warnings of danger.

Evie had always wondered why the normads had never done anything about the derelict sight and remembered asking her parents the question.

Magic dear, her father had told her with a smile. *The normads see the manor and wonder why it still stands, but then forget about it almost instantly. The Guardians imposed a protection spell of their own which causes the normads to forget what they have seen once they have seen it.*

The ground floor opened up to a large welcoming foyer with a grand staircase in its centre. Candlelight flickered from the sconces on stone walls, glowing brightly as Evie walked along a quiet corridor towards the common room.

The sound of muffled voices filled the halls, along with the smell of freshly cooked pizza, and her stomach rumbled as she found the door to the large, oval shaped room.

The common room was ablaze with light, and a welcoming warmth erupted from the open fire as the flames burned away in the hearth. Robyn, Tessa, Cora, Zac, and Lucas were spread out on the armchairs, each with a slice of pizza in their hand.

"I hope there's some left for me," Evie said, seating herself in between Robyn and Lucas.

The smell of freshly cooked pizza made her forget all about her damp clothes.

"Here you go," Robyn said, handing her the pizza box. "There's more in the other box Jack."

"Thank you, but I've got to go," Jack said. "I'll see you all in the morning."

"What about The Guardians?" Evie frowned. "Won't they want to know that I'm back?"

"They already know," Jack replied, and noting the expression on her face, he added, "don't worry about The Guardians. Eat and rest up. We can talk in the morning."

He left then, gently closing the door behind him.

Evie took a bite of pizza, sinking back into the chair.

"I forgot how good this tastes here."

"Better than London?" Tessa grinned.

"One hundred per cent!" she smiled.

"Traitor!" Robyn chuckled, and added, "Are you feeling better now?"

"A little. My head still aches," she replied. "But I think that's a combination of hitting it and all the questions I have."

"I'm sure you have lots to ask," Zac said.

"I need you to tell me everything that has happened since I left, so that I can make sense of it."

"Where do we even start?" Zac said, looking to the others for support.

"Maybe we could start with *your* story?" Tessa suggested, and Zac nodded in agreement. "I mean, it's how all this started really, don't you think?"

Zac nodded.

"Two years ago, I was conducting a training exercise in the Enchanted Forest with a group of third year students." Zac began his story, sitting on the very edge of the chair as he spoke.

"We were ambushed. Only we didn't realise The Dark Prince had recruited *others*.

"The werewolves took us by complete surprise. Myself and two students were bitten. We later found out that The Dark Prince had ordered the wolves to *bite* but not *kill*, as he hoped to recruit us to his side too. Well, he got two out of the three. I managed to escape and hid in the forest. It was Jack who found me. I was barely alive, but somehow he got me back to The Academy just in time. Thankfully, the werewolf who bit me didn't bite me for long enough, so the venom didn't fully enter my bloodstream. With a special tonic, I can still carry on as normal. It's only when the full moon is near that I struggle."

He paused, looking away as though embarrassed by his tale. Evie reached for his hand. "Zac, I'm sorry."

"It's taken me a while to come to terms with it, but I'm okay now," he told her, and added, "that was when The Dark Prince officially came out of hiding. The attack on myself and the others was his way of letting us know he was back."

"How did The Guardians react?" Evie asked. "They told us

The Dark Prince was dead."

"They acted just as surprised as us," Zac said angrily. "We never got an explanation."

"So, you're not truly a werewolf?" Robyn asked.

"I have werewolf healing abilities," he explained. "And my senses are more enhanced. The only time I struggle, is when there is a full moon, but thankfully, I have never transformed. The wolfbane tonic helps."

"That is bloody awesome!" Robyn exclaimed.

"I guess, in a weird way, it is kind of awesome," Zac said, grinning as he added, "I do heal super-fast!"

Evie smiled. "I guess it's bonus points for us then, to have both an almost-werewolf *and* a vampire on our side! You guys didn't really need me after all!"

"This isn't a joke!"

Cora's voice erupted within the common room, and as Evie turned towards her, she could almost feel the atmosphere in the room turn to ice.

"We have lived through this every single day for the past two years, whilst *you've* been wrapped up in London living your best life.

"Every day we train, and we fight to protect both our world, and the normads. We've seen so many murders and unexplained disappearances. You have no idea what it has been like for any of us. And you're right. We *don't* need you."

"Cora!" Tessa exclaimed, throwing Evie an apologetic look before twisting her head back to Cora. "What the hell is wrong with you?"

"No, Tessa, it's fine," Evie said, "let her get it all off her chest."

Cora glared.

"You left us Evie. You broke The Circle and left us weak, all because you couldn't handle being on your own. You're not the first person to lose their parents, and you certainly won't be the last. You're the reason our magic isn't strong enough to stand against The Dark Prince. You're the reason we are failing…"

Steadying her rising temper, Evie focused on her breathing, but with every venomous word that left Cora's mouth, Evie could feel the veins beneath her skin begin to pulsate as a wave of relentless power surged through her body.

And then, her hands were burning, really burning, and as she looked down, Evie saw the fiery flames once again, dancing within her palms.

Cora froze, staring at Evie with wide, terrified eyes.

"What are you doing?" she asked anxiously.

"Evie!" Robyn declared. "Evie, for Christ's sake, stop it!"

"I can't," Evie said urgently.

Her blood heated as the flames burned brighter, hotter. Her skin tingled, sweat licking her forehead. She felt her veins, pulsating wickedly. Crackling to life with the embers of her fiery flames as a menacing heat surged through her body, latching onto every piece of her being.

"Someone get Jack, now!" She heard Tessa yell.

"Are you planning to use that, Miss Gray?"

The fire in Evie's palms continued to burn as she slowly turned to identify the deep, husky voice which had spoken.

A man was stood by the door, his golden-brown face expressionless as he stared.

The man was tall and slim, with shoulder length, jet black hair that he'd tied into a ponytail behind his head.

The side of his neck was painted with a tattoo of Latin text that appeared to snake down to his chest. The new arrival was handsome, in a boyish way, but the confident yet arrogant way in which he stood made Evie feel instantly wary of him.

"Miss Gray?" The man repeated her name, crossing his arms. "Please could you put the flames out before you set The Academy on fire."

"I can't," Evie told him through gritted teeth. Pain crippled her now, her body shaking as her temperature soared.

"Has this happened before?" he asked curiously.

"Um," she began, unsure of whether or not she should tell the truth. She didn't know this man, and something was telling her not to trust him. "No. No it hasn't."

The man paused for a moment, contemplating her answer, but after a few seconds, he shook off whatever thought had crossed his mind and strode towards her, placing himself directly in front.

"You have to clear your mind. Empty every thought you have and focus. You control your magic. The magic does not control you. Do you understand? Focus and take control."

Evie listened, closing her eyes. The burning in her palms was unbearable, but she did as he said, focusing on the magic that raged within her. The heat that pulsated through her body began to slow, the burning replaced with a cold sensation as though someone or something was flushing her blood with icy water.

She knew the flames had gone before she opened her eyes. Her hands were her own again. Relief and exhaustion flickered through her as she lifted her head. The man was still there, staring at Evie with a puzzled expression. For a moment the room remained silent.

"Thank you," Evie finally said, meeting his dark eyes.

"Magic is connected to our emotions," he said. "If we give way to our emotions, then we allow our magic to seize control, and thus burn us out."

Evie nodded, clenching her fists by her sides as he continued to stare at her.

"I heard raised voices?" he pressed.

"It was nothing," Cora said hurriedly. "Just a minor disagreement. It's sorted now."

"I do hope so. Now is not the time for us to turn against one another," he said sharply. "It's rather late. You should all turn in for the night. The Guardians have requested a meeting with The Circle first thing, and it would not be prudent for any of you to be late."

"Of course. We were just about to head upstairs," Cora agreed.

"Very well then. Goodnight," he said, and without another word, he left the common room, closing the door behind him.

"Who the bloody hell was that?" Robyn asked in a hushed whisper.

"That was the Inquisitor," Cora replied. "We should all go to bed. Unless you want him back in here."

Evie sighed, spinning round to face the others, and whispered, "She really does hate me, doesn't she?"

"Just ignore her," Lucas said, wrapping his arm around her shoulders. "She'll come around eventually. Just leave her to calm down."

Evie nodded but said nothing as she wrapped her arms around herself. She felt utterly drained.

"Let's go upstairs, we can talk there," Tessa suggested, and everyone nodded in agreement.

Lucas cleaned the room with a swish of his hand. The pizza boxes disappeared, and the cushions straightened themselves on the old chairs. The fire in the hearth, burning merrily just moments ago, had now burnt out, leaving the room smelling of freshly burnt ash.

***

The Circle had their own designated quarters within The Academy, located on the very top floor of the manor. There were four bedrooms, a small kitchen, two bathrooms, and a spacious living room.

Evie smiled as she took in the familiarity of the room. She had only spent a year there before she decided to leave.

"You guys are in this room," Tessa said, pointing to the door on the other side of the living room. "The beds have already been made up for you both. Cora and I are right next door, and the boys are over there. Jack still has the privilege of having his *own* room."

"Perks of being a leader," Lucas said sarcastically.

"How many times have I offered to swap with you?"

Jack's voice sounded from the kitchen. He walked into the living room smiling.

"I thought you lot would have gone to bed already."

"I'm going. Goodnight," Cora said quietly.

She hadn't spoken a word since leaving the common room and silently left, shutting her bedroom door behind her.

"That girl!" Tessa sighed. "I honestly don't know what is with her lately. She's so moody and grumpy all the time!"

"So, it's not just because I've come back then?" Evie asked, as she sat herself next to Zac.

Tessa shook her head.

"She's been like it for months. I wouldn't take it personally."

"Has something happened?" Jack wanted to know.

45

"I just met the Inquisitor," Evie told him, and added with a sarcastic grin, "*you* could have warned me about him."

Jack frowned. "What happened?"

"He arrived just in time to stop super-witch over there from turning to common room into a darn furnace," Lucas teased.

"What?" Jack went rigid, his lips forming a tight line. "Why did none of you come get me?"

"Well, we were about to, but the Inquisitor walked in before we could," Tessa explained.

Jack took a shuddering breath as he ran his fingers through his hair, and said, "So Hayden knows about your ability?"

Evie nodded. She was exhausted, and her body craved the softness of the bed that she knew lay just beyond the closed door on the far side of the room. But one look at Jack's taut body told her she wouldn't be going anywhere just yet.

"He asked me if it had happened before. I lied and told him no. Should I have told him the truth? About it happening in London?"

"No, you did the right thing," Jack said. "Was anyone hurt?"

"Of course not!" Evie said, stung by the accusing tone in his voice. "I would never..."

"I didn't mean it like that," he said, before inhaling a deep breath.

As he did, Evie noticed the muscles in his arms tense. He looked, for want of a better word, *stressed*.

"There's something you're not telling us," Evie said, frowning. "What is going on?"

"It's nothing," he replied. "You should go to bed. It's late, and we have an early start tomorrow."

"I wish people would stop telling me to go to bed. I'm twenty-one not twelve!" Evie exploded.

The tips of her fingers tingled as a fiery rage rippled through her. She clenched her fists, inhaling a long, deep breath as she tried to calm her temper.

"Listen, it's been a very long day for me, and a lot has already happened. I want to know what the hell is going on. And don't you dare even think about lying to me, Saunders!"

Jack tensed for a moment, before sitting down on the chair opposite.

"I don't think it is *wise* for others to find out about your abilities just yet, *especially* the Inquisitor."

"But he already knows, he saw me do it," she said pointedly.

"I had hoped to keep this between us," he said. "Did Hayden say anything else to you?"

Evie shook her head.

"He helped me to control it," she told him. "He didn't say anything else. Why am I able to create this kind of magic but no one else can? Fire magic is an element of *dark magic*, Jack. It's demonic, I *shouldn't* be able to do anything like this."

"I don't know," he admitted. "Fire magic is an element of Fae magic, and until today, it has only ever been seen used by the Fae, and *certain* demons. As far as I know, you're the first witch who has been able to produce this kind of magic."

"The Fae?" Evie gasped, and added worriedly, "do you think I could have Fae in my bloodline?"

Jack shook his head. "It's a possibility. Hence why I think we should keep this between ourselves for now. The Fae aren't a popular topic amongst The Guardians."

Evie released a heavy sigh. "The Fae war," she said. "Should I be worried?"

"About what?" he asked, his eyes softening.

"That I could potentially have either demonic or Fae blood

47

running through my veins? They're both on par with each other! The Fae are just as evil as demons, Jack!"

"You're so bloody dramatic!" Robyn teased, rolling her eyes. "I think we would know if you possessed demonic blood. I mean, you can be *cranky as hell* when you want to be, but you're definitely no demon."

"Ha-ha!" Evie smirked and turned back to Jack. "So, what do we do? What should *I* do? I could barely control it downstairs. What if it happens again?"

She didn't tell him that it had almost happened again merely seconds ago.

"The only thing you can do right now is just focus on *trying* to control it," Jack said. "You've been away from magic for a long time, so it will be difficult to reconnect, especially with this new ability, but you're going to have to try. Keep your emotions in check, and you will be fine."

"Keep my emotions in check?" She gave him a flat stare. "Easier said than done, Jack, don't you think? Cora said a few mean words to me, and I almost set the common room on fire."

He smiled, and she noted his eyes glinting as he stared at her.

"Well, you're just going to have to work on that temper of yours, aren't you Gray," he said. "Listen, we are meeting with The Guardians in the morning. After that, we can look into your family's history to see if this kind of magic runs in your bloodline. Until then, can you do me a favour?"

"What?" she asked.

"Try not to set anything, or *anyone* for that matter, on fire." He smirked, and the sight irritated her beyond belief.

"Well as long as nobody pisses me off, I guess we will be alright," she huffed, and added, "I haven't used magic in five years. In case none of you have noticed, I'm a little rusty."

"I'd beg to differ," Zac said beside her. "You kicked ass in that field, Evie!"

Evie sighed.

"That was just pure luck, Zac. You saw what just happened downstairs. I lost control."

"Get some rest," Jack suggested. "A good night's sleep will help."

Chapter Six

Despite the bone-tired exhaustion that slammed into her like a ton of bricks, Evie barely slept.

Her body ached as she rolled onto her back and the dull twinges in her head made her stomach churn. She picked up her phone and saw it had just gone seven. She'd slept for a mere four hours. Sighing, she turned her head to look across the room.

Robyn was still sound asleep, her dreams sweetly undisturbed. Pulling herself up, Evie tossed away the covers, and quietly tiptoed out of the bedroom. The living room was empty, and after making herself a cup of strong tea, she settled herself onto the sofa, pulling her legs up and covering them with a soft, grey blanket.

Evie had been back in Wilmington for less than twelve hours and already so much had happened. Her magic was a silent drum beneath her skin, and though the flames were gone, she could still *feel* the heat of them pulsating through her veins.

This power that she had was *strong*. Strong and dark, and she did not like the way it made her feel.

Closing her eyes, Evie's thoughts drifted towards her upcoming meeting with The Guardians.

Would The Guardians welcome her back to The Academy after what she did? Would they send her back to London and strip her of her magic completely for breaking The Guardian Oath? And what would happen if they found out about her secret? Had the Inquisitor already told them? What if she lost her temper again? What if she lost control?

So many questions, with so few answers. Evie felt frustrated as she placed her empty cup onto the coffee table. She sighed, picking up her phone again.

It was now seven-thirty, but there was still no sign of anyone else waking up. She needed to clear her head. After a few seconds, Evie stood up and went back into her bedroom. She pulled on a pair of yoga pants and a sweater, before picking her sneakers up from the end of the bed.

After grabbing her headphones, Evie left the room again and silently made her way through the living room and out into the corridor.

***

Once outside of The Academy, the cold air against her face instantly made her feel better. It was still dark, but she knew sunrise would be soon. Evie turned on her music, and left The Academy grounds, heading towards the park with a gentle jog.

It had been a while since she ran, and despite the hard ache that punctured her lungs, she slowly began to enjoy the steady pace she set herself.

She ran and ran, allowing the morning air to hit her face and penetrate her body, clearing the cloudy mess that her mind had become.

The park was so peaceful, and for the first time in hours, her mind felt clear. Evie took a deep breath and smiled as she slowed her pace before finally coming to a stop. She lowered herself onto a wooden bench that overlooked the lake, her eyes fixed on the smooth surface as she turned her music off.

She remembered the days when she would spend hours in

this very park with her father. Talking about the past and the future, books, and music. She had always been close to both of her parents, but her dad, he had been her very best friend.

Her parent's murders would always remain a mystery to her. Both alive and happy one minute, then suddenly gone the next. Ripped away from her for reasons she could not find answers to.

The Guardians had told her that their deaths had been a terrible accident. They'd told her to accept it. To move on.

But she hadn't.

She couldn't.

And now, five years on, she still struggled with the mystery that surrounded that terrible day.

Their bodies had been found in the Enchanted Forest. The homeland of The Guardians. The forest was tucked away, protected over the centuries by powerful wards which prevented those who did not belong from entering the ancient land.

The Gray's bodies had been perfect in appearance other than having no life. There had been no sign of struggle. They had simply looked as though they were both in a deep, peaceful sleep.

The sound of oncoming steps pulled her from her thoughts and Evie twisted her head to see Jack. He too was wearing running gear. He smiled as he sat down on the bench beside her.

"I didn't expect to see you here," he said, his voice a little breathless.

"I woke ridiculously early considering the time we went to bed," she said. "And I needed to clear my head. Running helps."

"I know that feeling," he said quietly, his eyes fixed on the lake.

"What time do we have to meet with The Guardians?" Evie asked.

"Nine-thirty," Jack replied, glancing down at his watch. "We have just over an hour. Have you had breakfast yet?"

Evie shook her head. "Not yet."

"Come on," he said, smiling as he stood up. "I'll treat you."

Evie frowned. "Okay," she said, and added, "but only because I'm hungry. This doesn't mean that I have forgiven you for the Robyn situation."

Jack chuckled. "I thought you would be over that by now."

"I hold a strong grudge, Saunders," Evie teased as she rose from the bench.

"Why does *that* not surprise me?" he said with a smirk.

***

Together, they walked away from the lake, leaving the park behind. The main streets were quiet, with only the odd person or two walking on the sidewalk. Evie smiled, taking it all in. Wilmington was so different to the busy streets of London, and she felt somewhat relaxed as she walked beside Jack.

"Is it strange, being back I mean?" Jack asked, noting her expression.

"I didn't think I would ever come back," she replied.

"I'm sorry," he said softly.

"No, it's fine," she said quickly. "I understand the reasons, it's just odd being here. I'd forgotten how quiet it was."

"Not quite the hustle and bustle of London, huh?" he said.

"Something like that," Evie said, as Jack paused outside a small, red-bricked building.

"My favourite place to hide." He smiled, pushing open the door for her.

Inside, the café was small but cosy. It felt bright and homely. The smell of fresh coffee penetrated Evie's nose as they sat down at a small round table by the window, and a few seconds later they were joined by a young waitress.

"Good morning," she said happily. "Can I get you both a coffee?"

"Could I have a tea please?" Evie asked, noting the name on her badge. *Tilly.*

"Sure, any in particular?" Tilly replied.

"Do you have English Breakfast?"

"Absolutely." She smiled, turning to Jack. "Same for you?"

"I'll have a coffee please," Jack replied.

"Sure! I'll get your drinks and then grab your breakfast orders, unless you want to order now?"

"I'm ready to order now, Evie?"

"Yeah, I'm ready, could I just get a sausage bagel please?"

Tilly nodded, noting it down on her order pad. "And for you?" she asked Jack.

"Same for me, thank you Tilly."

"I'll be right back." Tilly beamed, then hurried back over to the counter.

"Cute place to hide," Evie said, taking in the small room, and with a glance in Tilly's direction, she added, "come here often do you?"

Jack shook his head. "Only when I need to get away from The Academy."

"Oh?" she said, raising her brows. "Being a Guardian Leader not all it's made out to be, Saunders?"

Jack smirked. "You could say that."

"Whatever makes you happy, huh?" she replied with a smile. "So, what are your thoughts on my...*problem?* The Fae..."

"We'll discuss it back at The Academy," he said, his eyes moving to the side of her as Tilly approached their table holding

54

a tray. "Thank you, Tilly."

"Enjoy guys!" She beamed before hurrying back to the counter.

Evie bit into her bagel and smiled. "This is so good."

"Of course it is, it's the best cafe in Wilmington!" Jack grinned.

"Robyn will kill me for this," she said.

"Better not tell her then," he said. "Cora will be peeved if she were to find out I made her go all the way to London, for you to end up killed only hours after arriving."

"Ha-ha." Evie frowned. "*Cora*. She definitely hates me."

"She doesn't hate you," he said softly. "Just give her time. She's stubborn, and she has a lot going on right now."

"Like what?" Evie asked.

"That's not my place to say," he said, and added, "can I ask you something?"

Evie nodded. "Go ahead."

"Why didn't you talk to me?" he asked. "Or any of us for that matter. We were all here for you."

Evie tensed. Any mention of that day, the day she left, hurt as if it had only happened yesterday.

"I don't know," she said honestly. "I didn't want any of you to change my mind. The day my parents died, I felt like I had lost everything, and then Elijah disappeared too. I guess I felt I had no reason to stay anymore."

"You had us, Evie," he said softly. "We were your family too. Still are."

Evie smiled. "I know. But at the time, I didn't see it like that."

"And now?" Jack asked. "How are you holding up?"

Evie shrugged. "I have my good days and my bad days. I

miss my parents like crazy but I'm dealing with it better now. I just wish I knew what happened to them. That part hurts the most, the not knowing. I don't believe The Guardians story of it being an accident. Something happened to them. I know it did. And as for Elijah, I have no idea what happened to him. He disappeared right after our parents died. He didn't even show up for the funeral. It's like he never even existed."

"The Guardians did spend some time looking for him," Jack told her. "They called the search off a year after he went missing. I'm sorry, I know that's not what you wanted to hear."

"Elijah is a very clever person," she said, pushing her empty plate away. "He had his reasons for running and if he wanted to be found, I think he would have been by now. I guess it's just something that I have to accept."

Jack reached for her hand, and as his fingers touched her skin, she felt an electricity pulse through her. If he felt it too, he didn't let on.

"You're home now, with us, and that's all that matters. Don't ever feel like you're alone because you're not."

"Thank you," she said, glancing down to where his hand held hers. "I promise I won't do another disappearing act."

Jack chuckled, pulling his hand back. "Even if you did, Gray, I'd find you. You're not very good at it."

"Well if I *was* to go, I would just have to learn from past mistakes." She grinned. "You don't have to worry. I won't be going anywhere anytime soon."

"Good," Jack said. "So, of all the places in the world you could have gone, why did you choose London?"

Evie shrugged.

"In all honesty, I really don't know," she said. "I didn't really plan anything. I just packed my bags and left."

"Were you happy?" Jack asked.

"Mostly," Evie said. "More so when I met Robyn, as I am sure you already know. I was in a really dark place before she came into my life, and I didn't know what the hell I was doing. She made it better."

He smiled. "I'm glad you had her," Jack said. He took a long swig from his mug before placing it back onto the table. "So, London, was it what you thought it would be?"

Evie shrugged, lifting her eyes to meet his.

"It was my home for five years. At first, I struggled to adjust. I didn't know anyone. I stayed in hotels for the first eight months, and then I met Robyn...and I guess you already know the rest.

"She offered me her spare room, and her apartment became my home," Evie said. "She helped me with a job at the restaurant where she worked, and after that everything else just sort of fell into place."

"Sounds like you found your feet." Jack smiled.

"Sort of. It wasn't easy, not at first," she said. "I had to tell a few white lies about my age in order to get a job with Robyn. Luckily, her boss at the time was a bit of a dimwit and didn't ask questions."

Jack released a low laugh.

"Why does that not surprise me?" he teased.

"Hey, I had to do what was necessary, and if that meant telling a little white lie so that I could make some money, then who can blame me?" She grinned and added in a serious tone, "I refused to use magic. I just wanted to be normal. Working as a waitress and meeting Robyn gave me that. It helped me forget all the bad things that led me to London in the first place."

Jack nodded, acknowledging that he understood.

"Will you go back?" he asked. "I mean, if we succeed in

capturing The Dark Prince."

For a moment, Evie remained silent contemplating his words.

"I don't think I could," she said, and noted his posture relax a fraction. "Not now that I've seen you all."

"Good. I don't think the others would let you leave without a fight anyway." Jack said, glancing down at his watch. "We should probably get going soon. How do you feel about seeing The Guardians?"

"Honestly? I'm scared," she admitted. "I know that I broke the oath when I left…and I also know the consequences…"

"You have nothing to be scared about," he said softly. "They understand why you left, Evie. You'll be fine."

"I hope you're right," she sighed.

"I'm *always* right," Jack teased, smirking.

Evie rolled her eyes.

"I see becoming a Guardian Leader has done so much for your ego, Saunders."

He laughed. "Time to go, Gray," he said flatly.

Jack placed a twenty-dollar bill on the table before standing up. Evie followed, and after saying goodbye to Tilly, she led the way out of the café and into the now bustling streets of Wilmington.

Chapter Seven

The sound of hushed voices filled the ground floor library, and as Evie pushed open the heavy, wooden doors, she sucked in a deep breath, trying to ignore the nerves rising in her stomach.

Several people were sat around a large oak table that dominated the centre of the library, each head lifting as Jack steered her closer.

The chatter ended and for a moment, everyone stared. Evie glanced to the side of the room, relieved when she spotted the rest of The Circle sat beneath the wall length, stained glass windows.

At the centre of the table sat a slim female with white-blonde hair that surrounded her oval face. The female stood, and Evie noted the emerald, green cloak she wore over a black, pin-striped dress.

Lydia Bowater, the Headmistress of the Guardian Academy, smiled as she rounded the table.

"Evie," she said, her voice soft and welcoming. "I can't even begin to describe how wonderful it is to see you!"

"Hello Madam Bowater," Evie said, as Lydia took both of her hands into her own.

"Just look at you." Lydia beamed. "You've grown into such a beautiful, young woman."

"Thank you," Evie replied, smiling nervously.

"Well, it is wonderful to have you back sweetheart," she said. "I couldn't quite believe it when Jack told us the news of your return. It must be strange for you to be back after all this time, I'm sure, but please rest assured, we are all very grateful to see you home at last."

"I was worried about meeting with you today. I know I broke the oath when I left…"

"Nonsense," she said, waving her hand in dismissal. "You had your reasons, which I, and the Guard, understand. The circumstances in which you were placed would have been difficult for any one of us to have dealt with. You did what you thought was right at the time. The main thing that matters now is that you are home, where you belong, and that you are safe."

Evie sighed, feeling relief flood through her.

"Thank you, that means a lot," she said.

Lydia smiled. "I'm sure Jack and the others have explained to you the situation we are currently in."

Evie nodded. "Yes. But I'm not sure how I can help. My magic is a little…*unpredictable* at the moment."

"Might I interrupt, Headmistress?"

Evie whipped her head and was greeted by the Inquisitor's dark eyes. His black hair was hanging loose past his shoulders this morning, and the long, leather coat he wore, swept the stone floor as he stalked towards the Headmistress.

"You might recall the conversation we had last night. The suggestion I made?"

Lydia lifted her head, pursing her lips to form a tight line.

"Yes, I do recall our conversation, but it will not be necessary Inquisitor. Evie is a born witch. I have no doubt that her magic will be just fine once she has climatised to being back within The Academy."

"Oh, I do not for one-minute *doubt* Miss Gray's magic, Headmistress," he said. "But you heard Miss Gray herself, her

60

magic is unpredictable. The Dark Prince grows more powerful with each passing day. Our mission is to capture him and put an end to his current reign. Miss Gray is a liability that we cannot afford to take a risk with."

"A liability?" Evie snarled. "What the hell is that supposed to mean?"

"Evie," Jack's warning voice echoed beside her.

"Yes, Miss Gray. A liability. Your lack of control is evidence of that. Surely you must agree.

"I suggest," he said, turning to face the table of other Guardian Leaders, "that Miss Gray undertakes an *initiation*...."

"Initiation?" Evie said. "I did that when I was fifteen years old. Every Circle member goes through the initiation process."

"Yes, but this would be different," he said. "The purpose of *this* initiation would be to test your skills as a witch, and to identify whether or not your magic is *worthy* of being part of The Guardian Academy. Of course, it will not identify how you were able to create a magic that does not belong to us, but it will give us an idea of the strength of the magic that runs within you. As we all know, *fire-yielding* abilities are an element of the Fae..."

"*Fire?*" Lydia said curiously. "What are you talking about Inquisitor?"

Hayden smiled coldly. "Miss Gray is able to produce fire from her hands, Headmistress," he said. "*Dark magic*. It must be investigated. Immediately."

For a brief moment, Lydia's eyes appeared dazed as she stared at Evie, but after a few moments, she quickly composed herself, shaking away whatever thought had crossed her mind.

"Is this true Evie?" she asked.

Evie nodded. "I'm just as perplexed as you are," she replied. "I don't know how, or why it happened, it just *did*."

"Interesting," Lydia mused. "Yes, I agree with the Inquisitor, this is something that we will have to investigate as a matter of urgency. Why did you fail to mention this last night, Hayden?"

"A mere slip of the mind," he said casually with a cocky grin. The sight of which infuriated Evie so much, it caused her fingers to tremble in response. "The initiation?"

Lydia shook her head. "Not necessary," she said. "Evie is a witch. She was chosen to become a Circle member by the Golden Sword of Leo Guardian, our founder. The suggestion of an initiation is outrageous."

"I must disagree, Headmistress," came a dull, and very bored voice from behind.

A short, frumpy looking man, with thick grey hair and a round face spoke from the far end of the oak table. His aging face looked tired as he inhaled a deep breath.

"Hayden has a point, Headmistress, surely you see it too. Miss Gray has been away from the magical world for a long time. It would be naïve to simply *carry* on as though she hadn't. Particularly after what the Inquisitor witnessed last night. *If* she possesses dark magic…"

"Quiet, Julias," Lydia retorted. "I agree that we must investigate the magic Hayden claims to have witnessed, but I do not agree to an initiation. I'm sorry, but my answer is no."

"It's okay Lydia," Evie said, forcing her eyes to meet with the Inquisitors as she bit back her rising anger. "If the Guardian's want me to have an initiation, then I'll do it."

The Inquisitor smiled. "I'm glad you agree Miss Gray."

"Evie, you don't have to do this," Lydia said quietly. "The final decision lies with me, and I do not agree with you having to do this."

"I'll do it," Evie pushed through gritted teeth. *Breathe.*

Lydia sighed. "Very well. I will decide on a date and time and let you know."

"Excellent," Hayden said. "Now that issue is sorted, shall we discuss more pressing matters?"

Lydia scowled but agreed as she made her way back to the table, signalling for Evie and Jack to join the rest of The Circle.

Lydia sat down and waved her hand across the table. A newspaper floated into the air as she spoke.

"Another body was discovered last night. The Dark Prince must be stopped. I fear we are running out of time."

"Where was the body found?" Zac asked.

"Near the University," Lydia said quietly. "Two more normads have also been reported as missing."

She raised her hand again, causing a large photo to rise into the air. Evie's body froze as her eyes focused on the image of a young man, his body naked and covered in wounds.

"We must up our game. More patrols will be needed to protect the normads. We have made the decision to allow the second and third years to assist with our patrols. It is not a decision I take lightly. They are still in training, but what other choice do we have. We made a vow to protect the normad world, and I will stick to that vow no matter what. I will be reducing the patrols in the Enchanted Forest to allow for this."

"You can't do that!" Cora exclaimed, thinking of her own family. "Who will protect the Forest?"

"The Enchanted Forest is protected, you have my word," Lydia replied. "At this present time, the normads are in far worse danger, and we have a duty to protect them. It seems The Dark Prince has taken a liking to the humans. What he hopes to gain, I can't even begin to fathom. But this death shall not be the last. And neither will the disappearances.

"I have devised a rota. Patrols will start this evening. Evie, until you have learnt to control this new ability of yours, I think it is wise that you stay in The Academy grounds."

"Why?" Evie chimed. "What good will I be hiding behind these walls? Let me help."

Lydia shook her head. "Evie, I trust your judgement. You are a good warrior, but we cannot risk you out on the streets right now with an element of magic that you can neither control nor understand."

"But…"

"That is my final word," Lydia said sympathetically.

"What of the students?" Jack said. "I've spent hours in the training room with them Lydia, they aren't ready for this. They can barely duel!"

"Worry not of the students, Jack," she replied. "I will ensure they are protected. You have my word."

Chapter Eight

"Well, I think it's absolutely insane that you have to do this initiation."

Lucas' deep voice seemed louder in the deserted courtyard. The anger in his tone was unmissable as he and Evie sat close together on a wooden bench that overlooked the stables. Two giant, chocolate brown horses stood in the barn, silently watching as they spoke.

"It's ridiculous." He growled.

"What's ridiculous, Lucas, is me having to stay cooped up in The Academy."

"Evie, I don't think you get it," he said, twisting his head to face her. "The Inquisitor's initiation is *nothing* like the one we did when we were fifteen. I've seen him with the new students; it wasn't nice to watch, and as for Lydia, she's just looking out for you.

"I saw how you reacted in London when Cora told you to remove the bracelet. You were terrified of the thought of using your magic. I'm not stupid, Evie. I know you. And I remember how you were after your parents died. What do you think this initiation will do to you?"

Evie sighed. "I'm not scared," she began, but quickly fell silent. She knew Lucas was right.

"You don't have to pretend with me Evie," he said softly. "I know what losing your parents did to you. I was there. And I get it. Whatever Hayden has planned for you, I can guarantee that it won't be a walk in the park."

"What do you suggest I do?" she asked quietly. "To stop me falling apart the second I use my magic."

"I don't know, but we are all here to help you," he said softly. "Talk to Jack. Maybe he will have some insight into what Hayden plans."

Evie nodded. "Do you think my parents knew, Lucas?" she asked.

"About your fire ability?" he asked, and she nodded once more. "If they did, I think they would have told you."

"Yeah," she said with a shiver. "My parents wouldn't have kept something like this from me. They were probably just as clueless as me."

"Come, let's get you back inside," Lucas said, and stood up.

***

Not wanting to eat with the rest of The Academy, Evie and Lucas headed straight upstairs to The Circle's apartment. Tessa and Zac were the only ones there, deep in conversation as they entered.

"Hey, pizza just arrived, get it whilst it's still hot!" Tessa grinned.

"Did we not just eat pizza last night?" Evie said. "Don't you guys eat anything else?"

"You can never have too much pizza," Tessa said pointedly.

"Hmm. I'll pass thank you. I'm not really that hungry," she said. "Where's everyone else?"

Tessa shrugged. "Suit yourself. Cora and Robyn are out patrolling the university until five, and Jack, well I have no idea where he is. Haven't seen him since this morning."

"I thought patrols were starting this evening. Has something happened?"

Tessa shook her head. "Nothing unusual. Lydia just wanted to get a head start. Me and Zac are taking over from them."

"Okay," Evie said with a yawn. "I think I'm gonna lay down for a little while, the exhaustion is finally catching up with me."

"I'm surprised you've made it this long," Zac said through a mouthful of pizza. "Go get some sleep. We'll wake you if we need to."

With a smile, Evie left. Someone had been in the bedroom she shared with Robyn. The curtains were open, allowing soft beams of cold, golden sunshine through the glass panels. The room smelled fresh, and she noted a bunch of pretty yellow and pink flowers had been placed on the dresser.

Smiling, she kicked off her shoes and lay down on the bed. Her body ached with exhaustion, and as she settled her head into the softness of the pillow, her mind tried to make sense of all that had happened.

Two days ago, she was in London, living a life that she had grown to love, but the more she thought about that life, she found herself feeling *different* towards it.

She couldn't quite explain the thoughts now rushing through her mind, but she had a feeling it had something to do with the bracelet that she was no longer wearing. Evie had always believed she was happy in London, but deep down, she had known there had been something missing.

She closed her eyes, allowing the exhaustion to take over, and suddenly, she knew exactly what had been missing.

The Circle.

***

"Evie!"

Tessa's frantic voice rang through Evie's ears, forcing her eyes to fly open.

"What's happened?" she said, her voice groggy with sleep.

Evie sat up, feeling dizzy as her eyes tried to focus. The room was dark, lit only by the flickering of yellow candlelight. Tessa was sat at the side of the bed, with Lucas and Zac standing close by. The look on each face staring down at her caused her heart to race with worry.

"What is it? What's happened?" she pressed.

"It's Cora and Robyn," Tessa said hurriedly. "They should have been back over an hour ago. No one has heard from them, and we can't reach Cora on her cell."

"What? Why are you only just waking me!" Evie said frantically, jumping out of bed.

She pulled on her boots, grabbing her jacket as she left the bedroom.

Jack was stood in the kitchen. His phone pressed against his ear, but Evie ignored him as she stormed through the living room.

"Evie! For God's sake will you just wait for one second."

Evie paused by the door and turned around to face Tessa and the others. Her face was red with anger.

"They could be in trouble," Evie said hurriedly. "We don't have time to stand around and wait, Tessa!"

"Not so fast," Jack said suddenly, leaving the kitchen to join them in the living room. "It will do no one any good if we go storming into the night, not knowing what we are going into. Lydia has already ordered searches to begin. Tessa, Lucas, and Zac are going to join the other leaders. I will head over towards the university and search that area. Don't worry, we will find them."

"And what am I supposed to do?" Evie said, although she already knew the answer.

"You're to wait here," Jack said, and added, "but I know you won't do that, so you're coming with me."

Evie nodded, surprised. "Okay, well let's go," she said and hurried towards the door.

Chapter Nine

There was an icy atmosphere in The Academy, and frantic voices could be heard all around.

Evie followed Jack out of the manor, and they walked in a hurried silence through the near deserted streets of Wilmington, moving further and further away from The Academy. It was still early evening, and she found it odd to find the streets so empty.

The bitterness of the cold air took Evie's breath away as they crossed a narrow street that opened up to a long, cobbled pathway.

"She'll be all right," Jack said quietly. "They both will."

"You don't know that" she replied. "This is my fault."

"Why would you think that?" he asked.

"I've dragged Robyn into this mess," she said. "She shouldn't even be here."

"You can't think like that," he said. "Robyn knew what she was getting herself into. She's a powerful witch Evie, trust me. She's no amateur."

"How are you so calm right now?" she gasped.

"I have to be," was all he said.

Jack stopped walking, pausing as his eyes scanned the quiet street. Evie followed his gaze, and suddenly, his hand gripped her elbow, pushing her roughly down a narrow alley.

Before she could protest, Jack raised his finger to his mouth, signalling for her to remain quiet.

Evie struggled to move as his body pressed against hers. She felt her back hit the wall behind her, but the shiver that now trickled through her body had nothing to do with *that*.

She looked at Jack, feeling her stomach ripple with nerves. His jaw was locked in concentration; his face taut with tension as he stared out onto the street.

Whatever had caught his attention had caused his entire posture to go rigid.

Evie adjusted her stance, placing her hands onto his firm chest, and pushed him slightly to gain his attention. When he didn't respond, she nudged him again, this time, with enough force to make him look at her.

Jack opened his mouth, and whispered, *"Demons."*

Following his gaze, Evie gasped. Fear and anticipation spiked through her as her magic thrummed through her fingers. She glanced down, quickly pulling her hands away from his chest as her palms erupted with fire, the flames illuminating the dark alley.

"Oh no!" Evie breathed, her voice hushed.

"Control it," Jack ordered. His voice thunderous as he stared down at her.

"I don't know how to," she barked back, flicking her hands in the hope that it would force the flames to disappear. "Jack, help me!"

A dark shadow crept across the alley entrance, and Jack quickly pushed Evie further into the darkness, his body blocking the flames as several ghostly figures sauntered by. Evie felt herself meet with another wall, and a wave of panic surged through her.

They had reached a dead end.

"You need to control it," Jack's voice was as cold as ice, but it was nothing compared to the look in his eyes.

70

"I'm open to suggestions," she breathed.

Jack glanced quickly to the entrance, before turning his head back to her.

"You're scared. I get it, and right now, your magic is wild and reckless," he said. "Magic stems from our emotions. You need to clear you head and calm down. I know you're scared. I'm here, Evie. Nothing is going to happen to you. I won't let it. I just need you to calm your emotions and gain control."

"It's not that easy," she mumbled.

Frustrated, Jack stepped away from her.

"You're going to attract them," he seethed. "Stay here. I need to see where they have gone."

"No!" she gushed, taking a step to follow him. "Jack I am not staying in this alley by myself. I'm coming with you!"

"Evie, if you take one step out of this alley with those flames, the demons will be on us in seconds," he declared. "It is a miracle they haven't sensed you already. Your magic is a liability right now. Stay here and wait until I come back."

"I'm *coming* with you," Evie protested and pushed her way forwards.

His hand gripped her elbow for a second time, tugging her back. "I said no. Wait here!" he said, and added with a feral hiss, "That's an order!"

"You can't tell me what to do Jack."

"I am a Guardian Leader," he said, his voice cold. "*You* listen to my orders, Evie, unless you want to get us both killed. Call the others and tell them to meet us here. If the demons are heading towards the university, then I have a horrible feeling about Cora and Robyn's location."

"Let me go," Evie snapped, and as she lifted her hands, she noted the flames had vanished.

Angry tears pricked her eyes as she pushed against Jack's chest, shoving him aside as she walked to the entrance of the alley.

The demons were nowhere to be seen, but the university was ablaze with light. Jack was close behind, and as he made a step towards her, his phone began to buzz.

"Lucas?" he said into the phone. "Thank God... they're both okay? Good. I'm heading back now with Evie... No... Yes... Okay. I will bring Evie back to The Academy, and then I think we should head back over to the university... Demons... I'm not sure how many, we had a situation arise... Okay. Bye."

He ended the call and moved towards her.

"Robyn and Cora are at The Academy," he said. "They're both okay."

Relief flooded through her, but as she met Jack's eyes, her relief was suddenly replaced with utter annoyance.

"You don't have to come back with me," she told him. "I can walk by myself."

"Now who is giving out the orders?" he mocked. "Evie..."

"It's fine," she said. "I'm a liability. I get it."

"I said your magic was a liability, not you," he said.

"Whatever," she said, forcing her eyes away. "It's the same thing. Just leave me alone."

"Evie, wait," Jack said, reaching for her arm. "Why are you mad at me?"

"You called me a liability," she said, and even as she said the words, she could hear just how childish they sounded. "Instead of helping me, you just pushed me to control something that I have no idea how to control.

"In London, when this power was first exposed, I actually did feel in control," she said. "But now I feel as though I have this terrible darkness running through my veins and I don't know what to do. I asked you to help me, not yell at me. I can't control this thing, Jack, because I don't know how to. So, I am sorry if I am not up to your standards."

"Evie, I wasn't yelling at you," he said. "Your flames were going to attract the demons. What else was I supposed to do? Hug you and tell you not to worry? That everything would be alright? I am sorry if I upset you. I didn't mean to. I just needed you to listen."

"Whatever Jack," she said. "Let's just go. I want to see Robyn.

***

Evie walked in silence, growing angrier with each step.

Control it!

Bleh! How on earth did people expect her to control something that she did not truly understand? Her new ability was stronger than the magic she'd been born with.

Evie could almost taste the strength of the magic as it coursed beneath her skin, eager for release once more. She clenched her hands into fists, breathing heavily as her eyes blurred with angry tears.

Why did no one understand?

Magic had destroyed her.

Broken every single piece of her mind and soul and left behind the nervous wreck that she was now.

Magic had taken her family. Her life. It had forced her to run. To run as far away as she possibly could, from the only life she had ever known.

They did not understand. They never would.

Swallowing the bile of rising anxiety that threatened, Evie hurried forwards, aware of Jack following only a few feet behind.

She would not talk to him. *How dare he*!

She had asked him to help her, yet his response had been frustration.

Why did he not understand?

Why did no one understand?

Jack… Lucas… even the Inquisitor.

They had each told her to focus on her power.

Focus and control.

But how on earth was she supposed to do that? Evie had spent the last five years living amongst the normads. The bracelet she'd worn had blocked her magic, as well as the magic of those around her.

Not only did she have to reconnect with the magic she had been born with, but now she also had this terrifying new ability to contend with.

And it scared her. More than she was willing to admit.

Frustrated, Evie released a heavy sigh and froze.

Deep in her thoughts, she had not noticed the air around her suddenly drop as a cold breeze whistled through the darkness. The streetlamps that had lit the path were as dark as the night sky, and the silence had now given way to the sound of hushed, menacing whispers.

Evie twisted her head to look over her shoulder, her eyes locking with Jack's.

Before either of them could speak, Evie was crippled with a surge of excruciating pain as her body was forced into the air, bound above the ground.

Demons.

Evie thrashed desperately against the invisible chains

holding her in place. She opened her mouth, screaming for Jack, but her voice failed her as a demonic, ghostly creature appeared before her.

Its hideously wicked face was the picture of nightmares. Haggard, with mottled grey skin and canines so sharp, the points could have shattered glass with the faintest touch.

The demon hovered for a moment. Its vivid green eyes focused on her as it tilted its head from side to side.

Assessing her.

And then its long, bony fingers were reaching forwards, caressing the side of her face with torturous delight. Evie screamed as the demon's pointy talons pierced her skin. She reached up, helplessly clasping her hands arounds its slimy forearm.

A wave of relentless power shot through her veins, igniting the tips of her fingers with a blinding, fiery light.

The demon screeched, the sound a deafening wail, and Evie fell to the ground with a thud as her head hit the path. She scrambled to her knees, her vision barely there as she tried to locate Jack.

She screamed his name, over and over, desperate to hear his voice, but was only met with the sound of another thud as her back hit the solid brick wall behind.

The demon hovered above her, its fathomless eyes gleaming with a deathly delight. Evie stumbled but remained upright.

"*The rumours are true,*" the demon said, speaking in the old demonic tongue.

It was barely a whisper, and though Evie had not heard the language before, she seemed to have no trouble understanding the words that replayed in her mind.

The demon smiled widely, and Evie gagged as its rotten

breath caressed her face. It lowered its head, closer and closer until she could feel the roughness of the demon's lips against her neck.

Evie screamed as the demon's teeth punctured her skin, tearing into her neck with a venomous bite. Fire surged through her veins, burning every inch of her rapidly weakening body as the demonic poison raced through her bloodstream.

Her magic sparked within her. Her blood thumping vigorously as her heart thundered against her chest.

Survive.

Evie heard the command clearly. As though someone had spoken it out loud. She forced her eyes to open, willing her rapid breathing to calm. The venom crashed through her bloodstream, seeking its way to her thundering heart.

Death was close. She could taste it. Her body could feel the darkness of it with each lingered breath she took.

Survive.

Fight.

Breathe.

With one final push of energy, Evie listened to the commands of her mind, willing herself to focus on the darkness that so desperately wanted to aide her.

She would survive this night. She had to survive. To fight.

Unclenching her fists, Evie eyed her palm, watching as the fiery flame flickered. The ball of flame grew hotter as more power surged through her body. Then she released her magic.

The demon screeched, vanishing into an eruption of bright, orange flames. Evie fell to the ground, panting as her palm now crushed against the side of her neck.

"Evie!"

Jack was on the ground beside her, pulling her up into a

sitting position. He looked at her, his mouth moving quickly, but she could barely hear the words he spoke.

"Evie, talk to me!" he urged.

"Burning..." she said and thrashed against his hold. "It's burning... My neck... Please... MAKE IT STOP! IT'S BURNING JACK... PLEASE... PLEASE MAKE IT STOP!"

"Get her to the infirmary now!"

Hayden's voice thundered as he approached them. His golden-brown face filled with undeniable fury.

"Go now! She's been poisoned!"

Chapter Ten

The Academy was bright with a soft yellow light as Jack's portal opened up into the courtyard.

He hurried inside, running towards the Infirmary. Seconds felt like minutes, but he quickly reached his destination, forcing the door open with a heavy kick.

He lowered Evie onto the closest bed as several healers crowded her. Jack watched helplessly as she thrashed against the healers attempts to bind her.

Watched as her frantic eyes, both as black as the night sky, flickered viciously in and out of consciousness.

Her torturous screams pierced every inch of his body, and he felt his own heart race dangerously fast beneath his aching chest.

He could barely breathe, but his eyes refused to leave her. Pain was all he could feel as he desperately fought against the urge to reach for her. To hold her hand. To do something. Anything…

"Wait outside," Merida, The Academy's chief healer, said urgently. "The poison is reacting with her magic. It's making it difficult for us to sedate her. We could be here a while."

Jack shook his head. His eyes never leaving Evie's agonised, pale face. He couldn't leave.

"I'm staying," he said. "I have to stay."

"There is nothing you can do Jack," Merida said softly. "Please, let us do our work. Let us help her."

His agonised mind screamed at him to listen to Merida, but

he could not ignore the ache in his heart at the thought of leaving. Minutes trickled by as he contemplated the healer's request, until finally, he nodded, spinning on his heel to walk away.

The screams grew quieter as he moved further away from the infirmary until finally, they could no longer be heard. He stopped once he reached the top of the staircase, racing through his mind as he tried to figure out where they had gone wrong.

What had he missed? Had he been so focused on Evie, that he had misjudged the situation? Had the demons followed as they left the alley?

Did they even leave?

Cursing himself, he pushed open the door to the ground floor foyer, unsurprised to see The Circle waiting for him. The Inquisitor was there too, deep in conversation with Lydia and Julias. They paused when they saw him.

"Where is Evie?" Robyn was rushing over to him. Her face blotched with dried tears. "Is she okay? Can we see her?"

Jack shook his head. "She's been poisoned," he said. "Her magic is reacting with the poison. It's making it difficult for the healers to sedate her."

"But they will be able to help her?" Robyn cried. "Jack, tell me they will help her!"

Jack said nothing as Tessa wrapped an arm around Robyn's shoulders, pulling her against her.

"She will be okay," Tessa said softly. "They will save her. I know they will."

"What the hell happened Jack? Were you that *blindsided?*" Julias' voice bellowed, bouncing against the stone walls.

"I didn't know we were being followed," Jack's voice was cold. "I assumed the demons had gone into the university."

"You assumed?" Julias mocked. "As a Guardian Leader, was

it not your duty to follow?"

"As a *Guardian Leader*, it was my duty to ensure Evie was brought back to The Academy," he almost growled. *"She* was my priority."

"And that was the right thing to do," Lydia said. "Miss Gray's magic is unpredictable. You couldn't have taken the risk."

"Organise a team and get back over to the university," Julius ordered. "For your sake, you had better pray there are no innocents in there."

"What about Evie?" Jack said with a calm fury. "You've not bothered to ask how she is."

"Miss Gray is a liability," he said coldly. "She harnesses an element of dark magic. Perhaps you will understand just why the Inquisitor has suggested an initiation for the girl. Her simply being here puts us all at risk.

"Come Hayden!" Julius growled. "I have matters to discuss with you."

Jack sneered, his face rigid with anger as he watched Julius and Hayden saunter away.

"Jack, you did the right thing," Lydia said. "Merida is one of our finest healers, and I am certain that she has dealt with far worse cases than this in her time. Evie will be fine. I can assure you."

"What are you orders?" Jack asked, his eyes now dazed with a look of relentless fury.

"We will investigate the situation at the university," she replied. "Take The Circle. If there are innocents inside, then you do what you must to get them out safely. If there are only demons present, then you come straight back, and we will re-evaluate the situation."

"Understood," he said.

"Jack, I know you will want to hunt the demon that did this, but for all our sakes, don't," Lydia said. She stood directly in front of him, her eyes filled with concern. "Leave that battle for another day. Go and investigate the university and come straight back. Evie will need you... *all of you*."

She turned and left then.

Jack didn't move. He knew he would have to go back to the university. He knew it was wrong to push aside the possibility of there being innocents inside there. Normads who needed their help. His help.

Yet he couldn't move. He was torn, and the pain that shredded his heart held his feet firmly to the ground.

He didn't want to leave *her*. Not again.

Cora stepped towards him, taking hold of his arm, and whispered so that only he could hear.

"I know what you're feeling Jack, so you can quit trying to hide it. You forget that I am an empath. Your pain is my pain. You stay here with Evie. We will go to the university."

Jack shook his head, desperately trying to contain his thoughts.

"No. I'll go. Lucas and Zac, you come with me," he said briskly. "You girls stay here with Evie. Call me the second she wakes up."

"We will," Tessa said, and added, "Be safe, all of you."

Jack nodded and beckoned for Lucas and Zac to follow him.

***

Cora bit her lip, watching as they left The Academy.

"Should we go to the Infirmary?" she heard Tessa ask.

"I need to tell you something first," Cora said quietly. "Come

81

with me."

Cora led Tessa and Robyn into an empty room just off the corridor, locking the door behind them. She waved her hand across the frame, casting a silencing spell.

"What's going on Cora?" Tessa asked, brows furrowed.

Cora glanced at Robyn before perching herself on the edge of a table. She crossed her arms as she spoke.

"I think someone planned the attack tonight," she said, her voice filled with undeniable anger. "Robyn and I didn't just go missing, Tess. Someone opened a portal that sent us to the other side of town. You guys couldn't get through to us because our cell reception had been blocked. All of this was planned, Tessa."

"The Dark Prince?" Tessa asked.

Cora shook her head.

"No," she said, "I think someone within these walls is responsible. You know as well as I do how much the Guard has changed over the last few years. Don't you think it is weird, the second Jack finds Evie, we are attacked?"

"Where exactly are you going with this Cora?"

"Listen, I know it sounds crazy, but it is the only thing that makes sense right now," Cora said. "Other than The Circle, no one else knew Jack had found Evie. We go to London to bring her home, and we are attacked. And then again tonight. Jack didn't tell The Guardians that he'd found Evie until we came back."

"I don't understand," Tessa said. "Why on earth would The Guardians want to hurt Evie?"

"Isn't it obvious?" Cora said. "This power that she has. They must want it. Whoever is behind this, must have known about Evie's magic, and the attack in London was their way of exposing it.

"Evie didn't know that she had this power, this ability, but I am willing to bet that The Guardians did."

"That is one crazy accusation, Cora," Tessa breathed. "Look, I know The Guardians aren't quite what they used to be, but do you truly believe that they would turn against their own people for the sake of magic?"

"You just want to see the good in everyone, Tess," Cora said pointedly. "You saw how powerful Evie's magic is. She destroyed those demons with one hit. She opened a portal without any help from us. She is powerful, and I think when she learns to control it, she will become an unstoppable force. Wherever this magic came from, it's dangerous. For Evie, and for us. We can't trust anyone. Not now."

"Who do you think is responsible?" Tessa asked nervously.

Cora shrugged.

"I don't know," she said. "I'm having a hard time reading any of The Guardians lately. Julias especially."

Tessa's eyes suddenly widened.

"The Inquisitor!" she said in one breath. "He's had it in for Evie since she arrived. This whole initiation nonsense proves that."

"That would make sense," Robyn said angrily. "I'd bet my money on him being responsible."

"It's not Hayden," Cora said. "I agree his methods are harsh, but it isn't him."

"You would say that," Tessa sniggered.

"What the hell is that supposed to mean?" Cora snapped.

"Oh Cora, enough of the bullshit. We all know about you and Hayden. We've known for months."

"Did I miss something here?" Robyn asked.

Cora blushed angrily.

"That has nothing to do with it. I just know it isn't him alright," Cora seethed.

"Oh Gods! Are you sleeping with the Inquisitor?" Robyn

asked, pretending to gag. "Christ, this night just keeps getting better and bloody better!"

"Shut up Robyn!" Cora ordered. "Look can we get back to the point please? Someone within these walls organised the attack tonight. I'm certain of it. We can't trust anyone."

"What makes you so certain?" Tessa asked.

"The portal was opened by a Guardian. It had the same shimmering glow as Jack's, though whoever did open it tried to disguise the glow. I know what I saw though," she said. "Whoever sent us through that portal, did so as a way to lure Evie out of The Academy tonight."

"That doesn't make any sense," Tessa said. "Lydia ordered Evie to stay at The Academy. All of the Guardian Leaders were in the library when she made that order. Why on earth would someone then create a diversion to lure her outside. It doesn't make sense."

"Fae magic," Cora said. "We all saw Lydia's face when Hayden told her about it. Don't you think it is strange? The Guardians are told about Evie's magic, and a few hours later, she is attacked? Lydia ordered Evie to stay here because she knew that Evie would do the exact opposite."

"You think Lydia had something to do with this?" Robyn asked angrily.

"I think…" Cora said, rubbing her temples to soothe the dull ache that had formed in her head. "I think we all need to watch our backs. Evie almost died tonight because of this power she has. I think tonight was a warning. Whoever is responsible will attack again. It's only a matter of time."

"We need to tell Jack and the others," Tessa urged.

"I know," Cora said. "But for now, I think we should go to the infirmary. Evie is not to be left alone. Not now."

Chapter Eleven

Jack watched as Lucas and Zac strode towards him, both looking as stressed as he felt.

They had searched the University grounds, both inside and out, but had found nothing other than an empty building. No demons. No normads. Nothing.

"The demons definitely came in here?" Lucas asked as they left the grounds.

"I assumed they did. They were gone by the time we left the alley," Jack replied, and added with a snarl, "I should have gone in."

"No, you did the right thing," Zac said. "Screw what Julias said. Your priority was getting Evie back to The Academy."

"Something doesn't feel right." Jack said, casting his eyes around the empty streets.

"Look, it's been a crazy night," Lucas said. "Wherever the demons went, they aren't here now. We need to go. Evie is our priority right now, not hunting demons. Screw Julias."

Jack nodded but said nothing as he opened a portal, and the three of them stepped through.

The portal closed with a shimmering blur, and Jack, Lucas, and Zac hurried into the manor.

The Academy was much quieter now. Jack knew that he would have to report to Julias and the other Guardian Leaders at some point, but that could wait.

The sound of Evie's terrified screams still echoed in his mind as he sprinted down the stone steps towards the basement.

The infirmary was near silent now, with the only sound coming from the whispered voices surrounding the nearest bed.

Evie was asleep. Her head tilted to the side, and Jack's eyes fell onto the pinkish scar that now ran the length of her neck. He felt his body tense at the sight of it.

"She's okay," Cora said, smiling. "The healers removed all the poison. Merida said you got her here just in time, any longer…well, it would have been a different story."

"Has she woken at all?" he asked, keeping his eyes fixed on Evie.

Cora shook her head.

"No, but Merida said that this is to be expected. She'll wake when she's ready," she said. "Her body will be exhausted from the poison and her magic."

"Okay," he said, inhaling a deep breath. "We should let her rest then. We might as well go upstairs, there is nothing else we can do until she wakes up."

"Umm, about that," Cora said, glancing around as if to make sure they were alone before speaking. "We can't leave her down here by herself."

Cora then repeated the thoughts she'd shared with Tessa, whilst Jack, Lucas, and Zac listened intently. When she was finished, she turned to Tessa and Robyn.

"Did I miss anything?" Cora asked.

Robyn shook her head. "No, I think you said it all."

"Have you spoken to anyone else?" Jack asked. His voice as cold as ice, but it did nothing to match the rage he felt.

"No. Of course not," Cora replied, knowing who he had been referring to.

"Good," he said sharply. "Listen, I've had my suspicions

about The Guardians for a while now. I agree with Cora. Someone within these walls is responsible for tonight. We can't trust anyone."

"Surely we can trust Lydia?" Zac said. "She's our headmistress. No way would she be involved in something like this!"

"No," Jack said. "This stays between us. Until we identify who was behind tonight's attack, we need to keep our heads down."

"Okay." Zac nodded. "Do you think this has anything to do with The Dark Prince? I mean, both attacks involved demons. The bastard has an army of the wretched things at his side."

"I don't know," Jack said. "But if it does, then it means whoever ordered the attack is working alongside him. We need to find out who is responsible sooner rather than later."

"There isn't much we can do tonight," Tessa said. "Maybe we should call it a night and get some rest."

"You guys go," Jack said, casting his eyes onto Evie's sleeping figure. "I will stay."

"Are you sure?" Robyn asked. "I'm happy to stay with her. You've had a rough night too, Jack. You need to sleep."

"I'll be fine," Jack said, and pulled a wooden chair closer beside Evie's bed.

Chapter Twelve

As midnight came and went, Evie still showed no signs of waking. Exhaustion kicked in as the clock struck two, and Jack struggled against the fight to keep his eyes open. He glanced around the infirmary, the dull, yellow light affecting his tired eyes.

He needed to shower, and he craved a hot cup of coffee, but he didn't dare leave her side. If Cora's theories were right, and he was certain they were, then Evie was in danger. His mind ran wild with questions as he tried to figure out who could possibly want to hurt her.

Like Tessa, his initial thought had been the Inquisitor. His clear dislike for Evie had been made apparent from their first meeting, but would he really stoop as far as to hurt her? Jack shook the thought away. As much as he didn't like the Inquisitor, he knew Hayden wasn't the one responsible.

Julias. It would make sense for it to be him. He was a wretch of man, who had always expressed a quiet interest in dark magic. It certainly wouldn't come as a surprise if Julias was indeed having illegal dealings with demons.

And then there was Lydia. She was a good headmistress and very popular amongst the students of The Academy. It couldn't be her...yet Jack could not brush off the nagging feeling irritating the back of his mind. The look on Lydia's face when Hayden told her about Evie's power...

He massaged his temples as a dull ache stretched over his

face. Perhaps if he closed his eyes, just for a second...

The sound of a creaking door forced Jack's eyes open. His conscious mind jumped into action, pushing away all thoughts of exhaustion. His vision clearing as he scanned the room, quickly turning his eyes back to Evie. Still sleeping. Her hand in his, and Jack breathed a sigh of frustration.

How long had he slept for? Seconds? Minutes? He looked at his watch and saw that it was three in the morning. He had been asleep for almost an hour. Jack looked back at the door and saw that it was closed. Slowly, he pulled his hand out of Evie's, and stood up, walking quietly across the infirmary.

He opened the door and stepped outside. The corridor was empty and very quiet. Had he imagined it? He cast a spell to detect other human presence but felt nothing. Jack shook his head again, annoyed with himself, and turned back, shutting the door behind him.

To his surprise, he was greeted by a pair of big, brown eyes. He smiled, relief flooding him as Evie pulled herself up.

***

"Jack?" her voice croaked.

"I'm here," Jack said, and with two large strides, he was back beside her bed.

He sat down, keeping his brilliant blue gaze on her.

"How are you feeling?"

"Everything hurts," Evie replied, wincing slightly. "How long was I out for?"

"A few hours," he told her.

"Have you been here this whole time?" she asked, staring at him.

Jack nodded. "Someone had to keep watch since you clearly can't be trusted to be alone."

Evie smiled, lowering her gaze.

"You didn't need to stay with me but thank you. Was anyone else hurt?"

"No, thankfully," Jack said. "Do you remember what happened?"

"Vaguely," she said. "My head is a bit of a blur. I remember us coming out of the alley and...Jack I am so sorry for the way I acted. I shouldn't have spoken to you the way I did."

"You don't have to apologise," he said softly.

"Yes, I do," Evie pressed, and she shuffled to the edge of the bed, ignoring the tingle of electricity that pulsed through her body as her legs brushed against his. "I'm sorry."

"I'm just glad that you're okay," Jack said, his voice quiet.

"Thanks to you!" she said and gave him an incredulous look. "Seriously, if you hadn't acted so fast..."

"Let's not think about the *what ifs*," he said, and she noticed a dark shadow flash across his face. "You're safe and that's all that matters."

"You look exhausted," she told him, noting the circles beneath his tired eyes. "Why don't you go and get some sleep? You don't have to stay down here with me. I will be fine."

"I'm not going to leave you down here by yourself, Evie," Jack said. "I can't..."

"Because you think someone within these walls planned the attack?" she asked flatly.

Jack frowned, but before he could speak, Evie continued.

"I may have had my eyes closed, but I heard what Cora said, Jack," she said. "The Guardians are corrupt, aren't they? I think you've known that for a while."

"The Dark Prince wasn't the only reason for you coming back here," Jack said. "A lot has changed Evie. The Guardians aren't what they used to be. I've had my suspicions for a while, but I can't figure out what is going on.

"As Guardian Leader, it is part of my role to attend meetings with The Guardians and The Elders, but so far, I haven't been invited to a single one, and when I question them about it, I get told that the Leaders are no longer required because Julias is dealing with everything."

"What do you mean?" Evie asked.

"Before The Dark Prince attacked Zac, I overheard a conversation between Julias and Hayden. They were talking about finding a weapon of some sort that held an incredible amount of power. Since then, there have been a lot of secret meetings, and they're using silencing spells to ensure their conversations remain private.

"The Elders no longer come here either," he added bitterly. "Which is odd in itself, because they have always had an input in the ongoings of The Academy. I can't even tell you the last time they were here."

"None of this makes sense," Evie said, feeling frustration sweep through her. "Why would The Guardians turn against us? Against their own people, just for a weapon."

"They want whatever this weapon is," Jack said grudgingly. "I've tried to figure out what the hell it could be, but each path I go down, I meet yet another dead end."

"And that is why you needed me to come back?" she asked. "To help expose The Guardians?"

He nodded. "Partly," he said. "Our magic weakened when you left, Evie. If The Guardians are corrupt and are searching for something that could be used against us, then we need to have

The Circle whole."

"Do you have any idea who was behind the attack in London?" she asked. "And tonight, for that matter?"

"I have a couple of suspicions. Julias being one of them." He sounded frustrated as he spoke. "He's been an ass ever since he came here, and I've never trusted him. The only problem is, I can't figure out who else would be working with him."

"Well, I thought that would have been obvious." She frowned. "Hayden. He's a complete asshole. And you already said, you overheard him talking about this weapon with Julias."

Jack shook his head. "I don't trust Hayden as far as I can throw him, but I don't think he is involved with either of the attacks, Evie."

"Okay, but if it *was* Julias, how did he order the demons to answer to him?" She mused. "Demons don't take orders from witches, Jack, especially Guardians."

"I know." He sighed, and added, "unless they are working with The Dark Prince. That would explain it."

"Do you know how crazy that sounds?" she mused.

He released a low laugh. "It makes sense though," he said, and added, "it's been a long night, and we are both exhausted. We can talk about this in the morning with the others."

Evie frowned, watching as Jack sunk back against the chair.

"In case you hadn't noticed, there are five empty beds in here."

"The healers would skin me alive for even considering using one of those beds," he said pointedly. "After the night we've had, I don't particularly fancy experiencing the wrath of Merida."

"That is the most ridiculous thing I have ever heard," Evie scoffed. "You're a Guardian Leader! Fine. Since you're so *scared*, we can both go upstairs and sleep in our *own* beds."

"We can't…well, *you* can't," he said. "You're not allowed to leave the infirmary until you have been officially discharged by Merida."

Scowling, Evie rolled her eyes.

"Fine," she said, and moved across the bed, making room. "Get in."

"What?" Jack said, perplexed.

"You heard me," she said. "I won't sleep knowing that you're sat in that darn chair, and since you're too scared to risk the wrath of the healers by sleeping in one of the perfectly unused beds, I am willing to share my bed with you…since you saved my life and all."

"I'm not sharing a bed with you, Gray," he said pointedly.

"I promise I will keep my hands to myself," she teased, and instantly regretted her words as embarrassment flooded her cheeks.

To her surprise, Jack chuckled. "You look like a tomato," he said. "I didn't realise I had that much of an effect on you Gray."

"You don't," she snapped, watching as he rose from the chair.

Jack chuckled but said nothing as he sat on the edge of the bed. He removed his boots before swinging his legs up and stretching them across the bed. The small frame was barely big enough for one person let alone two, and Evie felt her heart silently race as her body brushed against his. His muscular frame left her with no other choice but to lie on her side, leaving her forehead barely inches from his broad shoulder.

Evie inhaled a nervous breath, breathing in his intoxicating apple-spiced scent and felt her stomach erupt with a silent angst.

"You're shaking, Gray," Jack said as he too rolled onto his side. "Are you cold? Or do I make you nervous?"

"Don't flatter yourself," she replied, pursing her lips into a tight line to stop the smile that threatened to betray her.

"Why are you smiling then?" he asked.

"I'm scowling," she replied. "Why are *you* smiling?"

"I'm not," he said flatly.

"Stop staring at me," Evie warned. "I offered to share my bed with you so that you could sleep. Not stare at me."

"Is that the only reason you offered to share your bed?" he asked, brows furrowed as his mouth lifted into a teasing grin.

"You're insufferable!" she snapped. "I could easily change my mind and *make* you sleep in that darn chair."

"We both know you won't do that," he said.

"Get. Out. Saunders!"

To her annoyance, Jack didn't move as he released a low laugh. A second passed and Evie froze as he lifted his hand, resting his palm against her cheek.

If he felt her shudder slightly at his touch, he did not make it known. Instead, he tilted her head slightly, and within an instant, Evie was drowning in his brilliant blue stare.

"I shouldn't have brought you back here." His voice was quiet, and she could taste his minty breath against her face.

"What is that supposed to mean?" she asked, hurt by his words.

"None of this would have happened if I had left you in London...if I had just left you alone."

"You don't mean that," she said. "What happened tonight, it wasn't your fault, Jack. You didn't know any of this would happen."

"You almost *died,* Evie!" he said sharply, and she couldn't mistake the hurt in his voice.

"But I *didn't*," she said. "Thanks to you. You are the reason

94

I am alive. You got me to the healers in time, and because of that, you saved my life. Don't you dare blame yourself for any of this Jack because I certainly don't.

"No one could have foreseen tonight's events," she said. "So please stop with the guilt talk, because I would much rather you annoy me with your useless attempts at flirting."

He laughed, relaxing slightly. "You think I was *flirting* with you?" he teased, and added, "don't flatter *yourself,* Gray."

"Whatever," she said, lowering her eyes from his.

Resting her head against the pillow, Evie smiled as the heat from his body sent a sudden wave of relaxation through her, and she found herself edging just a little bit closer until she was completely nestled against his muscular frame.

She felt Jack tense slightly, but he lifted his arm, allowing her head to rest comfortably against his chest.

"I'm glad you're back Evie," Jack said, and added in a near whisper, "I missed you."

"Me too." Evie smiled against him, closing her heavy eyes as she succumbed to sleep.

Chapter Thirteen

Evie was officially discharged from the infirmary the following afternoon, though she had to beg Merida to even entertain the idea of letting her go.

If it had been up to the stern old witch, who had fussed over her the entire morning, she would probably have been in the infirmary for the remainder of the week. Merida had also warned her not to use any more magic until she'd learnt how to control her new ability, as another burnout would render her completely powerless.

Jack had stayed with her until Merida finally gave her the all-clear and had walked with her back to The Circle's apartment. Nothing was said about the previous night, and Evie could not shake off the nervous thrill that surged through her body whenever he was around her.

She was attracted to him. That she could not deny. He was good looking, kind, and though he irritated the hell out of her, she *liked* him a little more than she should.

But despite being part of The Circle, Jack was also a Guardian Leader. Evie was filled with conflicting emotions as she wondered if he felt the same as she did. His useless attempts at flirting gave her the impression he did.

He had also told her he'd missed her, but maybe she was looking into it more than she should. Maybe he had missed her friendship. The two of them had always had a friendly banter, even more so when she'd become a part of The Circle. But she could not ignore the spark she now felt between them.

Did he feel it too?

Frustrated with herself for even allowing such feelings to consume her, Evie had gone back to the apartment, losing herself in conversation with The Circle as she desperately tried to push all thoughts of Jack Saunders aside.

***

It was strange, being back in the one place that she had always told herself she would never return to. Yet she had to admit, despite everything that had happened since returning, she couldn't shake off the feeling of *relief* she felt.

As the days stretched into nights, Evie and The Circle spent long hours in the library, searching the many archives for links between the Gray family and the Fae.

So far, they had found nothing, and Evie found herself becoming increasingly frustrated with their lack of progress.

"Maybe we should call it a night?" Robyn suggested.

It was nearing midnight, and The Circle had already spent the last few hours tucked away in the depths of the main library.

Jack had shared his suspicions about The Guardians with the rest of The Circle, and though it was difficult news to process, they all agreed that The Guardians could no longer be trusted.

Evie sighed and rubbed her eyes.

"I don't think we will find anything here," she said. "We've already spent hours looking over the same things, and we are still none the wiser. I think we just have to accept the fact that there is absolutely *no* Fae blood in my family's history."

"Hey, don't give up so soon," Tessa said reaching for her hand and giving it a squeeze. "We will find something. We just have to keep looking."

"I guess," Evie replied.

Lucas and Zac both stood up and began to pile their books and papers together.

They all turned when the library doors suddenly burst open, watching as Jack stalked towards them. He looked disgruntled, his body rippling with tension.

Evie stole a glance towards him, noting a bloody wound above his right eyebrow.

"It's nothing," Jack said, meeting her panicked stare. "I've handled it."

"Clearly, looking by the state of your face," Evie retorted. "What happened?"

"It's nothing," he replied, wincing.

Evie rolled her eyes. "It certainly doesn't look like *nothing* to me," she said flatly, crossing the room to stand in front of him. "You should get the healers to take a look, it doesn't look very nice."

"I'll be fine," he said, followed by, "did you find anything?"

"Nothing," Lucas answered. "We were just about to call it a night."

Jack nodded. "That's probably a good idea," he said. "I heard voices in the common room as I walked by. I tried to listen in, but I couldn't make out what was being said."

"More evidence to prove that The Guardians are assholes?" Evie said, as she folded her arms across her chest.

Jack smirked. "I'll look into it tomorrow," he said.

"Come on, let's go upstairs," Tessa said quietly. "I don't feel comfortable discussing this in here, anyone could be listening."

One by one, they filed out of the library and along the silent corridors of The Academy.

The Circle's apartment was welcoming as they piled in, and offered an instant sense of protection as Cora locked the door.

Evie watched as Jack sunk into one of the armchairs, and she shook her head in disbelief.

"You don't always have to play the martyr, Saunders. I am certain the healers would have that wound cleaned up in seconds."

"There's a first aid kit in the bathroom," he said, lying his head back against the pillows.

Rolling her eyes, Evie turned and hurried into the bathroom. She found the kit in a cupboard beneath the sink, and after grabbing a towel and a bowl of warm water, she went back into the living room.

The girls had already gone to bed. Evie placed the bowl onto the small coffee table, along with the first aid kit, and turned to face Jack. She moved closer and twisted his head slightly in order to get a better look.

"Last chance," she said. "Merida could heal this wound in a heartbeat."

"I trust you," he said confidently.

Evie picked up a cotton gauze pad, soaked it in the water, and began to wipe the blood away from his face. Jack winced but said nothing as she continued to clean the wound.

"It's not that deep," Evie told him after a few minutes. "I think you will survive."

"Thank you. Happy to know I'll live to tell my tale," he replied with a sarcastic grin and lifted himself forwards.

The room was empty. Neither had noticed Lucas and Zac silently slipping away. Evie packed away the first aid kit and tossed the bloody gauze into the bin.

"Are you going to tell me what happened?" Evie asked.

Jack frowned. "I told you it was nothing," he said flatly.

"Okay so you got into a fight with *nothing*?" she said. "Quit the bullshit, Jack. Tell me how the hell you got hurt."

"Now who's being insufferable?" he teased, but noting the flash of rage in her eyes, he said, "I was walking through the park, and I was attacked. That's all you need to know."

"Who. Was. It?" she asked, anger flaring.

"It doesn't matter," he said. "Look it's done. I'm fine. I dealt with him."

"Who hurt you, Jack?" Evie demanded. She gripped the side of his face, forcing him to look at her. "Tell me the truth."

"I don't know for sure," he said after a few seconds of silence. "I didn't recognise the guy. But he was a witch, I know that much. He attacked me from behind. He managed a lucky shot at my face before I tackled him to the ground."

"Where is he now?" she pressed, fingers tingling as her magic sparked.

"He ran off," Jack said bitterly. "I've reported the incident. Don't worry about it."

"Jack, considering recent events, why the hell did you think it was okay to walk through the park by yourself? At this time of night... " she said.

Jack frowned. "Careful, Gray. People might start to think that you're worried about me."

"This isn't funny! I'm worried about all of us," she said sharply. "Did it not cross your mind that the same person who tried to hurt me, could also be the one who attacked *you* tonight?"

"It did cross my mind," he said thoughtfully.

"Is that all you have to say?" she asked, perplexed by his lack of concern. "Any lower, and you could have lost your eye!"

"I guess it was my lucky night," he said. "Gods forbid the

consequences losing my eye would have caused."

"You're an asshole," she said as he released a low laugh. "None of this is funny!"

"Lighten up," he said softly, and stood up. "I'm fine. I don't know who attacked me, but I can't exactly go running around making accusations. We are supposed to be keeping our heads low, remember?"

Evie nodded, crossing her arms as he moved around her. He walked into the kitchen, returning a moment later with a bottle of water and an ice pack.

"The healers would provide you with a tonic that would work much better than an ice pack," she said.

"The ice pack will work just as well." Jack smiled. "Thank you for seeing to my wound. Your hands were much softer than Merida's would have been."

Evie smiled, feeling her cheeks flush with heat. "Let's not make a habit of it shall we, Saunders?" she said quietly. "Well if that is all, I think it's time to go to bed."

"I agree," he said, and added with a smile, "It's Christmas Eve tomorrow."

At the mention of Christmas, Evie was filled with her usual feeling of utter dread. Within seconds, her heart was thumping dangerously beneath her chest. Clutching her arms around herself, Evie forced her eyes shut, and silently began to count.

One. Two. Three. Four…

"Evie?" Jack's voice sounded distant in her mind as he moved closer to where she stood. She felt his hand reach for her chin, tilting her head up. "Evie what is it? What's wrong?"

"It's nothing," she said through gritted teeth. "Leave me alone. Please…just go…"

"I'm not going anywhere," he said, gripping her cheek. His

thumb gently caressed her skin, soothing her. "Breathe. Whatever is going on, just breathe through it. You're safe. I'm here."

Seconds turned to minutes, and after a while, Evie felt the thumping of her heart begin to settle, until finally, a normal rhythm was restored. As her breathing eased, her chest slowly relaxed, allowing the anxiety that had overwhelmed her to evaporate completely.

"I'm sorry," she said quietly, feeling her eyes begin to burn. "That hasn't happened for a while."

"This has happened before?" he asked, as he lowered his hand.

Evie nodded. "Panic attacks," she told him. "I've been having them since my parents died. Certain things trigger them...Christmas was my dad's favourite holiday."

"I'm sorry...I didn't realise," Jack said.

"You weren't to know," she said quietly, inhaling a deep breath. "I'd appreciate it if you didn't tell anyone about this. I can usually hide them pretty well. I was caught off guard tonight."

"I won't say anything," he said. "You know you can talk to me, Evie. I'm here to listen."

"I know," she said, and lowered her head. "Thank you. I'm sorry you had to see that."

"You have nothing to apologise for," he said, and placed his finger beneath her chin, lifting her head once more. "Look at me."

"No," she said, forcing her eyes away. "I'm embarrassed."

To her surprise, Jack chuckled, and she felt his fingers slide along her jaw, his palm resting in a cupping position against her face.

"You have nothing to be embarrassed about." His voice was soft, and she lifted her head, her eyes meeting with his.

"We should go to bed," Evie said.

"We should," he agreed, but made no attempt to move.

He lowered his head, resting his forehead against hers. His lips inches away from her own.

For a moment, they stood still, and she felt his other arm lace around her back, pulling her closer against his muscled chest.

"Jack," she said in a voice that was barely a whisper.

With a deep breath, Jack pulled away, and Evie was certain she could feel the reluctance in his release.

"Goodnight Evie," Jack said, stepping aside and giving her room to pass.

Chapter Fourteen

The Academy was always quiet over the festive season, with many of The Guardians and students choosing to spend time with their families.

The Circle, however, had spent the majority of Christmas Eve in their apartment.

Lucas and Zac had been put on tree duty and had not long returned with a Christmas tree so big, they'd barely been able to fit it through the door. Cora had rolled her eyes, but the spirit of Christmas had soon taken over, and she was now busy co-ordinating the tree decorations.

Evie watched from across the room. She had a book in her lap, but she wasn't really paying attention to the words on the pages. Christmas was the one time of the year she always loved as a child, but since losing her parents, she had come to resent it.

"What do you think of the tree?" Zac asked, seating himself beside her.

"It's great," she said quietly.

"I thought you'd want to help decorate?" he said.

"Not really my thing," she told him, and added with a forced smile, "besides, you guys are doing such a great job."

Zac frowned.

"Are you alright? Has something happened? You've been quiet all day."

"No. I'm fine," she told him, and added with a sigh, "Christmas isn't my favourite holiday, that's all."

"Oh," he said. "I didn't even think. I'm sorry…do you want to get out of here? We can go for a walk if you like?"

Evie smiled. "It's all right Zac," she said. "I'm fine here, honestly. The tree looks great, really, it does."

"If you change your mind, just let me know," he said, and stood up.

He walked across the room and joined the others who were stood admiring their handy work. Evie closed her book and placed it on the table as the door to Jack's bedroom opened. He wore a pair of grey shorts and a black T-shirt, and it was the first time she'd seen him looking so relaxed since her return from London.

Evie watched as he crossed the room, disappearing into the kitchen. Frustrated, she stood up, not really knowing what to do with herself. After last night, she'd barely been able to talk to him coherently, let alone look at him. She was becoming increasingly annoyed with herself, and the overwhelming wave of emotions that threatened to explode.

Jack appeared, holding two bottles of soda. He passed one to her, his eyes trailing her movements as she took the soda from him.

"Thanks," she said.

He sat down and gestured for Evie to do the same.

"Lydia has agreed the date for your initiation," he said. "It's going to happen on New Year's Day."

"Oh," she said, raising her eyebrow. "How very dramatic of them. Why wait so long?"

Jack stiffened, and Evie noticed a dark shadow flash across his face. "The Guardians want to *investigate* your magic further before the initiation. Precautionary measures."

"Of course they do," she said, rolling her eyes. "Did you find

105

anything out about their meeting last night?"

Jack shook his head. "I mentioned it to Barnabas, but he had no idea what I was talking about."

"Barnabas?" Evie said, frowning. "How? I thought the Elders didn't come here anymore?"

Jack nodded. "They don't," he said. "I spoke to him briefly via a fire message."

"So, I guess your theories are right?" she said. "It is obvious The Guardians *are* up to something, but the question is, who was in the common room last night? Do you think Barnabas was telling the truth?"

Jack shrugged. "Again, I have my theories, but without evidence, we can't prove anything," he said. "As for Barny, he's an Elder, Evie. He would never betray his own people for the sake of gaining more power. I trust that old soul with my life."

"But not enough to tell him what's going on, right?" Evie asked, raising her eyebrow. "I get why you want to keep this between us, Jack, but don't you think it would be wise to have someone of Barny's status on our side?"

"Not until we have proof," he said. "Right now, all we have are theories."

"What about the demon attack? Isn't that enough proof?" she said.

"No," he said. "We need concrete proof."

Evie sunk back into the armchair with a sigh. "I guess we will just have to find more evidence then."

"The Guardians are meeting tonight," he told her. "I haven't been invited, but I'm going regardless. I'll see what I can find out."

"This evening?" she said. "It's Christmas Eve, I thought everyone would have left already."

106

"They're leaving after the meeting," he said. "The Inquisitor has already gone. Apparently, there has been some activity in the Land of Wonder. He left with Julias and Lydia to investigate about an hour ago."

Evie raised her eyebrows for a second time. "The Land of Wonder? The *Fae* realm?" she mused. "Don't you think that's a bit of a coincidence?"

"Yeah," he agreed. "It could be a ruse. But if they think your magic *came* from the Fae, what better place to start their investigation into *you*. It was Lydia's idea."

"Lydia?" she said. "How do you know?"

"I heard her talking to Julias," he replied.

"I have a real bad feeling about all of this," she said, and bit her lip. "I don't think The Dark Prince is the *only* one we should be worrying about."

Jack nodded. "We will figure it out, but for now, there isn't much that we can do," he said. He sounded annoyed. "We will just have to wait until after the holidays, but that doesn't mean we have to stop looking into your family's history. We must have missed something, somewhere."

"We're done!"

Cora's excited voice filled the apartment, forcing Jack and Evie to end their conversation.

"What do you guys think? Too much? Too little?" she asked. "Do you think we need more lights?"

"You've definitely outdone yourself this year." Jack smiled. "It looks great Cora."

"Excellent!" She beamed. "Well, now that is done, I guess I had better pack a bag and get ready."

"Where are you going?" Evie asked.

"Home." She grinned.

"That will be lovely," Evie said, and felt her heart sink a little.

"I didn't realise the time." Tessa gasped. "Zac, we had better get a move on. Gods forbid we're late, our parents might actually kill us."

"Do we have to?" Zac groaned. "We're too old for this bullshit."

"What are you talking about?" Robyn asked curiously.

Cora smirked. "Zac's parents and Tessa's parents still make them join in on the Christmas traditions…they're spending their Christmas Eve carolling in the Forest."

"That is super cute!" Robyn beamed. "I've always wanted to go carolling on Christmas Eve!"

"Why don't you come with us?" Tessa suggested. "You can stay at my house. My parents won't mind! In fact, they'll be excited to meet someone from the London Guardians! Zac's parents will love it too! You can join us for dinner tomorrow as well."

"Are you sure both of your parents won't mind?" Robyn asked.

"Of course, they won't mind! They'll be delighted!" Tessa smiled. "Go pack your things. I'll send a fire message to them now."

"What about you, Evie?" Robyn asked, turning to face her.

"Absolutely not," she said. "I'll be just fine with my books. You go though, you'll have so much fun."

"Are you sure?" Tessa said. "You know my parents will be happy to see you again, Evie."

"I'm sure," she said, and smiled. "Honestly, you guys go, have some fun."

"But what will you do?" Robyn asked, her tone sympathetic.

"You can't spend Christmas Day on your own Evie!"

"I'll be fine," she said. "Honestly, go pack your things already!"

***

On Christmas morning, Evie woke to find The Circle's apartment silent, and was surprised by how much she didn't like it. Christmas had always been a big event for her family, and she missed it.

She missed the sound of her dads laughter as they tore open their presents, and she missed her mother singing as she fussed over the stove.

Her heart ached with an agonising pain as she thought of her parents. The memories of them overwhelming her as her eyes began to burn.

A mystery. Their death had become a mystery that no one, other than herself, seemed keen to resolve. When her parents died, Evie had fought relentlessly with The Guardians. To make them see what she knew to be true; her parents had been murdered.

In the days leading up to her leaving, Evie had spent every waking hour looking for clues of who might have been responsible. But each time, she only reached a dead end. Not a single shred of evidence to suggest foul play. Just two bodies.

The Guardians had ordered her to accept the Gray's death as nothing more than a terrible accident and move on. Case closed.

"Evie, are you alright?"

Wiping her eyes on the sleeve of her shirt, Evie spun around. Jack had entered the kitchen and was leaning against the doorframe.

"Oh, I'm sorry, I didn't think anyone was here," she said. "Just ignore me. I'm having a moment."

"Has something happened?" he asked, concerned.

She shook her head. "You caught me again…I'm just being silly," she said. "Why are you here? I thought you would have left already."

"My parents are visiting my sister in Australia," he said. "She moved out there a few years ago…they take it in turns to visit each other."

"I'm surprised The Guardians let them go, with everything going on I mean," she said.

Jack smiled. "My dad has never been one to follow Guardians orders," he said. "He was disappointed when I became a leader."

Evie chuckled. "I'm sure he's proud of you really," she said, and added, "So, you're stuck with me then."

He nodded, smirking.

"Lucas left an hour ago. If you would rather be alone, I can leave."

"I don't want you to go," she said. "Being back here brings back so many memories of my parents."

"That's understandable," he said softly.

"Jack, will you go somewhere with me?" she asked before she could stop the words escaping her mouth.

"Sure," he replied.

"You can say no, but I want to visit my parent's grave."

"Of course," he said. "Do you want to go now?"

Evie nodded. "Are you sure you don't mind? I don't want to spoil your day."

Jack smiled. "I didn't exactly have anything planned," he said.

Chapter Fifteen

The small church was blissfully quiet, and Evie was filled with an instant sense of ease as Jack's portal disappeared.

The entrance to the graveyard was unlocked, and Jack pushed the old, creaking gate open to allow them in. In front of the old church, lay endless rows of headstones, each protruding from a blanket of fluffy white snow. Evie walked forward, slowly reading each name until she found the one she was looking for.

Paul Elijah Gideon Gray
Born 17.9.1973
Died 9.7.2016

Anna Eloise Gray
Born 6.5.1974
Died 9.7.2016

Gone in life, but together in death.
Their strength and love, forever as one.

Her eyes stung with built up tears, and Evie muffled a sob against her palm. She felt Jack's arm rest on her shoulder, pulling her against him. She melted into his embrace, welcoming the comfort of his arms as they wrapped around her.

"I'm sorry," Evie said. "I feel like an idiot. I'm not usually this emotional."

"This was always going to be hard for you."

"I just wish I had answers," she said, frustrated. "If I knew what happened to them, maybe I would have some closure. I have so many questions. I hate not knowing."

"What if there was a way?" he said.

"What do you mean?" Evie asked, raising her eyebrow.

"To find out what really happened to them," he said, and added, "as a Guardian Leader, I shouldn't even be suggesting this, but as your friend…"

"Jack Saunders are you suggesting that we do something *illegal*?" she asked, raising her eyebrow once more. "I didn't have you down as the rule breaking kind of guy—your dad would be very proud!"

His face held a mischievous smirk. "Do you want to do this or not?"

"Are you sure I will find out what happened to them?" she asked.

"I'm pretty certain, but this stays between us," he warned and held out his hand for her to take. "I don't think the others would approve if they found out."

Evie nodded, taking hold of his outstretched hand. She felt excited and a little nervous as Jack opened a portal.

Chapter Sixteen

The occasional hoot of a hidden owl was the only sound as Evie and Jack stepped out of the shimmering portal.

The darkness of the woods in which they now stood was frightening, and Evie had trouble shaking off the feeling they were being *watched*.

Jack lifted his hand, casting a spell that would reveal any other human presence.

"It's just us," he said quietly.

"Jack where exactly are we?" she asked, her eyes scanning the swaying trees that surrounded them.

"Albania," he answered.

"Albania!" Evie exclaimed in a hushed breath. "You didn't say we had to *leave* the country. Have you lost your mind?"

"*You* said you wanted to know what happened to your parents." His voice barely audible as he, too, scanned their surroundings.

"Who could you possibly know that lives in Albania?" she asked.

"The Seer," he replied.

"What*?*" Evie gasped, grabbing hold of his arm. "Christ, Jack! The Seer!"

"We can go back to The Academy if you like?" he suggested pointedly. "But you won't find answers from anyone there. The Seer is the only one with the sight. She will tell you what The Guardians didn't."

"*If* The Guardians find out about this," she said, "they will strip us of our powers! Do you really think this is a good idea? We already have enough problems to deal with. We're breaking the law."

"Evie, I wouldn't have bought you here if I didn't think it was safe," he said. "The Guardians won't find out. I promise. You just have to trust me."

Evie paused. "Wait a sec… *you've* been here before, haven't you?"

"Once," he said. "A long time ago."

"Why?" she asked.

"That's not important," Jack said. "Look, I know, The Guardians have filled our heads with poison about the Seer, but she really isn't what they say. They put her into exile and stripped her of her powers for a crime she did not commit, because they were afraid of losing their credibility as *protectors*."

Evie frowned. "So, who did obliterate the Scottish Guard?"

"No one knows, but it wasn't Lilibeth. We can trust her. She's helped me once before."

"Lilibeth?" she replied questioningly. "You're on first name terms with the most dangerous woman to exist in our world? I'm starting to think there *is* a lot that I *don't* know about you *Mr I am a Guardian Leader*."

"She's not dangerous. Not really. Let's go. Her cave is deeper in the woods," he said sharply.

"Promise me nothing is going to kill us? I've had my fair share of near-death experiences lately."

Jack smirked. "I promise I won't let you die. Besides, I cast a protection spell before I opened the portal. If there is anyone around us, they can't see or hear us."

"That makes me feel a little better," she said anxiously.

Evie became more nervous as they trekked further into the darkening woods, causing her heart to race rapidly. Jack walked beside her, silently. His body taut like a bow, but if he was nervous, he didn't voice it.

The temperature dropped the further they walked, and as a gush of bitterly cold air swept through the trees, Evie shivered then let out a gasp as Jack finally began to slow.

In front of them stood a large cave. The cave was surrounded by overgrown bushes, and in its centre stood a hole, wide enough to allow only a single person to pass through at a time.

"Exactly how far into the cave do we have to go?" Evie asked, her eyes widening.

"Not *too* far," he said, and on detecting the nervousness in her voice he asked. "Are you sure you want to do this?"

Evie nodded. "We're here now," she said. "Let's go."

The smell of soil, moss, and damp filled the air as Jack led her through the mouth of the cave. An icy chill settled along her bones as she followed him through the long, winding tunnel. With each silent step, Evie could feel the daunting anxiety rise within her. The flashlight that Jack held in his hand filled the narrow tunnel with a bright light, though it did nothing to calm the beating of her pounding heart.

As though sensing her fear, she felt Jack's hand reach for hers, and she gripped it with her own. The silence played on her nerves, but her voice failed her as she tried to muster a string of words together. She remained silent, ignoring the wild thoughts hurtling through her mind.

Evie lost track of time, and she wasn't sure how long they had been walking. The temperature of the cave chilled her deeply, and she did not realise the tightness of her hand in Jack's until he flexed his fingers slightly, releasing the pressure.

"Sorry," she said.

"I didn't have you down as the *scared of the dark* type of girl," he said, releasing a chuckle that seemed to bounce off the stone walls. She knew he was teasing her as an attempt to lighten her mood. "Relax, Evie. You're safe with me."

"It's not the dark I'm afraid of," she muttered. "How much farther?"

"We're almost there," he said. "Are you alright?"

"I'm fine," she told him. "I just don't like confined spaces."

Jack gripped her hand, acknowledging that he understood. They walked in silence until at long last, they reached the end of the narrow tunnel.

Though it was dark, Evie had no trouble seeing *her.*

***

Lilibeth did not move as Jack stepped closer to her.

The Seer wore a long silvery dress that was ripped in parts, and a dirty white cloak which hung from her frail body. Her silvery-blonde hair, which Evie imagined would have once been immaculate, was matted and hung from her head in a knotted mess.

Evie felt a wave of sadness rush through her as their eyes met. The Seers pale, oval face, though tired and aged, was beautiful, with eyes so dark, she could feel herself getting lost within them.

"Do not pity me," her musical voice echoed throughout the cave, "I neither need, nor want the pity of a Guardian."

"I'm sorry," Evie said, forcing her eyes away. "I didn't mean…"

"*Why* are you here Jack Saunders?" Lilibeth asked, cutting

116

Evie off. The sharpness of her voice felt like the edge of a dagger, and Evie felt herself recoil slightly. "I told you never to return."

"We need your help Lilibeth," he said.

Lilibeth laughed. "My days of helping The Guardians are *long* gone," she said quietly.

"Please," Evie pressed. "We aren't here because of The Guardians. They don't know we are here. I need your help. My parents, they were murdered five years ago..."

"I know who *you* are," Lilibeth said sharply. "But I cannot help you."

"Please, just listen to what I have to say," Evie said. "The Guardians lied about my parents' death. They said it was an accident. I know they were murdered. I just don't know why or how. Please, if you know anything, tell me."

"You have a pure heart, Evie Gray," she said, and Evie noted that some of the sharpness in her tone vanished. "There are many secrets and lies that cloud your past. Your parents died because of a secret they did not wish to share. The Guardians did not lie to you. Paul and Anna Gray were not murdered."

"Yes, they were," Evie said. "Someone, or something, killed them... "

Lilibeth shook her head.

"Your mother could not live with the idea of anyone else finding out about what they did. Your father had more faith, but in the end, he knew your mother was right. If anyone found out about *you*, the consequences would have been so severe. Your parents died in order to keep you safe. They *sacrificed* themselves, so that *you* could live."

Evie regarded the Seers words, shaking her head vigorously, "No...no! My parents would never...they would *never* do anything like that." She almost screamed. "It's a lie! They were murdered!"

"The Gray's were a very powerful couple. They pulled off the perfect death. There was no evidence of foul play. *They* took their own life, in the hope that they would take their secret to the grave. They died believing they were *protecting* you."

"I don't believe you," Evie cried. "It's not true! They wouldn't do that!"

"I am bound by an ancient magic. I cannot lie, nor do I have reason to." She sighed. "I know this is not what you wished to hear, but now you have, I must warn you, a darkness like no other is upon you."

"Darkness?" Evie repeated, ignoring the tears escaping her eyes.

Lilibeth smiled, inhaling a deep breath.

"Smell that," she said excitedly as her nostrils flared. "The Fae are powerful, magical creatures. Their magic sought by so many for centuries. That magic runs through your veins. Strong and pure, just like your heart. The Dark Prince is not the only one who seeks your gift. There are others who want it too."

"This doesn't make any sense," Evie said, before adding, "We have searched all the archives relating to my family, there is no mention of Fae in my bloodline. How is this even possible?"

The Seer sucked in a breath.

"Simple. There is *no* Fae blood in your family's history. *"*

"Then how am I able to create an element of Fae magic?" she asked.

Lilibeth said nothing, lifting her chin slightly as Evie continued.

"If my parents *knew* I had Fae magic, why didn't they just tell me? What about my brother? Elijah, does he have it too?"

The Seer shook her head. "I know nothing of him," she said, and turned away.

"You're lying!" Evie shouted. Rage flared within her, and

she felt the simmering spark of her magic as it flared beneath her fingers. "You know more. I know you know. TELL ME!"

The Seer did not answer.

Instead, Lilibeth raised both arms, lifting Jack and Evie into the air as she chanted words in a language neither could understand.

A surge of wind encircled the cave, spinning faster and faster with each word the Seer spoke, forcing Evie and Jack to crash violently into each other.

The Seers power was strong, and Lilibeth's dark laugh echoed wickedly through the cave. Evie screamed as she and Jack were carried by the wind, back through the caves tunnel, and into the darkness of the woods outside.

Jack landed hard on the moss-covered ground, cursing loudly as Evie fell next to him. The wind stopped, and Evie jumped to her feet, grabbing the flashlight out of Jack's hands.

The mouth of the cave had sealed itself.

"She's gone," Jack rasped, answering her unspoken question. "We need to go."

"No, we can't go. I still have a million more questions!" she cried. "Please, make her come back."

"We have to go," he said. "You won't get anything else from her tonight. She's gone."

"No." She sobbed. "You told me I would get the answers I needed. Make her come back!"

"She's gone Evie," he said, grabbing her shoulder. "I'm sorry. We need to go."

Evie inhaled deeply, flinching at the pain in her chest. Her eyes blurred with angry tears as Jack reached for her hand, and she watched silently as the portal reappeared, shimmering brightly.

She had no words left to say and remained silent as Jack gently tugged her forwards.

119

Chapter Seventeen

"So let me get this straight. The two of you just decided between yourselves to wander off to another country, without so much as a whisper to any of us about what the hell you were planning...to pay a visit to the *Seer?*"

Cora's sharp voice seemed to fill every inch of the living room. She was stood by the kitchen, arms folded across her chest, seething as she glared at Evie and Jack.

Evie rolled her eyes. She had spent the last ten minutes *trying* to tell The Circle what happened in Albania, but Cora's constant interruptions were making the task difficult. Sucking in a deep breath, Evie lifted her head to meet Cora's deadly glare.

"We didn't wander off anywhere," Evie said. "It wasn't a pre-planned day out Cora. It just sort of happened. Besides, you guys weren't here."

"We *all* have cell phones, Evie," Cora said. "A simple *hey guys we're just heading over to Albania to pay a visit to the Seer* would have been thoughtful. Anything could have happened to you, and none of us would have known.

"Considering recent events," she continued, throwing a dirty look in Jack's direction. "I would have thought *you* would have known better. I am surprised you even agreed to such a reckless idea. What the hell were you thinking?"

"If you're implying that this was *my* idea then please let me correct you," Evie said crisply. "It was *his* idea to visit the Seer. Not mine."

"Seriously, *Jack?*" She scowled. "I expected this stupidity from Evie, but not you! You're a Guardian Leader for Christ's sake! You're supposed to *lead* by example!"

"I am still in the room you know." Evie scowled, biting back the anger threatening to flare. "Nobody was hurt. We saw the Seer. We came home. Nothing bad happened, Cora. Not physically anyway."

"But something could have happened, Evie! And none of us would have known. What don't you understand about that?" She gasped and twisted her head to Jack. "What about you? Anything to say for yourself?"

"You're right," Jack said. His voice was flat. "We shouldn't have gone without telling you guys. It was stupid idea. I should never have suggested it."

"Good. I'm glad you agree with me," she said. "So, was it even worth the risk? Do you believe what the seer told you?"

Evie sagged slightly against the wall.

"I don't know. Her riddles have opened the doorway to a hell of a lot more questions. My parents were good people, I know they were. But this…this is huge.

"I don't know what to do. For five years, I've believed my own version of events, and now I just don't know what to believe. I am so confused."

"You have us," Tessa said softly. "We will do everything we can to help."

Evie nodded but said nothing as she closed her eyes, allowing herself a moment to switch off.

***

"If we hadn't bought you back here, your Fae magic would have never been exposed. We will do everything we can to help find out the truth about your parents," Tessa said. "We are in this together, Evie. We're family."

As Tessa spoke, Cora glanced across the room, and felt a dark chill trickle down her spine.

Jack had gone rigid. His lips forming a thin line as he stared ahead. His face white with fury, and as he twisted his head, Cora flinched as he gave her a look so scalding, it felt as though his dark eyes were burning right into her.

Cora balked at the intensity of his stare, gripping her sides as she felt his fury radiate from his taut body, hitting her like shards of shattered glass. She gasped, reaching for her throat, struggling to catch her breath.

Being an empath had its benefits, but right now she wished she didn't have the gift.

"Cora? Are you okay?" Zac's voice was filled with concern, and it took a moment for Cora to regain control.

"I'm. Fine. Just..." she managed through clenched teeth, "just a lot of emotions in here right now. It's giving me a headache."

"You look like you're about to throw up," Tessa said, and jumped up, rushing to Cora's side. "I really don't know how you deal with it all. Do you want some herbal tea? Maybe that will help?"

"Deal with what?" Robyn asked as Cora shook her head.

"Cora's an empath. Sorry, I thought you knew," Evie said, and crossed the room to stand beside Cora. She reached for her hand. "You're in pain...I'm sorry. Cora. Is it because of me? I know my emotions are unchecked right now..."

"No, it's not you Evie." She forced a smile. "Look, I think we should all take tonight off and relax. It's been non-stop since we got back from London. I think we all deserve a night off to just relax and enjoy what's left of Christmas. We can talk about this tomorrow."

"That sounds like a great idea," Lucas said.

"I'll grab us some food from downstairs. I bet there's still plenty left over from this afternoon," Tessa offered. "I'll get dessert too. We definitely need cake!"

"I have some things to finish up in my office," Jack grumbled. "You guys carry on without me."

"Screw whatever bullshit Julias and Hayden want you to do," Lucas said. "It's Christmas. Take the night off!"

"I'll be an hour," he said flatly.

He left without another word. Cora sighed and turned away from the girls.

"I'll be right back," she said, and hurried after him.

Jack was halfway down the hall when she finally caught up with him. He spun around, surprised to see her.

"What's wrong?" he asked.

"I know what's going on Jack. I told you the other night, your pain is *my* pain. You're in love with her."

"I have no idea what you're talking about, Cora," he said, and she could hear the defensiveness in his voice.

"Don't lie to me. I feel what you're feeling whether you want me to or not. So quit trying to push me out. I'm not an idiot. I've seen the way you look at her. I feel *everything* that you feel when she is with you. You can deny it all you like. You can attempt to mask your feelings, but you can't hide them from an empath.

"You've been a completely different guy since she came back. Your focus…your judgement…everything is *off*. I get it. Really, I do, but you have to find some way of dealing with it. Taking Evie to the Seer was stupid and reckless. You're a

Guardian Leader, for Christ's sake. Did you even consider the consequences?"

Cora paused, waiting for him to interject, and when he remained silent, she sighed.

"Listen, I don't want to be the one standing here giving you a lecture. It's not my place to do so, but I have to say something. Every single feeling that you had in that room tonight, I felt it too, and it hurt like hell. I know you blame yourself for the demon attack the other night, but that wasn't your fault. None of this is your fault."

"Have you told her?" he asked sharply.

Cora shook her head. "I wouldn't do that. It's not my place. But I think *you* should. You have to tell her how you feel."

"No," he said. "We have enough going on. Our main priority is to find out which of The Guardians ordered that attack. Everything else can wait."

"Your feelings are important too, Jack," she said softly.

"Keeping Evie safe is important," he almost growled. "Capturing The Dark Prince is important. Uncovering the truth about The Guardians is important. Nothing else matters right now, Cora. I have to keep my focus. I've already made two mistakes, one of which almost got Evie killed. I won't allow anything else to get in the way, do you understand? I can't afford to lose my focus again."

He spun on his heel then, storming away. Cora watched his retreating figure, sighing.

Being an empath truly did suck at times.

***

A few hours later, with the food long gone and the night drawing

124

to a close, Evie, for the first time since arriving back at The Academy, finally felt at home.

It was almost midnight when Jack returned. His face red, and his chestnut brown hair dripping with melting snow. If he looked agitated before, it was nothing compared to how he looked now. He was furious.

"That was a *long* hour." Lucas gave a flat stare as Jack sat down in an empty armchair.

"I got caught up with something else," he replied grimly.

"Dare I ask if there's any food left?"

"In the kitchen, but you will have to warm it up," he said.

"What kept you?"

"It was nothing, don't worry about it," he said.

"Well, it was your loss," Lucas teased and shrugged. "I'm going to call it a night. See you all in the morning."

"Me too," Robyn agreed with a yawn. "We all need a good night's rest, ready for tomorrow."

"What's happening tomorrow?" Jack wanted to know.

"If you'd have stayed tonight, you would know." Lucas grinned. "Evie and Zac can fill you in. I'm off to bed."

The bedroom doors closed gently behind them, and Evie pulled a thick blanket over her as she stretched her legs out across the sofa.

"So, what was so important?" she asked, watching as Jack opened a bottle of beer. "Do you think that's wise? You'll need a clear head tomorrow, Saunders."

"It's Christmas," he said moodily.

Evie raised her eyebrow, taken aback by the sharpness of his tone. "Oh-kay," she said, frowning. "Well, I wouldn't have too many Mr, because you and Cora have pulled the short straw."

Jack nodded. "Enlighten me."

"I've been thinking about what the Seer told us," Evie began, "and despite her riddles confusing the hell out of me, one thing was pretty clear. My parents didn't have Fae blood. I think we need to delve further. The magic could have skipped a generation or two, hence why we should look further back. My grandparent's parents, and so on.

"Unless I was adopted," she teased, chuckling at her own joke. "I also think we should look into my brother. You told me The Guardians stopped looking for him, and I think there is more reasoning to that, so Lucas and Zac are going to find out what they can about Elijah."

She barely paused for breath before she added, "You, on the other hand, have the wonderful task of helping me prepare for this initiation. With Cora's help of course."

"You still have a few days until the initiation, there's no need to worry about that right now," he said, and took a long swig of his beer. "But the rest of the plan sounds good."

"Actually, the initiation is tomorrow," she said flatly. "We found out about an hour after you left."

"What?" He looked angry. "Why did no one tell me?"

"*You* weren't here," Evie pointed out, rolling her eyes.

Jack scowled. "The date had already been agreed. Why the fuck has it been bought forward?"

Evie shrugged, raising an eyebrow.

"Maybe they discovered something in the Land of Wonder, and it's made them want to *test* me sooner rather than later."

"This isn't funny," he growled. "They wouldn't change the initiation date without good reasoning. This is worrying, damn it."

"Why are you getting so worked up?" Evie snapped, annoyed. "We knew it was going to happen. So what if it is a few days earlier?"

"This wouldn't even be happening if you could just *control* your damn emotions," he said coldly.

Evie recoiled, taken back by his outburst.

"What's wrong with you?" she asked sharply.

"Nothing," he said, before standing up. "I'm going to bed. Tomorrow is going to be a long day."

"No one is forcing you to help me," she snapped, frustrated by his attitude. "In fact, don't bother. I don't *need* your help. Cora will help me. Then you can do whatever it is you have to do as a stupid Guardian Leader."

"I didn't say that I didn't want to help," he snarled, and for a moment they glared at each other.

"I don't want your help," she said angrily, rising from the sofa.

She clenched her fists, feeling an unyielding rage boil within her. Her fingers tingled as a fiery heat surged through her veins, threatening to give way to the magic that so desperately wanted to escape.

Silence fell between them, and Evie took a shuddering breath, watching as Jack drained the contents of his bottle.

"You're losing your temper again," he said, and added coldly, "was that not the reason for you ending up in this position in the first place?"

"Fuck you Jack," Evie said, her words trembling as she fought against the overwhelming urge to put him on his ass. "One beer and you turn into a complete asshole."

"How do you expect to control your magic when you allow your emotions to *control* you?" he asked. "You're a mess, Evie. You have no fucking idea what this initiation will do to you unless you learn how to control your emotions."

"Enough," she said, ignoring the burn in her eyes as she met with his flat stare. "I don't know what has happened to you tonight to make you act like such a prick, but you have no right taking it out on me. I suggest you stay the hell away from me."

Evie turned around then, and after saying a quiet goodnight to Zac, who had remained silent the entire time, she stomped out of the room, slamming the bedroom door with a loud bang.

Chapter Eighteen

The afternoon of the initiation brought a change in weather, and with it came a tense atmosphere in The Academy.

Evie sat in one of the many training rooms, her head aching having spent hours with Cora practicing spells whilst attempting to master some sort of control over her new magic. No matter how hard she tried, she simply could not tame the flames.

"Focus!" Cora said for what must have been the tenth time that day. "You're not focusing, Evie. Your head is elsewhere. What is going on with you today? And where the hell is Jack? I thought he was supposed to be helping."

"He's not invited," she said moodily. "Can we take a break? We've been at this for hours and my head is going to explode."

"Your initiation is tonight. We don't have time for breaks," she said. "Try again!"

Evie scowled and closed her eyes, willing for the fire to show. Nothing happened. "It only seems to work when I'm angry or scared. Right now, I feel neither."

"So, get angry then! You certainly have a lot to be angry about," she said as the doors to the training room suddenly swung open.

Jack stood in the doorway; his muscular arms folded across his chest as he stared at the two of them.

As Evie met his dazzling blue gaze, she felt her palms begin to burn. She risked a glance down at her hands, and finally, there it was.

Only this time, the magic was...*different*. Instead of a fireball, her hands were engulfed in bright, orange flames, burning her skin with wicked delight.

Silent panic began to surge through her as she watched the flames flicker merrily against her skin.

"Well, would you look at that!" Cora beamed. "Finally. Progress!"

"I take it that was my doing?" Jack said sheepishly.

"I thought I told you to stay the hell away from me," Evie snapped, waving her hands in an attempt to stop the fire.

The flames continued to flicker, much to her irritation.

"Waving your hands isn't going to make it go away," he said, closing the distance between them. "You have to clear your mind completely and focus on the magic. Then you *will* it to stop. Our magic is related to our emotions. Control your emotions, then you will control your magic."

"I don't need or *want* your help," she said, but did as she was told all the same.

With her mind clear, the flames disappeared almost instantly. Cora smiled and picked up a pile of books that she'd placed onto the table.

"Well done," she said. "Keep practicing. I'll be back in a minute."

"Where are you going?" Evie demanded.

"Toilet break." She winked, and quickly left, leaving everyone in silence.

Evie grimaced. "Why are you here Jack?" she asked, crossing her arms. "I told you to stay away."

"To apologise," he said. "For last night. I didn't mean to upset you."

Evie frowned. "Well, you did."

"I know, and I am sorry," he said softly. "I was pissed off with Julias, not you. I'm sorry."

"Jack, you're a Guardian Leader, you have just as much authority as the Guard," she said. "These people don't control you."

"Sometimes, as a leader, you have to do things that you don't always agree with," he said, and she could hear the bitterness in his tone. "Some orders, you can't say no to. It's just the way it is."

"There's more," she pushed. "Something else is bothering you. What is it?"

"It's nothing," he said quickly. "Honestly. I just wanted to apologise for upsetting you."

She raised her eyebrow. "All right," she said. "I guess I accept your apology."

Jack smiled. "Good, because I've been worried all morning that you might *use* that newfound power of yours to put me on my ass for being such a prick."

Evie smirked. "I don't need magic to do that," she said confidently.

"Oh really?" he said, raising an eyebrow.

Evie rolled her eyes. "I've already said that I forgive you," she mocked. "Don't make me change my mind."

He released a low chuckle, grinning. "So now that I am here," he said. "Will you let me help you?"

"I really don't see the point. I can't control it." She sighed and added, "I was planning to just *wing* it tonight."

Jack frowned. "I'm not sure the initiation works that way," he said. "You have to be prepared for every eventuality. The Inquisitor will want to test your reactions as well as your new abilities. It's not something you can just *wing*, Evie."

"But as you've already pointed out, I can't control this *thing* without controlling my emotions," she said, annoyed. "I'm a mess, remember."

"No, you're not," he said softly.

He held her hands in his own, and she watched nervously as his thumb traced her skin back and forth.

"Close your eyes," he told her, smiling when she continued to stare at him. "Trust me. Close them."

He released her hands then, guiding them to rest at her side as she finally closed her eyes. Evie felt him move, placing himself behind her so that her back was flush with his muscled abdomen. She flinched at his touch, but kept her eyes tightly shut.

"Relax," he told her. She could feel his lips, brushing the side of her ear. "Clear your mind and focus solely on your magic. Try to separate your new ability from what you already know."

"You're not making it very easy for me to focus," Evie said accusingly. "Is it necessary for you to stand right behind me?"

He chuckled in amusement. "Yes," he said, his voice barely a whisper against her ear.

"You're insufferable," she jibed.

"And you're not concentrating," he said flatly. "Clear your mind. Focus on your emotions. Only then, will you learn to control your powers."

Chapter Nineteen

The Inquisitor stood in the centre of the courtyard that sat at the rear of The Academy.

Evie walked along the cobbled path, aware of the many eyes on her as she did.

Standing behind the Inquisitor, she saw Lydia and Julias. Several of the Guardian Leaders whose names she had not bothered to remember were also there, watching closely. Evie scanned the courtyard, searching for signs of the four ancient Elders, but saw nothing amongst the sea of faces that stared back at her. Their absence struck her as odd.

She scanned the crowd again, pausing when she found a pair of familiar, bright blue eyes.

For a few moments, Evie held Jack's gaze, feeling an invisible electricity pull through her. The corner of his mouth rose a fraction, and Evie welcomed the silent gesture.

"Miss Gray," Hayden said as way of introduction. "Apologies for the sudden change of date, it was an unfortunate necessity. I assume you are feeling better?"

"Much better, thank you," she said.

"I am glad to hear that. Luck was most definitely on your side," he said. "The magic that you hold is a rare phenomenon. Never have we come across a witch who happens to harness an element of magic as strong as the one you hold. The purpose of tonight is to identify the strength of the magic and the threat it may pose to our world. We are protectors. We are witches.

Warriors of the Guard. The flames you harness, have you always been able to do this?"

Evie didn't respond straight away. Her mind calculating the words he spoke.

Should she tell the truth?

"Miss Gray?" he prompted.

"No," she said. "It's a new thing."

"A new *thing*?" he repeated. "Interesting statement."

"I don't know how I did it. It just happened."

"Did your parents possess the ability to perform this sort of magic?" he asked.

"Not as far as I'm aware," she said. "I never saw them do it, and they never told me. I didn't know I could do it until it happened. The first time was in the common room. I was just as surprised as you."

"Interesting," he mused. "Shall we begin?"

Evie nodded, focusing all her attention on the Inquisitor. The courtyard was silent as the two stared intensely at each other, neither one removing their gaze from the other.

Her hands began to burn. Tingling with a wicked delight as the Fae magic slowly began to course through her veins.

Control.

She inhaled a long, deep breath, focusing on the magic that was so desperate to erupt.

Focus and control.

She stole a glance at her hands, relieved to see they were still her own. Hayden smiled, raising his own hand as he whispered silent words.

The spell hit her hard. Penetrating her chest with a pain so sharp, it ripped the breath from her. The power forced her off her feet, throwing her across the wet ground with a great force. Her

134

shoulder slammed into a metal bench, and it was all she could do not to scream out.

"That was a simple stunning spell, Miss Gray," Hayden said. "A Guardian Warrior should have been able to *anticipate* and *block* it. Get up."

Ignoring the searing pain in her shoulder, Evie crawled onto her knees, using the bench to pull herself up. The Inquisitor raised his hand again, but this time, she was ready.

Evie raised her own hands, willing the magic to release. It surged through her veins, heating her entire core.

But the flames did not come.

Droplets of water suddenly rose from the ground, rising into the air before her. She manoeuvred her hands, binding the droplets together and forced it forward towards the intended target.

The water engulfed him instantly. Trapping the Inquisitor in a watery cage. Darkness erupted within her. Clouding her mind with a shimmering veil as her magic crashed through her bloodstream, the burn of the surge amplifying with each passing second. For a moment, she heard nothing but silence. Her eyes fixed on the watery prison that held the Inquisitor firmly in place. His wide eyes met with hers, bulging with panic as his lungs begged for air. She could see the *pleading* in those eyes.

And then she heard a voice. *His* voice. Followed by his brilliant blue eyes, now standing before her.

Anxious voices filled the courtyard. Yelling and screaming her name, but it was *his* voice that anchored her.

Her fingers tingled with electricity. The darkness within her, fighting desperately to regain its control over her. She lowered her gaze, staring at her hands in horror.

What had she done?

The courtyard became a buzz of activity as Guardian after Guardian tried and failed to release the Inquisitor from his watery prison. He thrashed vigorously as their spells failed over and over to undo the magic that held him in place.

Evie stared. Her frantic eyes watching as Hayden finally stopped fighting.

His body weakened, flopping as the water filled his lungs, slowly drowning…

Something in Evie snapped. Regaining her focus, she pushed Jack to the side, and threw her hands forward, waving them over the cage. Within seconds, the water was gone, and the Inquisitor fell to the ground, gasping helplessly. Several Guardians, including Lydia, rushed to his side.

Evie stood frozen, conscious of the many eyes that now bore into her.

"Silence," roared the Inquisitor. He pushed The Guardians away, and strode towards where Evie stood, grabbing her hard by the shoulder, and whispered, "You're *Fae!*"

"What?" she said, terrified by the dark look in his frantic eyes.

"Follow my lead," he said, and suddenly began to clap. "An excellent initiation. One of the best in fact!"

"Hayden!" Julias' deep, angry voice grew louder as he walked towards them. "She almost killed you. Lock her up! Guardians, take her. She is a danger to us all!"

"Don't touch her!" Jack's voice was thunderous. He grabbed her arm, tugging her backwards to stand behind him.

"Calm down, Julias. No need for theatrics," Hayden said calmly. "Miss Gray has performed an exceptional bit of magic tonight."

"Fire! Water!" Julias spat. The rage in his voice unmissable as he shot Evie a vicious glare. "You know what this means, Hayden!"

"Quiet, Julias," Hayden said sharply. "The initiation is over. You are all dismissed."

Throwing a dirty look in Evie's direction, Julias twisted his body, and hurtled into the confines of The Academy. Once he was gone, Hayden turned to Evie, gripping her arms tightly.

"Are you alright?" he asked. His eyes were frantic as they bore into her own. "Are you hurt?"

"What the hell is going on?" Jack demanded.

"This is far worse than I thought," Hayden said, mostly to himself.

"What the fuck are you talking about?" Jack growled.

"Get inside," Hayden ordered, throwing a quick glance around the courtyard. "I will explain everything. Go. Go now!"

Then he left, spinning on his heel as he hurried away from them. Evie watched his retreating figure in silent panic, consciously aware of the others moving closer to her.

She felt her heart thunder against her chest as the blood pounded in her ears. Her vision blurred, and she was gripped with a sudden overwhelming urge to vomit. Evie clutched her arms around herself, trembling as she swallowed back the threatening bile. Breathe. She needed to breathe.

"Breathe, Evie." Jack's voice was like an anchor in her mind, guiding her back to the surface. He stood in front of her, his hands resting gently on her shoulders.

"Slowly," he said. "In. Out. In. Out. I'm doing it with you. You're not alone. I'm here. Look at me. Forget everything else. It doesn't matter. Focus on me. Nothing else matters."

Seconds. Minutes. Hours.

Time seemed to stop with every panic attack that struck.

Usually, she was on her own. Hidden away from the world whilst she rode out each painfully exhausting attack, but now she was surrounded by her friends. Friends who were all stood with faces as white as snow. She felt Jack's hands on her shoulders. Heard his calming voice through the walls her mind had built.

The tightness in her chest began to lessen, and her vision began to clear. Though she was aware of the others, she focused her eyes on Jack, imitating his breathing, until she reached a normal rhythm with her own.

"You're safe," he said. "I've got you."

Evie nodded, feeling her cheeks become wet with silent tears.

"Let's go," he said softly, taking hold of her hand.

***

The Inquisitor was already waiting in The Circle's apartment, sat in one of the armchairs, with his arms folded. His face, usually sharp and searching, was now filled with curiosity.

"What the fuck was all that about?" Jack demanded.

Hayden sighed, gesturing for them to sit down.

"I'm going to ask you a question, Evie, and I want the truth this time. The night we met, that wasn't the first time you've used this magic, was it?"

Evie shook her head, her hands shaking.

"The first time was in London. It happened right before the demon attack. And then again when Jack and I were by the university."

"I thought as much," he said. "You have Fae blood."

"I know," she said. "But I've only recently found out."

"Yes, your meeting with *Lilibeth* was quite informative," he said quietly.

"You know about that?" Evie said, casting her eyes to Cora.

"Rest easy, it wasn't Cora who told me," he said. "She and I may have a personal relationship, but I assure you, she would never betray her friends. I know about your meeting with the Seer because I was there. I followed you to the graveyard on Christmas Day."

"You followed me? Why?" she asked.

"I was sent here, Evie," Hayden explained. "To gather information and evidence to prove my theories of corruption. For a few years now, I've had my suspicions about the Pennsylvanian Guard meddling with dark magic and having dealings with demons. I have never been able to prove my theories...until now.

"I came here under the pretence of Inquisitor," he continued. "It was my only way to get closer to certain individuals within this Academy. When I heard of your return, it only furthered my suspicions. The magic that you hold Evie, it is no secret."

"I beg to differ," Evie said quietly. "I knew nothing of it."

Hayden smiled weakly. "Others knew," he said. "For years, there has been rumour of a witch who harnesses elements of Fae magic. Someone within these walls knew of this. The attack in London wasn't the work of The Dark Prince, Evie. It was the Pennsylvanian Guard."

Evie's heart sank, and she lowered her head slightly, silently absorbing every word he spoke. "We know."

"I'm sorry, Evie," he said, and she could hear the sincerity in his voice. "I'm sorry that I made you go through the initiation tonight. It was the only way I could prove my theories and keep up pretences."

"Who is responsible?" Jack asked, his voice burning with rage.

"It wasn't just one person," Hayden said, and added coldly,

"Lydia and Julias are the individuals responsible."

Evie sucked in a deep breath. "Lydia?" she said. "No. No, it can't have been Lydia. She was one of my mom's closest friends! You must be wrong…"

"There is a lot you don't know about Lydia Bowater," he said. "From a young age, Lydia has always been hell-bent on becoming more powerful. She puts on a very good act, but I can assure you, Lydia Bowater is not a woman you can trust."

"How long has she known?" Evie asked, feeling a steady anger begin to rise.

"She's had suspicions for years," he replied.

"This is so messed up," Lucas growled. "Are you certain it was Lydia and Julias?"

"Yes," Hayden said. "Lydia wants Evie's magic, and she is willing to do anything to get her hands on it. The demon attack won't be the last."

"I don't understand," Evie said. "Why bother with demons? Why not just go straight for me?"

"My only guess is that Lydia wanted to prove her theories. Prior to you running away, Evie, this power you now have hadn't manifested," Hayden said, frustrated. "I think Lydia discovered that Jack found you before he told her himself, and wanted to see for herself if she was right. I am guessing your power was somehow *bound* and then manifested because of your age perhaps."

"What do we do?" Lucas asked. "Are there others involved?"

"We have to leave. The Academy isn't safe," he said. "Lydia and Julias are the only Guardian's involved. I have found no evidence to suggest there is anyone else."

"The Elders, they know it's Lydia and Julias who were

responsible?" Jack asked.

Hayden nodded. "They have been informed," he said, "But I don't have solid evidence to order their arrest. It is my word against theirs."

"How do you know they were responsible?" Jack pushed.

"They aren't as smart as they wish to believe," Hayden said. "I overheard the two of them talking the night *you* ran into trouble in the park."

Evie frowned, now realising it had been Lydia and Julias inside the chamber Jack had passed on his way to the library the night he'd been attacked.

"Were they responsible for Jack being attacked too?" Evie asked bitterly.

"I believe Julias was the key instigator," Hayden said. "But again, it is my word against his."

"So, what do we do now?" Cora wanted to know. "Surely The Elders can do something?"

"The Elders won't do anything without concrete evidence. Julias has worked hard these past few years to keep The Elders away from The Academy, Cora," Hayden said. "Right now, all we have is my word to go on, and it isn't enough. I can't prove Lydia and Julias ordered the attack. I just have what I heard."

"Okay, so what about the attack before Christmas?" Zac asked. "Was that Lydia and Julias too?"

"I believe so," Hayden replied. "But again, I don't have any proof."

"Do you think they are working with The Dark Prince?" Evie suddenly asked, her voice hoarse.

"I have considered it," he said and added with a huffed sigh. "Again, without proof…"

"So how did Lydia order the demon attack?" Evie asked.

"Demons don't answer to witches, especially not *Guardian's*."

"That I am still trying to figure out," he told her.

Evie nodded, and said, "They're going to kill me."

"That is not going to happen," Hayden said fiercely. "Evie, I came here to protect you, and that is exactly what I will do. We all will. Until we have concrete evidence to order their arrests, The Academy is no longer safe. You need to leave."

"Hayden's right," Tessa said. "We will keep you safe, I promise."

"If she goes, we all go," Zac said from across the room.

"We are *all* leaving in two days," Hayden said. "My plan is to create a diversion to get everyone out of The Academy, so that we can leave without bringing attention to ourselves. The safest place for Evie right now is the Enchanted Forest, but it would be foolish to go directly there. I have a friend who lives just outside of town. We can stay there until we can make our way to the forest."

"We?" Evie frowned.

"I am coming with you," Hayden said.

"And in the meantime?" Zac wanted to know. "We can't stay locked up in here."

"I wouldn't expect you to," he said. "But I would limit the amount of time you spend downstairs."

"No," Evie said sharply. "No. I'm not running away from this. Running won't solve anything. We should confront them. You said we needed evidence, Hayden. Running away isn't going to help us get that. We have to stay. *I* have to stay."

"You aren't safe here," he said urgently. "You saw how Julias reacted tonight! You have shown two elements of Fae magic, Evie. Do you understand how serious this is? What *they* will do to you?"

"Running away isn't the answer..." Evie declared. "It won't solve anything Hayden."

"It is if it keeps you safe," Jack said sharply. "We're leaving."

"Listen, it's been a long night," Hayden said. "I've no doubt Julias will be seething right now, after what happened tonight. My advice is that you all stay here for the remainder of the evening. I will come back in the morning. No one is to leave this apartment until I return."

Without another word, the Inquisitor rose from his chair. Lucas saw him out, locking the door after him. He returned to the living room; his pale face filled with disbelief.

"Anyone else lost for words?" Lucas mumbled.

"Did you lock the door?" Jack asked, and as Lucas nodded, he said, "Good. I want you all to pack. We're leaving tonight."

"What?" Cora said. "Jack, did you not listen to a word Hayden said?"

"I'm sorry Cora," Jack said. "I don't trust him."

"Are you serious?" she gasped. "Hayden risked everything tonight, and you *still* don't trust him?"

"Cora, he wants to wait another two days before leaving," Jack said hurriedly. "You saw what happened tonight with Evie's magic. The entire Academy saw! And now everyone knows she harnesses *two* elements of Fae magic. What do you think will happen? Julias will not sit around and allow us to carry on as normal. I'm surprised they haven't already barged their way up here.

"We are getting the hell out of here. Tonight," Jack seethed.

"I agree with Jack," Lucas said, crossing his arms. "I'm sorry Cora, but we can't take the risk. I agree with Hayden on one thing though, we can't go directly to the Enchanted Forest. It's too

143

obvious. It will be the first place they look."

"I'm open to suggestions," Jack said.

"We could go to Henry's?" Tessa offered. "You know how much he hates the Guard. I'm sure he would want to help."

"If he hates the Guard, why on earth would this Henry guy, want to help us?" Robyn asked.

Tessa smiled. "He's a powerful warlock, and he has always been friendly with us," she said, before casting her eyes onto Evie. "Besides, wasn't Henry good friends with your dad, Evie?"

"Yeah, he was," Evie replied. "Actually, it's a really good idea, Tess!"

"No," Jack said.

"Why not?" Evie asked, raising her eyebrow.

"It just wouldn't work," he said. "We need to think of somewhere else."

"He's the High Warlock of Pennsylvania. His wards are stronger than any protection spell we could cast. You know it's our best option until we get to the Enchanted Forest."

"You might as well just tell her," Lucas said, rolling his eyes. "You know she will find out eventually."

"Tell me what?" Evie asked.

Jack frowned, throwing Lucas an annoyed look.

"Henry and I don't see eye to eye. We had a minor disagreement a few years ago. I haven't seen or spoken to him since, and I am not particularly interested in changing that."

"I wouldn't have called it *minor*," Cora smirked.

"What happened?" Evie asked, turning to face Jack. "Cat's out of the bag now, Saunders, so tell me?"

"It's not important," he snapped. "Look we don't have time for this. We need to pack and leave. So could everyone please get moving. We meet back here in ten minutes."

"What about Hayden?" Cora asked calmly. "I can't just leave without telling him, Jack. You might not trust him, but I do, and I don't think it is right to just go. He risked a lot for us tonight. We can't just leave him."

"Cora's right," Evie agreed, noting a flash of annoyance in Jack's eyes. "We can't just go. He's on our side. We need to at least tell him."

"Fine," Jack barked. "But we are leaving tonight. With or without him."

Chapter Twenty

"Are you alright?" Robyn asked quietly.

Evie was sat on the edge of the bed, her legs tucked up beneath her chin. Her eyes fixed on the bag that lay at the foot of her bed.

She'd barely said two words since Jack ordered The Circle to pack.

"I'm not sure," Evie replied, lifting her head. "Last month I was in London, living a magic free life. A life that I actually liked, and now I'm back here, about to run away again. So much has happened since I came back to The Academy. I just...I don't know, I guess I just feel really confused by it all. Running away isn't going to solve anything, Robyn."

"I understand," she said, sitting down beside her. "But I don't think Jack sees it as *running*. He just wants to keep us all safe, and he can't do that here. We can't plan anything here. Not now we know who was behind the attacks."

"I know, and you're right, but it still doesn't make sense," she said. "Say we go to Henry's, then what? How long do we stay there? And what happens when we finally do get to the Enchanted Forest? We still have The Dark Prince and whatever mad plan he is hatching to contend with."

Robyn shook her head. "I'm sure we will figure it all out Evie, try not to worry so much. Everything will work out, I promise."

"I'm scared Robyn," Evie said, lifting her head.

It was the first time she'd admitted her feelings, and even as she said it, she could *feel* the darkness of her magic simmering beneath her skin.

"This *magic* I have, it terrifies me," she said. "I don't understand it. I have no idea how to control it. I can feel it, Robyn. I can feel it tingling in my fingers, just waiting to be released. During the initiation, I could feel the darkness trying to take control. My parents knew. They knew the whole time and they never told me."

"I know you're scared, honey," Robyn said softly. "But we are all here to help you figure it out. I don't know why your parents didn't tell you the truth, but I am pretty sure they had good reasons."

"Reasons I will probably never know the answers to." Evie sighed, and added, "Listen, I've been thinking…"

"Don't even go there," Robyn said firmly. "I know exactly what you are going to say, and you can forget it right now. You're not doing this alone. We are in this together, and I'm pretty damn certain the others would say the same too."

"It was just a thought," she said as she stretched her legs so that her feet were now on the wooden floor. "Come on, we should go."

Robyn frowned but followed her all the same. She grabbed both their bags and led the way into the living room. The others were already there. To Evie's surprise, Hayden was back.

"Are you both ready?" Jack asked, and Evie nodded. "Good. Tessa has cast a non-detectable spell, so all our bags can go into one. We will travel by car. The Guard won't be able to track us."

"Okay," Evie said quietly. She still didn't feel entirely comfortable with the plan. "When are we leaving?"

Jack glanced down at his watch, before turning to Hayden.

147

As he did, a loud bang erupted from below.

Hayden smiled. "We leave now," he said urgently.

***

Evie sat in the back of Jack's SUV with Robyn in the seat beside her. Rain battered against the windows in a torrential pour, yet Evie kept her eyes fixed on the glass, watching silently as the outside blurred by.

They had been on the road for almost an hour now, but she had still not spoken. Her head too noisy to even contemplate a conversation. So much had happened. So many questions forming in her aching mind. Her magic drummed a steady beat beneath her skin, sending a tingling sensation as it travelled to the tips of her fingers. Since the initiation, her magic had remained a constant buzz. The drumming a continuous reminder that it was there. That it was ready to be released again.

Evie clenched her fingers, inhaling a deep breath as she did. She had felt so much power in that courtyard. So much power, it had scared her as the darkness had tried to consume her. To break her...

"How long will it take to get to Henry's?" Robyn's voice broke through the torment of her mind, forcing Evie's focus on the blurred window to break.

"Another hour or so," Jack replied, casting a quick glance in his mirror. Evie felt his eyes focus on her for a second before turning back to the road.

"So, The Guardians are corrupt?" Robyn said bitterly.

"Lydia and Julias are corrupt." Lucas said, flashing his razor-sharp teeth with a growl. "We can't tar them all with the same brush."

148

"We don't know that!" she argued. "It doesn't make sense. Why would Lydia turn against us?"

"Power." Jack said angrily.

"Where does Julias come into it?" she asked.

"Julias has been Lydia's sidekick for years," he said. "He will do whatever she tells him to do. Without question."

"It seems like a huge risk to take," Robyn said. "Do *you* think they could be working with The Dark Prince?"

"It is possible." Jack shrugged. "But it wouldn't explain why…unless The Dark Prince wants Evie's magic too…"

"Jack…" Lucas gasped suddenly, twisting his head to face him. "The Dark Prince…all this time we have questioned what his motives are…"

"Me," Evie said quietly. "All this time you have all wondered what this *weapon* could be, and it has been staring you right in the face. It's me. My magic. That is what he is after."

"We don't know that for certain," Jack said quickly, though Evie could tell from the tone of his voice, that he too, thought the same. "We will work it out once we get to Henry's."

"And how do you suggest we do that?" she said, her voice coming out colder than she intended. "Your first response was to run…*we* shouldn't be running, Jack. We should be confronting them. You're supposed to be a Guardian Leader, surely that gives you some kind of authority. Some kind of voice. Why are you so afraid of using it?"

"If running keeps you safe, then that's exactly what we will do," he retorted.

Silence filled the car, and Evie forced her eyes away from the rear-view mirror, away from the intensity of Jack's icy stare.

"We'll be okay Evie," Robyn whispered, but Evie only turned away, forcing her eyes back onto the road.

***

After what felt like hours, Jack finally began to slow the car as he pulled onto a long, twisting path. The rain still fell heavily as he drove, and after a few moments, a large farmhouse came into view. Its windows illuminated with a welcoming yellow glow.

Evie unbuckled her belt and opened the car door. She pulled her hood over her head and ran towards the porch with Robyn and Lucas close by.

The rickety wooden steps creaked as they took to them, finally sheltering from the rain. The others joined them, and Evie reached out to press the old doorbell before stepping back. It took a few minutes, but when the door swung open, she was surprised by the figure that stood before them.

Henry Martinez was a warlock. The High Warlock of Pennsylvania, and one of the most powerful she had ever met.

He stood in the doorway, his grim face brightened by the soft glow of his porch light. His dishevelled appearance caught Evie by surprise as she took in his long, shaggy black hair and thick, round face. On the one side of his cheek, she noted a long, red scar. It looked relatively new. Henry growled.

"What in God's name are you lot doing here?" he bellowed, and spat, "Guardians!"

"Hello to you too, Henry," Evie said, folding her arms.

Henry paused, focusing on Evie, and within a few seconds, his battered face stretched into a curious smile.

"You're supposed to be in London."

"Yeah, that didn't quite work out the way I planned," she replied. "I've been back a couple of weeks."

"What are you doing here?" he asked.

150

"We need your help," Evie said. "I'm in trouble, Henry."

"What do you mean, trouble?" he asked curiously.

"Can we talk inside? I know it's a lot, us just turning up like this. We probably should have called first or something," she said, "but we didn't have time."

Henry nodded, but his face suddenly turned ravenous as his eyes fell onto Jack.

"I told *you* never to step foot on my land again." His nostrils flared in fury.

"Not my choice to be here," Jack almost growled. "I'm here because of Evie. Whatever issues you and I have, I suggest we leave them out here. We have more important things to deal with right now."

Henry scowled but said nothing. Instead, he moved aside to allow them into his house. Once inside, Henry bolted the door shut and gestured for The Circle to follow him down a narrow hallway. He led them into a large, open-plan kitchen.

It was a typical farmhouse kitchen, with a large wooden table and a huge cast iron stove centred in the middle. On top of the stove, a cauldron was gently simmering away, emitting a delicious aroma of honey and lemon.

"Sit," he barked, pointing to the table.

The Circle followed his order and a number of teacups appeared in front of them, each filling with a creamy coloured liquid. Evie picked up her cup, smelling the tea. Whatever tea this was, it smelt and tasted divine.

"So," Henry said, "this *trouble* you're in, does it have anything to do with the demon attack that happened before Christmas?"

"How do you know about that?" Evie asked.

"I'm a warlock," he said, matter-of-factly. "It's my job to

151

know."

Evie nodded.

"It's complicated," she said. "Lydia Bowater was behind the attack. I don't really know where to start, but to cut a long story short? My parents weren't murdered, Henry. They took their own lives because they thought they were protecting *me*. But they were wrong.

"Lydia knew about their secret, long before they died, and now…well…I guess now she wants to kill me, along with many others apparently."

Henry remained silent for a few moments, taking in her words carefully.

"For your parents to end their own lives, it must have been one hell of a secret," he said. "What could Lydia possibly want so much that she would turn on her own people?"

"Evie has Fae magic," Tessa answered. "We didn't know, until recently. Lydia wants it, and so does The Dark Prince."

"Fae magic?" Henry repeated, and Evie nodded. "Your parents, they both knew?"

"Yes, which is why they took their own lives. They thought they were protecting me," she said. "They knew, but they never told me, Henry. Not once."

"When did the magic expose itself?" Henry asked.

"It was in London," Evie said. "We were attacked by demons, and it just sort of happened. That was the first time the fire showed. The water exposed tonight."

"You possess *two* elements of Fae magic?" he mused.

Evie nodded. "They're the only two that have shown. Are there more?"

"Yes," Henry said, sitting down at the table himself.

He clicked his fingers and a piece of old parchment appeared before him along with a pencil, and he began to draw.

"There are four elements. Fire. Water. Wind. And Earth. Each element belongs to the Fae, but separately. It is very rare for one to hold all four, but not completely unheard of, should we believe the rumours. If you say two of these have already shown themselves, it is a possibility that the other two could show too."

"I'm a witch Henry," Evie said desperately. "My parents were witches. How do I even *have* this power?"

"I wish I could tell you," he said thoughtfully.

Evie sighed. "We've searched through my history and found nothing to link my family with the Fae. It doesn't make any sense at all."

"There are a number of possible answers, Evie," he said softly. "Unfortunately, I cannot give them to you."

"But you're the High Warlock," Cora said. "Surely you must have some kind of magic that will help us."

Henry thought for a moment, and Evie felt her magic begin to stir.

"There might be a way," he said, finally.

"I'm listening," Evie said eagerly, and added, "we went to the Seer, but she was about as useful as a chocolate teaspoon. I just want answers Henry."

She noticed Henry's eyes darken at the mention of the Seer but said nothing as he cleared his throat.

"There is a magical stone that one has heard of," he said, straightening his posture. "A stone that holds the ultimate power. It has the ability to *tell* you what you want to know just by holding it."

"Are you talking about the Truth Stone?" Cora asked. "Because that was lost over five hundred years ago."

"That is exactly what I am talking about," he said. "But you're wrong. It wasn't lost. It was *hidden*. Hidden away to protect its magic. I am surprised the *Seer* did not tell you about it, since it was *she* who hid it."

"Yes well, the Seer was more interested in her riddles than actual information," Evie huffed and said, "so where is this stone?"

"Nobody knows," he said.

"So why bother mentioning it, Warlock?" Jack snarled, nostrils flaring in annoyance.

"That temper of yours will get *you* in serious trouble one of these days, boy," Henry barked. "I said *nobody* knows, not that *I* didn't."

"So, you know where the Truth Stone is?" Evie pressed, ignoring Jack's rising temper.

"I do," he said.

Evie grinned. "Excellent! Where is it? Will you take us? Can we go now?"

"Not so fast," he said. "It's late. We aren't going anywhere tonight. We can wait until morning."

"You're serious?" Evie said. "Oh Henry, you don't know how much this means to me."

"Believe me, I do," he said. "You can all stay here tonight. You will be safe. In the morning, I will take you to the Truth Stone. Get a good night's sleep, you're going to need it."

"All right," Evie said. "Well thank you, for letting us stay here, I mean. We're all really grateful."

"It's the least I could do," he said. "I was very fond of your parents. There are several guestrooms upstairs, make yourselves at home. My bedroom is downstairs, so we will not disturb each other."

Henry stood up then and waved his hand over the cauldron. Whatever was inside, suddenly stopped simmering. He left them alone, gently closing the kitchen door behind him.

"Anyone else find that conversation a little odd?" Zac asked.

"What do you mean?" Evie said.

"He's a warlock, Evie," he said, brows furrowed. "Why does he need a Truth Stone?"

"What's the problem?" she snapped.

"There's no problem," he said hurriedly. "I'm just being cautious. A lot has happened tonight. Come on, we should get some rest."

Evie frowned as she stood up from the table.

"Lead the way," she said.

***

Henry's farmhouse was huge, and as they climbed the stairs to the first floor, they found eight double sized bedrooms and four welcoming bathrooms.

Evie chose the bedroom at the end of the hall. Inside, there was a large double bed, a small wooden dresser, and a side table. An oil lamp sat on the side table, bringing the room to life with its gentle flickering glow. She kicked off her shoes before pulling off her leggings, and lay on the bed, grateful for the softness it offered.

Her head was beginning to ache. She stretched her legs, staring at the ceiling above her, willing sleep to come, but a gentle tap on the door forced her to sit up.

"Come in," she said.

The door opened and she was surprised to see Jack. He had her bag in his hands.

"Thought you might need this," he said, and his eyes fell onto her bare legs as he dropped the bag onto the floor.

155

"Oh, thank you," Evie said, tugging the covers up as heat flooded her cheeks. "I didn't even think about it."

Jack smiled briefly, and said, "It's been a long night."

"Yeah, it has," Evie agreed. "Jack, I'm sorry for snapping at you in the car. I lost my temper, and I shouldn't have spoken to you the way I did."

"You don't have to apologise," he said, twisting his body so that he was facing her.

"Yes, I do," she said. "You didn't deserve that, especially in front of Lucas and Robyn. I know you're just trying to help."

"We're all on edge. You really don't have to apologise. Get some sleep," he said.

Evie sighed, resting her head back.

"I don't think I can sleep," she said with a deep sigh. "My mind is too wired."

"I know that feeling," he admitted, running his fingers through his hair.

Evie shuffled over, giving him space to sit down.

"Are you okay?" she asked as he settled himself at the bottom of the bed. "I know you don't want to be here."

"I'm fine," Jack replied.

"Jack what happened with you and Henry?" she asked.

"I should have known better than to believe you would let that one drop." He huffed. "It was a long time ago. I wanted some information, but he refused to give it to me. I lost my temper...and, well it didn't end very well. I haven't seen or spoken to him since, until tonight."

"What did you want to know?"

"Does it really matter?" he asked.

"I'm sorry...it's none of my business."

"I wanted to find you," he said quietly. "Warlocks have the

ability to track people, but Henry wouldn't do it."

"You fell out with Henry because of me?" She felt her cheeks flood with warmth.

Jack nodded but said nothing. The small room suddenly felt smaller.

"You asked the Seer for help too, didn't you?" she asked, recalling the Seer's cold voice.

Jack nodded but said nothing.

"Why do you care so much?" she asked, unable to stop the words from escaping her mouth.

"I've always cared, Evie," he said, staring at her. "I should go."

He stood up, moving back towards the door.

"Wait," Evie said, climbing up off the bed.

She grabbed his arm, and he paused, twisting his body to her. "Stay with me."

For a moment, he said nothing, and she watched his eyes trailing her body. The silent seconds that passed between them felt like very long minutes.

Finally, Evie watched his posture relax, and a wave of relief swept through her. She twisted her body, guiding him back towards the bed.

Evie climbed onto the bed, watching quietly as Jack removed his boots. A thrilling sensation coiled in her stomach as he pulled his shirt over his head, revealing a perfectly toned and muscular abdomen. Aware that she was staring, Evie forced her eyes away as Jack lay down beside her. Her pulse quickened at their closeness.

"You're shaking again," Jack teased, twisting his head to the side to face her. "Nervous?"

Evie rolled her eyes.

"You're not my type, Saunders," she said through pursed lips.

"You're a terrible little liar, Gray." He smiled.

"And you're an insufferable flirt," she retorted.

Jack released a low laugh, and his eyes bore into hers. "Can you blame me?" he said quietly. "Are you sure you want me to stay? Unlike you, I can't promise that I will keep my hands to myself."

Evie rolled her eyes, biting her lip before her mouth could betray her.

Chuckling, Jack lifted his arm, pulling her closer as she nestled into his side, feeling his warmth radiate against her. For a moment, she forgot everything outside the bedroom door as she dared to trail her hand across his chiselled stomach. The heat of his skin prickled against her fingers.

He flinched at her touch, and Evie could no longer resist the smile that formed on her lips as she rested her leg on top of his. Jack's hand grew tighter on her waist, tugging her that little bit closer. His other hand rested on her arm, his own fingers stroking gentle patterns. Each touch reminding her that she was safe. That she wasn't alone.

"Sleep, little liar," his voice was soft in the darkened room, and the sound of it filled her with an instant sense of ease, allowing her mind to finally succumb to the exhaustion her body felt.

Chapter Twenty-One

When Jack woke the next morning, it was still dark outside.

Evie lay next to him, her dreams undisturbed. She had her head buried into his side with her arm resting across his chest. He was certain that she had not so much as moved from this position all night. Jack lifted his free arm and glanced at his watch. It had just turned five-thirty. He yawned. It was too early to wake up, yet his legs were itching to move.

Slowly, he pulled his arm from beneath Evie, careful not to wake her as he lifted her arm from his chest, and silently climbed out of bed. He pulled the blanket over her before leaving the room.

The house was quiet as he made his way downstairs, and as he neared the kitchen, he noticed the light was already on. Hayden and Lucas were sat at the table, both with a steaming mug of coffee in front of them.

"Hey," Lucas said, offering Jack a mug.

"Anyone else up yet?" Jack asked.

"Zac. He's outside," Lucas said. "Are you sure we are doing the right thing? We have no idea what we could be heading into, Jack. I'm just not sure it's worth the risk."

"Try telling Evie that," he said. "I'm not too happy with the plan either, but she's desperate for answers. If this is the only way that she'll get them, then I'm willing to try, but we have to be careful. Henry might have been friends with her parents, but that doesn't mean I trust him."

"I agree," Hayden said quietly. "We do not separate for one second, understood?"

Both Jack and Lucas nodded as voices emerged from outside the kitchen. The door opened, allowing Cora, Tessa, and Robyn to pass through.

"Where is Evie?" Robyn asked, glancing around the kitchen.

"She's still sleeping," Jack said.

He noticed a smile stretch across Cora's face and felt his own cheeks flush with heat.

"Sleep well, did you?" she asked.

Jack ignored her, and said, "We were just talking about our plans. We don't know what today holds, but we have to stay together no matter what happens."

"When are we leaving?" Tessa asked.

"In thirty-minutes," Henry's voice grumbled, and they all turned to see him lock the back door. He was wearing a travelling coat and had tied his hair into a ponytail. "There's porridge on the stove if you're hungry."

"I'll go and wake Evie," Robyn said. "I can't believe she's still sleeping."

"I'm here!"

Evie strolled into the kitchen, her hair damp and tied into a high ponytail.

"I wasn't asleep. I was in the shower," she said.

"Oh," Robyn smiled. "Are you okay?"

"I'm fine," she replied. "Are we leaving yet?"

"Soon." Jack said, his icy blue eyes falling onto hers. "There's porridge on the stove."

"Thanks," Evie replied, sitting down in the empty chair next to Lucas.

As she poured herself a cup of tea, she could feel Jack's eyes watching her.

She had woken to find him already gone, and a sense of disappointment had filled her as she lay back on the bed, her mind running wild with thoughts as she replayed the night.

Evie added sugar to her tea, and as she lifted the cup to her lips, she stole a glance across the table. Jack remained unmoving; his eyes still locked on her.

Her mouth curved at the corners, her cheeks blushing pink. Jack's answering smile was enough to set her nerves on fire, and she thanked the Gods when he finally looked away, disturbed by Henry's deep voice.

"We leave in ten minutes." Henry said. "We have quite a walk ahead of us, so wrap up warm. It's cold out this morning."

***

Henry led The Circle away from his farmhouse and across a very wet and muddy field. The rain had settled to a light drizzle, but it was still bitterly cold.

Evie shivered against an icy breeze, pulling the zipper up on her jacket so that it covered her neck. She walked alongside Robyn and Tessa, mindful of the others following close behind.

Henry led the way, leading The Circle along a small winding path that opened up to a dark forest.

Evie watched as Tessa lifted her hand, and a bright white light illuminated their path. Several deer were stood opposite, their tiny black eyes watching with intense curiosity.

Minutes turned to hours, and by the time Henry finally began to slow, the sky had turned a dull grey, but the temperature had become less bitter. Henry paused, twisting his head this way and that.

"What is it?" Evie asked.

"It's been a while since I travelled this forest," he said.

"We're lost?" Jack growled. "I thought you knew where this stone was?"

"I do," Henry growled back. "The stone isn't hidden in this forest boy! Anyone would find it."

"So where is it?" he asked.

"*Hidden*," Henry hissed, and turned away as he pulled out a compass from his pocket. He stared at it for a few moments, before deciding against whatever thought crossed his mind. "This way."

The morning grew lighter as the hours passed, and by lunch time they still hadn't found whatever it was that Henry was looking for.

He led them further into the forest and into a large clearing that was surrounded by fallen trees. Evie made her way to the nearest tree trunk and sat down, her feet throbbing. She took off her bag and pulled out a bottle of water, taking a long swig as Robyn sat down next to her.

"When Henry said we had a long walk ahead of us, I didn't think he meant literally." Robyn gasped. "We've been walking for hours!"

"I know," Evie said, watching as Henry picked up a large stick. "What is he doing?"

Henry stood in the middle of the clearing and, using the stick he held, he drew a large circle in the ground. Once done, he waved his hand over the circle and several candles appeared, each flickering to life as he muttered a silent spell.

Evie jumped up, grabbing her bag, before hurrying over to him. "What are you doing?" she asked.

"I told you, the Truth Stone is hidden," he answered. "This forest has a power of its own. In order to get to the stone, we must harness the power of the forest to create a portal which will then take us to the stone."

"Oh," she said. "And where exactly is the stone?"

"Unfortunately, I cannot tell you," he said. "The power of the forest will take us to it, but we will never know *where* it is. The Seer was very clever when she hid the stone."

"How do we get back?" Jack asked.

"Portal." Henry snapped. "Everyone step into the circle. Now!"

They followed his orders, each watching intently as Henry fiddled with something in his pocket. Evie leaned forward, trying to see what it was, but he pulled his hand out empty.

Evie glanced around the circle, meeting Jack's eyes. His rigid face was sharp, filled with concentration, but she noticed the corner of his mouth rise just a little to reveal the smallest of smiles. She smiled back, before quickly returning her eyes to Henry.

"Clear your minds," Henry ordered. "Allow the magic of the forest to run freely through the trees. Harness that power. Breathe it in with every fibre of your being."

They all remained quiet, and after a moment the sound of whistling wind trickled through the trees around them. Evie opened her eyes as a strange feeling passed through her. She glanced around and saw Henry silently step away.

What was he doing?

Evie gasped as her body became paralysed, her feet sinking into the mud. The panicked voices of her friends rang through her ears as the wind grew stronger, whistling viciously as she tried to gain control of the magic that roared within her. She forced her feet out of the ground, her Fae magic now soaring, and lifted her hands towards Henry's wind.

Evie clenched her fingers, forcing her mind to focus, and

after a few moments, the wind began to bind until finally it slowed. The trees stopped swaying as she gained more control, forcing the ball of wind into the sky.

Frantically, she scanned the clearing.

Where was Henry?

She felt the others move to her side, but as she twisted her head, she was gripped by a sight that filled her with utter dread. Jack remained on the far side of the clearing.

She knew something was wrong the second their eyes met.

Without another thought, Evie pulled away from the others, hurtling herself across the clearing towards him.

As she neared, a cloud of black shadows rose from the ground, stretching towards her. The tentacle-like shadows bashed against her, tossing her backwards and onto the ground with a thud.

Evie could hear the panicked voices of the others behind her as she rolled to her side, pulling herself up. Jack had fallen to his knees. The shadows twisted and looped around his body, binding him. Evie scrambled to her feet as a bone-chilling scream left his mouth.

"Jack!"

Evie screamed his name as she threw herself across the clearing towards him. Her hands burned as her flames erupted, but she paid them no attention as she kept her frantic eyes on Jack.

"Don't... Evie!" His voice stammered as he spoke, and she saw his jaw clench together. "Stay back!"

"No!" she yelled, rushing to him. She fell to her knees in front of him. "Tell me what to do!"

"Get. Out. Of. Here!" He grimaced. "Go..."

"I'm not leaving you!" Evie cried, reaching for his hand.

164

Jack jerked back, away from her touch.

"Don't," he said breathlessly. "This is dark magic...it's too strong. Please Evie...he wants *you*..."

"I won't leave you..." Evie said, frantic desperation filling her voice. "Tell me what to do Jack!"

"Listen to me," he said, and despite the nightmare that threatened so dangerously close, his voice was gentle. "We only have a little time, so please listen to me. You have to let me go. This is what he wants, and I'll be damned if I let this happen. You need to go, Evie.

"We didn't have enough time," he said, his voice rising slightly. "Not nearly enough time, but the little we did have, I am grateful for. I never stopped caring about you Evie."

A sob left her mouth.

Helpless. Broken. Powerless to do anything.

"Get. The. Fuck. Out. Of. Here!" he ordered.

She watched helplessly as the shadows gripped at Jack's body, the darkness slowly crushing him.

"Jack!" she screamed his name. Over and over as fear thundered through her pounding heart.

Fear soon turned to rage as her magic threatened to consume her. Her body shook vigorously, her blood heating with each passing second.

A pair of strong calloused hands suddenly gripped her, dragging her backwards. She fought against their hold, twisting her head to see Lucas.

"Do something!" she begged. "Please, Lucas! Do something!"

"It's too late," Lucas said, and the pain in his voice crippled her.

Evie twisted back to Jack, watching as the shadows engulfed

his entire body.

His eyes never left hers, still so brilliantly bright, even as death teased his soul.

She felt Lucas' arms around her, pulling her backwards until she met with his solid chest, but her eyes remained on Jack.

"I will find you," she whispered, sealing the promise with her thundering heart as the darkness finally ripped him from their world. "No matter what happens, I promise I will find you."

Chapter Twenty-Two

"Tell me why I should not kill you, Warlock?"

The voice which spoke was as dark as the night itself, the speaker standing in the shadowy depths of two large oaks. As Henry drew nearer, the man twisted his body away from the trees. His ruby-red eyes fell onto Henry, sparkling with a wicked amusement as Henry stumbled backwards. The man smiled coldly as he took a few tentative steps to where the warlock stood.

Henry balked at the closeness but did not remove his eyes as The Dark Prince positioned himself directly before him.

"Forgive me, but I do not understand," Henry mumbled. "I did everything you asked of me."

"*Everything I asked...* " he repeated, staring at Henry with an uncomfortable intensity.

"Yes." Henry snorted. "I thought you would be happy."

The Dark Prince thought for a moment, acknowledging the motionless figure that lay at Henry's feet.

"I told you to bring me the girl...*that* is not a girl."

"The plan changed," Henry pleaded. "But it will still work. You will still have the girl."

"I TOLD YOU TO BRING HER TO ME!"

The Dark Prince's wicked voice bellowed through the woods, hitting every tree in sight. Birds shrieked in the canopies above, their wings whirring furiously as the small creatures scarpered into the starless sky.

"You incompetent fool."

"My Prince, she would have escaped!" Henry protested. "The Fae magic she holds is too strong! I cast a spell to paralyse The Circle, but she broke through it instantly! *My* magic had no effect on her. It would have been foolish to continue with the plan you set out."

The Dark Prince laughed cruelly.

"So, we have *both* underestimated the power she holds..." he mused. His jaw tightened as he eyed the crumpled body lying at Henry's feet.

"Not quite," Henry said and glanced down. "This boy...he is one of the Guardian brats. Evie Gray will stop at nothing to save him. I plan to take him to the Unseelie Court. The place where it all began. Magic has not worked there for years. The girl will come for him. It is only a matter of time. Trust me, this plan will work.

"I have seen with my own eyes the power she holds," Henry continued. "To even attempt to harness it here would be a fools move."

The Dark Prince looked down at Jack's frozen body.

"What about The Guardians? Surely they will want to assist with his rescue?"

Henry shook his head. "The Circle mistrust everything to do with them right now. The Guardians will not be an issue, I can assure you of that."

"Is that so?" he mused.

"You are not the only one who seeks the girl's power," he answered.

"I know," he said quietly, flinching slightly as a soft *thump* greeted his shoulder.

The Dark Prince twisted his head a fraction, acknowledging his loyal companion with a brief nod. The raven sat beside his ear, almost statue-like as she too, glared at Henry.

Henry eyed the raven for a few moments before turning his gaze back to The Dark Prince.

"The Land of Wonder will aide your plan tremendously," he said. "She will come for him. And when she does, the magic she holds will be yours."

"Clever, Henry. Even for you," he said. "I myself had not entertained the idea of travelling to the Fae realm. How ironic? The very place where it all began. You are certain she will come?"

"My Prince, Evie Gray will follow this boy to the ends of the earth and back, there is no doubt about it," he said, smiling menacingly "Trust me, the plan will work."

***

"That lying bastard!"

Unyielding rage boiled, knocking the breath out of her as Evie paced the clearing. Blood pounded through her veins. Her magic roared, screaming for release.

Seconds, minutes, or could it have been hours? Evie lost track of time the longer The Circle spent in that wretched clearing. She needed to calm down. She needed to breathe.

Calm. Breathe. Think.

Her palms exploded with a fiery rage. Her hands shaking vigorously at her side. Leaves began to lift from the ground, spinning around her as the Fae magic rapidly took control. The voices of her friends filled her ears, yet her mind could not understand the words they yelled. The darkness was creeping in, slithering through her body like a snake taunting its prey.

A sense of grief suddenly washed through her, merging with

the rage until she felt nothing at all.

The flames vanished, and Evie swayed slightly as the reality of their situation suddenly overwhelmed her.

He was gone.

"This is all my fault," Evie rasped.

"Henry had us all fooled," Lucas said.

He stood a few feet in front, and as Evie lifted her head, she was suddenly stung by the distance he kept between them.

"Lucas…" she began, lowering her eyes to glance down at her hands. "Lucas… I… you don't think I would…"

"Gods no!" he almost growled, and within seconds, he had closed the gap, pulling her into his arms. "I'm sorry. I just wanted to give you space."

"I wouldn't hurt you." She sobbed, burying her head against his chest. "I would never hurt any of you…"

"We know," Lucas said as the others moved closer. "I know this might sound like a truly stupid question…but are you alright?"

"No," she said, and added bitterly, "Jack told us not to go to Henry, but I didn't listen. I insisted it was the right thing to do. I thought Henry would help. I thought we could trust him."

"We're going to find him," Lucas said. "I swear to you. On my life, we will find him."

Evie sucked in a deep breath.

"How?" she demanded. "He's gone Lucas, and none of us have any idea where Henry has taken him. Or why for that matter."

"Isn't it obvious?" Cora said, forcing all eyes to her. "Henry took Jack because he couldn't get to you, Evie. His magic paralysed us all, yet you were able to break through. I think he panicked, and that is why he took Jack instead."

170

"He didn't do this alone," Evie said suddenly, as realisation obliterated her heart. "He's working with The Dark Prince…"

"And when you broke through Henry's spell, he panicked," Cora continued. "He knew it would be foolish to even attempt to take you after seeing how powerful your magic is."

"But why take Jack?" Evie asked, frustrated. "What does he have to gain?"

She heard Hayden sigh heavily and twisted her body to face him.

"Because Henry knows that you will go after him. No matter the consequences," Hayden said.

Evie frowned and rubbed her temples. "That still doesn't make sense. Henry could have taken any one of you guys, and I would stop at nothing to save you."

"I know you would," Cora said, folding her arms across her chest. "I also know how Jack feels about *you.* The connection you both have. Henry saw this and used it to his advantage. If it is true, and Henry is working with The Dark Prince, then taking Jack was a very clever way to lure you to him."

"I don't understand," Evie sighed.

"Henry betrayed us," Cora said. "From the minute we walked into that darn farmhouse, he had his plans set in motion. But he didn't comprehend just how powerful your magic is, Evie. He's taken Jack somewhere…another realm perhaps? A place where he knows you will follow, and knows that The Dark Prince will have unrestricted access to you…"

"The Land of Wonder," Evie gasped. "Of course! It makes perfect sense."

"The Fae realm," Hayden said sharply. "A truly wicked land, and, of course, the perfect place. If we are correct, and Henry has taken Jack there, the Gods only know the horrors that await him. Time will be against us. Magic doesn't work in the Land of Wonder."

171

"Magic doesn't work?" Zac said, frowning. "So, Jack will be completely powerless?"

Hayden nodded. "Yes," he said, hurriedly. "We've already lost hours. We need to move."

"What about the Fae?" Evie asked.

Hayden shook his head.

"Long dead by now. The only thing *we* have to worry about, are whatever monsters the Unseelie's left behind."

Evie swallowed, feeling a bile of anxiety rise in her throat.

"How much time do we have?" she asked.

"Time works differently in the Fae realm," Hayden said. "An hour to us, could be a day in the Land of Wonder, maybe even more. We have to move fast."

"How do we get there?" Cora asked.

"That's where it gets complicated," Hayden replied "The Academy holds the only portal with direct access to the Land. It was sealed after the Fae war, but it is still accessible."

"We have to go back to The Academy?" Lucas grimaced.

"Yes." Hayden said.

"What about Lydia and Julias?" he asked pointedly.

"We will cross that bridge when we get to it," Hayden said and turned on his heel. "We need to move fast. This forest is protected by an old magic. We won't be able to open a portal here. We will have to walk back to Henry's farmhouse."

"Walk?" Cora exclaimed. "It took us *hours* to get here, Hayden!"

"Then I guess we had better start walking," Evie commanded.

She stormed ahead, pulling her bag onto her back. Her mind was frantic as she walked.

There were so many places on the planet that Henry could have taken Jack, yet he had chosen the Land of Wonder.

The realm of the *Fae*.

Chapter Twenty-Three

It had been many years since the Fae war.

When the witches had ambushed the land, leaving only death and destruction in their wake. But even with the Fae long banished, the Northern part of the Land of Wonder, and home to the Unseelie Court, remained a truly wicked and dismal place.

Heavy grey skies threatened the land with a constant thunderous storm, as blisteringly cold winds rattled through the deserted Court and its village.

The Twisted Castle stood upon a hill, overlooking the northern shore of the vast Black Sea. Its broken windows covered with rotting wood boards, whilst deep green ivy slithered like snakes over the crumbling brickwork.

In the days before the war, the castle had been a very fine and respectable home, belonging to Naida Thorne Wyre, and his wife; the notorious, and devilishly gruesome, King and Queen of the Unseelie Court.

When the war broke out, and the Fae were banished, the castle fell into disrepair. These days the Twisted Castle was nothing more than a derelict ruin.

Jack rolled onto his back, flinching at the pain in his shoulder. He pulled himself up, dragging his legs across the rotting floorboards, wincing as he did so.

A coppery taste coated his tongue and combined with the revolting tang of rot and decay, the blood in his mouth made his stomach churn. He keeled over, unable to stop the surge of vomit

173

that escaped his mouth. After several wretches, he collapsed against the stone wall, his head pounding viciously.

His body ached, but he could not remember anything physical happening to him. He closed his eyes thinking of Evie and the rest of The Circle.

It had been a mistake to trust Henry. He knew that from the moment it had been suggested. He was a warlock, and warlocks as powerful as Henry Martinez were a dangerous breed.

A cold breeze suddenly swept across his face, forcing his eyes to open.

The Dark Prince stood before him. For a moment, the two remained silent. Each assessing the other. A calm fury settled over him as The Dark Prince released a cruel sneer.

"Jack Saunders," he mused quietly. "What a predicament you've come to be in."

"Where is she?" Jack growled. "Where's Evie?"

"All in good time boy. All in good time," he said. "She will come. I have no doubt about that."

"Whatever you're planning to do, you won't get away with it." Jack winced. "The Circle *will* stop you!"

The Dark Prince laughed.

"Stop me?" he said. "You opened the very door I needed access to. I have spent the last twenty-one years searching for her you know. I was very nearly ready to give up.

"Until *you* opened that sealed door," he said. "Your first mistake was visiting the Seer. She may have been exiled by The Guardians, but you will find that she is *mine* to control. Your second mistake was thinking that you could bring Evie back to The Academy without any *consequences*."

He stalked towards him, grabbing hold of Jack's shirt with his long fingers. The Dark Prince only smiled menacingly as he lifted him from the floor before slamming into the wall behind.

"You should have left her in London, boy," his voice was barely a whisper.

He released his hold, and Jack fell to the floor with a heavy thud.

"A witch born with the magical elements of the Fae," The Dark Prince mused. "How extraordinarily rare…Evie Gray will come. I have no doubt about that, and then, then I will kill her, and take what was *promised* to me."

He left without another word.

Jack roared at the pain seeping through him, his body shaking as he forced himself onto his knees, biting back the vomit that threatened to erupt once more. Despite having no physical wounds, everything hurt.

His eyes frantically scanned the chamber. His mind evaluating his situation. There was no way out, and he was far too weak to even attempt an escape without his magic.

Cursing, Jack fell backwards against the stone wall, shivering as a gush of bitter wind swept through the room. He glanced around again.

No windows.

And the only door was undoubtedly guarded by demons.

Had he imagined the wind?

His head was so dazed. His eyes sore from exhaustion, and his heartbeat quickened with each painful breath he took.

Think. He needed to think.

He was a Guardian Leader…a powerful witch, but that would not help him here. Jack swore, kicking his heel into the broken floorboards.

His magic was useless in this realm, and he was too weak to fight whatever wicked creatures The Dark Prince had ordered to guard the door.

Sinking his head back in defeat, Jack allowed his eyes to close once more. A veil of darkness soon engulfed his body and mind, ripping him into a deep unconsciousness that he could not hope to resist.

***

The Academy glistened with a soft yellow light as Evie marched through the cobbled courtyard. Her legs ached. Her head throbbed, yet she barely noticed.

Rage motivated her. Henry's betrayal fuelled each furious step she took as she stormed through The Academy's rear courtyard and into the pristine gardens. There was no moon out tonight. Not a single star shone in the black canvas that stretched above. The only sound was that of Evie's thunderous footsteps, closely followed by the rest of The Circle, as she slipped into the manor through an unlocked side door.

Shuddering a deep breath, Evie did not stop as she stalked ahead, leading them to the main library. According to Hayden, this was where they would find access to the portal. She rounded a corner, her eyes falling onto the large doors that now stood before her. With a wave of her hand, the library doors exploded open.

They weren't alone.

From her spot near the hearth, Lydia smiled. Beside her, wearing an equally smug grin, stood Julias.

"Well, well, well," Lydia said, her voice quiet but sharp. "You have no idea just how worried we've been."

"I'm sure you have," Evie spat, her dark eyes fixed on Lydia. "Yet not enough to notice that one of your *own* is missing."

The two looked puzzled, and Julias shrugged.

"Do tell us exactly who it is you're referring to," he said in a nonchalant tone.

"Don't play the stupid card, Julias, it really doesn't suit you." Evie scowled, and added with a near feral sneer, "We know about the demon attack, Lydia. We know you and your *pet* beside you were responsible, so you can stop with the pretence."

Brow furrowed, Lydia shook her head.

"Oh Evie." She sighed. "I never intended to hurt you. Gods, no! The power you hold…it is phenomenal, but it's also very dangerous to someone like you. You are barely out of your training years. You will be a constant target…*a threat* to those who do not understand. I just wanted to help you…"

"By almost having me killed?" Evie glared.

"By taking the magic from you," she countered. "The Dark Prince will kill you…"

"Well, I guess he will just have to get in line," she said. "You knew about this magic all along. You knew Jack found me. That is why you ordered the demons to attack us in London. You knew the Fae magic would expose itself, didn't you?"

Lydia smiled, and Evie could not help but balk at the cruelty that rested within that smile.

"Your parents were fools. Fools to think they could take their dirty secret to the grave," she said, taking a tentative step away from the hearth.

She closed the gap with another two strides, stopping only inches away.

"I knew about *you*, little witch…"

With a deafening bang, the library doors suddenly exploded open, giving way to several heavily armed men.

Lydia froze and a shadow of dark rage flashed across her

cruel face.

During their journey through the woods, Hayden had sent word to his friends at the New York Academy, requesting their presence immediately.

Francis Dubois strode forwards, towering over his companions. He had thick black hair, that sat in tight curls upon his head, and his dark brown skin, radiated with beauty and elegance.

The leader of the New York Guardians frowned as his eyes surveyed the room. First Evie, and then The Circle, before finally settling with Lydia and Julias.

"So, it is true?" he said, his voice almost shattering the silence that had erupted. "Lydia Bowater, you never cease to surprise."

Lydia smirked. "How lovely to see you, Francis," she said.

Francis threw his hands up.

"You're done, Lydia," he roared.

Evie could sense a wildness about him, but said nothing as two more Guardians stepped forwards, each gripping Lydia and Julias tightly around the elbow. They both wore typical Guardian fighting gear, the leathers gripping at their sharp muscular figures. Neither spoke, and their silence was deafening.

"What do you plan to do?" Lydia remarked as she glared at Francis. "You know this is a mistake."

"You have betrayed the Guard," he said. "And for that, you must face the consequences."

Lydia huffed a laugh.

"Consequences," she spat. "You know nothing of the *consequences,* Francis. The power that *she* holds…it will end us all; you mark my words. We both know what The Dark Prince is after… *who* he is after…"

"Enough," Francis ordered, and barked to The Guardians who held Lydia and Julias, "take them to the infirmary!"

The two Guardians nodded, and with thundering steps, they urged Lydia and Julias forward. But as Lydia brushed past Evie, her hand stretched forwards, suddenly clasping around her throat. Evie snarled as her own hands lunged for Lydia's wrist, gripping them tightly against their hold. Lydia screamed.

Evie jumped backwards, horrified as her frantic eyes fell onto Lydia's scorched wrist.

"You little bitch!" Lydia screamed. "Look at what she has done. With her bare hands! She is a danger to us all Francis! The power that she has…"

"I said enough," Francis barked. "Get them out of my sight!"

The two men nodded, and escorted Lydia and Julias out of the library. Once they were gone, Francis turned on his heel to where Hayden stood.

"Your message was very blunt," Francis said, casting another quick glance to Evie, who was stood staring at her hands. "You need to explain what the fuck is going on here."

"We don't have time to stand around talking," Evie said, pulling herself out of her daze. The tips of her fingers still tingled. "We need to leave. Now."

"After what I have just witnessed, I don't think you will be going anywhere young lady," Francis said firmly. "The magic Lydia speaks of…"

"It's Fae magic," Evie said. "Long story short…I was born with it, but it only manifested a few weeks ago, after *Lydia* ordered a bunch of demons to attack us in London. Until that point, I didn't know I had this ability.

"But right now, I don't have time to stand around and discuss this. Henry Martinez has kidnapped Jack Saunders and has taken

179

him to the Land of Wonder. We need to leave now!"

"Henry Martinez is the High Warlock of Pennsylvania," Francis said, frowning. "Why on earth would he kidnap a Guardian?"

"Because he is a lying bastard," Evie snarled. "Look, Mr, I really don't have time for this. Jack has already been gone for hours. You know as well as we do how time works in the Fae courts. Now please, stand aside and let us go."

"Why would he take him to the Land of Wonder?" he questioned. "There is no magic in the land…"

"I don't know," she said, and feeling the frustration build within her, she turned her head to Hayden, pleading with him to help.

"Francis, we think Henry is working with The Dark Prince, and the reason that he has taken Jack, is an attempt to lure Evie to him," Hayden said.

"If that is true, then you are walking directly into a trap," Francis said. "If it is true, and this girl does have Fae magic, then I cannot allow you to simply wander off into the Land of Wonder…"

"I appreciate your concern," Evie said, "but we are going with or without your permission. Jack needs us…"

"But your magic…" he began.

"I don't care about my fucking magic!" Evie roared. "I care about Jack! And right now, you're wasting precious time. We have to go!"

For a moment, Francis said nothing as he turned to face his two remaining guards, gesturing for them to join him.

"Very well. You cannot go alone," he said. "Cillian Broadhurst and Jamie Mathieson are two of my strongest warriors. They will accompany you to the Land of Wonder and assist with your rescue mission."

"Thank you," Evie said, releasing a sigh of relief.

"You are to find Jack, and come straight back, do you understand?" Francis ordered, and she could hear the warning in his tone. "I will inform The Elders."

Evie nodded but said nothing as she whipped her head to face the others. Hayden stood on the far side of the library, whispering an array of words to the wall before him.

To anyone on the outside, this would have looked strangely odd. Frowning at his actions, Evie hurried across the library to stand beside him. As she approached, a solid oak door appeared in the wall.

He stopped chanting almost instantly as the door swung open with a small *click*, revealing a water-like hole that now glimmered brightly. Behind them, The Circle stared in momentary awe.

He had opened the portal that would take them to the Land of Wonder.

Mesmerised, Evie edged forwards, her eyes eager to see more. She felt as though she was staring into the depths of the great ocean. Moving forward another inch, Evie paused quickly as the sound of distant voices suddenly broke.

Taking a tentative step, Evie eyed the portal, but saw nothing other than the shimmering whirls beyond the doorway. The whispering voices remained.

"I've never seen a portal like this," she said, her voice thoughtful. "It's strange, but beautiful at the same time. The voices…I can't tell what they're saying, can you?"

"Voices?" Hayden threw her a concerned look. "I don't hear any voices, Evie."

Oh, they were most definitely there.

Whispering. Calling. Beckoning…

"Strange," she said a moment later. "So, what happens now?"

"We walk through," he replied. Her comment about hearing voices had bothered him, but he quickly shook it off as the others moved to stand behind them. "The portal will take us directly to the Land of Wonder, but it won't take us to Jack. Finding him will be down to us, and it won't be easy."

"Okay," Evie said. "Then let's not waste any more time."

"Henry knew exactly what he was doing by taking Jack there," he said firmly, gripping her forearm. "After the Fae war, magic was banished along with the Fae of the Unseelie Court. The Guardian Leaders who fought the battle agreed the land should remain magicless. It was their way of ensuring the Unseelie's would never find a way of returning."

"Should we be worried?" Zac suddenly asked.

"I would be lying if I said no," he said. "It is important that we stick together at all times. No matter what happens. I don't know what horrors await us. We find Jack and we get the hell out of there. Understood?"

The Circle nodded in agreement, and Hayden waved his palm in a clockwise motion over the doorway.

One by one, they stepped through the doorway, vanishing into the shimmering whirls.

Chapter Twenty-Four

The Land of Wonder was divided into three courts, each ruled by three very different rulers.

To the South sat the home of the Seelie Fae. Basked in endless golden sunshine, the court was ruled by a Fae Queen who had very little interest in war and battle. For the love of her people, Queen Arabella had cast a protective shield across the Seelie Court as soon as the war between the witches and the Unseelie Fae had begun, making her court inaccessible to those who were not of Seelie blood.

The Hollow Court was to the East of the land. Hidden within the depths of Blood Thorne Forest, the ruler of the Court, Prince Hunter Meadows, also liked the company of his own people. Unlike the other courts, the Hollow Court had no King or Queen. Instead, the rebellious crown prince, known for his tyrant ways and wicked humour, ruled the court under the constant influence of brandy and chaos.

And finally, to the North, sat the court of the Unseelie Fae. Prior to the war, before the witches had trampled the land and forced the Unseelie's into exile, the court had been ruled by the notorious King Naida. The King had been a formidable bastard, with a nature so vicious and cruel, that even those within his own court strongly disliked him.

A heavy storm threatened the Land of Wonder, teasing the Northern shores with a torrential downpour.

Lifting her head from the soggy black sand, Evie's frantic

eyes scanned the beach. It was quiet. Too quiet. Even the sounds of the waves, lapping against the blackened shore made little noise, leaving her with an intense feeling of unease.

The others were close by. Each brushing grains of wet sand from their leathers. The two Guardian warriors who had been ordered to accompany The Circle were stood a few feet away, each male wearing a grim look upon their faces. The shorter of the two, whose name she remembered as Cillian, turned to face her. His eyes flashed with silent fury as the pair locked gazes.

Her mouth curved, breaking into an innocent smile. Cillian's only response was to quickly turn his head back to his companion who muttered something under his breath, and the two quickly submersed themselves in silent conversation.

Evie huffed a sigh, rolling her eyes.

This was going to be fun.

"So, this is the Land of Wonder?"

Robyn's voice filled her ears, forcing her to turn away from the warriors and face her friends. They were stood on a long stretch of beach. On one side, the Black Sea roared angrily, its colossal waves raging beneath the stormy sky above. A dark forest dominated the other side of the beach. Evie glanced towards the forest and felt a cold chill trickle down her spine. Sucking in a deep breath as she attempted to calm the rising anxiety, Evie closed her eyes for a moment.

Breathe.

"The land is separated into three courts."

Hayden's deep voice forced her eyes to flicker open. He was stood a few feet in front, his eyes glancing briefly at the compass which lay in his outstretched palm.

"The Seelie Court. The Unseelie Court. And the Hollow Court. Jack could be in any one of them," he said.

A deep frown was burrowed in his forehead.

"We should split up," Lucas said. "We would cover more ground."

"Not an option," Cillian barked from behind. "It's too dangerous, especially without magic. We stay together."

"But it will take us forever to search *three* courts," Evie said desperately. "Jack could be dead by the time we find him. I agree with Lucas. Splitting up will enable us to cover more ground."

"I said *no*." His voice was thunderous. "We stay together."

He was a brute of a man, despite his height. With thick, broad shoulders, and a head full of grey, wiry hair. Evie could see why Francis considered Cillian one of his strongest warriors. The man oozed a confident swagger, which left Evie with no doubt that those under his command would do exactly what he ordered.

Unfortunately for him, she was not *his* to command.

"You are forgetting who *we* are," Evie said sharply. "We do not take orders from you, regardless of who you are. Jack has already been here for far too long. Time works differently here as you are very well aware. We're splitting up."

"And you're forgetting *where* you are girl," Cillian challenged. "Your *status* here means nothing. Magic is forbidden, which therefore makes you no stronger than a normad. We stick together, or we leave.

"Mark my words girl, I will have no trouble dragging you back to The Academy should you decide to refuse."

Seething, Evie clenched her fists at her sides. She could feel the eyes of The Circle bearing into her, yet nobody spoke. A silent rage stormed through her, and she could almost feel the drum of her now dormant magic, beating quietly beneath her skin. She wanted to argue. To tell the warrior who stood before her *exactly* what would happen should he even think about laying his violent

185

hands on her, but a quick glance at Hayden kept her silent. He said nothing as he stared at her with sharp, warning eyes.

"Fine. We will stay together." Evie scowled, and from the corner of her eye, she was certain she saw Hayden relax.

"Wise choice," was all Cillian said.

Ignoring the warriors, Evie whipped her head to Hayden.

"Where exactly are we now?" she asked.

"North. The Unseelie Court lays just beyond this forest," Hayden said. "Well, what's left of it."

"The Unseelies were exiled, but the Seelies weren't. Why?" she asked.

"That's right," Hayden answered. "The Unseelie Court is ruthless...*was* ruthless I should say. The Seelies, well, they were different. The Seelie Queen refused to take part in the war, which was why The Guardians granted her court their freedom."

"Was magic banished there too?" Evie asked.

Hayden nodded. "The Guardian's cast a very powerful spell to ensure Fae magic was banished across all three courts," he said, and added with a bitter growl, "they did not realise their spell would also stop *our* magic from working."

"Seems a little dramatic," she mused. "To banish magic across all three courts. The war was with the Unseelie Court right?"

"For someone who is so desperate to search these lands," Cillian snickered, grimacing as Evie turned to stare at him, "you're doing a wonderful job of wasting precious *minutes*."

"When I want your opinion," Evie spat, and scowled, "I'll ask for it."

Cillian only smirked before twisting his head towards the dark forest.

"Nightfall will soon be upon us," he said. "We should move

now, whilst we still have daylight on our side. The Gods only know what lurks within that forest when night falls. As Hayden has already said, the Unseelie Court lies just beyond the forest. It will take a good couple of hours for us to reach the village.

"So, unless you want to cross paths with the wraiths and other ungodly creatures of this vile land, I suggest we get a move on."

***

In the depths of the darkening forest, Evie walked with unease beside Lucas, her eyes carefully tracking the movements of the others who walked ahead. She had said nothing else to the two Guardian warriors, despite the roaring rage that coursed within her veins, silently begging her to lash out.

She had questioned The Circle about their magic. Asking each of them if they too, could still feel it, despite it not working.

They had each given her the same answer.

No. They could not.

On that, Evie decided to keep her thoughts to herself.

She could feel her magic within her. Feeling it simmering quietly and tingling the tips of her fingers. At first, she thought she had been imagining the sensation. But the further they walked through the Black Forest, the more the sensation grew.

It wasn't possible, yet she could not deny what she felt. Her magic was simmering, clutching at the darkness that threatened to overwhelm her.

Breathe.

Breathe.

In and out. One… two… three…

Sucking in a deep breath, Evie lifted her head. Gigantic

spiders clutched at their snare strings in the canopies above, whilst goblins of all sizes lurked nearby, hiding quietly amongst the trees and overgrown shrubs.

The Circle walked on, and every few minutes, Evie found herself casting a nervous glance behind. Nothing followed, but that did not stop the feeling of unease rushing through her chilled body. The smell of pine needles and rich earth filtered through the air as a gentle breeze slipped through the trees.

The smell reminded Evie of the Enchanted Forest, and she found herself wishing they were in the homeland of The Guardians, instead of this dark and wicked place.

A caterwauling sound, somewhere between a screech and a tortured cry, suddenly echoed through the forest.

The Circle froze. Heads spinning in every direction, each set of eyes searching the endless trees for the source but finding nothing. The forest had once again fallen into a near silence.

"We all heard that, right?" Tessa whispered, gripping onto Zac's arm.

"Wraiths." Cillian sneered as he and Jamie stalked towards the front. "I did warn you. We need to move. Now."

***

Evie shuddered beside Lucas, both from the deep chill of the forest and the unease that taunted her. Lucas said nothing as his golden eyes continued to monitor ahead. She reached for his arm, wrapping her own around his tense muscles.

The silence gave time for her mind to drift. She thought of Jack. Flinching as her mind gave way to the images that haunted her. The look on his face when the darkness engulfed him.

We didn't have enough time…

His voice pierced her mind, dragging a muffled sob from her throat.

What if they were too late?

No. She wouldn't allow herself to think like that. Jack was strong. He was a powerful Guardian Leader and witch.

But what if...

STOP!

The order echoed through her head, loud, and as clear as ice. Strong.

Powerful.

We didn't have enough time...

Frustrated by her thoughts, Evie loosened her hold on Lucas, pulling her arm out of his.

"The village is on the other side of the forest," Hayden said, twisting his head to the side as Evie approached. "Maybe a couple of miles or so."

Evie nodded. "Should we be worried about the wraiths?"

"They won't bother us if we don't bother them," he said.

"And the village?" she mouthed.

"The village has been deserted for almost twenty-two years," he said. "The Fae are long dead, trust me."

"I wasn't talking about the Fae," she said grimly. "We don't know what lives there now."

"No, we don't," he agreed.

Evie fell silent, her mind racing with the terrifying thoughts she desperately wanted to forget.

Bravery was one of her traits, but there was something about the Black Forest that truly frightened her.

Chapter Twenty-Five

At long last, the moss-covered path began to open, and the dark and gloomy forest gave way to an even gloomier sight.

The village was deathly quiet. With not a single creature in site. Several small cottages stood before them, battered and derelict from years of neglect. Windows were shattered and doors hung dismally from their rotted frames.

Evie froze. Her eyes becoming blurred as she took in the scene before her. The pull of invisible strings latched painfully against her vision, dragging her into the depths of the darkness that teased her mind and soul, slithering with a wicked thrill.

A baby lay in a crib. Its cries piercing every corner of Evie's mind as she was pulled further into the vision.

Evie was stood beside the window inside a large, circular room. She glanced behind her, looking out of the shattered glass, feeling an anxious bile rise within. The Black Sea raged below. The dark waves illuminated by a sudden strike of bright, white lightening.

Evie gasped as she realised where she stood.

She was inside a tower of the Twisted Castle.

The room in which she stood was almost destroyed, with broken pieces of furniture scattering the majority of the wooden floor.

Beside the crib, the crumpled body of a woman lay in a curled heap, unmoving. Thick brown hair covered the woman's face, hiding it from view. The infant's screams grew desperate, crying out for a mother that would no longer answer.

The vision changed swiftly, and Evie twisted her head as another figure entered the room. A voice so gentle, and so achingly familiar began to sing, soothing the terrified cries of the baby almost instantly.

Evie watched as the figure moved towards the crib, reaching down to lift the baby. Despite being cloaked from head to toe, the baby cooed happily, nestling its head against the figures chest as the voice erupted into a beautiful, enchanting lullaby...

"Evie!"

Evie's eyes snapped back into focus, her mind reeling. Anxiety tore at her body, crippling her chest as her lungs begged for air. She clutched at her sides, clenching her fists as her eyes clamped shut.

Breathe.

Breathe.

Breathe.

The vision remained painfully clear in her mind as Evie desperately tried to control her unsteady breath.

In. Out. In. Out...

"Evie are you alright?" Robyn's voice was soft before her, and Evie lifted her head. "Evie, talk to me."

"I'm... fine," Evie said, forcing the words out. She was trembling as she cast her eyes down to her hands. "I..."

"You saw something," Hayden said sharply. "What was it?"

"I..." she began, swallowing back the bile in her throat. "I... I don't really understand it... I... this *vision*... I was inside the Twisted Castle. Everything was destroyed. I saw... I... a baby... yes, a baby... crying... and a woman lying on the floor next to the crib, but she was dead, and then... it changed. Someone else came into the room, but whoever it was, their face was covered."

191

"Did you see anything else?" Hayden asked urgently.

Evie shook her head. "Nothing," she answered.

Her head was beginning to throb.

"Did you see the baby?" Jamie suddenly asked from behind her. "Was it a boy or a girl?"

"I don't know. I couldn't tell," she said, twisting her body to face the New York Guardian. "Why do you ask?"

"Curiosity," he said flatly. "The Land of Wonder has a way of distorting the mind and making things that aren't real, seem *very real*. We should find some shelter until this storm blows over. We won't find anything in this rain."

Evie nodded and felt an icy shiver as she watched the New York Guardians exchange weary glances. The two men said nothing, and turned away from The Circle, leading the way into the gloomy village. She watched the Guardian's stalk forwards, and for a moment she allowed her mind to process what she had seen. The lullaby had been so achingly familiar…

Evie shook off the thought as Robyn came to her side. She felt her arm loop through her own and the two set off after the others. Night had fallen over the land. The sky a starless black canvas above. Evie shuddered as she cast her eyes upwards. She had never seen the sky look so…empty.

The village was small, but big enough to have accommodated at least a hundred Fae before the war had forced the Unseelie's into exile. There were numerous buildings dotted around. Some were single storey, others were at least three, towering over the smaller buildings crumbling beside them. They walked through the village for another ten minutes before the Guardian warriors came to a sudden standstill outside the garden of a small, grey-stone cottage.

The cottage stood alone and was by far the only building that appeared liveable. Granted, the glass in the front windows was missing, but it had a door that stood firmly in its frame, and it looked big enough to house everyone until the storm had blown over.

Unsurprisingly, the door was unlocked. Lucas pushed the handle down, and the wood creaked as the door swung open.

Lucas and Zac pulled out a flashlight each, and the cottage was suddenly filled with bright, yellow light. They were stood in a small hallway. On either side stood two doors, both of which were shut, and in front, a narrow, rickety staircase led to the first floor.

Zac opened the door on the left, revealing a small and grim looking sitting room. He held his flashlight up, shining it around the room. A large open fireplace dominated the main wall, and several armchairs had been crammed into the small space. Tessa hurried over to the fireplace, noting a large metal bucket filled with coal.

"These are dry," she said, and she began to place the lumps of coal into the grate. "They should light."

"Here, I have matches," Zac said, handing her a box.

"I need something to get the fire going," Tessa said. "Paper or something."

"Here you go," Robyn said, edging closer to her. She took off her bag and pulled out a notebook. "Use this, it's not important. You can burn the whole thing."

Tessa nodded, taking the notebook from her, and begun tearing pages. She scrunched them into little balls before placing them evenly into the grate.

To her surprise, the paper began to burn away, and it wasn't long until the fire hit the coal sending a much-needed warmth into the small room.

"As soon as this storm passes, we are heading straight back out," Evie said defiantly.

She was stood by the window, her eyes fixed upon the empty street outside.

"Agreed." Hayden nodded. "We should at least try and rest whilst we are here though."

"We will stand guard," Jamie said, and with a small nod towards Cillian, the two warriors headed towards the door.

"We will take it in turns," Lucas said, brows rising slightly. "You take the first hour. Zac and I will take over after that."

Jamie nodded but said nothing more as he and Cillian left.

"I don't like them," Tessa said, frowning.

Zac chuckled. "I'm glad someone voiced what I was thinking," he said. "I'll be glad to get to be rid of them."

Whilst the others settled themselves, Evie remained by the window. The heavens had opened now, giving way to a torrential downpour. It was difficult to see anything through the pouring rain, but she kept her eyes focused on the cobbled streets. The heat from the fire was now stifling, and the warmth made her uncomfortable. Moving closer to the glassless window, Evie closed her eyes for a moment, allowing the icy breeze to caress her face.

Behind her, she could hear the soft chatter of her friends, but she couldn't focus on the words being said. She could not stop thinking about the vision. The sound of the gentle voice that had soothed those terrified cries so easily. The lullaby had been so gentle and so full of love, and she found herself thinking of her own mother.

Evie…

Evie froze. The Circle were still chatting quietly behind her, but she was certain she'd heard her name. She turned to look at the others, yet none of them acknowledged her as they continued with their conversation.

A whisper.

That is all it had been. Yet it had been so clear. Almost as though someone within the room had called her name. Evie turned back to the window and saw the flash of a figure shimmer past. Her eyes widened as she tried to see past the rain, but she saw nothing.

Evie.

She turned away from the window, her heart suddenly racing.

"Guys, I'm just going to stand on the porch for a few minutes… it's too stuffy in here," she said, moving towards the door.

"Are you okay?" Robyn asked.

"I'm fine. I just need a little air," she said, forcing a smile. "I'll be right back."

Evie left the sitting room, pulling the door shut behind her. She couldn't see Cillian and Jamie. Good. She didn't need any more hassle.

Evie stepped out, sucking in a deep breath as she did. Her head was beginning to throb. The Land of Wonder had a way of playing tricks on the mind, especially a mind that was tired. And boy was she exhausted!

The rain continued to fall heavily, splashing against the cobbled ground. She thought of Jack and felt a sudden ache within her. He had been gone for almost twenty-four hours.

Evie Gray…

Her head shot up. The figure she had seen was back. Its weightless body gliding down the cobbled path as it drifted away from the cottage. Evie hurried down from the porch, pulling her hood up to cover her head as she followed the ghostly figure. She picked up her pace, her steps turning into a run as the figure moved further away.

"Wait!" Evie shouted. Her voice barely audible through the heavy downpour.

The figure continued to glide away, before finally stopping beside a large stone memorial in the middle of the village.

Evie stopped running, clutching her sides as she tried to even her breathing. The figure didn't move. Hovering before the memorial. When her breathing finally returned to its regular rhythm, Evie took a few tentative steps forward.

"Who are you?" she asked.

"You shouldn't be here." The voice was harsh, forcing the hairs on Evie's neck to rise. "*You* should not be here, Evie!"

"How do you know my name?" she asked, eyes widening. "Who are you?"

"It matters not who I am," the figure barked. "Leave this wretched court. Leave now and promise to never return!"

"I can't," Evie said, confused. "Not without Jack."

"He warned you not to follow. Yet you came anyway," the figure whispered mournfully. "It is too late for him. The land has already taken him. *Save yourself*, you are too important. Go, Evie Gray. Go and never return to this land."

"No!" Evie shouted. "I'm not going anywhere. Not without Jack."

"Then it will have all been for nothing." The figure slowly twisted around, pulling its cloak away from its face.

The scream that left Evie's mouth was excruciating. She stumbled backwards, falling onto the cold ground in a panic as the ghostly woman floated towards her. Her pale face was mottled, with eyes so dark, she felt as though she were drowning.

Her long bony fingers stretched forwards, gripping hold of Evie's hands, but not in force. With a gentle grasp, Evie was lifted to her feet.

"Do not fear me girl," she whispered quietly. "I won't harm you. But there are others here who wish to do so. They are waiting for you, and without magic on your side, you stand no chance. Leave now, whilst you still have time."

"Who *are* you?" Evie asked again.

"It matters not who I am," she repeated, and slowly turned away. "They have waited so long for this moment. I truly believed...leave now. I beg you. Please. Go."

The woman vanished as an eruption of fretful voices suddenly filled the square. Evie spun around to see Lucas, Hayden and Zac hurtling towards her. Behind them, she saw Cillian and Jamie.

"Evie!" Lucas shouted. "What the fu–"

"I'm sorry," she said quickly. "I'm sorry... I..."

"Start talking, now," Lucas said, grabbing hold of her hand and pulling her towards him. "Gods, Evie!"

"I'm sorry," she said again. "I should have said something. I heard a voice calling my name, and then I *saw* something in the street. I thought I'd imagined it at first, but when I went to stand outside, I saw it again."

"Saw what, exactly?" Hayden asked.

"I think it was a ghost. I didn't see its face until now," she said. "I followed her, and she spoke to me. She told me to leave."

"*She?*" Hayden asked.

Evie nodded. "Fae," she said. "Well, the ghost of one anyway."

"Impossible..." he said.

"I know what I saw, Hayden!" she snapped. "She told me to

leave."

"Did she say anything else?" Zac asked.

Evie relayed her conversation with the Fae ghost, feeling the burn of their eyes as she spoke. By the time she finished, Hayden was marching her back to the cottage.

***

"Is it possible that Evie *imagined* the ghost?" Cora asked quietly. "The land distorts reality, confuses what is real and what is not real, right?"

"I don't know," Hayden said, twisting his head to Evie. "It was definitely Fae?"

"She had pointy ears," she said sharply. "What else could it have been?"

"What did she look like?" he pressed urgently. "Tell us again, every little detail."

"I already told you. Her face was scarred and mottled," Evie said, frustrated. "She had pointy ears. She *looked* terrifying, but I got the impression that she didn't want to be. It was weird...she said *they*...do you think she was talking about Henry and The Dark Prince?"

"I'd rather not find out," Lucas said sharply. "What do we do now?"

"We stick to the plan," Hayden said. "We find Jack, and we get the hell out of this land. The sooner we leave this place, the better."

"Plan of action?" Tessa asked, jumping to her feet. "We can't wait until this storm passes. Not now. We need to find Jack."

"I know, but it won't be easy in this rain," Hayden agreed.

"Hayden what if we're too late," Evie said painstakingly.

"She told me the land had already taken him…what if he's not in this court?"

"Then we move on to the Seelie Court, and we keep searching until we do find him," he said softly. "We will find him, Evie. I promise. Jack is stronger than you think. He will be okay."

Chapter Twenty-Six

The wind roared with a ferocious growl, battering the crumbling walls of the Twisted Castle. Its weakened structure trembled against the waves of the Black Sea as they crashed violently into the ruin.

Jack rolled onto his side; his vision blurred as his eyes tried to regain focus. He had no idea how long he had been unconscious for, or what had rendered him unconscious, but he did know that his body ached. Exhaling as deeply as he could, Jack forced away the pain that rippled through his body, ignoring the urge to vomit as he did so.

He pulled himself up, wincing.

Darkness filled the chamber, bringing with it a coldness like no other. Shivering, Jack clenched his chattering teeth together. Within seconds, the small chamber plummeted to freezing. He shuddered as his head met with the stone wall once more. His shirt lay crumpled in the corner. Covered in vomit and blood, he had no choice but to remove it. His eyes scanned the chamber, looking for something, *anything* he could use to wrap around his shoulders. But he found nothing.

The darkness swirled once more, gripping tightly as it clung to his weakening body. It slithered through his blood, moving slowly towards his slowly beating heart. He closed his eyes as pain lanced his body, the curse of the land pulling him back into a slumber he could not resist.

*   *   *

"He is stronger than I first thought," The Dark Prince said quietly as he stood over Jack's body.

"He's a Guardian. What did you expect?" Henry spat. "The curse is working. It is only a matter of time before it consumes him completely."

"Unfortunately, time is something that I do not have," he mused. "You've felt the *changes* since we arrived. Something has changed within the land since Evie Gray and her Guardian friends arrived."

"My Prince?" Henry said, confused. "I've noted no changes."

"Hmm," he said thoughtfully, twisting his head slightly so that his eyes fell onto the raven that sat upon his shoulder. "If the girl does not find him soon, I fear my plan will not work. I need the madness to overtake him before she finds him. The sight of him weak and near death will *weaken* her, and I will have no trouble extracting the Fae magic from her then."

"Do not worry, my Prince," Henry said, trying to sound positive as he too looked down at Jack's unconscious body. "A few more hours and he won't even know his own name. A little patience is all you need."

"Patience is a trait that I do not have," he said as he strolled towards the door. "I must go back to the normad world. There are things I must see to. You will stay here and guard the castle. The minute Evie Gray arrives, you do what you must to get her and bring her to me. Do not harm her, Henry. She is *mine*."

"Understood. But what of the others?" Henry said.

"Do what you must with them," he said coldly. "I want Evie

Gray alive. I *need* her alive for what I must do."

"Will you share your plans with me?" Henry asked. "I have proven my loyalty to you, my Prince. You are already powerful. You have magical abilities that many have only ever dreamed of. You could rule without so much as flicking your finger. Why do you require the girls magic? What do you plan to use it for?"

"That, Henry, is my *secret* to keep," he mused. "You will find out in due course. For now, all you need to know is that I require the girl."

"Understood," Henry said, his voice flat. "Will I be having any assistance guarding the castle?"

The Dark Prince laughed. The sound of it almost as cold as the chamber they stood.

"Tell me, Henry, why would a high warlock of your status require assistance? Are you unable to handle a bunch of Guardian children?"

"I can handle them," he said bitterly.

"You will handle them alone," he said. "They do not have magic; therefore, you have nothing to worry about. Kill them. Kill them *all* if you so desire. Just bring Evie Gray to me."

The Dark Prince left then, and Henry swore angrily. He hated being told what to do, and he especially hated being made to feel inadequate. Using his foot, he kicked Jack's body so that he rolled onto his back.

"You fool," Henry said quietly. "You should have left her in London."

***

The rain finally slowed to a gentle drizzle as The Circle spread out through the Unseelie Court.

They had searched every cottage and building, finding nothing but empty, derelict canvases. The Circle found no sign of Jack, or anyone for that matter. The voice that Evie had heard did not return. Neither did its ghostly figure.

Several more hours passed before Hayden paused, ordering The Circle to regroup at the top of a small hill that overlooked the Black Sea.

"We still have one more place to look," Hayden said, turning to point ahead of them. "The Twisted Castle is three miles from here."

With the rain settled, it was much easier to navigate their way through the Unseelie Court, and the Twisted Castle soon rose in the distance before them.

As she led the way, Evie felt something change within her. She couldn't explain the feeling, but it reminded her of the first time she had *felt* the Fae magic rise. Her fingers tingled with each step closer to the castle, and by the time they had reached the long-cobbled path that would lead them inside, her hands were burning.

"Guys, not to cause a panic, but I feel odd," Evie said suddenly, holding her hands up. She twisted them, this way and that, expecting to see the fiery flames, but nothing happened.

"What is it?" Lucas asked.

"I...my hands feel weird," she said. "They're tingling..."

"It's probably the land. You're more connected to it than we are because of the Fae." Hayden said. "Magic doesn't work here. Remember?"

Evie didn't respond. She knew what she had felt, and she was almost certain it *wasn't* the Land of Wonder playing tricks with her head again. She lifted her head to look at the castle.

"You guys stay out here and keep watch. I will go in."

"No. We will all go in," Lucas said swiftly. "Have you seen how big that thing is?"

Evie shook her head.

"He's here," she said quietly, her eyes almost lost in a trance. "He's here Lucas. I can feel him."

"What are you talking about?" he said, throwing a nervous glance towards the others.

Ignoring him, Evie hurtled towards the castle, her fingers tingling with each hurried step. She felt something tighten in her chest, forcing a gasp to escape her mouth. Her hands reached for her chest, her fingers massaging the ache that had formed. Ignoring the surge of pain that threatened to overwhelm her, Evie forced her feet forwards.

Her magic roared beneath her skin as Evie pushed open the rotting oak doors. They creaked with life as she stepped inside, and her eyes automatically adjusted to the dark entrance.

Evie...

She found herself smiling as a soft voice whispered her name. In front of her, she found a grand spiral staircase. Mindful of the rotting wood, Evie took to the staircase, taking each step slowly. The carpet that covered the stairs was spongey, filled with years of mould and decay.

"I thought I told you to leave."

Evie paused as the ghost of the Fae woman hovered at the top of the stairs. Her face was less mottled now, and Evie could see the beauty that would have once radiated beneath her ghostly form. Even in death, this woman, whoever she was, was beautiful. Evie paused, her mind reeling. Only a few hours ago, this ghostly figure had been the image of nightmares, but now...

Evie shook her head. She didn't have time to allow her mind to wonder. Jack didn't have time...

"And I told *you* that I wasn't going anywhere without Jack. So, either get out of my way or help me find him," Evie retorted.

"They know you are here," she said quietly, and added with a muffled whisper, "What have you done..."

"If you're talking about The Dark Prince, then good," Evie snapped. "Now tell me, *where* is Jack? I know he is here."

"The dungeons," she whispered. "He isn't alone. Be careful."

Evie nodded and said without thought, "Will you come with me?"

"Yes," she said quietly.

Evie spun around and darted back down the stairs. Though it was dark, she seemed to have no trouble navigating her way around the dingy castle. The wind outside had picked up once more; the broken windows allowing the bitterness easy access to the castle.

Evie shuddered as she continued her search. The ground floor was scattered with broken pieces of furniture. Shards of glass crunched beneath her feet as she stalked forwards. She continued along a narrow corridor, aware of the ghost who followed silently behind. When she came to a dead end, Evie twisted her head. The Fae said nothing. Instead, she raised her hand and pointed to a door that stood to Evie's left. With a hurried breath, Evie reached for the handle and pushed the door open.

The door opened to what once would have been the kitchen. It was a large space, with an even larger wooden table in the centre of the room. On the far-right side, a gigantic hearth dominated the stone wall, whilst opposite, a sink sat, still filled with numerous pots and pans. Evie stood for a moment, allowing her eyes to absorb everything. With a shudder, she noted bowls caked with mould and rot upon the table.

Bile rose within her stomach as the smell penetrated her nostrils. With a grimace, she swallowed the bile back down and turned her head back to the Fae who hovered behind.

"You will find the door beside the sink," the Fae said quietly, "will lead you to the dungeons."

Evie nodded and hurried over to the door, ignoring the scuttling of little feet as she did. She squirmed as several rats hurtled behind a small cabinet. The door was bolted shut, locked with a heavy golden padlock. She moved closer, and as she did, she felt a surge of power racing towards her fingers. She raised her hands, her eyes widening at the faint yellow glow that was emitting from her fingertips.

Evie turned to look at the Fae.

"What's happening to me?" she asked nervously.

"It would appear," she said in a voice that echoed with sorrow and despair, "that *your* magic is an exception to the spell that was cast over this land."

"What the hell does that mean?" Evie asked.

"Unlock the door," was all she said.

Confused, Evie lifted her hand towards the padlock, gripping it with her trembling fingers. The padlock grew hot beneath her skin as her magic grew stronger and with a loud *click,* the heavy lock fell to the floor.

She pulled the door open, and with a final glance behind her, Evie began to descend the winding stone steps. The shimmering glow from the Fae provided her with light as she took each step two at a time. By the time she reached the dungeon floors, a cold sweat slithered down her back.

The hallway was very narrow, giving her a sense of claustrophobia. She felt her anxiety rise, threatening to explode within her. She hated confined spaces.

Evie pushed forwards until she came to the end of the hall and found two more doors. Surprisingly, both were unlocked. Reaching out, Evie pushed down the metal handle of the first door and pushed it open.

Chapter Twenty-Seven

Henry was stood with his arms crossed; a wicked smile spread across his face, as Evie stumbled into the dungeon.

"Alas," he said excitedly. "I do love it when a good plan comes together. The Dark Prince will be so pleased."

Evie scowled, her hands burning as her eyes met with Henry's.

"You bastard!" she growled. "You were *friends* with my parents, and you *betrayed* us!"

"Warlocks do not have friends," he said bitterly. "Your parents were fools to trust me, and as for you, you're just the same, and look at the price you've had to pay."

"Why did you do this?" she whispered bitterly.

"You have something so many of us in this world desire," he said. "The magic that filters through you blood wasn't just *given* to you. You were born with it, and that is what makes you so powerful. Half witch. Half Fae. What a beautiful combination."

"I don't understand," she said. "My parents were witches…"

"There are things you do not know," he said. "Things your parents did not want you to know. Yes, you are correct, they were indeed both witches. But you were never *theirs*."

Evie's heart seemed to accelerate as she processed Henry's words, and suddenly, the invisible strings that had latched to her mind outside the cottage were back again, and she could feel the darkness clouding her vision once more.

The baby had stopped crying, its little hands reaching out to the one who had settled it. The figure pulled down the hood of their cloak, revealing a soft, oval shaped face and a smile that was filled with so much warmth and love. Her wavy blonde hair fell past her shoulders and the baby reached for it, giving it a gentle tug.

"It's all right, my little precious," Anna Gray whispered. "You're safe. You're mine now."

"Do you understand now?"

Henry's voice was so sharp, the mere sound of it was enough to shatter the vision and pull Evie back.

"You were *taken,* and now, the stolen child of the Unseelie Court has returned. What a terrible shame the wretched Fae are not here to see…"

"No!" she screamed. Her blood was boiling. Simmering beneath her skin as her magic roared ferociously. "No! You're lying! I'm not…"

"Oh, but you are! Even *you* must realise the truth by now. The Guardians initiated the Fae war. They knew of a child born to both Fae and witch…and they knew of the consequences that would follow if that child was to exist in our world. The war wasn't started over a little conflict between Fae and witch, Evie. It was started because of *you.*"

Evie shuddered, stumbling backwards slightly at his words.

"Your parents were fools to believe their death would keep you safe. Keep you hidden. Fools blinded by the love they had for *you.*" Henry's voice was a wicked snarl. "And now you're here. In the very place where it all began. Powerless and *mine!*"

Henry rushed forwards with menacing speed, his black eyes filled with wicked malice as he reached for her, but Evie was fast. She jumped aside and twisted on her heels. Henry followed and released a low gasp as his eyes fell onto her hands. Evie sucked

208

in a deep breath, thanking the Gods, as the flames burst to life, snaking around her fingers and wrists.

"*It can't be,*" he hissed.

"Guess you were wrong about magic not working here after all," she said. "Now where the fuck is Jack?"

Henry snarled, exposing a wicked grin as the dungeon door exploded open.

Following Henry's gaze, Evie froze as a familiar figure walked through the open doors, but before she could even begin to appreciate the relief, the ache in her chest became unbearable.

Jack stood motionless. His usual blue eyes were the colour of black ink and fixed intensely on her. His naked chest rose with each heavy breath he took. Evie made a noise, somewhere between a gasp and a sob as her frantic eyes searched his silent figure.

She flinched at the sight of his perfectly sculptured abdomen, covered with lacerations and dried blood – physical reminders of his imprisonment.

What had they done to him?

"Jack?" she said his name, her voice almost a whisper, forcing the flames to vanish as she took a tentative step towards him. "Jack, look at me…"

"He doesn't know who you are," Henry mocked. "You're too late. The curse of the land has already done what it was designed to do."

"Jack," she said his name again, closing the gap between them. "Jack, listen to me. You have to fight this. You have to fight! Whatever image you see in your mind, it's not real. *I am real.* Jack, I see you. Now I need you to see me."

"Evie?" his voice broke the shield she had over herself, and for a moment, she forgot where they were and rushed towards him.

A pair of warm calloused hands clasped around her throat, squeezing with a menacing tightness. Gasping, Evie clutched at Jack's wrists, fighting against his hold as he dragged her across the dungeon floor. Henry chuckled from the side, watching with a gleeful delight as Jack lifted Evie, tossing her to the ground. Evie screamed, scrambling to her knees, but Jack was on her before she could stand, forcing her back to the ground with a deafening thud.

"Have your fun boy, but do not kill her," Henry's voice teased from the side-line. "Our Prince needs her alive for what he plans to do…"

His fingers laced themselves through her wavy hair as he dragged her head up. His eyes bore into her own, and she gripped his arm once more.

She had to fight back.

Evie lifted her free arm, bringing it down with such force against the arms that held her in place. Jack buckled, loosening his hold on her hair, allowing her to swivel out from beneath him. She scrambled to her feet, raising her hand as she did, welcoming the sight of the fiery flames in her palms.

"Jack, STOP!" she screamed as he advanced towards her. "Jack, please! Please don't make me do this! I don't want to hurt you…STOP!"

Jack didn't respond, and within seconds he was stood before her. His dark empty eyes rested on her.

"Kill me…it's the only way…" he gasped. "Evie do it!"

"No!" she cried, forcing the flames to vanish for a second time.

Her hands became her own again, and she placed her palms onto his shaking chest, shoving him backwards. His heart thundered beneath her trembling fingers.

"Jack, fight it! This is the curse talking! Fight it! You're strong...please."

A wicked smile stretched across his face, but as he went to move forwards, he found himself rooted to the spot.

Evie glanced behind him, filled with both relief and panic as several figures sauntered towards them.

Fae.

"Impossible," she heard Henry say, but she did not remove her eyes from the new arrivals as he darted out of the dungeon.

"Stand back child."

The female who led the Fae spoke with a soft voice, enchanting almost. She moved with such grace towards where Evie stood, and her eyes, Evie noticed, were the colour of the sun.

"The curse of the land is strong," she mused, "but, with a little assistance, it can be broken."

"How?" Evie pleaded. "How do I break the curse? Please, help me. I'll do anything. Please! Just save him!"

"You need not ask," she whispered, gesturing for her companions to join her. "We are here to help, Evie Gray."

The Fae twisted her head then, focusing her eyes on Jack as he fought against the invisible chains that bound him. His arms thrashed as whirls of black ink began to spiderweb across his chest.

Jack fell to his knees as an agonising scream rippled from him. The female stood in front of him, placing a pale hand on either side of his face. Sweat licked his forehead, and his entire body shook rigorously against her touch.

"What are you doing to him?" Evie yelled, as a painful tug erupted within her chest. "You're hurting him. Stop!"

"She is extracting the curse." A male Fae who stood a few

feet from Evie moved towards her. He too had yellow eyes. "The pain he feels comes from the curse. Not her."

Seconds felt like minutes, and Evie could do nothing but watch in desperation. Finally, Jack's body stopped shaking, and as the Fae removed her hands from his face, Evie noticed his shoulders sag a little.

He gasped, inhaling a long breath of air before lifting his head. His brilliant blue eyes were his own again. The tightness in her chest lessened.

"Evie?" Jack's voice was barely a whisper as he rose to his feet. Paying no attention to the woman who stood beside him, he closed the space between them with two large strides, his eyes never leaving hers. "Gods, Evie…"

His mouth found hers, his lips hot and insistent. His hands gripped at her waist as her own curled around his neck, pulling herself closer against the hard lines of his body.

The kiss deepened with an explosive force, a clash of tongues and fireworks, deliciously fierce as he cradled her head, angling her for an even deeper kiss. Her lips parted eagerly, allowing his tongue to move against hers with torturous strokes. Desire consumed her. Consumed every rational thought, replacing it only with her *need* for wanting more.

The kiss was *obliterating*.

She couldn't stop.

Wouldn't stop.

Each kiss a reminder that he was safe.

That he was alive.

That she had found him.

Jack shuddered, releasing a low growl as her teeth bit into his lower lip.

"Sorry." Evie trembled as he pulled back slightly, his eyes

never leaving hers.

"Did I hurt you?"

The hurt that resonated in his voice was enough to break her as she realised what he was referring to.

She shook her head, gripping the side of his face with her palm.

"That wasn't you, Jack," she said breathlessly. "It was the curse. It wasn't you."

He pulled away further. "I could have killed you," he said. "Gods Evie..."

"Stop," she ordered. "I don't want to hear that kind of talk. You were under the curse of the land, Jack. It wasn't you."

He said nothing.

"Jack," she whispered, feeling a tear escape her eye. "I thought we would be too late..."

"I thought *I* told you not to come for me," he said, and she noted the corner of his mouth rise slightly.

"When did I ever listen to your orders, Saunders?" She grinned.

He smiled, and said, "The others?"

"They're outside. Waiting for us," she said, and added with a smile, "you're safe now. We all are."

He released a sigh of relief as she reached up, looping her arms tighter around his neck.

"And you?" he asked.

"What about me?" she asked, confused.

"You came in here by yourself." His eyebrow raised a fraction.

"Well, I figured it was my fault that you were in this mess, so it was my job to fix it," she said. "I'm not sure you would have had the same response to that *kiss* had it been Lucas or Zac standing here…"

Jack released a low laugh, gripping her waist as he lowered his mouth back to hers.

"Then I guess I need to thank my lucky stars that it was you," he whispered against her lips before pulling back. "Thank you…for not giving up, I mean. I know I told you not to come for me, but I am glad you came."

She smiled. "You clearly don't think very much of me if you thought I would have even contemplated listening to your ridiculous order."

His head dipped slightly.

"I wouldn't have blamed you, Evie." He sighed.

"Jack, I'm here, and I would have kept searching for you, day and night, for as long as it took until I found you," she told him, and added with a smile so wide, she could barely contain it, "come on Saunders, let's get the hell out of here."

***

The Circle were stood in the courtyard, watching intently as Evie and Jack emerged from the Twisted Castle.

The rain had stopped. The blustery wind nothing more than a gentle breeze. Evie lifted her head slightly as Jack's arm brushed against her own. She didn't know how long they had remained inside the dungeon.

Jack had pulled her back into his arms, his lips knocking all sense of reason out of her.

"Jack!"

Lucas' voice erupted with relief and utter joy as he rushed across the courtyard, embracing his friend with wide arms.

"You look like hell, mate."

"Feel like it," Jack said, grinning. "It's good to see you all."

"It's good to see you too," Lucas replied, as the others joined them.

Tessa stumbled forwards, crying as she wrapped her arms around Jack's neck.

"Oh Jack, you have no idea how worried we have all been!"

"I can imagine," he said softly as she pulled away. "I want to thank you all, for coming. I think another day in that place...well, I don't even want to think about it."

"You're safe now, that's all that matters." Cora beamed, as she, too, pulled him in for a hug.

"What do we do now?" Evie asked.

"We should go back to the cottage," Hayden said, before adding, "and *you* can explain what the hell you were thinking, running off like that."

"What are you talking about?" Jack asked, and Evie rolled her eyes.

"Does it really matter?" she said. "We're both safe and alive, aren't we?"

Hayden raised his eyebrow.

"Nice try," he said. "Back to the cottage. We can discuss things there."

Chapter Twenty-Eight

Evie held back the retort that danced on her lips, and hurried forwards to walk with Tessa, Cora, and Robyn.

She turned her head, casting one final glance at the derelict ruin, silently thanking the Fae, wherever they had disappeared to. As she walked, Evie tried to piece it all together, to make sense of everything that had happened.

If the Fae had been exiled, *how* had they appeared by her side? Hayden had been certain the Fae were long dead, yet she had seen them.

Very much alive.

And what about her magic?

Magic was forbidden, yet hers had come to power when she needed it most. She had known Jack was inside the Twisted Castle. But how? She could not explain the feeling she had felt as she had stood outside. The crippling ache within her chest as her magic had roared beneath her skin. Her mind was buzzing with questions.

So many questions. Yet so few answers.

Where was Henry? Why did he run away? And more importantly, *where* was The Dark Prince hiding?

"You okay Evie?" Robyn asked, her gentle voice breaking through Evie's thoughts.

"I've got a headache," Evie replied.

"I'm not surprised, after tonight!" she said. "You scared the hell out of us you know, running off the way you did."

"I'm sorry," she sighed.

"We couldn't even follow you because the door sealed itself the minute you entered the castle," Robyn said incredulously.

"Seriously?" Evie gasped, and Robyn nodded.

"Can we agree that you won't do it again?" Tessa said quickly. "I think we've had enough excitement for one night."

"Speaking of excitement." Cora smirked. "The sexual chemistry between you and Jack is *killing* me right now...what the hell happened between you two inside that castle? I want every little detail, right now!"

Evie blushed, forcing her eyes to remain ahead.

"Nothing happened," she said.

"Bullshit," Cora said. "I'm an empath. I can read you both like a bloody book. Tell us!"

"Leave her alone." Tessa grinned. "It's none of our business..."

"We're friends, aren't we? Friends share this kind of information with each other!" She grinned. "You agree with me, right Evie?"

Evie smiled but did not respond as they neared the cottage. Something was different. The windows were no longer broken, the pearly glass now emitting a soft yellow glow through each pane. The thatched roof was no longer destroyed, and a small chimney was emitting pale grey smoke.

"Am I imagining this?" Evie said, looking at the girls with the utmost confusion.

"We see it too," Robyn said quietly.

Evie stepped forward, climbing the two stone steps that led to the cottage. She pushed open the door and was instantly hit by a welcoming warmth. The cottage was bright, and the smell of lavender filled the air as Evie pushed open the sitting room door.

In the centre of the room, a table had been placed, and was filled with the most exotic looking fruit, and an array of foods that Evie had never seen before.

"What the hell is going on?" Cora asked as she, Tessa, and Robyn entered the room. "Who did this?"

"The Fae," Evie said, smiling.

"Fae?" Hayden's voice was sharp as his eyes scanned the room. "What are you talking about Evie?"

"They're alive, Hayden," she said. "They did this."

Evie stood by the fire, welcoming the heat it radiated as she spoke. She began with the ghostly figure she had met, and then again inside the castle. She told them how she had known Jack was inside the castle but could not explain *how* she knew, just that it had been a feeling she knew to be true. Everyone remained silent as she told her story of the events that happened, and how it had been the Fae who saved Jack from the curse.

She told them of Henry, avoiding eye contact as she repeated his tale of her parents and the war, and how he had vanished when the Fae had appeared.

"I don't know where Henry went," she said quietly. "I assume he panicked and made a run for it."

"It's not Henry that worries me," Hayden said. "The Fae *should* be dead, Evie. They were banished into exile over twenty years ago. Their prison was one of the strongest magical fortresses ever made. So, the fact that they're here and *you* can see them, causes us a problem...a really big problem."

"Why is it a problem?" Evie asked. "Had it not been for *them*, Jack would be dead. They saved his life, Hayden. They removed the curse. We should be thanking them."

"At what cost? The Fae don't just *help* because they feel like it, Evie," he told her. "They are untrustworthy, malicious, and cruel, *especially* those of the Unseelie Court. They saved Jack because they want something in return."

218

"I don't believe that," she snapped. "Has it not crossed your mind that maybe the reason they saved Jack is because I am half-Fae? Their blood runs inside me, maybe they just had an obligation or something to help one of their own. They could have let Jack die, but they didn't."

"I don't buy it," he said sharply. "And you shouldn't be so trusting either. You know nothing about the Unseelies."

"Hayden is right, Evie," Lucas said softly, and added as he glanced around the sitting room, "witches were responsible for their exile. *We* are witches. *We* are Guardian warriors. Why would they want to help us?"

"Lucas we had nothing to do with that war. We were babies," Evie snapped, wiping angry tears from her eyes as she turned back to Hayden. "You say the Fae are untrustworthy and malicious, so what does that say about me? *I am* half-Fae, Hayden."

"We don't know if that is true," he said. "Henry is a compulsive liar. We can't trust a word he says. Until we have proof, we can't believe anything."

"What Henry said is the only logical thing that makes sense, Hayden. You know it is," she said, feeling anger rising within her. "I am the reason the Guardian's initiated the Fae war. The vision I saw, it was real. It *happened*, and the woman I saw, that was my mother, Hayden."

Hayden shook his head.

"Evie, you are in the Land of Wonder. A land that distorts reality and truth. We can't know for sure until we have solid proof. That memory could have been a false projection placed in your mind by the Fae to gain your trust."

"You know what, I'm done talking to you," she snapped and stormed towards the door. "I know what I saw, Hayden. It was real, whether you want to believe it or not."

***

Evie left the room, ignoring Tessa's calls for her to stop, and climbed the narrow staircase to the first floor.

The landing was lit by flickering candles, and as she opened the first door she came to, she was welcomed into a small, but cosy bedroom. Evie slammed the door shut and curled up into a ball on the bed.

"Do not let your anger consume you child," a delicate, musical voice spoke from across the room. "They do not understand."

Evie shot up, watching as the Fae removed the cloak from her head. Her face, unlike the first Fae she had met was beyond beautiful, with silky smooth skin and eyes as yellow as the sun.

"Who are you?" Evie asked.

"My name is Adeline," she whispered. "We did not have chance to speak whilst at the castle. Your friend? I assume he is well?"

"He is, thanks to you!" Evie said. "You knew my name...at the castle, you said my name. How do you know who I am?"

Adeline smiled, tilting her head slightly to the side.

"I have waited a very long time to meet you," she said. "Evie Gray. Longed and most awaited child of the Unseelie Court. Stolen and concealed by the witches...until now."

"So, it is true?" Evie gasped. "Everything that Henry said about my parents, it's true?"

Adeline nodded her head.

"You are the stolen child of the Unseelie Court," she said. "For years my people have held onto the hope that you would

220

one day return to the homeland and break the spell that has kept us trapped for so many years. I want to thank you, Evie. You have no idea what your being here has done for my people."

"Hayden told us the Unseelies were banished into exile," Evie said. "He said you would be long dead by now. How are you still alive?"

"He is correct, in part." Adeline shrugged. "The Guardians banished the Unseelie Court into an unforgiveable exile, but they were foolish, and young. They did not understand the true magic of the land. Yes, their spell trapped us, and for years we have tried tirelessly to break that spell. The enchantment that was cast was created to trap *all* Unseelie Fae. However, *not all* were captured."

Adeline shifted slightly, pulling herself upright as she repositioned her posture.

"One Fae, *a baby*, was taken. That simple act was The Guardians downfall. When your mother took you from our land, it weakened the spell enough for me to cast my own. I remained hopeful that one day *you* would return, and in doing so, you have broken the spell cast upon us by The Guardians."

"Why did my mum take me? If the Guardian's initiated the war, why did she take me?" Evie asked. Her mind reeling. "I need to know the truth. They kept all of this from me. They *killed* themselves to *protect me*."

"You are special," she replied. "You are both witch and Fae, a rare phenomenon. Your birth mother was a rebellious little tinker who did not always make the right choices. She fell in love with a witch. The Unseelie Court did not expect to find her pregnant, but when they did, they were so very angry and disappointed. She had bought terrible shame upon our court."

"You knew her?" Evie gasped. "Tell me about her. What was her name?"

221

Before Adeline could respond, there was a gentle tap on the door. She raised her finger to her mouth and whispered, *"Ssh,"* before vanishing.

"Evie?" Jack's voice echoed from behind the door.

Evie pulled herself up, and said, "It's unlocked."

Jack stumbled inside and closed the door softly behind him. "Not sure about you," he said, eyeing her on the bed with an incredulous look, "but I'm having a real bad case of Deja vu."

Evie rolled her eyes, and said, "Well the last time we spent the night on a bed together, you got yourself kidnapped the very next day."

"Maybe I should go," he teased. "Wouldn't want recent events to repeat themselves, would we?"

"I'm far too exhausted to go on another rescue mission. You'll have to give me a few days," she said and gestured for him to join her. "I'm not coming back downstairs."

"I'm not here to ask you to," he replied. "Can we talk?"

Evie nodded and shuffled across the bed to give him space to sit down.

"Are you alright?" she asked, as he made himself comfortable.

"I'm fine," Jack said. "Tessa has cleaned up most of my wounds."

"I can't even begin to imagine what you went through inside that horrid castle," she said. "Jack, I'm so sorry."

"It's not something I will forget in a hurry," he said quietly. "But I'm glad it was me. The thought of *you* or any of the others in that castle...I can't even think about it."

"I'm sorry," she said. "I should have listened to you. You told us not to go to Henry's..."

"None of us could have foreseen what would happen, Evie,"

he said. "Henry fooled us all."

"I wish there was something that I could do to make you forget all the horrid things they did to you," she said quietly. "You didn't deserve…"

"Don't worry about me. I'm fine." He smiled, then added, "My worry is you. What is going on Evie?"

Evie sighed. "I just feel…lost," she said. "Everything I thought I knew; well, I guess none of it was real. I am so confused about everything…"

"You can talk to me, Evie," he said gently. "None of us can even begin to understand what you are feeling right now, but we all want to help you. You have to understand, up until today we all thought the Unseelies were dead. It's a lot to take in."

"Jack, I have to tell you something," she said quietly.

"What is it?" he asked.

"Before you came upstairs," she began. "The Fae who saved your life…she was here."

"What?" he gasped, anger flaring in his eyes.

"Please, let me explain," she said.

With a deep intake of breath, Evie told him everything the Fae had told her.

"And your father?" he asked when she had finished. "Did she talk about him?"

Evie shook her head. "She didn't say," she replied. "But this must mean something right? I think we should find her, maybe she can tell me more."

"I'm not sure how Hayden will take to that," he said. "We are leaving at sunrise."

"I can't go. Not without speaking to Adeline again," Evie said sharply. "I have to speak with her."

Jack nodded.

"Okay," he said. "But we discuss it with the others first. Agreed?"

"I just need to know the truth." She sighed. "It's hard to believe any of it. Despite what they did, I know that my mum and dad were good people and they loved me."

"I know," he said softly, wincing slightly.

"You're in pain," she said, eyes widening. "Jack you should be resting, not listening to me go on about my problems."

"Do you want me to leave?" he asked, smirking.

"Of course not," she replied. "But I also don't want you to sit here listening to me whilst you're clearly in pain. You need to rest, and sleep is the best healer."

"I know my limits." He shrugged. "I'm fine."

"No, you're not," she said, her voice incredulous.

"I'm fine, Evie, I promise," he said. "Don't worry about me."

"How can I not?" she asked, picturing him inside the castle. "The curse..."

"Is gone," he said firmly. "Look, Evie, it's over. We're safe, and tomorrow we are going home...together."

Evie nodded, twisting her head to face him.

Placing his fingers beneath her chin, Jack lifted her head gently, lowering his mouth to hers. His lips were gentle, his kiss soft. Evie lay back, pulling him down with her so that his body hovered over hers. She welcomed the weight of his body against her own, the sensation sending tiny electric pulses through her as his lips caressed her neck.

She shivered at his touch, and his hand found her bare thigh, his fingers gripping and squeezing as his mouth crashed back onto hers. Her tongue met his with a satisfying urgency, and she held on to him savouring the minty taste of him.

Jack pulled back, never once removing his eyes from hers. "I never stopped thinking about you, Evie," he said, and she knew he wasn't referring to recent events. "I never stopped caring about you."

"I know," she whispered, holding his cheek in her palm.

Her cheeks flushed as she broke the intensity of his stare, forcing her own eyes onto the hand that rested against his cheek.

"Stay with me tonight."

It wasn't a question, and his answering smile was enough to cause her butterflies to erupt once more. His lips brushed against her own with a breath-taking gentleness, lingering for the briefest of seconds before pulling away.

"Always," Jack promised.

He lifted himself up then, moving to the edge of the bed as Evie climbed under the covers. It really was like Deja vu, as she watched him pull his shirt over his head, and she silently thanked the Gods when he climbed into the bed beside her, keeping his trousers firmly in place.

She wasn't quite ready for *that* just yet.

"Come here," Jack said, lifting his arm so that she could nestle herself against him. "Sleep, Evie."

"I'm not sure that I can," she said, sheepishly. "I'm afraid to close my eyes."

"You're safe, Evie," he told her. "I promise. I won't let anyone, or anything hurt you."

"That's not what I'm afraid of," she said.

Jack frowned, confused by her words.

"What are you afraid of then?" he asked her.

"Losing you," she said quietly. "I saw you in that castle. I saw what the curse did to you. I'm terrified of falling asleep because I don't know what will happen when I wake up. I worry for the others too. I just…I can't go to sleep."

"Evie," Jack said softly, gripping her cheek with his hand. "We put our trust in Henry because we thought he would help. None of us knew that he was going to betray us. We have to take this as a lesson learnt. What Henry did, it was unforgivable, but you can't allow that to control you. We are safe because we are together. The Circle is strong, and now we have Robyn and Hayden with us, and your magic, we are even stronger. You don't have to be afraid. Everything is going to be all right. We will figure this out together once we get out of this land."

Evie sighed as Jack pulled the blanket up to cover the two of them, and she wrapped her arm tightly around him.

"We have so much to worry about," she said quietly. "We need help, Jack. We can't do this alone. The Dark Prince wants me. He wants this power I have, and the Gods only know what he plans to do with it."

"I swear on my life, Evie, we will stop The Dark Prince," he said. "I promise. We will get help."

Evie nodded, trusting his words. "What about the Fae?" she asked.

"What about them?"

"They saved your life, Jack," she said. "I think Hayden is wrong about the Unseelies."

"Evie," Jack said. "Listen to me, the Unseelie Court is known for its ruthlessness and cruelty. You probably feel an obligation to trust them, because you have Fae in your blood, but don't. You don't know them. You were raised by witches, and that is what you truly are. The Unseelies had a reason for saving my life, and I am willing to bet that they want a favour in return. Never trust a Fae, no matter what they offer in return."

"Maybe you're right," she said quietly.

226

"I'm always right." He smiled. "Sleep Evie. I'm not going anywhere. I promise."

He lifted his hand, stroking his fingers up and down her arm. The sensation sent a wave of security through her, and after a few moments, Evie felt her body relax. She closed her eyes, finally allowing the exhaustion take over.

Chapter Twenty-Nine

Hayden stood outside the cottage, his eyes overlooking the quiet Fae village with distinct curiosity.

The early morning, before the rest of the world awoke, had always been his favourite time of the day. It gave him time to think, and right now, he needed this time.

He had barely slept, and he was anxious. He worried for Evie, and the rest of The Circle. Something didn't feel right, and it made him feel uneasy. The information Henry had shared with Evie had been playing on his mind.

Things had changed since their arrival in the Land of Wonder. The grey clouds that masked the land in a gloomy blanket, had given way to pale blue sky, that was dominated by the very rare sight of golden sunshine. He ran his long fingers through his hair, frustrated as his mind buzzed with questions he could not answer.

He hated not being in control.

He hated not knowing what to do.

The cottage door suddenly creaked open, and Hayden spun around to see Evie looking back at him.

"Morning," she said sheepishly.

"Good morning," he replied.

"I need to talk to you. All of you," she said quietly. "Do you mind coming inside?"

"Of course," he said.

He followed her into the cottage and found everyone in the

sitting room. Including his friends from the New York Guardians.

"I just wanted to apologise to you all for last night," she said. "I shouldn't have stormed off like that, and I'm sorry."

"We understand," Tessa said. "None of this is your fault, Evie."

"It feels like it's my fault," she said. "I was the one who convinced us to go to Henry's. We wouldn't even be here if we had just stayed away from him."

"Everything happens for a reason, Evie," Cora said softly.

"Maybe," she mused. "But it still doesn't change the fact that you are all involved in *my* mess, and I totally understand if you want to stay out of it."

"Evie, why would you even think we wouldn't want to help you?" Lucas asked. "I think I speak for everyone here when I say *we* are your family too, and we are in this together."

"The Fae who saved Jack's life was here last night," she said the words as quickly as she could.

"What?" Hayden's voice erupted.

"I know you're probably furious but listen to what I have to say," Evie said. "Everything that Henry told me was true…"

***

Evie retold the tale she had told Jack. The Circle and the New York Guardians listened intently, sharing curious glances with each other every so often. When she finished, it was Cora who spoke first.

"So let me get this straight," Cora said. "An Unseelie Fae fell in love with a witch, a witch who did not return that love, fell pregnant with you, and then died anyway? That is so sad…"

"Cora!" Tessa warned.

"What? Evie knows what I mean," she said. "Who was the witch?"

"No idea," Evie said, trying to fit the puzzle pieces of her life together. "Which makes this whole situation even more frustrating, because I have no idea who he was, or any idea of how I can find out."

"You know what troubles me," Robyn said thoughtfully. "Witches hate the Fae. There has always been a rift between *us* and *them*. Why did your mum would take you? You were the child of a Fae... an *Unseelie* Fae. It doesn't make sense."

"It makes no sense at all," Evie agreed. Frustrated, she added with a heavy sigh, "Everyone who *could* give me answers, are dead. And I have no idea who my real father could be, or if he is even alive. If I could just talk to Adeline again..."

"Not happening," Cillian's voice was deathly sharp, forcing all eyes to turn to him and his companion. "Our orders were clear. We find Saunders. We get the hell out of here. There will be no *talking* to the Fae..."

"I'm sorry, I do not recall anyone placing you in charge," Evie snarled. "This has nothing to do with you."

"I think you will find that it does," he barked. "We are here under the orders of Francis Dubois, and you will do well to remember that. Our mission is complete. We have rescued Saunders. Now we leave."

Evie's face scrunched in anger, her nostrils flaring as she glared at the New York Guardian. A vicious pull on her magic pulled a snarl from her lips as her fists clenched tightly to her sides. Her power, relentless and dark was snaking over her, slithering desperately as rage boiled within her.

Cillian only stared, the corners of his mouth curling into a wicked smirk.

"Easy now," he said. "We wouldn't want any accidents to happen."

"Trust me, putting you on your ass would *not* be considered an accident," Evie said. "The Fae have answers to the questions I need answering. Adeline has information that could potentially solve the puzzle my life has become."

"Evie, I understand why you would want to talk to her again," Jack said, gripping her elbow to gain her attention before Cillian could respond. "But Cillian is right. Our priority right now is getting the hell out of this land."

Evie said nothing, feeling her fingers tingle with frustration. Her magic was screaming beneath her skin. The darkness of it surging with an uncontrollable frenzy. She turned away from Jack, pulling out of his grasp, and inhaled deeply.

Control.

She was losing control.

"Magic is connected to our emotions," Cillian's voice broke once more, forcing Evie's eyes to meet with his. "It reacts to the way we feel. If we are sad, our magic is weakened. If we are content, our magic has balance—it becomes more controllable. The anger you feel right now is affecting your control Miss Gray.

"You are allowing it to take over because you have *no* control." He shook his head, casting his eyes towards her trembling fingers. "You need to look at the bigger picture. Magic was banished within this land over two decades ago. Yet yours appears to be working—ask yourself why? The Fae did not just walk out of their exile—they were *let* out. You cannot trust them."

"I don't trust *you*, yet here I am, tolerating your bullshit commands," she said, her cold voice barely recognisable. "You are not in charge of us Cillian. You were sent here to *assist*, not command."

231

"Oh, Evie." Tessa sighed from behind. "We will figure this out, surely there must be another way of finding answers?"

"Well, I did have one idea," Evie replied, ignoring Cillian's taunting stare. "But it's a long shot."

"Just tell us?" Tessa pushed.

"Well, my brother would have been ten at the time all this happened, surely, he'd know something. He was old enough to understand that my mum was never pregnant with me. I just thought maybe he might have answers."

"But Evie your brother is…"

"Missing. I know." She sighed, finishing Tessa's sentence for her. "Like I said, it's a long shot."

"But it's not a bad idea," Jack said. "I agree. It is something we could look into. We should try to find him, but I don't think it will be easy. Elijah could be anywhere."

"The Guardians have never found any trace of him," Lucas said. "But they only conducted a local search."

"Their actions make more sense now," Jack said bitterly. "Lydia was more interested in Evie. Why bother wasting resources with Elijah."

"You're wasting your time," Jamie scoffed. "Elijah Gray has always been a worthless piece of shit."

A ruthless surge of power had Evie twisting her head towards the New York Guardian. The bastard only smiled.

"You know nothing about my brother," she said.

"Oh, I know *enough*," he said.

The look in his eyes left her reeling. But before she could question him, Jack spoke.

"We will try to find him." Jack threw The Guardians a look that said *shut the hell up* and reached for Evie's shoulder.

"And the Fae?" Evie asked. "You're going to completely ignore the fact that Adeline could save us a whole lot of time?"

"The Fae cannot be trusted," he said sharply. "I've agreed to find your brother because I believe it is right thing to do. We've no business tangling ourselves with the Fae."

"Jack..." she began but closed her mouth as she met with his icy glare. "Fine. Where do you suggest we begin this search?"

"The Enchanted Forest," Hayden said from across the room. "We can make contact with The Elders and go from there."

"How are we going to get to the forest?" Cora wanted to know. "Portal?"

"We need magic to open a portal, and with only Evie's working, it won't be enough," he said. "We will have to travel by sea. It will take a little longer. Two days at most, but the Black Sea has a direct link to the northern shores of the Enchanted Forest."

"The *sea*?" Robyn's eyes widened. "Like, on a boat?"

"Are you afraid of the sea?" Lucas asked.

"I prefer to *look* at the waves from the safety of solid ground, Lucas," Robyn said flatly.

"I didn't think you were afraid of anything," he teased, and added, "don't worry. I'll hold your hand for the entire journey."

Robyn blushed, and Evie raised her eyebrows at them both.

"We'll be fine," Zac said, breaking the brief tension that had risen. "I'm a very good sailor, Robyn. You'll all be safe in my capable hands."

"You fill me with so much confidence, Zachary," Robyn said and looked back at Hayden. "Is there no other way?"

"Unfortunately, no," he said.

"Not to point out the obvious here," Cora said. "But we don't have a boat."

"We will." He grinned. "Get ready. We leave in ten minutes."

Chapter Thirty

The harbour glistened beneath the unfamiliar shine of the golden sun as The Circle walked along the cobbled path. To Evie's surprise, the dock was already inhabited.

Three motionless figures stood waiting.

Fae.

Evie recognised Adeline and returned her smile as they neared. The two Fae that stood either side of Adeline remained expressionless, their silken beautiful faces sharp and tense.

"Wait," Hayden said, pulling Evie back by her arm.

"You see them?" Evie asked.

Hayden nodded but said nothing.

Adeline sauntered forwards, stopping when she was a few feet away from The Circle.

"You've no need to fear us," she said softly. "No harm will come to you."

"What do you want?" Hayden demanded.

"A trade," Adeline said. "I trust you have a number of questions for me, and I do not blame you. For years, you children have been led to believe that my people are to be feared."

"Enlighten us," Hayden said coldly. "How the hell did you escape your prison?"

Adeline smiled.

"There was never a prison to escape," she said. "The Guardians were foolish. The Unseelie Court was never truly imprisoned. The arrival of Evie Gray has broken the spell cast

234

upon us by The Guardians."

"How so?" he said.

"You will see. In time," Adeline mused. "The Dark Prince knows of Henry's failed attempt to capture Evie...oh yes, we know all about *him*. The Dark Prince has killed the warlock and plans to unleash his demons upon your world. The consequences will be *disastrous*. My court is willing to help you stop him."

"How do you know all this?" Lucas asked suspiciously.

"We have our ways," she replied, smiling. "And you will know, the Fae cannot lie. So, my information is very much true."

"How do we stop him?" Evie asked, edging forwards to stand beside Hayden. "You said you could help us."

"Yes," she said. "That is where my trade comes in. We will stop The Dark Prince. We will put an end to his war and to his plans, but we ask of one thing in return. Evie Gray, you must stay in the Unseelie Court. You were stolen from us by the witches. Stay with us. We are your true family. We will teach you. Guide you..."

Jack suddenly pushed his way forwards, his hand reaching for Evie's. She could feel the tension ripple through his fingers as they squeezed against her own.

"No," he said darkly.

"Why don't we allow *Evie* to make the decision for herself. After all, it is *hers* to make," Adeline mused, and tilted her head to the side. "Evie?"

"No," Evie said, and she felt Jack's hand relax in her own.

"You are half-Fae. The magic that lives within you will never reach its full potential unless you embrace who you truly are. You belong to the Unseelie Court. Come with us."

"I do not *belong* to anyone," Evie said sharply.

"You so easily cast us away without giving us the chance to

know each other," Adeline said. "Very well. I am sure, in time, you will come to realise...I thought I sensed something in you...but I was wrong. How disappointing."

She left then with her guards closely by her side. The Circle moved closer, each wearing a hostile look upon their face.

"Do you understand what I said now?" Cillian said. "The Fae cannot be trusted."

"The sooner we leave here, the better," Hayden said with a nod in Cillian's direction. "They won't forget this. The Fae don't take kindly to being told no. Our problems just got a whole lot messier."

"What are you talking about?" Lucas snapped. "They're gone, Hayden. The Fae are the *least* of our problems."

"Evie was taken from this land. You heard what she said: *you belong to the Unseelie Court.* Cillian was right. The Fae didn't just walk out of exile Lucas. They were *let out...*"

"By me," Evie said. "The spell Adeline cast when they were put into exile was broken because of me."

"We need to go," Jack said urgently.

"Wait," Evie said, pulling her hand out of Jack's grasp. "They won't forget this. The Unseelies have spent years bound to this land. I don't know why my mother took me, and I probably won't ever know, but she did so for a reason, and I think that reason was to protect me.

"This isn't the last we will see of them, I know it." She sighed.

"If your mother hadn't taken you, do you think the Unseelies would have *killed* you?" Robyn asked and everyone turned to look at her.

"I don't know," Evie said. "I feel this strange connection with her... with Adeline. I can't really explain it, but I feel like I *know* her."

"You have a connection with this land," Hayden said. "You're half-Fae, and you being here has strengthened the magic in you that has lay dormant for so long. As long as you remain here, the connection will continue to grow. We need to leave. Now. The Enchanted Forest is the safest place on earth right now."

"Do you think they will follow us?" Evie asked.

"Not to the Enchanted Forest," Jack said. "The Fae can't step foot there. It is protected by an ancient law that was set thousands of years ago. We will be safe there. For now."

Hayden twisted his head, carefully scanning the glistening dock of boats.

"Let's go," Hayden ordered, and pointed to the nearest boat in the dock. "This one looks the most stable."

"*Stable?*" Robyn said, her eyes widening.

"We'll be fine," he said, offering her a reassuring smile.

***

The boat swayed gently as they climbed aboard. It was old but had a solid, and firm, wooden structure.

Hayden had been right. Compared to the few others that surrounded it, this boat did appear to be the most stable.

Evie hovered behind, her mind reeling.

"What's wrong?" Jack asked. His voice was gentle, and she turned to look at him.

"Nothing," she said, hoping he would believe her lie. "I'm fine."

"No, you're not," he said. "You don't have to be brave all the time, Evie. Feel whatever it is you're feeling, just don't bottle

237

it up."

"It just feels like the last twenty-one years have been an utter lie," she said, folding her arms across her chest. "I wish my mum and dad were here, so that I could talk to them. I feel so…lost…like I don't even know who I am anymore."

"You're Evie Gray," Jack said, placing his hands onto the sides of her face. "It doesn't matter whose blood you share. You're still Evie Gray. *We* know who you are…*I* know who you are, and I see you, Evie. I see everything that you are, and nothing will ever change that."

Evie smiled.

"Are you sure about that?" she said with a sigh before walking along the wooden plank.

Once everyone was onboard, Evie sat down next to Jack, allowing herself one final glance behind.

Adeline was stood facing the retreating boat, her hands risen slightly in the air with her lips moving rapidly as she chanted. Evie tensed, turning her head away.

"What is it?" Jack asked.

Evie turned her eyes back to the harbour, but Adeline was gone.

"It's nothing," she said as the boat finally picked up speed.

"Promise me we will never ever step foot in this wretched land again." Cora grimaced. "I can't wait to go home!"

"Where exactly *is* home?" asked Lucas.

"My parent's ranch," Cora replied. "It's big enough for us all to stay, and my parents won't mind. My dad already has a number of protective wards on the place. No one will find us there. We will be safe there until we contact the Elders."

"Are you sure your mum and dad won't mind?" Evie asked.

"Evie, you know my dad, he's always up for rebellious

activity." She giggled, but then fell silent as her eyes rested on Robyn. "Robyn? Are you alright?"

Robyn was sat on the opposite side of the boat. She was sat beside Lucas with her knees clenched to her chest, and her arms wrapped tightly around her legs.

"Peachy," she replied. "How long are we going to be on this thing?"

"If the wind picks up a little, maybe just under two days," Hayden answered. "Just try not to think about the water."

"Pretty hard to *not think about it* when you're floating on it, Hayden," she snapped. "I think I'll go below deck for a while."

"I'll go with you," Tessa offered.

"Me too," Cora chimed, tilting her head towards the sky. "I don't like the look of those grey clouds."

"Grey clouds?" Robyn said, looking up at the sky.

The sun was slowly beginning to fade, giving way to thick, grey clouds that threatened the land with another downpour of rain.

"Do you think there will be a storm?" Robyn asked. "Storms mean waves…waves mean…"

"Robyn, relax, there won't be a storm," Tessa said with a soft smile. "Those clouds are miles away. We'll probably just get a little bit of rain, that's all. Come on, lets head below, you'll feel better. Coming Evie?"

Evie nodded. "Sure," she said.

"Good, a bit of girl time is exactly what we need right now." Cora grinned. "No offence guys."

"None taken." Lucas rolled his eyes. "Just remember, I can hear everything you say."

"Good!" She smirked before opening a small wooden hatch that led below.

Surprisingly, the lower decks were much more comfortable. The girls found thick woolly blankets, placing them onto the floor so that they could all sit together.

"Crazy couple of days huh?" Tessa said once they were all seated.

"Crazy couple of weeks you mean." Evie sighed. "I'm glad I have you guys. Thank you for being here."

"Well, we don't really have anywhere else to go," Cora said, smirking. "Just kidding. We're family, and family sticks together. Now, I want details. What happened between you and Mr *Hot Body* in the Twisted Castle?"

"Can we please not refer to Jack Saunders as *Mr Hot Body*. It's really disturbing to have that image in my head!" Tessa grimaced.

Evie rolled her eyes. "He is very hot," she said over the girl's laughter.

"So, what *did* happen in that castle?" Cora asked. "Come on, give us details!"

"He kissed me," she said, feeling the heat rise against her cheeks. "A lot."

Cora sighed, smiling. "And last night? We know he stayed with you all night!"

Evie chuckled.

"Sorry to disappoint you, but nothing happened. That's not me and I don't think it's Jack either," she said. "We just talked."

"He's always been a gentleman," Cora said. "I wish Hayden was more like that."

"What's the deal with you two?" Robyn asked. "Are you actually a thing, or just *friends with benefits*?"

Cora scowled.

"I don't know what kind of girl you think I am, but I am

240

definitely not the kind to allow a *friends with benefits* kind of relationship. I do have morals thank you very much."

"I was kidding," Robyn said quickly, and Cora grinned.

"I know. I'm pulling your leg," she said. "We haven't been together very long. He doesn't really show his feelings, so I don't know where I stand with him. I really like him, like a lot and I think he likes me too…"

"You're an empath, you should already know how he feels," Evie said.

Cora shrugged.

"It's not always that easy," she said. "I know when he is anxious, and when he's worried or if something is bothering him, but that's all I get from him. He's very skilled at closing off his mind, and I struggle to break through the shields. I just wish he was more open with me."

"Why don't you talk to him?" Robyn said, and added with a sigh, "I wish I had a *guy friend*."

All three girls giggled.

"You can have Lucas," Cora said. "He thinks you're hot."

Robyn laughed, blushing.

"I'm being serious," she said. "You have Hayden, Evie has Jack…I'm pretty sure there's something with Tessa and Zac!"

"Absolutely not," Tessa said, giggling. "Zac is practically my brother! There are no romantic feelings there at all thank you very much."

"If you say so." She smiled. "Gods I'm starving!"

"Seriously, you were ready to hurl your guts up ten minutes ago." Evie chuckled, but at the mention of hunger, her stomach suddenly rumbled. "I'm pretty hungry too, but we're going to have to wait."

"Don't worry, my dad will rustle us up a great meal as soon

as we get home," said Cora. "That man loves to cook."

"Does he still make his amazing lasagne?" Evie asked.

"You betcha." She grinned. "I wonder what the boys are talking about up there?"

"I doubt their conversation is as interesting as ours." Evie said, rolling her eyes.

Chapter Thirty-One

Hours trickled by, and as the day finally turned to night, the temperature dropped to almost below freezing.

Evie shivered as she pulled a woollen blanket tightly around her shoulders. She had left the girls below deck, craving the feel of the cold air against her face. She had never been one for small spaces, and the space below deck had become stifling.

"I would attempt to use my fire magic to warm us all up," she said, dithering, "but I might set the boat on fire."

Jack smiled. "Better we freeze than burn," he teased. "How are you feeling now?"

"Tired. Hungry. And in desperate need of a ridiculously hot bubble bath," she replied. "I'll just be glad when we get to Cora's ranch."

"Me too," he agreed, as she shuffled closer to him. He lifted his arm, wrapping it around her back. "It's freezing up here, why don't you go back below?"

Evie shook her head. "No. I'm fine here," she said sheepishly.

"I'm not going anywhere, Evie," he promised her.

"Obviously," she said. "Unless you're planning to go for a swim."

"Would you help me to dry off afterwards?" he said, flashing her a teasing grin.

"You're insufferable," she muttered, and added with a smirk, "I'd let you freeze because you're a terrible flirtatious ass."

"I didn't hear you complaining when you were kissing me last night," he said.

"You kissed me, actually," she retorted.

"You enjoyed it," he said, releasing a low laugh as she glared at him.

"I might just push you over the side myself in a second." Evie grinned, watching as Zac and Lucas adjusted the sails. "Has Hayden said anything? About the Fae I mean?"

"No," he replied. "He's not really said anything at all."

"Hmm," she said, lowering her head slightly. "Do you think they will follow us?"

"Who?" Jack asked.

"The Unseelie's...you saw Adeline's face," she said. "She looked almost...distraught."

Jack shook his head.

"Forget about them, Evie," he said softly. "The Fae can't cross over into the Enchanted Forest. You'll be safe there. We all will."

"I wish it was that simple." She sighed. "It's weird, since I met her, I've had this strange...feeling, and I really can't describe it. But I can almost feel this *pull* towards her."

"You have a connection with them," he said. "That's all it is."

"Maybe you're right," she said. "Do you think she was telling the truth about Henry? Do you think The Dark Prince has really killed him?"

He nodded. "Fae can't lie," he said, wincing slightly.

"You're still in pain," Evie said, turning her head to look at him. "I wish there was something I could do to help Jack...I'm so sorry."

"I wish you would stop apologising, Gray," he said, smiling at her. "It's over now, Evie. We're safe, and that's all that matters. When we get to Cora's ranch, we will send a message to The Elders, and then we can plan our next move. Now that we know what The Dark Prince wants, it will make it easier for us to stop him."

Sighing, Evie pulled her hand out of his grip and made a move to stand. Jack's fingers caught hold of her wrist, and he too, stood.

"A lot of shit has happened these past couple weeks," he said, gently forcing her to face him. "Don't push me out, Evie. Whatever you're thinking, don't bottle it up. You're not alone in this, and I promise you I will be by your side no matter what happens."

With the threat of angry tears, Evie lowered her head.

"I'm not sure how to handle this. Any of it," she said quietly. "My parents lied to me, Jack. They lied to me and then they *left* me. They left me alone, without ever telling me the truth. And now, I'm expected to just accept *this* magic. Accept everything that I have been told and just…deal with it. I'm *half-Fae,* Jack…"

"We will handle this together," he said softly, lifting her chin with his finger. "Your parents had their reasons for keeping you in the dark. They wanted to protect you. We will figure this out Evie. I promise, we will. Your bloodline changes nothing."

"We don't know that." She pulled away from him. "We don't know how everyone else will react when they discover the truth about me. How can you be certain that The Elders will want to help? I am the reason The Guardians started the Fae war. Why the hell would they want to help me? They wanted to *kill* me because of this power…this *darkness*…."

"Where is all this coming from?" he asked, frowning.

"I'm just stating the obvious," she said sharply.

"Well, I think you're wrong," he said, wrapping his arm around her lower back and pulling her against his chest. He grinned at her reluctance.

"Stop looking at me like that," she breathed against him.

"Like what?" His voice was soft as he brushed his lips across her jaw, settling on the corner of her mouth for the briefest of seconds. "Like *what,* Evie?"

"I know what you're doing, Saunders." She scowled, unable to contain the shiver that his lips against her ear brought. "It's not going to work…"

His lips trailed back to her mouth, kissing her with a gentleness that forced her to forget as his fingers gripped the nape of her neck, cradling her closer. She was lost the second his tongue clashed against hers.

A distraction.

That's what this was.

And she wasn't in the mood to resist anymore as the kiss deepened.

"Jesus, get a room already!"

Cora's teasing voice forced them apart, and Evie could not hide the embarrassment from her flushed face as Cora joined them.

"I mean, I get it, really I do," she teased. "The sexual chemistry between you two is on *fire…*"

"Seriously." Evie grimaced.

Cora giggled. "All I'm saying is that if you guys want to trade places, Robyn is feeling a little better now so I don't think she would mind swapping places with you both, if you wanted some privacy."

"You really don't have a filter," Evie said, rolling her eyes as she pulled out of Jack's hold.

"My cue to leave," was all he said before disappearing.

He left, and Cora settled herself next to Evie, wrapping her arm through hers.

"Sorry, I didn't mean to interrupt you guys," she said. "Tessa and Robyn have both fallen asleep and Hayden said he wants to be alone."

Evie's eyes drifted towards the port end and saw that Hayden was stood with his back towards them.

"Jack said he was quiet. What do you think is wrong with him?"

Cora shrugged.

"He's worried," she replied. "He hates not knowing what is coming, and he's worried about you."

"Me?" she asked.

"Yeah, we all are," she said. "This whole Fae situation has spooked him. It's spooked all of us. God knows how you must be feeling about it."

"Confused, mostly," she admitted. "I thought Adeline wanted to help. Everyone just wants my magic, and to be honest, I wish they'd just take it so we can all just go back to normal. Whatever *normal* may be."

"Are you serious?" She sounded astonished. "Evie, the magic that lives within you is truly unique and special, and it is *yours*."

"You don't understand. Yes, it is unique and special, but it's also *dark*, Cora. I can feel it, even now, just sitting here. I can feel it simmering beneath my skin, desperate for release, it's exhausting," she said. "And it's dangerous Cora, surely you must see that."

Cora sighed but said nothing.

"I felt myself losing control with Cillian," Evie said.

"You were angry," Cora said, and added with a hiss, "Cillian is a prick."

"That doesn't excuse the fact that I almost lost control," Evie said flatly. "This magic...this power...none of us know anything about it."

"Listen to me Evie," Cora said, her voice softening, "you have questions, we all do. But you're not alone in this. We will all do whatever we can to discover the truth. Everything happens for a reason, and I truly believe that your mum had a damn good reason for taking you all those years ago.

"We will find out the truth. You *will* learn to control your magic. We will ensure justice is served to Lydia and Julias. And together, we will put an end to The Dark Prince."

Chapter Thirty-Two

Stormy grey clouds dominated the sky as morning finally rolled round, bringing with it winds so strong, they forced the boat to sway vigorously on the bumpy surface of the Black Sea.

Below deck, Robyn sat with her arms wrapped tightly around her knees. Her pale face, and wide eyes were enough to send a silent panic through anyone. Tessa and Cora were sat on either side of her, trying to calm her, but nothing they said had any affect.

"The boat won't be strong enough if these waves get any bigger," she said. "They will *crush* us."

"Robyn, will you quit that negative talk already," Cora said. "We're going to be fine. Zac is a natural sailor. He will get us all back safe and sound."

"I knew this was a bad idea," she cried. "I knew it. Surely there must have been another way to get back."

"It's our only way back," Evie said softly. "Robyn, everything will be all right. Just practice your deep breathing...it will help your anxiety."

"I'm not bloody anxious, Evie," she shouted. "I'm terrified! I hate the water. *You know* I hate the water!"

"We will be in the Enchanted Forest soon," Cora reassured her. "I promise. Just do what Evie said and practice your breathing. All of this will soon be over."

"I think I need some air," Robyn stumbled forwards, pushing both Evie and Cora as she did. "My chest feels so tight... I just...

I need to breathe."

"I'm not sure that's a great idea," Tessa said.

"Please," she pleaded. "The air will help."

Reluctantly, Evie, Cora, and Tessa agreed, and followed Robyn as she hurried through the small hatch.

The winds howled as heavy droplets of icy cold rain fell from the sky, flooding the wooden deck. Evie slipped as she struggled forwards, holding on to Cora for support. A sudden feeling of dread rushed through her as her eyes fell onto the angry swollen waves of the Black Sea, bashing the boat from side to side with a violent force.

"We should go back down!" Cora shouted, and Evie nodded.

Evie turned, her eyes focusing as she tried to find Robyn and Tessa. Tessa was stood at the stern. Jack and Lucas both stood by her side. Evie hurried over, holding onto anything she could reach to maintain her balance.

"Get back below! It's not safe up here." Jack's voice was barely a whisper against the roar of the vicious winds. His hands locked around her arm, gripping her tightly.

"Where's Robyn?" Evie yelled, but as she spun her head, another wave crashed into the boat.

Evie tumbled, hitting the deck of the boat, forcing the timber planks to buckle and bulge as she righted herself. Evie heard Jack shouting her name, but she couldn't concentrate.

Where was Robyn?

Hayden, Jamie, and Cillian were stood at the port, their voices muffled by the howling wind. She looked at Jack, and the two of them forced their way across the slippery deck, holding onto each other as another swell of angry waves attacked the boat.

"There was nothing I could do!" Hayden's voice echoed with

panic as Evie gripped onto his arm. She looked at Jamie and Cillian, both of them looking intently into the depths of the ocean. "She was right there! Then the wave hit…and she was…Evie, I'm sorry…"

"What are you talking about?" Evie screamed. "Hayden!"

"The wave hit and…"

Evie's eyes widened with fear at his words. She pushed him aside, gripping onto the side of the boat. She saw nothing but the rising swell of dark waters.

The others were stood close by, each voice screaming Robyn's name over the howls of the blustery wind. The bedlam of the storm caused her heart to race rapidly as she scanned the water.

"Robyn!" Evie screamed her name, praying to hear her voice respond, but nothing came.

"Oh my God!"

It was then that she saw her. Surrounded by the depths of the black, murky water, her lifeless body bobbing up and down as the rage of the angry sea threatened to swallow her.

Evie screamed Robyn's name, her chest tight with angst as she pushed past Hayden, gripping onto the side of the boat. Icy rain splattered against her face, restricting her vision as she hauled herself up onto the boats edge. Panic burned through her body, and for a moment, she stopped breathing as Robyn vanished from her sight.

Evie screamed her name.

Over and over, ignoring the calls of her friends from behind.

She squinted her eyes, desperately searching the blackness before her. The wind howled in her ears, and she gripped the sides of the boat, securing herself against a powerful gush. The boat swayed dangerously, but her eyes remained on the water.

Seconds turned to minutes, but Evie sighed a desperate breath of relief as Robyn came back into her line of vision.

The relief barely lasted a second. Robyn's body remained lifeless as the waves ripped and dragged her, before finally pulling her beneath the depths of the ocean.

"ROBYN!"

Evie screamed as the colossal waves roared with victorious delight, and without further thought, she plunged herself into the ocean.

Salty water filled her lungs as the force of the waves dragged her away from the boat, pulling Evie deeper beneath the murky surface. The Black Sea swallowed her whole, its violent currents tugging her deeper from the surface. Evie kicked her legs, her body fighting against the pull of the ocean as she swam.

Wind roared in her ears as her head broke the surface, and with a gasp, she called to her magic. For a moment the waves stilled, her magic controlling their constant attacks as she scanned the dark waters.

Cold pelts of rain battered her face, but before she could inhale the air her lungs so desperately craved, Evie was dragged back beneath the depths; her magic failing as the Black Ocean regained its control.

She tried to fight. She tried to swim. But with each kick and push, she felt her body become weaker, tired.

Yet she couldn't stop.

She *wouldn't* give up, not now.

Not when her friend needed her.

Swim!

Her conscious mind screamed within her, forcing Evie to push her body forwards, and as she did she felt something change. She opened her eyes, surprised by how focused they had become.

The darkness had vanished.

Her vision cleared as her magic roared within her, simmering with a violent rage. Pulling her hand forwards, she forced a bubble of air to appear. She tugged it towards her face, allowing the bubble to encase her mouth and nose. Silent relief rushed through her as her lungs inhaled the air she'd created.

And then she saw her.

Adeline smiled, beckoning Evie forward with her long, bony fingers. Evie swam forwards, and as she did, a flash of red caught her eye. She twisted her head slightly and felt her heart race. *Robyn.*

Adeline raised her hand, pointing it towards Robyn's lifeless body. Within seconds, Adeline had her hands gripped around her neck, pulling Robyn's body into her arms. Evie swam forwards.

"This is the consequence of your decision." The depths of the ocean carried Adeline's musical voice. "There was nothing I could do to change his mind. The Unseelie King is *furious*. A price had to be paid."

And then she was gone.

Evie swam forwards and grabbed hold of Robyn's arm. It took all her strength to get them both to the surface, and as the cold air finally hit her face, Evie gasped and dragged Robyn's head from beneath the water.

The wind had stopped howling.

The waves no longer roaring.

"EVIE!"

Jack's voice bellowed through the air as he, Lucas, and Zac swam vigorously towards her. He was fast, and as his hands gripped the sides of her face, Evie suddenly felt the world around her stop.

"You're so fucking stupid!" he shouted, forcing her to look at him. "What the fuck were you thinking?"

"She's dead Jack," her voice was muffled from the tears that now escaped her eyes. "She's dead."

"No…" Jack's voice quivered. "No… "

"I couldn't save her." Evie sobbed as Lucas and Zac finally reached them, both of their eyes falling onto Robyn's lifeless body.

"No!" Lucas' angry voice was pained as he pulled Robyn towards him, holding her tight against his chest.

Evie wrapped her arms around Jack's neck and sobbed. "She's dead because of me," she whispered. "*They* did this…"

"Ssh," Jack said softly. "We need to get back to the boat."

"Go," Zac said, his own voice quiet as he stared at Lucas and Robyn. "Go. We will bring her."

Jack nodded, and gently pushed Evie forward.

"We have to go," he said. "Lucas and Zac will bring her bod… they'll bring Robyn."

***

The boat remained motionless. The ocean calm beneath the wooden structure. Reaching for Jack's hand, Evie allowed him to pull her back onto the boat.

"Gods Evie!" Hayden gasped, tugging her into his arms. "What the fuck goes on inside that head of yours! Thank the Gods you're okay! Where is Robyn? Is she okay?"

Jack shook his head.

"Lucas and Zac are bringing her…"

"No," Cora cried. "Robyn's not… she can't be…"

"She's dead." Evie trembled, and suddenly the weight of the

world became too much, and she felt herself falling as she pulled out of Hayden's hold. Her knees buckled as she collapsed to the floor, sobbing.

Both Cora and Tessa knelt beside her, with Tessa pulling her close as she wrapped her arm around her shaking body. "Someone get a blanket," Tessa ordered.

"I don't understand," Cora cried. "She was on the boat. How did she even get in the water?"

"The wave that hit us…it must have pulled her in," Hayden said quietly.

Evie shook her head, pulling back slightly.

"This was no freak storm Hayden," she said. "*They* did this!"

"What are you talking about?" Hayden said, his eyes widening as he met with Evie's glazed stare.

"Adeline," she quivered. "*She* did this! My best friend is dead because of me. Because I refused to stay here with *them*!"

"This isn't your fault, Evie," Tessa whispered. "None of this is your fault! Don't you dare blame yourself…"

Evie said nothing. Despite the pain that drummed in her aching heart, Evie watched as Zac gestured for Hayden and Jack to join him.

Evie froze at the sight of her best friend.

She rose before walking the short distance to the stern of the boat and lowering herself to kneel beside Robyn's frozen body.

Nobody spoke.

Nobody moved.

Evie reached forwards, placing Robyn's head in her lap. The only sound audible was that of her muffled cries, breaking the silence with a heart-breaking sound. Evie buried her face against Robyn's, her hand gripping tightly against her tangled hair.

"It should have been me." Evie choked a sob.

"Evie," Lucas whispered, placing his hand onto her back. "We need to take her below."

Her head creased with grief as she lifted her eyes to look at him.

Evie barely nodded.

"I will stay with her," he said gently. "It's okay, Evie, she won't be alone. I won't leave her."

Lucas and Zac carried Robyn's body below, and Evie felt her shoulders sag, her heart breaking.

Robyn was gone.

The girl who had been her best friend for five years.

The girl who had been most precious to her.

Gone.

Evie cried until she had no tears left to shed.

Nobody spoke for what felt like a very long time, but Evie didn't want to talk. Jack sat beside her, but as he put his arm around her, she pulled away.

She didn't want sympathy.

She didn't want pity.

She wanted revenge.

Chapter Thirty-Three

Lydia sat with her head against the stone wall, watching her cell mate as he failed for what must have been the hundredth time to unlock the door to their temporary prison. She had lost track of how many days they had spent together, and the sound of Julias's voice was beginning to irritate her.

Lydia was angry.

Angry that she had allowed herself to become so caught up in obtaining the Fae magic that she had not realised she had been discovered.

The New York Guardians were a problem.

The Circle were a problem.

A problem that would need to be eliminated if she was to escape this wretched place, but no matter how hard they tried, the infirmary door simply would not budge. Lydia closed her eyes, using all the strength she had left to drown out the sound of Julias's whining, when suddenly, a loud bang erupted from the floors above.

Screams followed, and the sound of petrified voices soon filled the infirmary. Lydia jumped up from the metal framed bed and scuttled over to the door. She placed her ear against the wood and listened.

"Perhaps The Circle have returned?" Julias suggested, raising his eyebrow.

"For your sake, we had better hope not," she said, and gestured for him to remain silent.

Lydia exhaled, and as she did so, she could see the breath escape her mouth. The infirmary was as cold as ice. She glanced towards Julias, and the two of them stumbled backwards as the heavy wooden door made a distinctive *click*, before slowly swinging forward.

Two hooded figures floated into the infirmary. They both had their heads covered, but Lydia did not need to see their faces to know that they were demons.

The demons moved aside, allowing room for a third figure to enter.

The Dark Prince stood motionless as his ruby red eyes glared intensely at the two witches before him, sending a feeling of unease through both Lydia and Julias. Neither dared to break eye contact.

"Well, well, well. This is rather surprising." The Dark Prince's voice echoed through the chamber, bouncing heavily off the stone walls. "Witches imprisoned by witches. Do tell me the tale. I would very much like to hear this one."

"An error on my part," Lydia said, keeping her voice steady.

The Dark Prince smiled, flashing a set of perfectly white teeth. "Ahh...*you* seek the girls magic too. You need not deny it, I can see it all in your head. You've craved the Fae magic for so long, haven't you. Yet it was *right* there, completely within your grasp to take, but you failed Lydia...and now here you are. You witches never fail to surprise me."

"What do you want?" Lydia asked sharply. "You are clearly not here to exchange pleasantries. We heard the massacre upstairs."

"Hmm, such a sad loss of life," he said quietly. "If only they could have seen the *bigger* picture. I'm here to offer you a deal. We both seek the same...*prize*, shall we call it? I think we can help each other."

"Why would I consider helping you?" she said. "You're the enemy, are you not?"

The Dark Prince laughed coldly, sending a shiver down Lydia's spine.

"You would be surprised Lydia...there are *many* who have chosen to work with me, rather than against me," he said. "You're just as *evil* as me, Lydia Bowater. It seeps from your pores. Did you not attempt to kill the girl yourself? Interesting, I've been dying to know...just *how* did you order *my* demons to attack?"

Lydia smiled. "That information is mine to keep," she said. "You were not *displeased*, I take it?"

"Quite the contrary, I thought it was quite a bold move," he mused. "However, I am happy you did not succeed. I need the girl alive."

"For what reason?" Lydia pressed. "The only way to harness her magic is by her death."

"Her death by another's hand would only serve to cause me more problems," he said. "Problems that I do not have time to deal with."

"Enlighten me, *Prince*." She smiled wickedly. "You are already so powerful. Why do you seek her magic?"

The Dark Prince cast a wicked smile of his own and said, "That is my secret to keep, Headmistress. However, I do think you and I would make the most formidable team."

"Lydia?" Julias's voice quivered nervously as he spoke.

The Dark Prince twisted his head. His wicked red eyes burning into Julias's trembling body.

"I didn't have you down as a weak man, Julias. Clearly, I was wrong. You're afraid, and you have every reason to be. However, I can assure you, I am not here to kill you. Not today anyway.

"Help me and I will help you. I will give you both my protection. No harm will come to either of you as long as you serve me."

"How do we know that you won't just kill us both the minute you get your hands on the girls magic?" Julias asked nervously.

"I give you my word," he replied flatly.

"And what of the others?" Lydia asked. "The Circle? The rest of The Guardians?"

"You need not worry…The Circle have a bigger problem on their hands," he said pointedly. "Do we have a deal?"

Lydia nodded. "We do," she said.

"Excellent," he said coldly. "During my attempt to capture the girl, my journey took me to the Land of Wonder. The Fae that you witches *supposedly* banished over twenty-one years ago are no longer in exile. I don't know how, and I don't know why, but somehow, they have escaped."

"Impossible!" Julias barked. "I was there. I saw The Guardians cast the entrapment spell…it is unbreakable!"

"*Possible*," he corrected in a bored tone. "Henry Martinez witnessed the Unseelie Fae himself before I killed him. They are very much alive, and they are angry. They too seek the girl."

"Lydia, you understand what this means?" Julias's voice was fretful. "War, Lydia! A war I do not wish to fight!"

"Then leave," The Dark Prince ordered coldly. "I have no time for the weak. Either you fight with me, or you fight against me. I have offered you my protection and have given you my word. The girl is our *weapon*. With her magic combined with my own, I will be untouchable. So, I will ask you one final time. Are you with me?"

"Yes," Lydia said, throwing a dirty look at Julias. "We *both* are. But where do we start? I was here when The Circle bombarded this place before we were locked in this pitiful room. Are they still in the Land of Wonder?"

The Dark Prince smiled.

"They are not," he said. "Time is fragile. We must work fast. The Unseelies have had years to prepare for this moment. I must have the girl, before they come."

"We will bring her to you," Lydia said, and added nervously, "how will we stop the Fae, should it come to a fight?"

"Oh, there is no *should* about it," he said. "The battle *will* come, and we must be ready when it does."

Chapter Thirty-Four

The Enchanted Forest loomed into view as Evie sat alone at the stern; her eyes fixed upon the glistening surface.

She had not moved. Had not spoken. Her mind and body numb from the chaos her life had become.

She stared at the vast approaching shoreline, wondering what their next move would be.

What would happen to Robyn's body? Who would tell her family? What did fate have in store for them next?

So many questions, with so little answers. Frustration overwhelmed her as the boat finally docked.

The Circle climbed onto the sandy shore, watching silently as Evie followed. She stalked past Cora, feeling her friend's eyes fall onto her retreating body, and felt a shiver trickle down her spine. With a sigh, Evie paused, and turned to face Cora's tear-stained face.

Everything Evie was feeling, the empath felt too.

"Evie…" Cora whispered, taking a few tentative steps towards her. "You didn't do this. None of this is your fault."

"I…" Evie began, but words seemed to fail her as she fell against Cora's chest, feeling her friends' arms wrap tightly around her trembling body.

"Ssh, you don't have to say anything," she said softly. "Let's get you home. You'll feel a little better after a hot shower and something to eat."

"What about Robyn?" Evie asked, glancing towards the

stationary boat. "We can't just leave her."

"We will take care of her," Jamie said quietly.

Evie's head whipped towards the New York Guardians, both staring with solemn faces.

"You will take her back to London?" Evie said. "Back to her parents?"

"I said we will take care of it," Jamie said once more.

Evie stepped away from Cora, turning her body so that she was fully facing The Guardians.

"If anything happens to her," she said, her voice deathly calm. "I swear on the Gods, I will kill you both. You take her to London, and you treat her with the upmost respect. Is that clear?"

"Threats will get you nowhere Miss Gray," Cillian said coldly.

"Come on," Cora said hurriedly, gripping Evie's elbow. "Let's go."

"Not until I have their word..." she said, tears slipping down her face as she stared at the two warriors. "Please."

"You have our word," Jamie said, and she could hear in the Guardian's tone that he meant it.

"Tell her parents..." she cried, "tell her parents that I am sorry."

The Guardian nodded but said nothing as he and Cillian turned back towards the boat.

"I'll open a portal," Hayden said. "The faster we get to Cora's ranch, the better."

***

"Home."

Cora's strained voice echoed with relief as the portal

disappeared. Evie paused, watching as The Circle hurried towards the ranch.

"I know you're hurting." Jack's voice was quiet beside her.

Evie said nothing as she forced her legs to move forward, but Jack reached for her arm, gently pulling her to a stop.

"Evie don't shut me out," he said. "I know that anything I say right now won't change how you're feeling. But I am here when you're ready to talk."

Evie nodded, hearing Jack's heavy sigh as she walked towards the ranch.

"Cora!"

Rebecca Jenkins was very much like her daughter. With the same facial features and silver, metallic hair, it was possible that the two could have passed as sisters rather than mother and daughter.

Rebecca rushed forwards, taking the porch steps two at a time before finally embracing her daughter. Evie watched as Cora fell into her arms.

"Oh Gods! Mom!" Cora cried.

"Oh, my girl!" Rebecca sobbed. "We have been so worried. Your father and I heard what happened at The Academy. What were you thinking? Running off like that! Anything could have happened to you!"

"Mom, I'm fine, everything just happened so fast," Cora told her. "Look, my friends need somewhere safe to stay. I told them it was okay for them to come here."

"Of course," she said, looking at the others. "You're all more than welcome. You'll be safe here…"

Rebecca paused as her eyes fell onto Evie, and she suddenly let out another sob.

"Evie…" she said, clasping her palm to her mouth.

"Rebecca." Evie said, forcing a smile.

Rebecca gasped, before clutching her heart.

"Your pain... I've never felt anything like it..." she gasped.

Evie sighed. Like her daughter, Rebecca too, was an empath.

"I'm okay, Rebecca..."

"Cora!"

A deep, masculine voice filled the air as Cora's father hurried towards them. Evie's body twisted just in time see a tall muscular man, with thick auburn hair, and bright green eyes, scooping Cora into his arms.

"Dad!"

"Why didn't you come straight to us?" he asked, as he placed her back onto the ground. "Your mother and I could have helped! Running off like that! Cora..."

"We didn't have time, Dad," she replied. "Jack's life was in danger. We did what we had to do."

Tom Jenkins sucked in a deep breath as he looked at the others.

"I suppose you had better all come inside," he said quietly.

***

Evie stood by the door as the others made themselves comfortable.

The room was warm, with a fire crackling in the large hearth. Overstuffed chairs dominated the cosy room, and a small coffee table sat in the centre, laden with a tray of steaming mugs of coca. On either side of the fireplace, were a set of double wooden doors that led out onto a porch that overlooked the vast countryside views that surrounded the Jenkin's ranch. Evie kept her eyes on the lush green views of the Enchanted Forest, basking in the scent of cedar and ash, and for a moment, she felt time pause as a flurry of blurred images flooded her mind.

New pieces of her life's puzzle began to emerge as the images flitted from one to another, but no matter how hard she tried to piece them together, none of them would mould together.

She felt Rebecca move to stand beside her, reaching for her hand as she did. Evie twisted her head slightly, removing her gaze from the forest that lay ahead.

"Stop punishing yourself, Evie, your friend would not want that," she said softly.

"I can't," Evie said, her voice low as she forced the blurred images to the back of her mind. "We...this is all my fault. Jack was kidnapped because of *me*. The Fae are free, because of *me*. They killed Robyn because *I* refused to stay in that wretched land. I should have stayed. Robyn would still be here if I'd just stayed with them."

"They would have killed you too." Jack's voice was like thunder as he spoke.

"Better me than her," she said countered.

"Evie, listen to me," Cora said from across the room. "Robyn didn't die because of you. *You* didn't kill her. Adeline did. There was nothing more you could have done. She was already gone when you jumped into the water."

"I didn't do *enough*, Cora," Evie said coldly, hearing her voice rise. "I need some air."

***

"I really don't know how we are going to get through this." Cora said, massaging the dull ache that had erupted in her temples.

"You need to tell us everything that has happened," Rebecca

266

said, as Tom brought a second tray of hot drinks into the room an hour later. "From the beginning."

They were back in the den, having spent the last hour showering and finally changing into clothing that did not smell of dirt and grime.

"I don't even know where to start." Cora sighed. "So much has happened these past few weeks. Evie has literally been to hell and back. We all have…"

"Her pain is…unbearable," Rebecca said, holding her chest.

"Mom, I think you and Dad had better sit down," Cora said quietly. "We have a lot to tell you."

Only when her parents were both seated, did Cora begin to tell their tale. From the very first demon attack, to Henry kidnapping Jack. Cora told them about Lydia and Julias, and Evie's Fae magic, and the events that happened in the Land of Wonder.

At the mention of the Fae, both Rebecca and Tom exchanged nervous looks, but neither spoke as Cora continued her tale.

"And then, our friend, Robyn…" Cora's voice broke at the mention of Robyn, and she felt her eyes burn with angry tears. "They killed her, mom."

Cora cried, burying her head against Hayden's shoulder.

Rebecca released a heavy sigh.

"I am so sorry darling," Rebecca said. "You have all been through so much…I just wish your father and I had been there…"

"It wouldn't have changed the outcome." Cora sobbed.

"I don't understand *how* the Unseelies were able to escape. We were there, during the Fae war. The spell cast upon them by The Elders was one of the most powerful entrapment spells devised. It was unbreakable…"

"The Elders underestimated the Unseelie Court!" Lucas

scoffed. "Their spell didn't work because of Evie. Adeline cast her own spell before The Elders trapped them. The second Evie stepped foot in the Land of Wonder, the enchantment was broken."

"Because Anna took Evie," Rebecca said. "Evie is half-Fae. The spell didn't work because Anna took her and bought her back to our land. She had no idea…"

Cora nodded, lifting herself away from Hayden.

"Mom, I need you to tell us the truth," she said. "You and dad have known about Evie for a long time, haven't you? You knew who she really was."

"We have," Rebecca said. "You have to understand, Anna and Paul were our very best friends. They were like family, and family protect each other, no matter how crazy or insane things might be."

"Why did Anna take Evie from the Unseelie Court?" Lucas asked.

"It was a difficult time for Anna," she said. "We were young and had been forced to fight a battle none of us wanted to fight."

Rebecca shuffled slightly in her seat, sucking in a deep breath before continuing.

"It was an awful time. So many innocent people lost their lives. Anna and Paul had Elijah so young, but Anna craved a girl. She loved her son, but there was always something very odd about him. Sometimes, it was almost as though she was scared to be in the same room as him. I know, it is horrible to say, but that's the way it was. Elijah was a troublesome child. Always getting into fights and meddling with things he shouldn't. His mind worked differently to ours.

"A few months before the battle began, Anna discovered she was pregnant, but she lost the baby. The miscarriage tore her

268

apart, and it was as though she went into the war blinded. She didn't care what happened, she just wanted to mourn for the child she would never meet."

Rebecca muffled a sob, and Cora stiffened at the feelings that now surged through her mother.

"We were ordered to search the cottages. The Elders did not tell us what we were searching for, but we obeyed their command all the same. We were Guardian Warriors. We followed their orders without question," Rebecca said. "The Twisted Castle was the final search, and Anna came out holding a small bundle in her arms. I remember the look on her face as though it were only yesterday. *She was so happy.* I didn't say anything to her. I didn't ask any questions. I just let her go home."

"The Elders gave you orders to search the Unseelie Court, but they didn't tell you *what* you were looking for?" Cora asked, casting a nervous look across the den to the others. "Didn't that strike you as odd?"

"At the time, no it did not," Rebecca said. "You have to understand, things were different back then. We were told of a threat that had emerged within the Fae lands. A threat that had to be eradicated immediately. We were given no details. Only that it was for the greater good."

"Evie," Cora said.

Rebecca nodded. "We later found out the truth," she said, and added, "Anna knew, the second she found Evie, what The Elders were looking for."

"How did she know? Evie was just a baby," Tessa asked, and Cora could feel the confusion tearing from her.

She felt confused too.

"The *only* baby that we came across within the Unseelie Court," Rebecca said.

"A witch born with the elemental powers of the Fae," Hayden's voice was barely a whisper as all eyes turned to him. "A rumour, that was in fact, truth. Why did Anna take Evie?"

"I do not know," Rebecca said. "I didn't ask any questions. We found Paul and Tom, and we left before the others realised."

"This still makes no sense," Cora said, exasperated.

"Anna knew Evie was only half-Fae," Tessa said suddenly, eyes widening. "Of course! It would have been obvious just from looking at her. Evie has no resemblance to the Fae. She inherited her birth-father's genes, hence the lack of pointy ears and other Fae genetics!"

Rebecca nodded.

"Anna knew the bundle she held was indeed, the child The Elders sought," she said.

"But how did she get away with it?" Cora asked. "You said you left before the others realised, but surely they would have known Anna was not pregnant."

"It was a different time back then, Cora," Rebecca replied. "Anna and Paul moved away as soon as the war ended. They stayed away until Evie was about eight years old, by that time, everyone had moved on. Facts became a rumour once more. They thought they were safe."

"But they weren't safe," Lucas said. "Because Lydia knew their secret."

"That's right," she said. "Which is why they decided to bind Evie's Fae magic. It was their only way to protect her. But they were short sighted. Magic can only be bound for a certain amount of time, Lucas. A witch comes of age the second they reach their twenty-first birthday.

"Am I correct in saying that this is when the Fae magic was first exposed?"

"Yes. In London, when Evie removed the bracelet, it just sort of *exploded* out of her," Cora said. "Evie had no idea. She was just as surprised as we were to see it. We have no idea what we do next, Mom."

"I have sent a message to the London Guardians. I am still awaiting their response," Tom said. "But we have a bigger problem. The Academy was attacked two nights ago."

"Attacked?" Lucas exclaimed. "Was anyone hurt?"

"Most of the students and staff were able to get out, but not everyone survived," he said, and added with a deep fury, "The Dark Prince has taken Lydia and Julias."

"Are you certain they didn't go *willingly*?" Lucas spat.

"With Lydia, anything is possible," Tom said briskly. "Until I hear word from the London Guard, there is not much we can do. For now, you are all safe here. Our ranch is protected, but it would be foolish to remain here indefinitely."

"What do you suggest we do?" Lucas asked. "Now that we know what The Dark Prince wants, shouldn't we be focusing our efforts on capturing him? You know as well as we do, what will happen if he succeeds…"

"That won't happen," Tom said. "We will all do what we must to ensure Evie's safety. I have suggested a safe haven, for all Guardians to meet. There, we can discuss our plans. We will need help to stop The Dark Prince, Lucas. He has an army of demons at his call, and none of us know why he seeks the magic Evie holds."

"Are you sure you can trust anyone else?" he asked. "The Elders started the war against the Fae because of Evie. How do you know they won't just turn on us now that Evie is with *us*?"

"Lydia and Julias are bad seeds," Tom said.

"And the Elders? They gave the orders, did they not? Yet

271

they still remain in power. The Fae were still exiled," he said, raising his brow. "I'm sorry, Tom, but you have to understand my hesitation. Evie is one of my best friends and I will protect her with my life."

"I know." Tom nodded. "As will I. We can trust The Guardians. Like I said, Lydia and Julias are bad seeds, and they will be punished for their betrayal. Evie will be safe. I swear on my life. As for the Elders, they have learnt from their mistakes. We can trust them."

"What of the Fae?" Cora asked. "They aren't just going to sit back, not now they are free."

Tom sighed. "I don't think they will be a problem, Cora," he said. "Right now, our problem is The Dark Prince. We know what he's after, we just need to find out *why.*"

"And Evie?" she asked. "She's been through so much already, Dad. She deserves to know the truth about her parents, and I think you and mum should be the ones to tell her."

"I know, honey," he said softly. "Your mother and I will talk to her. But for now, I think Evie needs space and time to grieve."

***

The slowly descending sun reflected in the crystalline waters of the lake that lay beyond the paddock of the Jenkins ranch.

Evie stood with her arms against the wooden fence, staring out across the paddock and onto the calm waters.

Two large, brown horses stood to her left, staring absently as a gentle breeze filtered through the brisk evening air. Jack approached her with a steady caution, leaning against the fence beside her, but remained far enough to give her space.

"I know you're not okay," Jack said quietly. "I know you're

hurting, and you have every right to feel hurt. Be angry, be upset. Feel whatever you have to feel, but don't shut us out. Don't shut *me* out. Robyn was our friend too, and we are all hurting. You can't blame yourself for what happened to Robyn. She wouldn't want you to either. You didn't do this Evie."

"You're right Jack," she said, her voice void of any emotion as she turned to stare at him. "I didn't do this. *You* did. *You* made The Circle go to London. *You* made me come back, and *you* made the choice for Robyn to come too. Robyn would still be alive right now if you had just *left me alone!*"

"You don't mean that," he said, stung by her words.

"She was my *best friend,* Jack!" Evie sobbed. "Robyn was my best friend! And now she's gone, and I don't know what the fuck I am going to do without her! She was my *family,* Jack! Everyone I have ever loved has been ripped away from me. I have *nothing left!* Robyn didn't deserve to die. She didn't deserve any of this. She would still be alive if you'd left us in London!"

"I'm sorry for what happened to Robyn. She didn't deserve any of this. She was a good person, and I'll be forever grateful that you had someone like her in your life.

"But don't stand there and blame this on me. I didn't kill her Evie."

Evie sobbed, letting the tears cascade down her cheeks.

"It should have been me."

"Don't say that!" he growled, gripping her arm, and pulling her to face him. "Don't you dare fucking say that Evie! What happened to Robyn was terrible. We are all hurting! We are all broken, but don't you stand there and say that it should have been you. It shouldn't have been anyone!"

"Let me go," she said, and placed her hand onto his wrist.

Jack's hand jerked away at her touch; his skin now burnt

where her flames had seared his skin. Evie's eyes widened, her heart thundering as the realisation of what she'd done hit her. She pulled her hand back, stumbling away from him.

Evie turned then, and hurried away, ignoring Jack's calls for her to stop.

Chapter Thirty-Five

"Dinner's ready!"

Tom, waving his hand, lifted several plates, his magic forcing the fine crockery to land softly in front of everyone, before placing two large dishes of piping hot pasta in the centre of the table.

"Dig in," he said. "There is plenty more on the stove."

"Thank you, Tom," Tessa said, scooping the pasta onto her plate. It smelt divine. "This is our first meal in days!"

"Well, I hope you enjoy it," he said, glancing around the table. "Where's Jack?"

"He's taken one of the horses for a ride in the fields," Rebecca said. "He will eat later."

Evie looked down at her food, feeling a surge of remorse in the pit of her stomach. Her hands were clenched in her lap, and as she lowered her gaze, she felt utterly ashamed.

She had been so angry when she had spoken to Jack. Angry and broken, and she had taken it out on him. Not only had she said words she did not mean, but she'd also hurt him.

Hurt him with the darkness that now sang a wicked melody as it danced through her veins.

"Are you all right, Evie?" Zac asked from across the table.

"I'm fine," she said, and after a moment, she pushed her plate away and stood up. "I'm just…I'm not hungry."

Rebecca smiled sadly, and for a moment, Evie was certain Cora's mother had the ability to read her mind.

She needed to find him. To make things right.

"I'll put it in the oven for you sweetheart," Rebecca said softly.

Evie said nothing as she hurried out of the room.

***

Evie found Jack in the stables at the back of the Jenkins' house. His back was to her, and she sucked in a deep breath before slowly moving forwards.

The horse he stood with noticed her, and neighed, highlighting her presence. Jack twisted his head, but quickly turned his attention back to the horse as he stroked him.

"You can tell me to go away," Evie said. "I wouldn't blame you."

Jack said nothing and continued to stroke the horse.

Evie sighed, clutching her sides.

"Jack, please. I would prefer it if you would just tell me to go away rather than ignore me," she said. "I'm sorry. I didn't mean...Jack I'm so sorry..."

"It's fine," he said flatly.

"Is that all you're going to say?" she asked.

"What do you want me to say, Evie?" he said, and finally turned to face her.

"I hurt you," she stammered, her eyes falling onto the redness of his wrist. "With my magic...Jack..."

"You were angry," he said. "You lost control. It's fine."

"No, it is not fine!" she gasped. "I lost control with *you*. The one person that I...Jack I..."

"I'm fine, it's just a little red. No harm done," he said. "You should go back inside."

"Jack please," she cried, tears finally breaking free. "I'm sorry. I didn't mean a single word I said to you. I was angry and you were *there*...I took it out on you, and I had no right to do that. You didn't deserve..."

"You may not have meant it, but you were right about everything," Jack said quietly. "If I'd left you in London, none of this would have happened. Robyn would still be alive. It was a mistake to bring you back here."

"Please don't say that." She flinched. "I didn't mean it. I was angry and upset. Of course I don't blame you. I shouldn't have said it."

"But you did say it, Evie," he said coldly. "And it's fine. I get it."

"I was angry, Jack," she cried, and wiped her eyes with her hand.

Jack sighed.

"Don't cry," he said, and she heard his voice soften slightly. "What's done is done. It's fine. Just forget about it."

"What is that supposed to mean?" she asked.

"Go back inside," he said, ignoring her question. "It will be dark soon."

"Not until you explain to me what you mean," she said, feeling an explosion of angst surge through her.

The world spun, and Evie felt her breath catch in her throat as Jack made a move to turn.

"Evie, I don't want to talk to you," he said solemnly, before walking away.

***

Sitting in the corner of the Jenkin's den, Evie sat with her eyes

277

fixed upon the orange flames, dancing wildly in the hearth. After leaving Jack, she had returned to the house, her mind racing with angst and torment. It had been hours, but Jack had still not joined The Circle, and she could not shake off the overwhelming anxiety that seeped through her body.

I don't want to talk to you.

The sound of his voice pierced her mind, shattering every inch of the walls she had built, until she felt nothing at all.

"Did you find Jack?" Lucas said, his soft voice breaking her thoughts. "I haven't seen him come back in for dinner yet."

"I left him with the horses," she replied, barely looking up.

"That was hours ago," he said. "Think I should go look for him?"

"Jack's a big boy, Lucas. I'm sure he will eat his dinner when he's ready," she snapped, forcing everyone to look at her. "Sorry."

"What happened?" Cora asked.

"Nothing," she replied.

Before anyone could respond, the door to the den suddenly swung open, and Tom stepped in.

"Sorry to disturb you, but I've just received a message from the New York Guardians."

"What is it, Dad?" Cora asked.

"It's not good news," he said. "The London Academy was attacked last night. A few have escaped, but the rest..."

"Robyn..." Evie said urgently. "Jamie and Cillian were taking her back..."

"I'm sorry, Evie," Tom said. "I don't know if they made it there or not."

"Is there a way to find out?" she pleaded, ignoring the tightening of her chest as she spoke. "Please Tom, I have to know…"

"I will do what I can," he told her. "The Guardians have agreed to a safe haven. We're leaving at sunrise."

"Do you have names of those who survived?" Hayden said urgently.

Tom shook his head.

"It was a terrible attack. I'm sorry, I wish there was more I could tell you."

"Damn it!" Hayden swore as he jumped to his feet. "Where is your office? I need to send an urgent fire message."

"Down the hall," Tom said. "Hayden what is going on?"

Hayden didn't reply as he hurried out of the room, slamming the door shut behind him.

"I'll go," Cora said, and hurried after him.

Tom turned back to the others.

"We leave at sunrise," he told them urgently.

Silently, Rebecca and Tom left the room, and the atmosphere grew tense. Nobody spoke for a while, each lost in their own thoughts.

"I wonder where this safe haven is?" Zac asked.

"God knows," Tessa said, and added with a desperate sigh, "Does anyone else have a bad feeling about this?"

"A lot has happened to us over these past few weeks Tess, it is understandable to feel paranoid," Lucas said. "Tom knows what he is doing. We can trust him."

"It's not Tom I don't trust," Tessa said with a sigh.

Chapter Thirty-Six

Pausing outside the door that stood nearest the stairs, Evie inhaled a deep breath, waiting for the others to disappear until she was completely alone on the large landing.

Her hand hesitated as she reached for the handle, magic swarming beneath her fingers.

Breathe.

Slowly, Evie pushed the handle down, and forced the door open.

Jack was stood by the window, his back towards her. He turned around, and Evie struggled *not* to look at him. His chest and arms both rippled with tension as she was met with his icy blue stare, and for a moment, she almost forgot how to breathe.

"Evie," he said her name softly, and she felt something flutter beneath her rib cage as some of the tension disappeared in his stance. "What's happened?"

"We are leaving at sunrise," she said. "The Guardians have agreed to a safe haven."

"I know," he said.

"Oh. Well, that's all I needed to tell you," she said, and turned away.

"Evie, wait." Jack's voice was sharp, and she felt her hand pause for a second time as she reached for the handle. "We need to talk."

"Now you want to talk?" she mused.

"Don't you?" he asked, brows furrowed.

"I feel so ashamed," she said, lowering her head. "I hurt you, Jack. I hurt you with this *darkness*, and I will never forgive myself. I lost control.

"Everything that I said, was said out of anger. I was angry, and I took it out on you. I know that's no excuse, but Jack I truly never meant to hurt you."

"You were upset," he said, pulling the towel from his shoulders and letting it drop to the floor. "I understand that. I wanted to come to you sooner, but I thought we both needed time to cool down."

"Oh," she said, feeling her shoulders sag a little at his words.

"*Oh*," he repeated, and with two short strides he closed the gap between them.

He reached for the side of her face, gripping her gently.

"I'm sorry for what I said," Evie said. "Robyn was my best friend...I shouldn't have said those things to you."

"We all say things we don't mean when we're angry, Evie," he said. "You loved Robyn, and I'm sorry that she was taken away from you. She was an amazing friend to you, to all of us."

"I miss her so much," she cried, nuzzling her head into his shoulder. "I couldn't save her, Jack."

"Ssh," he whispered, kissing her forehead. "Evie, there was nothing any of us could have done. She was already dead when you got in the water. Adeline knew what she was doing when she murdered her. She chose Robyn because she knew it would hurt you the most. You can't blame yourself for this. Robyn wouldn't want that."

"I should have protected her." She sobbed. "I knew she was afraid of the water. I should have made sure she stayed below deck. I should never have allowed her to leave."

"It wasn't your fault, Evie," Jack said, and the sharpness of

281

his tone forced her to look at him. "There was nothing that you, or any of us, could have done to save her, but I promise you, Adeline will pay for what she has done. They all will. Robyn won't have died in vain."

Evie muffled a sob as Jack pulled her against him, holding her tightly in his arms as she cried.

Pain lanced at her heart as the tears cascaded down her cheeks. Reality was crashing down on her with each tear shed. Everything that had happened erupted in her mind, flooding her with images she did not wish to see. Breathing became hard, her lungs screaming as anxiety and guilt taunted her entire being.

Robyn. Robyn had been her friend, her sister. The person she trusted the most. The person who had held her hand during her darkest days and helped her smile through the tears.

Robyn had been her very best friend.

And now she was gone.

Everyone she loved...gone.

"I don't know what to do," Evie said. "I don't know how to move forward from this."

"We have to," Jack said, wiping a tear away with his thumb. "For Robyn. For us...we have to move forward. It would be easy to simply hide from it all. To run away from what has happened, and what is yet to come. But in doing so, that would be an insult not only to Robyn's memory, but also to yourself. We move forward, Evie. We move forward and we fight for tomorrow."

Evie nodded, not quite sure of the words she wanted to say as she met with Jack's heavy gaze. He leant forwards, tugging her face gently towards his, brushing his lips against hers. She kissed him back, welcoming the warmth of his mouth against hers as she ran her fingers across the hard lines of his chest. The gentle caress of his mouth was enough to mask the nightmares that plagued her, and for a moment, she allowed herself to forget.

Jack wrapped his arms around her waist, clutching her against him. Evie gasped as his fingers slid beneath her shirt, shivering slightly at the roughness of his calloused fingertips against her trembling body.

Jack pulled away, moving his lips to the corner of her mouth and down, tracing her jawline before reaching the hollow of her neck. Evie sighed, arching back as each of his kisses ignited the fire within her, causing her tummy to erupt with desire.

Jack looked up, his eyes dark with hunger and impatience. She placed her hands onto his chest, nudging him slightly towards the bed.

"Evie," he rasped, pausing slightly. "We don't have to do this."

"I want to," she said, and slowly, she pulled out of his arms, and climbed onto the bed, gesturing for him to join her. "I want to forget it all, Jack. Please."

Jack followed, and as she lay down, he climbed over her, his body hovering slightly above, gentle with his movements, even now.

"Are you sure you want this?" he asked, smiling as she rested her hand against his cheek. "We can wait…you're not thinking straight…"

"Tomorrow isn't promised," she told him. "I don't want to think anymore. I just want to *feel*. I want *you*."

Her words were his undoing, snapping the control he had placed over himself. He crashed his mouth to hers, his lips hot and insistent. She kissed him back, her tongue dancing with his as she wrapped her legs around him, tugging him closer. The kiss was an explosion, and Evie trembled beneath him as his fingers gripped the back of her head.

After a few moments, Jack tore his lips away, watching her intensely as he slipped his hand beneath her shirt, teasing the edges of her bra before sliding back to her shirt. Evie grinned as he pulled his hand back, giggling as his fingers clumsily failed to undo the tiny buttons on her shirt.

"Want some help, Saunders?" she asked as he released a deep sigh of frustration.

With a smirk that had her heart dancing, Jack peeled away the shirt with one easy swoop and pulled back for a moment. His brilliant blue eyes lost in an insatiable daze as Evie reached for him. His mouth found hers once more, and the warmth of his chiselled chest caused the butterflies in her tummy to return. His hands found her waist, and Evie lifted her hips as he tugged at her leggings, pulling them down with ease. He made quick work of his shorts, tugging them down before tossing them behind him.

Evie's heart thundered against her chest as she lay bare before him, heat flushing her cheeks as she eyed every inch of his perfectly sculpted body, and the considerable size of a *certain* body part.

Jack grinned and pulled back, his eyes ablaze with a desire that matched her own as he stared down at her, gripping her thighs tightly, before gently parting her legs.

"Are you sure?" he asked.

"I want *you,*" she breathed.

She tensed beneath him, burying her face in his neck as he finally pushed into her with a devastating gentleness, muffling her sharp cry of pain as he began to move.

Gods.

"You need to relax, Evie," he murmured, pulling her mouth to his.

She did, allowing her eyes to close for a moment as his hips

284

rocked against hers, allowing the pain to turn swiftly into pleasure. Her breath rose with each slow, insatiable feel of him. She felt her fingers digging into his shoulders. Felt his tremor as she trailed them up his neck, forcing the kiss to deepen. Jack shifted slightly, the movement pulling a gasp from her lips as he lifted his head to look at her. His eyes were filled with a hazy lust, and she felt his hand travel down the side of her body, hooking around her thigh with a torturous clasp. She wrapped her leg around him as his hips thrust faster, deeper.

Pleasure erupted in waves, and she felt her own power clashing with his, ricocheting between their bodies. Heat flared through her, burning every inch of her body with desire so powerful, she could feel her control beginning to ebb.

His lips were torturous. A torturous delight that she could not get enough of. She could feel her magic simmering. Wild and reckless as sparks crackled between them.

"Look at me." Jack kissed her jaw, hooking his hand beneath her thigh as he buried himself deeper.

Bliss. Pure, unyielding bliss. And she wanted more. Needed more.

Evie opened her eyes. Every inch of her body yearning for *more*. It was a feeling so alien yet so natural to her, as his lips teased her neck once more with a breath-taking gentleness.

She embraced it all.

Every sweet kiss. Every gentle touch. Every little word he whispered against her ear.

Their powers collided then, as they both found their release, her body trembling beneath his. He stilled against her, moving his hand to cup her cheek as he pulled her mouth to his.

"I love you," he whispered against her lips.

For a second, her mind paused, allowing only room for this

intimate moment.

A moment her mind and body had so desperately wanted.

No magic.

No war.

No grief.

Nothing but them. Together.

"I love you too."

***

The gentle flicker of soft candlelight filled the dark room with a gentle glow. Evie rolled onto her back, pulling the sheets over her as she twisted her head slightly to her left.

Jack lay beside her, his face peaceful as he slept, his dreams undisturbed. He lay with one arm resting above his head, and the other stretched across his stomach. Evie watched him sleep, watching the gentle rise and fall of his bare chest. Her eyes drifted towards his left arm, admiring the black whirls of ink that dominated his tanned skinned, and she wondered what the meaning behind the tattoo was.

His entire left arm was covered, and the ink stretched all the way to his shoulder. An image of a clock filled the top half of his arm, and on either side, two angels stared back at her. Slowly, her fingers moved towards his arm, and as she traced the whirls of ink, Jack shifted slightly, and his eyes opened.

"Hey." His voice was croaky with sleep, but he smiled as he rolled onto his side, resting his head against his palm.

"Hi." Evie smiled nervously. "I'm sorry, I didn't mean to wake you."

"What time is it?" he asked.

"A little after four," she replied, and added, "I'm an early riser, sorry."

Jack chuckled. "Are you okay?" he asked her.

Evie nodded as he reached for her hand.

"I'm okay...are you?" she said.

"I've never lost control before," he said softly. "I...our powers..."

"I know," she said, remembering the feel of their powers colliding. Heat flushed her cheeks, "I'm guessing that isn't normal?"

He chuckled, "With you, I'm not sure *what* is normal anymore," he teased.

"Should we be worried?" she asked, biting her lip.

"We have enough to worry about," Jack said, and added with a teasing grin, "you were incredible... both times."

She rolled her eyes and said, "You weren't too bad yourself, Saunders."

Jack grinned and said, "I wish we could just stay in here forever and forget the world outside of these walls."

"I would drive you crazy eventually." Evie grinned.

"You already drive me crazy," he said, releasing a low laugh as he lifted his arm and pulled her against him.

Evie rested her head against his side, stretching her arm across his stomach. He kissed her forehead as she snuggled against him, wrapping her leg over his between the sheets.

"Did you ever think that you and I would ever be like this?" Evie asked. "Together, I mean."

"No," he said. "But I also didn't think that I would ever see you again after you left."

Evie lifted herself up and cupped his cheek with her hand. "So many things in my life don't make sense right now, but you, *you* I am certain of, Jack. I love you."

"I love you, Evie," he said, brushing his lips against hers.

"It is so easy to forget everything when I am with you." She sighed, pulling back slightly. "Jack what are we going to do?"

"I have a few ideas." He smirked.

"Very funny," she said, raising her eyebrow to him. "I was referring to our current problems. So much has happened."

Jack sighed, wrapping his arm around her a little tighter.

"I don't know. I wish that I could tell you everything is going to be all right, but none of us know what tomorrow will bring," he said. "Our only saving grace right now, is the safe haven. All of the major Academy's in the world have been ordered to go. It will be the safest place on earth for you, and our chance to figure out our next move."

"And when they discover the truth? About me I mean…" she asked quietly. "Do you really believe The Guardians of the world will still want to protect someone who is *half-Fae?* They were once ordered to kill me, remember."

"If anyone even *dares* to look at you in the wrong way, I will kill them myself," he said firmly. "You may share their blood, Evie, but you will *never be Fae.* I know who you are, and you are *nothing* like them. I'm with you, Evie, and I love you. For as long as the stars remain in the sky, I will love you, and even when they no longer shine their precious light, I'll still love you then."

The adoring tone of his voice surged through her, and she smiled as his fingers caressed her jaw. A wave of emotion filled her as she kissed him, hoping that he would understand the words she wanted to say but didn't know how to. Jack kissed her back, and she shivered as his fingers trailed the length of her thigh, each calloused touch leaving behind a beautiful insatiable tingling trail.

Evie pulled back, her eyes meeting with his as she rested her palm against his cheek.

"For as long as the stars remain in the sky," she whispered, repeating his words, as she lowered her lips back to his.

***

A few hours later, after telling Jack numerous times that they had to leave, Evie strolled into the Jenkins' den, closing the door softly behind her. Heat filled her cheeks as she spotted Tessa and Cora, both of whom were staring at her with pursed lips.

"Good morning," Evie said, yawning.

"Cut the crap." Cora smirked. "We want details! Now!"

"I have no idea what you're talking about," Evie said flatly.

"Where did you sleep last night?" Cora asked. "Because you certainly did not sleep in the same room as Tessa."

"Leave her alone, Cora!" Tessa giggled. "It's none of our business."

"We're friends, Tessa!" Cora said matter-of-factly. "Friends talk to each other. Now spill!"

"You're so annoying." Evie chuckled. "Fine, I stayed with Jack. I went to talk to him, and I...*it just happened,* okay! I didn't *plan* for it to happen, neither of us did..."

As she broke off, Tessa and Cora fell into a fit of giggles, earning them a pillow toss across the room.

"Hey!" Tessa laughed. "I'm sorry, we shouldn't laugh...but seriously, Evie? Your face is a picture right now!"

"Yours would be too, if your friends were being insufferable," Evie said, but the corners of her mouth rose, and she too started giggling.

"Was it your first time?" Cora asked, earning a nudge in the ribs from Tessa. "What?"

289

"*You're* insufferable," Tessa said, rolling her eyes. "Evie, you don't have to tell us anything you don't want to. What happened between you and Jack, is *between* you and Jack, isn't that right, Cora."

Rolling her eyes, Evie sighed.

"It's fine," she said, and added with a blush, "Yes, it was my first time, and I'm absolutely mortified that it happened in *your house* Cora…"

Cora chuckled, clasping her palm to her mouth.

"Don't apologise for that," she said, laughing. "How do you feel? Tell me everything!"

"I don't know," Evie said, blushing. "Neither of us planned for it to happen, it just *did*. One minute I was a blubbering mess, and the next…"

She clamped her palms to her face, ignoring the chuckles from across the room.

"Why are you so embarrassed?" Cora said.

"Shut up Cora," Evie grimaced.

Cora only chuckled as she said, "Tell us details! I want to know everything!"

"Do we have to talk about this?" Evie said, rolling her eyes.

"It's been a shit few weeks." Cora shrugged, and said with a grin, "How was it?"

"Gods," Evie groaned. "It was my first time. It's not like I can really compare it to anything…"

"But you enjoyed it?" Cora said, and from the grin that now spread across her face, Evie knew the empath already had the answer.

"Of course I *enjoyed* it," Evie said, eyeing them both. "But something weird happened…"

"Oh Gods, please tell me you were careful?" Cora suddenly

shouted.

Evie's eyes widened. Her chain of thought broken as Cora's words replayed in her mind.

She hadn't even thought about *that.*

"*Oh Gods!*" she said, biting her lip.

She had been so reckless.

They had *both* been so darn reckless. So caught up in the moment, the thought hadn't even crossed her mind.

"Don't worry, I've got you," Cora said. "I have a contraceptive tonic. I have more than enough for you to take a vial. We have enough to worry about without adding *babies* to the equation."

"Okay, can we *not*..." Evie grimaced, ignoring both Cora and Tessa's quiet outburst as the door to the den swung open.

As Hayden and Lucas seated themselves around the small table, Evie felt her butterflies return as Jack sauntered into the den. His face was glowing and his eyes, so bright in the early morning light, pierced every inch of her. For a moment, she almost forgot how to breathe. And then he smiled, completely knocking the breath out of her.

"Morning," Jack said as he poured himself a cup of coffee.

"Good morning." Cora grinned, but quickly lowered her head after meeting Evie's warning stare and giggled. "Umm, my mum has made breakfast, it's in the dining room. Go help yourselves, she said we all need to fill up."

"Is there no food at this safe haven?" Lucas asked, raising his eyebrow.

"Not as good as any food you'll get here," Cora replied, and added, "Mum has managed to get you a batch of your *special* dietary requirements too."

"I'm good with normal human food, Cora," he said, rolling

his eyes.

It was true, despite him being a vampire, Lucas was still able to tolerate human food, though the taste was a little blander, Evie knew he *preferred* normal food over the vampire equivalent… blood.

"We have an hour before the portal opens," Hayden said. "Tom has said to only take what we need. Warm clothes especially, which thankfully, Rebecca has sorted for us all. We're going to be taking an array of weapons…as a precaution."

"Weapons?" Evie said. "I thought we were going to a safe haven?"

"We are, but we can't rely on our magic alone to protect us," he said. "Tom is sorting through what he has now."

Hayden stood up, stretching his neck as his did, the tension clear in the veins that bulged in his throat. He picked up his cup, draining the last of his coffee before placing it back onto the table.

"I guess we should all go eat something," Tessa said, and after a moment, both she and Cora rose to their feet.

Evie followed suit, but before she could leave, Jack reached for her arm, pulling her back as the others left. Once they were gone, he pushed the door, closing it behind them and turned back to her.

"What's wrong?" Jack asked, brows raised.

"I'm fine," she said, suddenly feeling anxious as her eyes fell onto the redness that still remained on his wrist.

"You're not still worrying about last night?" he asked, frowning. "What happened with our powers was just a coincidence. We were both lost in our emotions."

"I know. I'm sure you're right," she agreed, though she was not truly convinced.

"Everything is going to be okay," he told her. "Just relax."

"Easier said than done," she said as his hand moved to rest against her cheek. "I haven't told the others about what happened...about your wrist, I mean."

"No one needs to know," he said. "It was an accident. Stop worrying about it."

"I *hurt* you," she said.

"You seriously want to argue about this right now?" he teased.

"Jack..." she said, pulling her head back slightly. "I'm being serious. What if I really hurt you next time? Or someone else?"

"Where is all this coming from?" he asked.

"I'm just scared," she said. "I don't want to hurt any of you because of this magic I have. Robyn *died* because of me..."

"Robyn did not die because of you, Evie," he said firmly. "Adeline killed her. Not you."

"If I lose control again..."

"You won't," he said softly. "I trust you, and so do the others."

"I don't trust myself," she said, lowering her gaze. "I've already lost Robyn. I can't..."

"Stop," he ordered, forcing her eyes back to his with a tilt of her head. "Stop talking like this. Nothing is going to happen to any of us. We are going to the safe haven, and then we are going to plan our next move."

Evie nodded but said nothing as he pressed his lips to her forehead.

"Come on," he said. "We need to eat something before we leave."

Chapter Thirty-Seven

Evie could hear Cora's sigh of relief as she watched her parents, and her beloved horses cross through the portal.

Cora had explained briefly to the others just why the horses needed to join them. They were two of the finest, and oldest steads to walk the earth, their hearts filled with an ancient magical source which enabled the steads to live an immortal life. Akhara and Wrenthorpe were more than just your average horses.

"We made it," Rebecca said, hurrying forwards.

Francis Dubois was stood waiting, along with Jamie and Cillian. Another man, who Evie did not recognise, was stood with them. He was tall, with olive skin, and thick curly brown hair. His posture radiated with a tension that made her feel utterly uncomfortable, and Evie forced her eyes away from his burning gaze.

On seeing the two guardians who had escorted The Circle to the Land of Wonder, Evie rushed forwards.

"Robyn..." she breathed. "What happened to her bod..."

"Your friend was safely escorted back to her parents," Jamie said quietly.

"The attack in London...were her parents there?" she asked. "Are they okay? Are they here?"

"Perhaps we could save the questions for later," Francis said softly, fixing his gaze onto Evie's trembling hands. On noticing his stare, Evie clenched her fists to her sides.

"Welcome," Francis said after a few moments, lifting his

gaze to look at the others. "To Guardian Sanctuary."

"Francis, it is good to see you," Tom said, holding out his hand. The pair shook hands. "My wife, Rebecca, and daughter, Cora. I believe you've already met The Circle."

"Indeed, I have. You have already been acquainted with Jamie and Cillian. This is Christian. Leader of the London Guardians," Francis replied, nodding his head to the man who stood to his left.

Evie tensed as she met Christian's sharp stare and felt herself moving subconsciously closer to Jack's side. She slipped her hand into his, gripping it tightly. Whoever this man was, he made her nervous.

"I'm glad to see The Circle were successful in their mission to save you, Mr Saunders," Francis continued. "Please, follow me. I'll show you to the camp site."

***

They followed Francis along a snow-covered path, climbing a series of rocky hills that opened up to a large clearing.

Hundreds of tents had been dotted around the makeshift camp, with small campfires emitting puffs of pearly grey smoke. The smell of freshly burnt wood lingered through the air, as numerous voices filled the clearing.

"Where are we?" Lucas asked.

"Colorado," Francis replied. "The magic that lives here is stronger than anywhere else in the world, with the exception of the Enchanted Forest, of course. We have four of the most powerful Guardian Academies right here, together in this safe haven. The protective enchantments that we have imposed are impenetrable. We will be safe here, for now."

"Four?" Lucas said, brows furrowed. "I thought every major Academy in the world had been ordered to come here. Where is everyone else?"

Francis smiled. "Unfortunately, we cannot have everyone arrive at the same time. It would cause such a strain. The other Academies shall arrive in due course."

"Thank you, Francis. Have you heard anything of The Dark Prince's movements?" Tom asked, as Christian, Jamie, and Cillian led the others down into the clearing.

Francis shook his head. "No," he told him. "Nothing since the devastation he caused in London, and there is still no sign of Lydia and Julias. I won't lie to you, Thomas, I am worried."

"I am worried too," Tom said, glancing towards Evie. "What will we do, Francis? We have allowed The Dark Prince to continue for so long. I fear we are too late now."

"There is not much we can do at the moment," he replied. "I have spoken with the other Guardians, and we're all in agreement—we must sit, and we must wait. It would do none of us any good to go looking for a fight. We need to prepare ourselves for what might come."

Tom sighed. "Yes, I agree with you on that too. I didn't think we would ever face a situation like this again, Francis," he told him. "The Fae war was the last battle The Guardians fought, was it not? We swore we would never allow anything like that to happen again! How did The Dark Prince become so powerful? How did we let it get this far?"

Francis inhaled a deep breath.

"It is not only The Dark Prince we should be worried about, Thomas," he said, and quickly glanced around to ensure they were alone, "I...Tom, I need to ask you a question, as a friend. You have a wife and daughter, both of whom you love very much.

296

I have a family of my own that I will do anything to protect. Is all of this worth it? All for the sake of *one* girl? She is *half-Fae!* Unseelie blood runs through her veins! We should think our next steps through very carefully Thomas. You and I both know the dangers of the Fae. We were both there, all those years ago. They are vicious, and manipulative...and they...we cannot trust them..."

"What are you suggesting, Francis?" Tom asked, and there was a tense change to the tone of his voice.

"I just think *you* need to be careful who you trust," he said. "Evie Gray is...she has the magical abilities of the Fae. None of us truly know where her loyalties lie. How can you be so trusting? The magic she holds...it is *powerful,* Tom. I felt it the moment I met her at The Academy. Lydia might have betrayed us, but she is right about one thing. The magic Evie Gray holds...it is *dangerous.* To all of us!"

"My wife and I have known Evie Gray since she was a child. We were very close to Anna and Paul, as you very well know. She is my daughter's best friend, which therefore makes her family to us. I trust her, as do my wife and daughter. No harm will come to her, do you understand? We will protect her, and we will fight if we have to.

"Evie may indeed have Fae blood in her veins, but she is still a witch. She was raised by witches and that is where her heart truly lies," Tom said. "She was given the choice to join the Unseelies, and she chose us, Francis. If that does not prove her loyalty, then I don't know what will."

"Forgive me, Tom," Francis said hurriedly. "I did not mean to cause offence. Of course, the Guardian's will do everything we can to protect her and everyone else within this clearing. You have my word, old friend."

Tom nodded. "I should check in with my wife and daughter," he said quietly.

"Yes, of course," Francis replied. "We have set up camp for you and The Circle on the farthest side of the clearing, nearest the river. I have arranged for all Guardian Leaders to meet at six this evening to discuss plans going forward."

"I'll see you this evening," Tom said briskly.

He left then, hurrying down the hill and into the noisy campsite. Tom nodded his head several times as he passed families he knew, but he didn't stop to talk. The conversation he'd had with Francis was bothering him, and he couldn't quite shake it off.

By the time he reached the river, he was completely mithered.

"Darling, is everything all right?" Rebecca strolled towards him, frowning when she noted his expression. "Tom?"

"Where has everyone gone?" he asked shortly.

"The girls are inside," she said, pointing to the tent on the left. "I've asked the boys to collect water and firewood. Tom has something happened?"

"I...it's nothing," he said. "Just something Francis...I'm probably just overthinking...a lot has happened..."

"Tom, I know you. You *never* overthink," she said flatly. "What did Francis say?"

"Rebecca, something doesn't *feel right*. Coming here was a mistake," he said quietly, and ushered her inside the other tent. "Talk to no one, do you understand? We must all stick together. I don't want anyone wandering off by themselves. Especially Evie."

"Tom, you're worrying me," Rebecca said. "Evie is safe here. We all are."

Tom shook his head.

"Francis…" he began but quickly paused. "Listen to me, sweetheart, I could be completely wrong on this, but…my instinct has never let me down yet. Just trust me on this okay. Until I know for sure."

"Of course," she said.

Tom smiled briefly, and they both went back outside.

Cora, Evie, and Tessa were stood outside the tent, each holding a steaming mug in their hands.

"Where did you get those from?" Tom chimed, trying to keep his voice steady.

"There's a canteen on the other side of the campsite," Cora replied. "Best hot chocolate ever, Dad. You should go get some before it all runs out."

"Canteen?" He smiled. "And here I was thinking we would have to go fishing in the river for dinner tonight!"

"Ha, ha." Cora giggled. "So, we thought you guys could have this tent, and we will take the other. It's big enough for us all to fit in."

"There's plenty of room if you girls want to come in with us," Rebecca offered.

"No, that's okay, Mom," Cora replied, glancing towards Evie and Tessa. "We'll be fine; besides, someone has to keep an eye on the boys to make sure they stay out of trouble."

"Okay, well you're Dad and I will go and take a look at this canteen," she said, and reached down to hold Tom's hand. "Be sure to check on the horses, alright?"

***

"Plan of action?" Cora's voice was like thunder in Evie's ears.

Evie shook her head. "I'm all out of ideas," she said, replaying Tom's words over in her mind. "I wonder what Francis said to make him react like that?"

"I doubt it was anything nice," Cora replied sharply. "My dad is the most laid-back guy you'll ever meet. Whatever Francis said, it's spooked him, which means we have a problem."

"What problem?" Hayden's voice filtered into the tent as he, Jack, Lucas, and Zac came through. Their faces red from the cold wind outside.

"Umm…" Cora began, but Evie stopped her.

"Tom doesn't trust Francis," she told them. "We overheard him talking to Rebecca. Something is going on."

"What?" Lucas said. "Francis set this whole place up to keep us safe. What is there not to trust?"

"He didn't say," Evie said. "We overheard him talking to Rebecca. Whatever Francis said, it's spooked him. He doesn't want any of us wandering off, especially me."

"Did he say anything else?" Jack asked.

"That's all we heard," Evie said.

"I've known Francis a long time. He is loyal to The Guardians. Tom might be reading into things a little…" Hayden began.

"My dad isn't stupid, Hayden," Cora snapped. "He can read people, and he knows when something isn't right."

"I'm not doubting that for one second, Cora," Hayden said. "All I am saying is that I have known Francis for a long time. *I know him*. We can trust him."

"Well, I guess we will find out, won't we," she said, before slumping down onto a make-shift bed.

"What else did Tom say?" Jack asked, pulling Evie to one side.

"Nothing," Evie told him. "It's probably nothing. Don't

worry."

"Well, we can't take any risks," he said. "We barely know anyone here, it would be foolish to be so trusting, despite us all being on the same side."

"I thought this was supposed to be a *safe haven*." Evie sighed, crossing her arms over her stomach. She suddenly felt nauseous. "Not another place where we would need to hide."

"Everything will be okay," Jack said softly. "Hayden and I will go to the meeting and find out what we can. In the meantime, *you* are not to leave this tent, understood?"

"Do I have any other choice?" she asked quietly.

Jack smirked before pressing his lips to her forehead.

"No, you don't. Just do as you're told for once and stay out of trouble," he said.

Evie sighed. "Trouble tends to find me remember?"

Chapter Thirty-Eight

With a deep breath, Tom led the way into the marquee with Rebecca, leaving Jack and Hayden to follow behind.

There was a small chatter of voices which appeared to grow quieter as the four of them sauntered forwards. Francis, who was stood a few feet away, suddenly stopped talking as Tom approached. His dark eyes following every movement.

"Tom," he said by way of greeting, and bowed his head to the others, before gesturing to the two men who stood beside him. "I believe you already know Christian Brentford, and this is…"

"*Elijah Gray?*" Tom's voice was thunderous.

The man who stood to the right of Francis twisted his head. He was tall and slim, with hardly any weight to his scrawny figure. His torn, baggy clothes hung from his small body, and his greasy, jet-black hair fell to his shoulders in matted clumps.

Elijah Gray smiled wickedly.

"Impossible!" Rebecca's voice sounded panicked as she turned to meet her husband's fretful eyes.

"Oh no, quite the contrary, Rebecca," Elijah said. His small black eyes were filled with the utmost hate as he stared at Rebecca and Tom. "Very much possible."

***

"What the fuck is going on?" Jack growled, breaking the small, uncomfortable silence that had filled the marquee.

"Why don't you ask Rebecca," Elijah answered bitterly. "Or maybe I should just tell you? Since she'll probably just spill you a bucketful of lies."

"Elijah," Rebecca warned. "*Don't* do this!"

Elijah laughed. The sound of it was cold enough to make the hairs on the back of Jack's neck rise.

"Oh, what a tale I have to tell!" Elijah beamed. "I've spent the last five years in hell because of what dear old Thomas and his busy-body wife did. Had it not been for the attack on the London Guardians—*God rest their souls*—I would still be there now. Hiding in the shadows because of *your* lies!"

"Elijah now is not the time for this," Francis said. "We have more important things we must concern ourselves with."

Elijah scowled. "Oh yes," he said, and rolled his eyes. "My *sister.* Where is the little delight anyway?"

Both Jack and Hayden tensed at the mention of Evie.

"I'd very much like to see her," Elijah continued. "Caused *quite the stir*, hasn't she? Well, I guess it was only a matter of time before my parent's dirty little secret was exposed. All those years they spent trying to conceal her. *Idiots*. They *deserved* to die for what they did. And now look at the consequences. Guardians *hiding* in this pitiful excuse for a safe haven! Protecting the spawn of the Fae. It repulses me! What on earth have we become!" he spat.

"She's your sister," Jack said angrily.

Elijah laughed coldly.

"*Sister*? She is no sister of mine. My parents *kidnapped* her because they were not happy with the child they already had. Now look at us! All hiding here because of what they did!"

"Elijah," Francis warned. "I told you when you arrived here, that The Guardians will do everything to protect your sister. Jack is right, she is one of us, despite the tainted blood that runs in her veins. However, not all hope is lost. We cannot do anything about her heritage…but we can purify her. The Fae darkness that lives within her…we can bind it…"

"Are you serious?" Jack's voice was murderous as he stepped closer to where Francis stood.

"Fellow Guardians, it is time you heard the truth," Francis said, holding his palm against his throat to amplify his voice.

"Twenty-one years ago, there was rumour of a child who had been born with an immense amount of power. A child born to the Unseelie Court, with the abilities of both witch and Fae," he said, keeping his voice steady. "The Elders were concerned enough to start a war with the Fae. *Evie Gray* is the child the rumour spoke of."

A mummer of hushed voices suddenly broke out, but it did not pause Francis and his speech.

"There is nothing that we can do about the blood she shares," Francis said. "The magic on the other hand…there is a spell that will allow us to bind her magic until we learn of a way to extract it. Once this terrible darkness has been removed, Evie Gray will be trusted amongst our people."

"I was right about you!" Tom roared. "You had no intention of protecting her, did you? You agreed to this *safe haven* as a way to get her here!"

Francis jerked his head towards the sea of faces that stared back at him.

"Fellow Guardians," Francis said. "A darkness like no other is upon us. We must protect ourselves. For years we have questioned what The Dark Prince seeks, and now we know. He will stop at nothing until he gets what he wants. The Fae magic. We cannot allow this to happen. Evie Gray is a danger to us all, and the longer we wait, the more powerful she will grow."

"Should have killed her when you had the chance!" a voice bellowed from the centre of the marquee. "Before her powers had a chance to manifest!"

"He's right!" Another, thunderous voice agreed.

"We cannot trust the girl," Francis continued, ignoring the outpour of angry voices. "She is half-Fae. The *weapon* The Dark Prince seeks. We cannot even begin to understand her true loyalties. The Unseelie Court are no longer trapped by the spell cast by The Elders. For all we know, Miss Gray could be working with the Fae to seek revenge. We must bind her magic!"

"Hear! Hear!" Several voices erupted in agreement.

"Not happening," Jack's voice roared through the marquee, and he brushed past Hayden, placing himself before Francis. "If you touch a single hair on her head, I will kill you myself."

Elijah laughed, and there was a hint of madness in his eyes as he began clapping his hands.

"Bravo Jack," Elijah said. "How very loyal of you, to protect her. You're a fool, she could turn on you, you know? Kill you whilst you sleep…"

"Evie is a witch," Jack said. "Regardless of what blood runs through her veins, she is a witch. She could have stayed with the Unseelies. She could have chosen them, but she didn't. She chose us and that is where her loyalty lies. Bind her magic and she will be defenceless when they come. She will be fucking powerless!"

"Jack," Francis sighed. "I understand your loyalty to the girl, but we have to think of the bigger picture. The safety of our people is more important, and as a Guardian Leader, it should be of great priority to you."

"Evie is my fucking priority!" he roared. The marquee shook violently around him. His own magic surging with a thunderous delight, sending sparks crackling at his fingertips. He did not remove his eyes from Francis' widened stare.

305

"Francis is right," Hayden said quickly, moving forwards to stand beside Jack. "We have to think of everyone here. If it makes The Guardians feel *safer*, then who are we to argue. I don't want to make a show of this Francis, understood? Evie has been through enough already."

"Of course." Francis nodded. "I just want what is best for our people."

"I will bring Evie to you," Hayden said.

"Hayden what the fu…"

"Quiet Jack," Hayden ordered. "It is for the best. We don't have another choice."

"It's in the girl's best interest," Francis replied. "Bring Evie here. We will not make a spectacle of this, I assure you. No harm will come to her. It is a simple binding spell. Elijah will accompany you back to your tent."

"I don't want him anywhere near her!" Jack hissed.

Elijah smiled wickedly.

"That's alright. I think I'll wait here," he said.

"Very well. Tom, I would like you and Rebecca to stay, if you will. I have something that I would like to discuss with you both," Francis said, and suddenly twisted his head to the side. "Christian, go with Hayden and Jack. Take Jamie and Cillian."

"Why the escort?" Jack growled. He could feel his temper flaring as Hayden brushed his arm. He wouldn't look at him. *Couldn't,* for fear of his temper.

Like hell would he stand back and allow Hayden to toss Evie to the wolves…

"Precautionary measures," Francis said. "Christian?"

Christian moved forwards, placing his hand onto Jack's shoulder to usher him forwards. Swiftly, Jack reached for his hand, twisting it away from him.

"Touch me again and I'll do more than break your fucking hand," he thundered as Christian yelped in pain.

Christian cradled his hand, whimpering an array of vulgar words as his eyes threatened Jack with a deathly glare.

"What the hell man?" Christian spat as he followed Hayden and Jack out of the marquee, and added in a hushed voice, "I'm on your side, you idiot!"

As soon as they were away from the marquee, Hayden spun around, using a silent spell to stun both Jamie and Cillian. The two Guardians both stood motionless, their eyes glazed from the spell.

"We need to hurry," Hayden said.

"Hayden, if you think I'm going to stand aside and let you toss Evie to them, then you can think again."

Hayden rolled his eyes.

"Francis trusts me. He trusts me enough to believe the bullshit I just fed him," he said, smirking. "We made a mistake coming here."

Without another word, Hayden stormed across the snowy clearing, as Jack and Christian followed close behind.

***

"That was a quick meeting," Evie said, but on noticing Jack's murderous expression, she quickly jumped up from where she sat. "Why do you look like you want to kill someone?"

"Probably because he does. *Several* people in fact," Christian spat, clutching his hand. "Is he always such a loose cannon? I swear he's broken my hand!"

"What the hell did you do?" Evie gasped as her eyes fell onto Jack.

"*I* didn't do anything," he grumbled. "Tom was right about Francis. None of The Guardians trust you. They want to *bind* your magic!"

"What?" Evie said, startled.

"We have to leave. Now!" he said urgently. "Oh, and your brother is here. He's with Francis right now."

Evie froze. Eyes widening as his words thundered in her mind. For a moment, the world stopped.

Elijah was here.

He was alive.

"*What did you just say?*" Evie said, closing the gap between herself and Jack. "Jack, what the hell did you just say?"

"We have to leave." His nostrils flared slightly. "Now. Pack up, we're leaving in five minutes."

"Elijah is *here*. Like, as in *here?*" she gasped. "Where is he? Did you speak to him? Is he okay? Jack talk to me! Is Elijah okay?"

Jack turned to face her, and she recoiled at the darkness in his usual blue eyes.

"Don't get too excited," he said bitterly. His words were sharp and cold. "He hates you, Evie."

"What?" she said, stung by his words. "He's my brother..."

"We don't have time to stand around and chat," Hayden said sharply. "Long story short? The Guardians want to bind your magic. Francis is deluded. He thinks you're going to turn on us. He's ordered me to take you back to him. Your brother is here, and I have no idea *why* or *how*, but right now, we don't have the time to find out. We need to go."

"Where are my parents?" Cora asked, worried.

"Francis ordered them to stay in the marquee with him," Hayden replied. "I'm sorry, Cora, but we either leave now, or let

308

them bind Evie's magic."

"So what? We just leave my parents here. Is that what you're saying?" she demanded.

"Cora, we don't have a choice," Hayden said, trying to keep his voice soft. "Francis wants to bind Evie's magic. Do you understand what that means? It won't just bind her Fae magic; it will bind *everything*. She will be completely defenceless. Your parents aren't stupid Cora. They know full well that I have no intention of following Francis' orders."

"It's okay," Evie said quietly. "We aren't going anywhere. Let them bind my powers. I really don't care. As long as we can all stay together, then I don't care what they do to me."

"Have you lost your mind?" Jack said, and she could hear the growl in his voice. "You will be defenceless, Evie. If The Dark Prince finds this place, you will be powerless..."

"We can't just leave Rebecca and Tom!" she yelled. "Not after everything they have done for us."

"Rebecca and Tom are more powerful than you think, Evie," Jack said. "They aren't stupid. They will find a way out, but right now, *you* are my concern. Everyone in that tent agreed with Francis. I saw Elijah's face, Evie. Whatever happened to him, it wasn't good. He hates you. He hates your parents. I am not risking your life..."

"Maybe if I just talked to him..." she began.

"No," he warned, and turned to Hayden. "We need to get the fuck out of here now."

"I can open a portal, but we will have to be quick," he replied. "The Guardians are probably already on their way down here. Cora, you have to decide..."

"I can't leave them," she said. "I'm sorry, Evie. They're my parents. I have to stay and make sure they're all right...I can't just leave them."

"I understand," Evie replied, crossing her arms around herself. "You should all stay here. At least you'll all be safe, and the rest of your families will be arriving soon. I'll go with Jack. The rest of you stay."

"How many times do we have to say this to you," Tessa said pointedly, "we are in this together. I understand Cora's reasons for staying, but *you* are our family too, Evie. We protect each other, and if that's mean we have to run, then we run. We stick together, no matter what happens."

Evie nodded, smiling briefly. "Thank you, Tess."

"Same goes for us," Lucas said. "Zac and I are coming. We already lost you once, Evie, and I'll be damned if I allow that to happen again."

Cora sighed heavily. "Great, now I feel awful."

"Don't," Evie told her. "They're your parents. I get it. I really do. You've already done enough for me, Cora."

"I'm coming with you," she said after a few moments. "My parents *are* powerful, and they aren't stupid. I know they will be fine. Jack is right. Our priority is keeping you safe."

"Are you sure?" Hayden said softly, taking hold of Cora's hand.

"Yes," Cora replied. "Let's do this, before I have time to change my mind."

"Okay," Hayden said. "We need to open a portal…"

"Good luck with that," Christian said, flexing his fingers. "Francis has this whole place portal proofed. The only way out of here is on foot."

Jack swore loudly. "We won't have time! Surely there must be a way to open a portal?"

Christian shook his head.

310

"The entire clearing is protected by Francis's magic. Combined with that of the other Guardians, there is simply no chance of breaking through the bonds. The only way is to get off the campsite. The enchantments only stretch so far. If you can make it to the woods, you will be able to open a portal."

"Then we do that," Jack said fiercely. "But we will have to move fast. I'm surprised Francis hasn't alre…"

He broke off, and Evie watched his face drain of colour as an eruption of voices suddenly broke outside the tent. She turned to Hayden. He too had a look of panic stretched across his face, but after a split second, he raised his finger to his lips, urging everyone to remain silent.

"*You can't hide in there forever, sister!*"

Evie's eyes widened at the sound of Elijah's voice.

A voice that sounded so familiar, yet so…*different*.

The manic excitement in his tone filled the tent as she turned her eyes back to Jack.

"Come out, little sister." Elijah's voice was taunting. "You don't have to be scared of *me*. I'm your brother! I've waited a long time for this reunion!"

"Enough Elijah." Francis's voice was sharp. "Lower your shields. I don't want to hurt anyone. This is a safe haven. We just want to keep everyone here safe, and to do so, we must bind the girl's magic before it is too late. See reason and lower the enchantments."

"*Out the back*," Hayden ordered in a hushed whisper, before grabbing Jack by the shoulder. "Go. Now. And don't stop until you are out of the clearing. The second you're out of the perimeter, open a portal and get as far away from here as possible."

"We're all going, right?" Evie gasped, her eyes widening as

she glanced from Hayden to Jack.

Hayden shook his head. "I will stay. It will give you time," he said, ignoring Cora's protests. "I can hold them off, but it won't be for long."

"Hayden, no!" Cora snapped. "We're *all* going. We will make it! I know we will."

"Cora, we don't have time," Hayden told her. "I want you to go. All of you, go. I will stay and hold them off."

"I'm staying with you. It was one thing to leave my parents, but I am not leaving you too," Cora said. "I'll stay and help you."

"This is ridiculous!" Evie said. "None of this would be happening if you would just let them do what they want to. Lower the shields, Hayden."

"What do you not understand about this?" Jack raged. "The Guardians want to *bind* your magic. They want to *take* your birth right away from you. I am not about to stand here and let them do that to you."

"*Tick tock, little sister*!" Elijah's voice cackled. "Come out now and nobody will get hurt. Promise. I just want to talk to you! I've missed your annoying, charming little self."

"Go! Now!" Hayden's sharp whispered voice forced The Circle to move.

Chapter Thirty-Nine

Hayden waited for Christian to disappear before turning his head to face Cora. For the first time, he felt as though he was *truly* seeing her, and a surge of gratitude ran through him.

He was glad that she'd chosen to stay by his side. He kissed her softly on the lips, and Cora melted into his tense embrace, soaking in every emotion that he had kept bottled up for so long. Hayden pulled away, and after a split second, he finally lowered his shields.

The tent was ablaze with light, and manic voices filtered through as The Guardians burst inside, pushing Cora and Hayden further in.

"They're gone!" A deep, manly voice roared.

"No!" Elijah's voice growled viciously.

"Clever move, Hayden. Or foolish?" Francis sighed. "I should have seen it coming. I should have known not to trust you. You have no idea what you have done, Hayden."

"How could you, Francis?" Hayden said. "I have spent years by your side. I trusted you. How could you betray us like this? What exactly do you have to gain from all of this?"

"You have no idea," Francis said quietly, "of the storm you have created…"

"How long Francis?" Hayden demanded.

"Hayden, what are you talking about?" Cora asked.

"Hayden…" Francis began. "You don't understand…"

"How long Francis?" Hayden spat. "How long have you

been working with The Dark Prince?"

"None of your damn business!" Elijah spat angrily, then rushed towards him so their faces were just inches apart. "I will give you one chance. Tell me where she is. Where is my sister?"

"Go to hell," Hayden snarled at him.

"You chose the *wrong* side, Inquisitor," Elijah warned. "You know the Fae will come, and it is only a matter of time before they do. The Dark Prince needs that power before they arrive, or we all die!"

"So why not let her fight with you?" Cora demanded.

"The girl cannot be trusted," Francis answered. "She could turn on us at any second."

"Yet you will happily hand it over to a *monster?* Have you considered what will happen if The Dark Prince turns on *you*?" Hayden said, glaring at them. "He is a monster. A murderer, and you've chosen to trust him over Evie Gray. You're a fool, Francis! You have so easily sworn your alliance to a man you know nothing about, and for what? Power? Greed? You are a *Guardian!*"

"He's just the same as Lydia…a traitorous bastard!" Cora suddenly snapped. "And for the record, Evie would never turn against us, because she is *one of us*. She is our friend, and she is *family.*"

"She is a *half-breed* brat that should not even exist in our world!" Elijah almost screamed.

"Enough," Francis warned, and turned to Jamie and Cillian, both of whom were stood to his left. "Take them to the cage. You are not to leave your positions until I return. No one goes in, and no comes out, understood?"

"Understood." Cillian nodded. "And what of the others?"

"Elijah and I will join the search group," he replied. "They

314

can't have gone far. My spells stretch well over a three-mile radius. We must move fast; The Dark Prince will arrive tomorrow. We need to find the girl before he arrives, is that clear?"

"You'll never find them!" Hayden barked. "I trusted you, Francis!"

Francis tilted his head slightly to the side.

"I thought you of all people would have understood the bigger picture," he said. "I guess I was wrong about you, Hayden."

"You won't get away with this, Francis!" Hayden spat. "The Elder's will not allow you..."

"You know *nothing* about the Elders," Francis said smoothly.

"We don't have time for this, Francis! Torture it out of them!" Elijah exploded. "That should loosen their tongues!"

"No harm is to come to them, understood?" Francis said sympathetically. "Take them away, Cillian."

Cillian stepped forward, and placed his thick hand onto Hayden's shoulder, shoving him forwards out of the tent. Jamie followed close behind, keeping close to Cora's side.

***

They walked across the darkened campsite in silence before finally stopping outside a large, wooden-fenced cage.

"Oh my God, Cora! Hayden!"

Rebecca's fretful voice filled the silence that had enveloped, followed by a look of relief as they met each other's eyes.

"Mom!" Cora rushed towards the cage, grabbing hold of her mother's hand. "Mom, are you alright? Did they hurt you? I swear to God, I'll kill them…"

"We are both fine…where are the others? Where is Evie?"

"You'll have enough time to catch up inside," Cillian shouted, as he unlocked the heavy padlock.

Using the momentary distraction, Hayden hurtled forwards, and threw his arm around Cillian's neck, before kicking the back of his legs to bring him to the ground. He landed with a heavy thud, and before he could fight back, Hayden raised his hand, stunning him.

Cillian lay at his feet, his eyes glazed as they stared at the black sky above. As Hayden stood, he was greeted by a pair of thick hands as Jamie reached out to grab him. Jamie was strong, but Hayden was *fast*.

He ducked, and swiped Jamie's legs, bringing him to the ground as Cora used her own magic to bind him. Jamie fought manically against the binds, but they didn't budge. Cora smiled, and waved her hand over him, watching as his body went rigid.

"Now what?" Cora asked, swiping a set of keys from Jamie's pocket. She rushed towards the cage, unlocking it quickly before pulling the door open.

"We need to get out of here, and fast," Tom told her. "The others?"

"They're gone. We had no choice," Hayden told him. "Tom…Francis and the others, they're working with The Dark Prince. That is why he agreed to this safe haven, it was all a lie!"

"I know," Tom barked bitterly. "I'm sorry, Hayden, I shouldn't have bought us here."

"You weren't to know," Hayden said. "I trusted Francis too."

"Is there anyone we can trust?" Cora asked.

"The Elders," Tom answered. "They aren't here. We need to find them; they are our only hope."

"Seriously? They started this whole *manhunt* with Evie," Cora sneered.

Tom sighed. "The Elders are not who they used to be Cora. We can trust them," he said, though Cora could hear the hesitation in his voice.

"Francis is already looking for Evie and the others," Hayden said. "We need to go."

"Where have The Circle gone?" Rebecca asked.

Hayden shook his head. "I have no idea," he said. "I told Jack to open a portal and go. We didn't have time to plan a location."

"We'll worry about that later," Tom said hurriedly.

"Dad, why is Francis doing this?" Cora asked. "Why have The Guardians betrayed us?"

"I have a feeling this is much bigger than we first anticipated," he said. "We will fight, and we will protect her, Cora, even if it means fighting against our own people."

Chapter Forty

Evie swore viciously. There was an unyielding rage in her voice. Her fingers tingled angrily as her magic ignited. The anger that she felt danced within her, leaving a determined melody of hatred and fury in its wake.

This nightmare she was living had to end. She had already lost her best friend. She was not going to lose anyone else.

"Evie, will you stop!" Tessa demanded for what must have been the hundredth time. "You're going to set the place on fire if you're not careful!"

Evie glanced down at her hands, and saw the sparks of fire, dancing in her palms. She clenched her hands shut and crossed her arms over her chest. They were stood in an abandoned warehouse, a few blocks away from The Academy.

Jack's portal had unknowingly bought them home, and after casting every protection spell that they knew, they'd made themselves a safe haven of their own.

"I'm sorry," Evie said. "I don't know I'm doing it."

"You need to control it," Jack told her. He looked exhausted. There were dark circles beneath his eyes. "Practice some meditation or do whatever you have to do to control it. We have to be ready to fight."

Evie scowled.

"I don't know how to control it!" she yelled at him. "It's worse when I am angry, and right now, I'm fucking raging, Jack. Look at us! We're hiding in an abandoned warehouse! Hiding from our own people. So, I'm sorry, Jack, I can't go *meditate!*

"We have no idea what is happening to our friends, or how to save them. For all we know, Hayden and Cora could be dead, and there is nothing that we can do about it, because we are *hiding.*"

"We aren't hiding," Jack seethed. She knew he was annoyed by her refusal to understand. "We're keeping *you* safe. Hayden and Cora aren't stupid. They will be fine."

"Are you sure about that?" she said, her voice deadpan. "Because Robyn wasn't stupid either, but she still wound-up dead. Don't you see what is happening here? Hiding isn't the answer, Jack. We have to go back. They're our friends, we can't just leave them!"

"And do what?" Jack demanded. "The Guardians don't want to help us, Evie. The safe haven was just a way to get you to them. We are not going back. I'm sorry. Hayden knew what he was doing when he chose to stay behind, and so did Cora. We have to protect you at all costs. Your magic in *their* hands, is a death sentence to us all. We will figure this out, but we aren't going back there. Hayden and Cora will be fine. I know they will."

"You don't know that! I have sent endless messages to Cora's phone, and not once has she replied!" she said through gritted teeth. "The only reason you are dead set against us going back, is because of *us*. Their life is just as important as *mine* Jack!"

"Sorry for caring about you," he growled, and added with a vicious snarl, "we aren't going back."

"So, we just sit here?" she snapped. "Jack please, just listen to me. We have to go back for them..."

"No," he told her sharply, before turning away.

She watched as he stormed across the warehouse,

319

disappearing behind two large silver containers, and she inhaled a deep, angry breath.

"You know, Robyn told me a lot about you, but listening to you right now, I'm starting to think that she was talking about someone else," Christian said flatly. "I didn't have you down as the type of person to just *sit back* and be ordered around. Jack might be your boyfriend, but he doesn't own you."

"He's just worried," Evie said. "But I don't agree with his decision to just leave Hayden and Cora. They're our friends, we should be doing something to help them."

"I agree," he said, stepping closer towards where she stood. "If you want to go back, I would be more than happy to join you."

"Ha! Thanks for the offer, but I think Jack would probably kill me himself," she said, sighing.

"Suit yourself." Christian shrugged. "So, Elijah? He's your brother huh?"

"Yes," she said, twisting her head to face him. "Did you see him? How long was he with the London Guardians?"

"He came to The Academy about three years ago," he told her. "He was a complete mess when he arrived, and he hasn't changed since. He's crazy, Evie, and completely obsessed with *you*."

"He wasn't like this before," she said, grimacing at the thought. "What happened to him?"

"I'm not sure if I'm the right person to tell you this," he said. "But since Tom and Rebecca aren't here, I guess someone has to…"

"Tell me what?" she asked. "What are you talking about?"

Christian paused for a moment, and reached for her arm, pulling her away from the others.

"You might feel differently about Tom and Rebecca once

you hear this," he said. "It is their fault Elijah went missing all those years ago. After your parents died, they told The Guardians that Elijah was responsible, and that is why he ran. Tom and Rebecca were powerful…they still are, and they have a lot of influence with the Guard."

"What? That's not true," she said. "Why would they lie about that? They knew about my parents; they knew exactly how they died. Why lie and blame Elijah?"

"You tell me." Christian shrugged. "I'm just telling you what Eli told me."

"He's lying," she said through gritted teeth. "Tom and Rebecca wouldn't make up something like that. Elijah has lost his mind. Whatever happened to him, it was probably his own doing."

"You should know though, Elijah is what the normads would classify as mentally unstable," he said, and suddenly reached for her shoulder. The minute his fingers touched her, Evie felt an uncomfortable sensation surge through her body. "Don't worry though, I've got your back, he won't get to you. I promise."

Evie pulled away.

"I'm pretty sure everyone here does, but thank you," she said. "I should go and talk to Jack."

"Sure," Christian mused. "If you change your mind about going back for Hayden and Cora, you just have to say the word. I meant it when I said I would go with you."

Evie nodded but said nothing as she crossed the warehouse to find Jack. He was stood on the opposite side, his eyes and face expressionless as he leaned against a metal cupboard.

He said nothing as she approached him. She could almost feel the tension radiating off him. She stood next to him, and after a few seconds, she felt his body relax slightly.

"I'm sorry," he said quietly.

"It's fine," Evie said, and turned to face him. "I'm sorry too."

"We are all worried about Hayden and Cora," he told her. "I know they will be okay. Hayden is a powerful witch, and so is Cora. They would agree that our priority is keeping you safe Evie. I wish you could just see...just *understand*...how important you are. Not just to me, but to everyone. You hold a magic that is so rare, and so unique, Evie. In the wrong hands...we have to protect you, no matter what the cost."

"I know. I just can't help but worry, Jack. What will we do now?" she asked him. "We can't stay in here forever."

"I don't plan to," he replied. "But right now, we are staying until we figure out our next move. The Elders weren't at the safe haven, which means they weren't invited. We need to find a way of contacting them. We will need them on our side."

"The Elders agreed to the safe haven," Evie said flatly. "How can we trust them? So much of this links back to them Jack. The Fae war, the orders to *kill* me when I was a baby."

"I don't think The Elders had anything to do with the safe haven," he said bitterly. "That was all Francis' doing."

"And the Fae war?" she prodded.

"I... " he stammered.

"Exactly," she frowned, knowing the truth. They could not trust anyone. Not even the Elders.

"What were you talking to Christian about?" he asked suddenly.

"He offered to go with me back to the safe haven," she said, smirking as she added, "and before you kick off, I told him no. I'm not stupid."

"I didn't say you were," he said. "He's a leech. I don't trust him."

"Yet you trust the Elders," Evie rolled her eyes. "He said something strange though. He told me Tom and Rebecca were the reason Elijah ran away after my parents died, and that they told The Guardians that Elijah was responsible for their deaths."

"Seriously?" he said. "He said that to you?"

"Yeah," she said. "Elijah was obviously lying. Why would Tom and Rebecca lie about something like that?"

"It would be interesting to know *why* Elijah disappeared," he said. "Do me a favour? Stay away from Christian."

"Why?" Evie asked, raising her eyebrow to him.

"I don't like him. He's pissing me off, actually. He hasn't stopped staring at you since you came over here," he said, glancing across the room.

Evie chuckled. "*Oh!*" she said and turned to follow his gaze. Christian was staring at them both but quickly looked away as Evie's eyes met his.

Evie smirked as she turned back to Jack and said, "Jack Saunders are you jealous?"

Jack grinned as he pulled away from the wall. His hand found her waist, twisting her gently, before pushing her until her back met with the cold metal behind. His other hand reached for her face, tilting it upwards until his lips were inches from her own.

"Of course I'm jealous, Gray," he whispered, and kissed her. "You're *mine*, and I don't like to share."

"You're insufferable." She grinned against his lips. "Enough kissing, Saunders!"

Jack pulled away, twisting his head round, before turning back to her with a smug grin. Christian was gone. Rolling her eyes for a second time, Evie tugged at his hand, pulling him across the warehouse to sit with the others.

Evie sat down opposite Tessa and Zac, waiting for Jack to join her, but he remained standing.

"Aren't you sitting down?" she asked.

Jack shook his head. "We need to eat," he said, and looked down at his watch. "It's still early. We should get something before it goes dark."

"What if someone sees you?" Evie asked, worried.

"We'll be careful," he said. "Lucas?"

"Yeah, I could do with stretching my legs," Lucas said, jumping to his feet. "Zac?"

"Actually, I was going to ask you to stay with the girls Zac, do you mind?" Jack said.

"Sure, just make sure you bring something good back, I'm starving," Zac replied as Christian stalked towards them.

"I can stay with the girls," he said.

Evie rolled her eyes, grinning as a flash of annoyance spread across Jack's face.

"Why don't you *all* go? We don't need babysitting, do we Tess?" she said.

"Absolutely not," Tessa agreed. "Go, and don't forget to bring back something to drink. I'm so thirsty."

They left then, and Evie and Tessa rejoiced in the quietness.

"Do you think they're all right? Hayden and Cora, I mean?" Evie asked, worried.

"If I know Cora, she's probably already kicked some serious ass out of those Guardian traitors," Tessa mused. "Don't worry, I am sure they're both fine."

"I hope so," Evie said. "Hey Tess? What do you think of Christian?"

"He's a little odd," she replied thoughtfully. "I can't really read him. Why do you ask?"

"Jack doesn't trust him," Evie told her.

"Jack doesn't trust anyone," Tessa said with a smirk. "Has something happened?"

Evie shook her head. "No, I think it's just Jack being Jack," she said. "I'm sure it's nothing."

Tessa smiled softly. "Hey, I've been thinking about our situation..." she began.

"Have you discovered some kind of miracle that will somehow put an end to all of this madness?" Evie asked hopefully.

"Unfortunately not," Tessa replied. "Listen, everyone wants your magic. What you have is so incredibly rare, Evie, and so very powerful, once you learn how to control it. If The Dark Prince was ever to harness it, we would be screwed. I think there is a much darker reason behind him wanting your magic.

"As for the Fae, you were stolen from them. They believe your magic belongs to them, and that is why they are so hell bent on getting you back. I'm pretty sure Adeline didn't just want you to stay in the Land of Wonder for a family reunion. She proved that when she killed Robyn. Witch magic combined with that of the Fae is rare Evie, and one of the most powerful combinations in the world. You've already demonstrated three of its elements."

"Where exactly are you going with this, Tess?" Evie asked.

"Look, it's a long shot, but I think it could be our only option. We can't fight The Dark Prince alone. He has too many demons at his call, and now he has the Guardian traitors as well. We also can't go up against the Fae. We don't know how many of them there are, and we also don't have the numbers on our side.

"But...if we were to somehow bring them *together*...we might stand a chance," she said. "The Fae would stop at nothing to ensure The Dark Prince doesn't harness your powers, and vice versa. I think it might be our only option."

"It could work." Evie thought, then added, "But I'm not really sure how. We don't even know if the Unseelies are here...or if they will really come."

"They will come," Tessa said sharply. "Now that they know you're alive, they won't stop until they get what they want. They will come for you. We have to bring them together. It's our only chance."

Evie nodded. "If the Fae do come here, we use me as bait," she said. "I can't think of another way to bring them together."

"That was my thought process," Tessa said, "just one problem..."

"Jack." Evie sighed. "I'll deal with him. I'll talk to him."

***

An hour later the warehouse was filled with the delicious smell of hot, aromatic spices.

"We got Chinese," Zac said, handing Tessa a container of piping hot food.

"Good call," Tessa replied as Zac, Lucas, and Christian all sat down.

Jack was the last to enter, casting his shields across the door before joining them.

"Any trouble?" Evie asked as Jack sat down in-between her and Lucas.

"Nothing," he replied. "We walked by The Academy, but no one was there. It was in complete darkness."

"So, are we planning on staying in this dump indefinitely?" Christian asked.

"Until we find a safer place, yes," Jack said. "Unless you have any better suggestions."

Christian shrugged but didn't respond as his eyes fell on

Evie. She quickly looked away. The intensity of his stare made her nervous.

"Just thinking about the girls," he finally said. "I wouldn't want them to be uncomfortable."

"We aren't pampered little princesses who need a soft mattress to survive the night," Tessa snapped. "If you're that bothered by our current living arrangements, feel free to leave."

Christian tilted his head. "I didn't say you were," he said, and stood up. "I guess if we're staying, I'll take first watch."

He left the room, stepping outside and closing the door behind him. He'd barely touched his food.

Tessa rolled her eyes. "Asshole." She scowled.

"What's his problem?" Zac said bitterly. "He was an ass whilst we were getting the food as well."

Lucas shrugged. "Let him stand out there all night,' he said, smirking. "Why is he even here anyway?"

Evie placed her own plate onto the table and turned to look at Jack. He was wearing the same annoyed expression he had earlier.

"What happened?" she asked him.

"Nothing. Don't worry about it," he said moodily.

"Seriously?" she said, raising her eyebrow before turning to Zac and Lucas. "What happened?"

"Nothing really." Lucas shrugged. "He's just a cocky prick."

"Right," she said, and rubbed her temples. "So, why is Jack so worked up?"

"I am here you know," Jack said.

"Well, I already asked you, but your current mood and your response to my question don't add up," she said, annoyed. "Does this have anything to do with what we spoke about earlier?"

Jack twisted his head to look at her.

327

"No," he replied, and she noticed the corners of his mouth lift slightly as he tried to hide his smirk.

"*Guys!*" Tessa chuckled as she stood up. "Jack, you know you have nothing to worry about, right?"

Jack smiled. "I didn't say I was worried," he said.

"Good," said Tessa with a yawn. "Right, we need somewhere to sleep."

She lifted her hand, waving it in the air and several bedrolls appeared before them. Tessa arranged them across the floor, bringing the bedrolls close to the small fire burning in the centre of the warehouse.

"Sorry it's not quite *Academy* standard, but it's better than nothing."

"It's perfect, Tess," Evie said.

After finishing their food, they each chose a bedroll, and Tessa waved her hand again, providing them with fluffy pillows. Evie climbed into hers, choosing to sleep in-between Jack and Tessa.

Once inside, she rolled onto her side, meeting Jack's piercing blue gaze. She reached her hand out and he grasped it with his own, tangling his fingers with hers.

"Are you okay?" she asked.

He nodded but said nothing as he continued to look at her. Beneath his eyes, Evie noted the dark smudges—physical indications of the exhaustion he felt.

"Go to sleep, Jack," she whispered, but he only pulled himself closer, resting his forehead against hers.

"I wish this bedroll was a little bigger," he said.

"Me too," Evie whispered.

She watched as his eyes drifted shut, keeping hold of his hand.

Evie sucked in a deep breath, allowing the exhaustion to take over her tired mind, and finally fell into a dreamless sleep.

Little did she know, the darkness that chased her was quickly closing in.

Chapter Forty-One

"Dad, where exactly are we going?"

Cora's fretful voice seemed louder amongst the silent streets as she and Hayden hurried after Tom and Rebecca's retreating figures.

"The Academy." Tom's voice was barely a hushed whisper as he led the way forwards.

"How can you be sure that it's safe?" she asked, throwing a nervous glance at Hayden. "Dad I'm really not sure about this…"

"I'm not either, honey," Tom said. "But we don't have many options. We need to find the others, and the only way we will do that is with the tracking crystals."

"Are they definitely at The Academy?" Hayden asked.

Tom nodded. "Yes, they are there," he said, and added in a low voice more to himself, "they have to be."

They continued to hurry through the quiet streets for another fifteen minutes before Tom finally began to slow down. He led them around a sharp corner.

The usual illuminated windows were dark and empty, and the once thriving Academy now stood abandoned.

Tom paused outside the iron gates, indicating for the others to stand with him.

"What's wrong? Cora asked.

"We need to be certain that there's nobody inside," he said, his expression solemn.

"I can check," Hayden said in a quiet voice.

He moved towards the gate, whispering an enchantment. When nothing happened, both Tom and Rebecca breathed a sigh of relief.

"Nothing," Hayden said.

Tom waved his hand over the padlock and the iron gates swung soundlessly forward.

***

"Well, well, well. Look who we have here."

A cold shiver ran the length Cora's spine as Lydia's voice filtered through The Academy.

She was stood by the stairs, her face glowing as an array of candles suddenly exploded to life, filling the foyer with a yellow flicker of light. Lydia smiled; her face filled with a wicked excitement as she stalked towards the new arrivals.

Behind her stood Julias, who looked equally excited. Though the candles illuminated the entrance hall, there was a blast of cold air surrounding them. Cora didn't have to think twice about where that coldness came from. She looked at Hayden with fretful eyes.

Demons.

"You must be very brave to return here, or perhaps very foolish," Lydia pressed. "Where is Evie Gray?"

"As far away from you as possible," Cora growled.

Lydia smiled once more, and with a click of her long pale fingers, Cora fell to her knees, screaming as she clutched her head.

Lydia's spell burned through every inch of Cora's body. Hayden dropped beside her. His lips moving rapidly as he whispered a counter-spell, and after a few, agonising minutes,

Cora began to relax in his arms. Hayden lifted his head, his eyes filled with rage as they fell onto Lydia.

"Excellent spell work, Inquisitor." Lydia smirked. "Now I suggest you all listen very carefully to what I am about to tell you, or I will cast *more* than a burning spell, do you understand? You have caused quite the storm, Thomas...quite the storm indeed.

"A darkness far worse than the Unseelie Court is coming," Lydia said. "The Dark Prince has offered to make a deal with you. Give the girl to him. She is nothing to you. Let The Dark Prince harness the elemental magic of the Fae. They're coming. Those wretched Fae *bastards* are coming, Tom. Give The Dark Prince what he wants. Let him harness the magic, and he will protect us. He will stop the Fae before they even have a chance to enter our world."

"We will take our chances!" Tom spat. "You can tell The Dark Prince that he can stick his deal. We will take our chances with the Fae, so thank you, but no thank you. I don't make deals with the devil."

Lydia laughed, cold and sharp.

"You're a fool, Tom," she sneered. "A fool! Evie Gray is one of them. She is half-Fae! She does not belong in our world. She shouldn't even exist!"

"Evie Gray is a witch!" Tom thundered. "She is one of us, and my family and I will protect her with our lives. You, Lydia, are a disgrace and a traitor. The Elders should burn your soul for your treacherous actions."

"The *Elders*," she said quietly. "Your precious Elders are just as corrupt as me, Thomas. We have all spent years searching for her you know. You have no idea..."

"We will stop you," Tom said angrily. "You won't get away

with this, Lydia."

"I look forward to seeing you try," she said coldly. "You should know that we are not alone here tonight. So, whatever you are planning to do, I wouldn't bother. There are demons close by, and they answer to *my* orders, so you might want to start doing what I say."

"What do you even have to gain from all of this?" Tom asked, perplexed. "The Dark Prince is a murderer. He has murdered *our people*! Yet you have willingly chosen to stand beside him."

"Power," she said thoughtfully. "Without power, we are nothing, Thomas, you, and I both know that. We will not survive without it. Think about it, Tom. Evie Gray was born to a witch and a Fae of the Unseelie Court! A very rare, unique phenomenon. The magic that runs through her blood is more powerful than you could ever imagine. The Dark Prince can harness that power. He would be unstoppable, and the Fae would simply be a memory. *We* would be powerful."

"You're the fool to think The Dark Prince will share that power with you." Tom laughed coldly. "He will kill you! He will kill all of you!"

"You know nothing of what The Dark Prince will do," Lydia said. "Reconsider your options. You owe nothing to Evie Gray. Think of your family."

"Evie is our family, Lydia," Rebecca warned. "How could you do this? You are a *Guardian*! You swore an oath to protect both the human and magical worlds. How could you betray us like this?"

"The Guardians are the past, Rebecca." Lydia smiled. "A new leadership is on the horizon."

"We will stop you." Rebecca seethed. "You won't get away

with this!"

Lydia smiled. "You have chosen the wrong path my old friend," she said, and lifted her hand into the air.

Nothing happened.

Cora grinned as she felt Hayden's magic bounce against her skin. His protection spell deflected Lydia's enchantments and she swore in frustration.

"You fools!" she shouted.

"The only fool around here is you, Lydia," Hayden growled.

He lifted his own hand then, and Lydia's body slammed back against the stone wall. She crumpled to the floor as Tom rushed forwards, binding her hands with his own magic before she could compose herself, and then quickly turned to Julius.

"You'll regret this," Julius stammered. "Demons…"

"All sent back to the hell hole in which they crawled from!" shouted a loud, angry voice from across the hall.

Cora lifted her head and was overwhelmed by a mixture of emotions as Evie and Tessa hurried across the stone floor towards her. Cora stood up and swung her arms around the girls, pulling them closely to her.

"Thank the Gods you're all okay!" Cora cried as she pulled away. "How did you even know that we would be here?"

"We didn't," Evie replied. "It's a bit of a long story, which I will happily tell you once we have this place secured."

"What about the demons?" Cora pressed. "Lydia said…"

"Didn't you hear what Evie said?" Tessa grinned. "They're gone! We have *little miss super witch* to thank for that!"

Evie smiled as she met Cora's eyes.

"We have a lot to tell you."

"Every door and window is secure," Jack's voice filled the entrance hall as he and Lucas stalked towards them. "No one is getting in here tonight. We are safe."

"As happy as I am to see you all, would you mind telling us what is going on?" Tom asked. "What happened when you left the safe haven?"

"Jack's portal bought us to Wilmington last night, near the abandoned warehouse. We had no clear idea of where were going," Evie said. "I'm not sure if it is a coincidence, but here we are."

"Coincidence indeed," Tom said, his voice sounded suspicious.

Evie nodded. "Weird, huh? Jack thought there might be something here at The Academy that could help us locate you."

Tom nodded, looking at the faces that stared back at him. "Where is Christian?"

"Gone," Jack seethed. "He was gone when we woke up. No doubt he's gone back to Francis and the other traitorous bastards."

"That little weasel!" Cora growled.

"So, what's the deal here?" Evie asked, casting her eyes across the foyer to where Lydia and Julias were bound.

"Tried to offer us a deal. You know, we give them you, The Dark Prince gives us his protection," Cora rolled her eyes.

"Interesting deal," Evie mused. "We should take it."

Cora's eyes widened with utter shock.

"Excuse me?" she snapped. "Did you even hear what I just said to you?"

"The Fae are here Cora. My magic is *stronger*," Evie said, holding up her hands. "I can feel it, buzzing beneath my skin, more than I could before. They're here, and they want me.

"Right now, we have enemies in every direction. The Guardians. The Dark Prince, the Fae. And all we have, are each other. We haven't been able to contact The Elders, which means

335

we are on our own. The Fae have had years to plan their revenge. I was taken from their court. This magic I have, it is *more* than just elemental Fae magic. I know it is, but I just can't figure out what. The Dark Prince is already powerful. Why does he want *my* magic too? There is a reason for everything, and to be honest, I don't particularly want to find out what that reason is. We need to stop him. And we need to stop him now."

Evie sucked in a deep breath, and when nobody spoke, she continued.

"Listen," she said. "The Fae are here, and they aren't going to be offering any more deals like they did in the Land of Wonder. We need to act now. We don't know how many Unseelies have crossed over to our world, but we do know that The Dark Prince has hundreds, if not thousands, of demons at his side. He also has the asshole Guardians who have betrayed us.

"The Dark Prince and the Fae both want the same thing. They want me. So, let's give them what they want. Let me go. Let me bring the two together. It is our only chance."

"She's lost her fucking mind," Lucas cursed.

"It's the only logical thing that makes sense, Lucas!" Evie frowned. "They both want me. Either way, one would have to destroy the other in order to get what they want. Don't you see how this would help us."

"Help us how, exactly?" Hayden said, casting his eyes to Jack's incredulous face. "This is one of the craziest ideas I have ever heard."

Jack shook his head and crossed his arms over his chest and gave him a *this has nothing to do with me* look.

"Not crazy, no," Evie said. "Just logical."

"And you're okay with this?" Hayden asked Jack incredulously. "You're okay with this ridiculous plan?"

"I think the idea is fucking stupid," Jack seethed, and added

336

bitterly, "but when has she ever listened to me."

"I don't understand how this plan will even work?" Rebecca said. "Evie, offering yourself as bait…it is dangerous! We can't take the risk!"

"My life has been at risk since the second my parents decided to lie to me," Evie said bluntly. "Look, every minute we spend hiding, is a minute wasted. My life right now is a fucking disaster. I am done running. I'm done hiding from this *magic*. I have spent the last five years hiding, Rebecca, and I refuse to do it anymore. That isn't how this works. I've run before and look how that turned out. We need to end this before it truly begins."

"We will protect you," Tom said. "Whatever happens, we will stand by your side."

"Thank you," Evie said, grateful for his words. "I have a plan, and I think it will work, but I need you all to trust me."

"Go on?" Tom said.

"Adeline is here, and she isn't far. I sensed their arrival the second they crossed over," she told them. "The Fae won't attack until they are ready, and neither will The Dark Prince. They both want the same thing—me. So, I will give them exactly what they want. Once I have them both together, they will have no other choice but to fight each other. That's when we take advantage of their distraction."

"Evie this is crazy," Cora said. "They're going to kill you. If The Dark Prince harnesses your magic, he will kill you!"

"The key word there, being *if*," Evie replied. "My plan will work, Cora. Trust me."

"And if it doesn't?" she said sharply. "Then what? We stand around and watch one of them take you? You've lost your mind!"

"It will *work*," she said defiantly.

"I don't like this plan," Rebecca said worriedly. "Surely

there must be another way!"

"There isn't," Evie said. "We can't trust anyone anymore. The Guardians of New York and London are both with The Dark Prince. Francis lied about the safe haven. He only invited the Guardian Academies who were in league with The Dark Prince. This is our only option. The Dark Prince is too powerful, and the Unseelies will have regained most of their magical strength by now. We have to do this Rebecca."

"I still don't like it," she sighed. "Tom, what are your thoughts darling?"

"I don't like it either, but Evie is right," he replied. "I can think of no other option, and without The Elders, I really don't know what else to do. I will reach out to a few old acquaintances and send another message to The Elders. In the meantime, I think it's wise we take Lydia and Julias somewhere secure."

With everyone in agreement, Tom and Rebecca left, and with the help of Zac and Lucas, they escorted Lydia and Julias away.

Once they had left, Cora turned her head towards Evie. "How're you holding up?" she asked.

"I'm fine," she replied, looking sideways towards Jack. He was stood across the hallway, talking quietly to Hayden and Tessa. "I think he wants to kill me right now."

"He's killing *me* right now," Cora groaned. "I can practically taste his rage."

"He doesn't agree with my plan. He thinks I'm being reckless," she said, and added with a sigh, "I wish he would stop being so over-protective. I'm not a stupid little girl. I know we are taking a huge risk, but it is a risk we have to take."

"You *are* reckless, but he loves you," Cora said. "He blames himself for all of this you know."

"What are you talking about?" Evie asked.

338

"He's struggling with his guilt." She sighed. "And anger, and resentment. He thinks that if he left you in London, where you were safe, none of this would have happened. He hates himself and yes, he is majorly pissed at you."

Evie sighed.

"I should go talk to him," she said.

Cora nodded. "Yes, you should," she said. "Go. We don't know what will happen tomorrow. Go make your peace. Oh, and Evie? *Try* to understand where he's coming from as well. He cares about you. We all do."

Turning away from Cora, Evie made her way across the foyer. The conversation instantly fell quiet as she approached, and she had the distinct impression that *she* had been their topic of talk.

"Jack, can I talk to you?" she said, and added, "privately?"

Jack nodded, and she swiftly turned to walk away.

Chapter Forty-Two

The Circle's apartment was exactly as they'd left it. Evie shut the door behind them, hearing the lock click into place as she stalked towards the living room.

Jack had propped himself against the wall, his arms folded across his chest. His face was the picture of pure thunder.

"I know you're angry," Evie said quietly. "If you have any other suggestions, then please feel free to throw them at me, because I am open to suggestions. Jack, you know that this is our only option. The Dark Prince has an army of monsters at his call, and God only knows how many Unseelie's Adeline has with her. We have to do this, Jack. We have to at least try."

"You've already made your decision," he said, and she balked at the coldness in his voice.

"I need to know that you are with me, Jack," she said.

"I don't *want* you to do this." His voice was sharp as he pulled himself away from the wall. "I don't want you to do this, Evie. None of us want you to. You see this plan of yours as the only way forward, but it isn't. There has to be another way. One which doesn't involve you dying."

"Jack, I'm not going to die," she said. "You will all be there! We're doing this together. You have to trust me. I wouldn't do this if I didn't think it would work."

"Do you know what I hear when I close my eyes? I hear your screams, Evie. When you were poisoned and thrashing about on that hospital bed. I still hear your fucking screams. I can't watch you go through that again... I won't..." He broke off, forcing his eyes onto hers. "You were right. I should have left you alone. I should have left you in London."

"Everything that has happened...it didn't happen because you sent The Circle to London." Her voice rose with frustration. "Jack, you bought me home, to you. My powers would have shown eventually. It was inevitable. We are going to get through this, because we have each other, and we have The Circle. You guys are my family; I will do anything to protect you. I've already lost my best friend, Jack. I refuse to lose anyone else. We have to do this. We have to do this for *her*."

"Your bravery and faith really do inspire me," he said, and added with a slight smirk, "but your stubborn heart and reckless head are driving me fucking crazy, Evie."

He lowered his head then, gripping her cheeks with his hands as he pulled her mouth to his, brushing her lips with the softest of kisses. His mouth lingered on hers for a moment, and Evie felt some of the tension in his posture slowly evaporate as she kissed him back.

"I react the way I do because I care about you, Evie," he said, pulling away slightly to look at her.

"You have to trust me, Jack," she said.

"I do trust you," he said. "I also have this need to protect you, Evie, but deep down I know you can protect yourself. You're brave, and you're strong and you are a credit to Anna and Paul."

"I'm strong because I have to be," Evie said as his lips moved teasingly along her jawline. "But right now, you're making me feel rather weak at the knees, Saunders..."

His mouth curled into a smirk as he moved his head, his lips finding hers with a crushing force. Evie pushed up on her toes, wrapping her arms around his neck, fingers twisting through his hair. His own hands dropped to her waist, pulling her against him.

The kiss deepened, and she could feel the *demand* of it, the *claim*, as his tongue clashed against her own.

Evie gasped as his hands trailed lower, hooking beneath her thighs to lift her. She wrapped her legs around his back, as his lips moved along her jawline, each tentative touch igniting the fire within her. Jack carried her across the living room, kicking open the door to his former bedroom before lowering her onto the bed. Evie pulled his mouth back to hers, trailing her hands down his side until she reached the hem of his shirt.

Jack pulled away only long enough to tear his shirt over his head before crashing his mouth back to hers. Evie felt his own hands slip beneath her top, his calloused fingers leaving a prickling sensation over her bare skin.

Jack pulled his mouth away again, tugging the top upwards, his eyes feral with insatiable lust. Evie smiled and lifted herself up.

As she lay back down, his hands moved to her trousers, and she could barely stifle the groan that left her mouth as he began to tug at them. She lifted her hips, and Jack eased them away, returning his brilliant blue eyes to hers.

"*Gods*, you drive me so fucking crazy," he rasped against her as his lips trailed down her chest. "You can tell me to stop, and I will stop, Evie. I don't know what will come of tomorrow, or the day after, or the day after that. I don't know how this shit storm will play out, but I do know how I feel about you.

"I love you. I have always loved you," he said, his voice prickled her skin as he placed his hand against her face, cupping her cheek. "And I will love you until my last breath, and in whatever life comes next, I will love you then. You have my heart, Evie. You always have."

"I don't want you to stop," she told him softly. "Whatever happens next, just know that I would endure it all again, just to

342

be with you. You're mine, and I am yours, and *nothing* will ever change that."

His piercing blue eyes were radiant as he lifted her head to his, his lips meeting hers once more. Energy crackled between them, sparking the ignition to her magic as it danced excitedly beneath her skin. His kisses sent sparks of pleasure throughout her body. His calloused touches were as hot as the flames that teased her fingertips. Her magic started to howl as he finally settled between her, pushing into her with a powerful thrust. She moaned as he set a beautiful, punishing pace, his eyes never once leaving hers.

Her fingers gripped at his neck, her nails digging into the rock-hard muscle. She could feel her magic. Could feel *his* magic as it flowed desperately between their trembling bodies.

"I love you." The words were barely a whisper, but she said them, kissing his lips as he gripped her thigh, pushing deeper to adjust his angle.

Fire exploded in her core, sending a release of pure pleasure cascading through her body. She tightened her grip, pulling his mouth to hers before he could pull away. Power simmered as she felt him find his own release, and she felt her legs tighten around his waist as he shuddered against her.

"That was… " he began, but words seemed to fail him as he tried to steady his rapid breaths.

Evie smiled against his mouth, knowing in that moment, and every moment after, Jack Saunders would *always* be her safe place.

Chapter Forty-Three

Adeline drew in a deep heavy breath as she stared intensely at The Academy.

Her yellow, grim eyes filled with an emptiness only she could feel. The Unseelies had waited a very long time for this moment. Revenge had fuelled the years they had spent isolated, forced into exile by the *witches*.

For twenty-one years, the Unseelie Court had been forced to live in exile. Their magic at the brink of disappearing completely.

Adeline had felt the power within Evie Gray. Had tasted the strength of the ancient Fae magic that lived within her blood the second the girl had stepped into their court, unknowingly breaking the spell that had been cast to entrap her people.

Time was ticking.

And her patience was beginning to ebb.

Adeline would have to act soon if she hoped to bring Evie back to the Unseelie Court.

She sighed heavily at the daunting task that lay ahead. It would not be simple. The girl had already refused her once, and after murdering her friend, Adeline knew it would be foolish to ask a second time.

Killing the girl had not been her choice, and regret rippled through her as she thought of the cruel order imposed upon her by King Naida.

Naida.

She grimaced as his unruly face cemented in her mind. His

cold words piercing every inch of her as she replayed his wicked order over and over again.

"You are to bring her to me, Adeline," Naida had ordered as he sat upon his throne. *"I care not for who she is to us, only of what she will do for us. For me. I need her blood. I need her magic. Bring her to me."*

Adeline looked up at the sky, feeling the chill of the demon's aura, and pushed all thoughts of the wicked king to the back of her mind.

The Dark Prince was nearby. She could feel it…feel his *want*, his *need* for the magic in Evie's blood. It would be disastrous were he to get his hands on the magic.

She would have to stop him. One way or another.

Adeline closed her eyes, willing a plan to present itself in her mind's eye.

Frustratingly, she saw nothing, and she cursed bitterly.

"My Queen, what is it?" Morgana asked, moving forwards to stand beside her.

"A complication." Adeline sighed. "I'm tired. I must rest in order for my mind to work as it should. The journey here has weakened me. You and the others will stay here and watch The Academy. I must be alone in order to think clearly."

"Adeline. My Queen, are you sure this is a wise decision to make?" Morgana pressed. "I feel him near, and he knows of our presence too. It would be unwise for you to be alone, without protection."

"I can protect myself, Morgana, you need not worry," she told him quietly. "I do not plan to travel far. I will be gone only a short while. I trust that you will stand guard."

"Yes, of course," he said. "And if The Dark Prince should appear?"

"Do nothing," she said. "Retreat and wait for my return. I want to see to The Dark Prince myself. He and I have much to discuss, and I would hate to be the one who doesn't end his pathetic existence. Do I make myself clear, Morgana?"

Morgana bowed his head.

"Crystal clear, my Queen," he answered.

***

"I'm going to ask you one more time, where is The Dark Prince hiding?"

There was anger in Tom's voice as he spoke. Hayden, Lucas, Tessa, and Zac watched from afar as Tom questioned Lydia and Julias. It was early morning and the sun had only just begun to rise, filling the library with a misty orange glow as its rays shone through the stained-glass windows.

Lydia and Julias were in the corner of the library, bound by Tom's magical chains, but neither would speak. Their lack of co-operation had forced a surge of frustration to rise within Tom, and the veins in his temples pulsated angrily as he stared at the two.

Lydia looked down at her feet, smirking as she did.

"I can do this all day you know," Tom warned.

"Do carry on," Lydia said quietly. "He will soon call his demons, and when they do not respond to his call, he will come, and then it will all be over for you, Thomas. There is still time, for you to change your mind you know. The Dark Prince is true to his word. He will protect you—*all* of you."

"I'd rather die than align myself with a monster!" Tom spat.

Lydia laughed a cold, hard laugh.

"Then die you will, Thomas," she said. "If the Fae don't kill you, then The Dark Prince certainly will. He is strong and clever. One way or another, he will harness the Fae magic. He will put an end to the bastard Fae once and for all, and he will lead this world."

"Not if we stop him first," Evie's voice echoed through the library, forcing Tom to spin on his heel.

She walked towards him, her face barely readable. Jack and Cora followed, closing the library door behind them.

"Where is he?" Evie asked with a lethal calm.

"I am sorry it has come to this." Lydia sighed. "But this could have been so *avoidable*."

"How so?" Evie demanded.

"Your parents could have ended this years ago," she said. "They could have harnessed the Fae magic from you—could have had it all to themselves. They would have been incredibly powerful, but they were fools. Your mother so badly wanted a daughter, but her body failed her—and then she found you," Lydia laughed, and added, "she should have killed you there and then."

Evie's hands burned at Lydia's words, but she forced her magic to remain tethered. She could not lose control. Not now.

Her racing heart began to slow as she forced her breathing to slow—forcing her mind to ignore the bitter words. Her palms felt hot, but the fire remained hidden. She breathed a sigh of relief then inhaled deeply.

"My parents, unlike *you* and the rest of the Guardian traitors, were good people," Evie said. "Mark my words, Lydia, we will end this, and you will all pay for your treachery."

Lydia smirked. "You're a fool to believe that you won't be turned, Evie. Your mother was Fae...*Fae blood is strong*. In the end, you will have no choice but to join them. The need will overcome you. Like calls to like, Evie. Remember that."

"I know who I am, and you're wrong," Evie warned.

"You're a fool, Evie," she said. "A stupid fool. You have no idea of the war that is about to come. A war that none of us will survive unless you give The Dark Prince what he wants, then all of this will be over."

"We have enough sociopaths in this world, Lydia," Evie said. "You won't win."

"Oh, but what if we already have?" she said. "I know things, Evie. Things that your precious parents kept hidden from you. Release myself and Julias. Release us, and I will tell you everything."

"Do you really think I am going to believe a word you say?" Evie sneered. "You're a liar!"

Lydia smirked. "I can tell you who your birth father is," she said quietly.

Evie recoiled, frowning as she met with Lydia's cold, dark eyes. "What?"

"Release me and I will tell you," she said flatly.

"Nice try," Cora snapped, grabbing Evie's arm. "She will say anything to get what she wants, Evie. Don't fall for it. She doesn't know anything. She is lying."

"Try me," Lydia teased.

"I'm done listening to your bullshit," Evie said, and spun away.

Evie hurried out of the library, slamming the door behind her. She rushed through the silent corridors and out the front door, welcoming the gush of cold air that swept across her face as she stepped outside.

It was bitterly cold, but she did not care, ignoring the chill against her bare arms. She hurtled across the courtyard, rage burning within her, but as she reached the empty stables, she suddenly froze.

"Hello sister."

The sound of her brother's voice sent a terrifying shiver down her spine, and as their eyes locked, she felt a wave of anxiety ripple through her. Her heart thundered beneath her chest as she eyed the man who stood before her.

Gone was the quiet, almost timid, older brother she had always loved, now replaced by a stranger. A stranger with thick, greasy, black hair, and a face that was gaunt and pale, filled with a bleak expression. His clothes hung off his frail frame, but his eyes—his eyes were full of a wicked excitement as he stared at his sister.

"Long time no see," Elijah said. "I would say that I have missed you, but we both know that would be a lie."

"Elijah," Evie struggled to say his name out loud as she looked at his frail figure. "What the hell happened to you? I don't understand..."

"Life," he said quietly. "I got dealt the shorthand, as you can see. Born to a mother who craved a daughter. Our *mother* made her disappointment in me very obvious, Evie. She hated everything about me. She couldn't even bring herself to *comfort* me when I needed her the most. What mother does that? What kind of mother ignores her crying child?"

"Mum and Dad loved you!" Evie declared. "I know they did. I saw how they were with you. They loved you!"

"You saw what they wanted you to see, Evie!" He raised his voice, clenching his fists into balls. "You had everything that should have been mine. You weren't even *their* child, yet they loved you enough to sacrifice their own lives to protect yours.

"They were fools. They didn't think. They believed their death would protect their secret—that it would go to the grave

349

with them and stay safely buried, but *I knew. I knew everything.*

"The Fae war," he said, grinning wickedly. "The Elders never truly had proof, you know. They initiated the war based on a rumour...a fucking rumour. One which I *proved* to be true. I still remember the day they bought you home. They were so deluded. So fucking happy and deluded. They truly believed that I was nothing more than a stupid child. I knew exactly *what you were.* I *saw* the magic you had, even as baby. I knew you were not like us. Like me. I knew you were not *normal.* I told Lydia about you. I told her what our parents had done..."

"I'm your sister," Evie stammered, as her eyes suddenly blurred. "Why would you do that, Elijah?"

"You are no sister of mine," he seethed. "You took everything from me! You took my parents. You received a love that I was never welcomed to. I've lived my life in *your* shadows. I promised myself that I would find you again and end this. I promised myself that I would get my life back."

"You've lost your mind Eli."

"Don't call me that!" he screamed and rushed across the cobbled courtyard towards her, throwing his hands around her throat. "Don't call me that, you fucking half-breed! You don't belong in this world, Evie. People like you *shouldn't exist!*"

Evie struggled against his hold, gripping her hands onto his as she tried to loosen his hold. Elijah, though frail, was stronger than she anticipated, and his hold grew tighter. She closed her eyes, willing for her magic to come. Willing for the fire to burn the hands that held her. Yet nothing came.

She felt *nothing*...

A flurry of angry voices filled the courtyard as The Circle hurtled towards them, shouting spells into the misty courtyard. Elijah let go, slamming her body to the ground, as a golden spark smashed into his chest, and he fell to the floor, panting.

Hayden and Lucas grabbed his arms, pulling him up as Tessa cast her own spell over him, immobilising his frail body.

***

Jack was by Evie's side in a flash, lifting her head up. Fresh blood trickled down her face and he noticed a deep cut just below her hair line. He helped her into a sitting position as Cora, Rebecca and Tom hurried over to them.

"Evie!" Cora said her name in a panicked whispered.

"I'm..."

"*Do not* say your fine," Jack bellowed angrily. "You're not fine."

"I wasn't going to," she said quietly, as Rebecca waved her hand over her head. The pain instantly disappeared and as she brushed her fingers across her forehead, she was thankful to feel that the blood had gone.

She turned to Jack. He was furious.

"What the hell were you thinking?" he asked. "Running out by yourself. Evie, even with our protection spells, we can't guarantee your safety!"

"Jack, please, I can't do this right now," she said, annoyed. "I need to speak to Lydia."

"To hell you do," he said bitterly. "You're not going anywhere near her."

"You don't understand," Evie said, her teeth grinding with frustration. "*Eli* told Lydia about me. He confirmed The Elders suspicions by telling her my parents secret, Jack. He is the reason my mum and dad are dead. I have to talk to Lydia."

"He told you that?" Cora asked.

Evie nodded, feeling the back of her eyes sting with the threat of angry tears. "He is the reason my parents are dead," she said, biting back the bile that rose in her throat.

"Unbelievable, bastard!" Rebecca scowled. "Anna and Paul died because of *him*. I told them to erase his memory! I told them he could not be trusted."

"What?" Evie said.

Rebecca sighed. "Evie, I'm sorry, I shouldn't have said that," she said.

"Cat's out the bag now," Evie snapped. "I am sick to death of being lied to. Whatever it is your hiding, you need to tell me the truth, Rebecca."

"Maybe we should go back inside," Cora suggested.

Chapter Forty-Four

Once inside, Evie hurried into the common room, waving her hand towards the fireplace. A warming buzz of air soon filled the room as they all piled in.

"I want the truth, Rebecca. Now," Evie demanded, folding her arms across her stomach.

"Sweetheart, we don't have to do this," Rebecca said, but Tom silenced her.

"It's time to tell the truth, Rebecca," he said quietly. "Evie is right. She has spent her whole life being lied to. She needs to know."

"Tom…" Rebecca warned.

Tom sighed, turning his attention to Evie.

"After we left the Land of Wonder, we returned home to find Anna and Paul on our porch. We weren't expecting them—we had already said our farewells, so it was a shock to see them there.

"Of course, both you and Elijah were with them. I remember the look on his face—it still haunts me to this day. A boy of ten, yet he looked much older. His eyes were filled with so much…*resentment* and *anger.*"

"Why did they come to you?' Evie asked.

"To tell us that they were leaving," Rebecca said. "They wanted to tell us because we were friends, and also because they needed someone to keep up their secret. Of course, we said yes. They were our very best friends. They stayed for a long while and we talked in depth. Elijah played in the other room, and none of us gave him a second thought really.

"Anna loved him, but she had always been wary of him. He wasn't a *normal* child. He had always been *odd*. We talked about their plans and about what the future might hold for you, Evie. They had to protect you, and the only way to do that was for them to leave."

"Elijah heard everything we said that evening," Tom said. "Rebecca told your parents that they needed to erase Elijah's memory, as a safety precaution, but Paul refused. He didn't think it was right. Elijah was just a boy, what did he know."

"More than they thought." Jack's voice was bitter.

Tom nodded.

"Elijah hated your parents from the very first moment they bought you home, Evie," he said. "He had been an only child for ten years, and then, all of a sudden, he wasn't. Your parents went to fight in the battle and returned home with a baby. They expected him to love you instantly. Anna and Paul were so blinded by you, they neglected him. He was much older than you. In their eyes, he was old enough to understand that their time would be devoted to you."

"I don't understand," Evie said. "I feel like we are talking about a completely different person. Elijah, the man who is outside right now, is *not my brother*. He was nothing like the way his is now. We were close! We were a close family. None of what he said makes any sense. I don't remember him being like that at all."

"Anna saw how he was," Rebecca admitted. "Like I said, he was a very odd child, and there were times that she worried when he was around you. There was an incident, a few years after your parents moved you all away. You almost drowned in the river that lay at the back of the cottage where you were living.

"You almost died, Evie, but by some miracle *you* were able to save yourself. Whether it had been sheer luck or *your* magic, somehow, you got yourself out of that river and back onto the embankment. You were six years old. Elijah swore it had been an accident. He said you had slipped. Anna didn't believe him, and you wouldn't talk to her. She'd already seen the way he was around you, and it terrified her, but Paul refused to believe it."

"I don't remember that happening," Evie said. Her mind was swirling with images, but nothing she saw made sense.

"You wouldn't," Anna replied. "Anna cast spells to make you forget. I'm sorry, Evie. Your Dad thought Elijah was just going through a rebellious stage, that he would eventually learn to love and accept you. But he didn't. And things only grew worse."

"What do you mean?" Evie asked.

"Your mum and I kept close contact during the years they were away," she said. "We wrote to each other every week. There were several more *incidents* over the years. But it was the one that happened the summer before you returned that tipped Anna over the edge.

"You were eleven," Rebecca continued, sucking in a deep breath. "Elijah was out of control. You outshone him in everything, Evie. Your magic was beyond what a child could do, and everyone was in awe. Of course, *we knew* it was because of the Fae lineage, and we knew it would only grow in strength as you grew. Academically you were incredible too. Jealously crippled Elijah. He despised you. Your parents were invited to celebrate the Summer Solstice with the Elders at the Palace of Light. They did not want to take you, for fear of your magic being exposed. They left you at home that night. With Elijah."

As Rebecca spoke, Evie scrambled with her mind, trying to

355

remember a past that was so clouded. She frowned, frustration falling heavily in her aching head.

"Elijah poisoned you that night," she said, and Evie could hear the anger in her voice. "Had your parents not arrived home when they did, you would have died. Paul gave you an anti-dote and found the poison had been laced in your drink. Elijah swore on the Guard that he had nothing to do with it. That you had opened the bottle from new."

"If they knew how he felt about me, why did they leave me alone with him?" Evie asked, frowning.

"I don't know," Rebecca said. "That was the point in which your mother decided you could no longer stay where you were. She begged your father to return to Wilmington. You were almost of age to apply to The Academy, but Anna knew they would have to bind your Fae magic. So that's what they did."

Evie nodded, contemplating her words.

"I'm so sorry Evie," Rebecca sighed. "I am so sorry you have had to deal with this. Anna and Paul should have told you the truth. They should never have kept this from you."

"Did you tell The Guardians that Elijah was responsible for my parents' death?" Evie asked flatly.

Rebecca sighed. "I'm so sorry Evie," she said. "I know it was wrong, but in a way, he was responsible. Without your parents' protection, you were vulnerable. Even with you being in The Academy, you were still at risk of exposure. Elijah knew too much. I told The Guardians in the hope they would arrest him, and it would give us time to erase his memory ourselves, but I was too late. He'd already disappeared."

Evie nodded. "Okay," she said, and turned to look at Jack. "I want to talk to Elijah—come with me if you must, but don't try to stop me. I have to talk to him."

"Evie..." Jack began but stopped himself suddenly. "Okay, ten minutes, and I'm staying with you."

"Fine," she said, and rose to her feet.

As she did, her vision suddenly blurred, and a quiet, musical voice filled her ears.

I feel the pain and confusion that rages within you.

Adeline's voice was soft, delicate almost. She was near—Evie could almost feel her presence as she spoke.

I can make that pain go away. You deserve to know the truth...all of it.

"NO! GET OUT OF MY HEAD!" Evie screamed, clutching the sides of her head with her hands as she attempted to drown out Adeline's wicked laugh. Jack rushed to her side, grabbing her arms.

"Evie!" he yelled her name as the others gathered around. "Evie, look at me!"

"She's here!" Evie gasped, her voice sharp as she finally regained control.

"Who?" Jack asked, forcing her eyes to look at him.

"Adeline...the Fae," Evie said. "They're not far. I can feel them. We need to go..."

"Evie, we can't just go storming outside," he told her. "We don't have a plan. We aren't prepared!"

"Jack, if the Fae are here, then we can't waste time sitting around devising a plan!" she yelled.

Jack paused for a moment, inhaling a deep breath as he turned towards Tessa.

"Can you ask Hayden and the others to come inside—Elijah won't escape, not with the spells they've cast. Tell them it's time."

He turned back to Evie, his eyes intent on hers. "I won't lose you," he said quietly enough for only her to hear.

"You won't," she said, believing her own lie.

She forced her eyes away from his, unable to look into his mesmerizing gaze. She wanted to believe that her plan would work. She wanted to believe that they would get through this— that when the battle came, they would win. But even she knew it wasn't going to be that easy. Evie knew, that when the time came, she would have to fight, whether she wanted to or not.

She cast her eyes towards the window, staring at the early morning sky. She pictured her parent's faces and wished for them to hear her silent thoughts. She felt Jack beside her, but before she could say anything to him, a loud explosion erupted, causing The Academy to shake rigorously beneath them.

Chapter Forty-Five

"What the hell was that?" Cora's panicked voice echoed through the common room.

"We need to go to the others," Evie said. She marched towards the door, but before she reached it, the door flew open.

Tessa hurtled forwards, closely followed by Hayden, Zac, and Lucas.

"They're here," she said. "Francis and the others! They're outside. We just about managed to get away."

"Elijah?" Evie asked, eyes widening.

Tessa shook her head. "I'm sorry, Evie," she said. "He's gone."

"We need to go," Evie warned, composing herself. "We have to make sure they follow us. Once we are in the park, I will call out to the Fae."

"How are you going to do that?" Lucas asked.

"I'll figure it out when we get there," she said hurriedly. "We're connected. That is why I can hear Adeline's voice."

"You go," Tom said, looking at Evie and the others. "Rebecca and I will stay. We will give you time to get to the park and ensure they follow you there."

"Dad, no," Cora said. "They'll kill you! Just come with us, we're stronger together."

"Sweetheart, your dad is right," Rebecca said. "Go, now! Hurry!"

Hayden opened the large glass window and gestured for the

others to follow. One by one, they climbed through, and Evie's heart raced as The Circle left The Academy grounds. The streets of Wilmington were quiet; they had the early hour of the day to thank for that.

The brilliant orange rays from the rising sun illuminated the park. As The Circle moved further in, a coldness suddenly filled the air. The leaves on the trees around them swayed rapidly as a forceful breeze swept through.

Evie looked at the others as Hayden came to an abrupt stop. Though no one else was visible, she knew they weren't alone in the park.

Demons.

"What's the plan?" Lucas asked quietly.

"We split up," Evie said. "You, Hayden, and Cora cover the west of the park. Jack, Tessa, and Zac, you guys take the east. I'm going to head towards the lake…"

"No." Jack said, and she could hear the panic in his voice.

Evie shook her head.

"Jack, don't," she said. "This *will* work, but you have to trust me. Go, now."

Jack kissed her forehead, his lips lingering on her skin for a few moments as he silently fought against his need to stay with her. He pulled away and reluctantly turned towards Tessa and Zac.

Evie watched as he walked away, noticing the tightness in his shoulders as he did. He was angry, furious even, and as much as Evie hated herself for making him feel this way, she couldn't afford to think about that now.

With the others gone, she slowly made her way deeper into the park. The sun was higher in the sky now, its rays bringing the park to life. It was bitterly cold, and she shivered as she walked.

The lake shone in the near distance, and she was momentarily dazzled by its beauty. Evie stopped walking, fixing her eyes on the lake. Several figures stood in the middle of the water. Their pale skin shining beneath the sun.

They were already there.

Adeline smiled as Evie moved closer to the lakes edge, and slowly glided across the shimmering surface. Adeline stopped and signalled for her soldiers to remain behind.

Evie did not move an inch as she finally met with Adeline's yellow eyes.

"We meet again." Adeline's voice was quiet, but the sharpness remained. "Have you changed your mind? Have you decided to join us and finally accept who you truly are?"

"I know who I truly am," Evie replied.

"I disagree," Adeline mused. "Your body craves what your heart misses—*family*. I can see your true desires—the very thing your heart seeks, but your mind denies. You need us. Come with me now. Leave this world and join mine..."

"No," Evie said defiantly. "This is my home."

Adeline smiled. "You're confused child," she said. "You only think this is your home because it is the only home that you know. Fae lives within you. It runs through your veins, and it is stronger than you could possibly imagine. You just have to embrace it. Embrace who you truly are."

"I thought there was a disgusting smell lingering about."

With her heart racing, Evie spun around. Elijah stood before her. His wicked smile revealing a set of yellowing, crooked teeth. He was surrounded by several others. Francis stood to his left, his face unreadable. And to his right...

The Dark Prince stepped forward, his demon's remaining close by his side. Evie gasped as she met his deathly red eyes and was momentarily surprised. The Dark Prince was not whom she was expecting. He wore mundane clothing. Black, tight-fitting jeans, and a pristine white shirt that clung to the chiselled body that lay beneath. The leather jacket he wore echoed with richness. He tilted his head slightly to the right, and Evie's eyes fell onto the small raven that perched upon his shoulder.

"Evie Gray."

His voice was quiet, yet the sharpness hit her hard, like throwing knives.

Unable to remove her eyes from his ruby red ones, Evie somehow managed to regain some form of self-control. She breathed in a deep gulp of air, conscious of the Fae who stood close behind. The Dark Prince made no acknowledgement of the Fae. He only had eyes for the girl who stood before him.

Evie gulped, casting a quick glance towards her brother. Elijah smiled.

"How I have waited for this moment," The Dark Prince said, his voice quiet and steady. "I did not expect you to come alone. Brave, some might say…or foolish? You have something I want."

"That makes two of you," Evie said, and quickly glanced towards Adeline and the Unseelies. "They want it to."

"Ahh," He smiled wickedly, and lifted his ruby eyes, "Welcome to the land of the living, Queen Adeline, it has been a while, has it not? Even after all these years, I see King Naida still prefers to hide behind his throne and let his loving wife carry out his dirty work."

"Twenty-one years, to be exact."

Unbeknown to Evie, Adeline was stood only a few feet behind her. Evie froze, unsure of her next move. The Circle were close by, but she didn't want to risk her plan not working by calling for them too soon.

"How the years have disappeared," The Dark Prince mused. "It was a cruel war, was it not? So many of your people slaughtered. Do tell me, how *did you* escape your exile?"

Adeline huffed. "Ahh, we were never truly exiled foolish boy," she told him. "You see, witches are powerful, cunning, and *sometimes* clever, but your minds shall always remain clouded. You allow your emotions to control you. That terrible day, you witches made a mistake. You believed you'd captured us. Believed in your minds that the Unseelie Court was finally under the control of the Guard, but you were wrong. So very wrong and *foolish*."

"Lies!" he spat. "I was there, Adeline. I watched The Elders banish every last one of you. The Seelie Queen was the only one granted freedom."

"Indeed, the Seelie Queen played no part in the war, thus earning her continued freedom within the Seelie Court. I believe she continues to sit upon her throne, completely disillusioned by the world around her," Adeline said, focusing her eyes on Evie. "Unfortunately for the witches, the banishment spell cast upon the Unseelie Court was broken the very second Anna Gray decided to take *this* child from our Court. Evie was born to an Unseelie Fae. The spell did not work because the Elders did not capture us *all*.

"And thanks to that minor error, my people have had years to plot our revenge. Years trapped within our court; time frozen as we dreamed of our freedom. And now here we are." Adeline smiled coldly. "I do hope you have put all your affairs in order, Matthew. Tonight could very well be the last one you see. *Unless* you stand aside. Order your demons to stand down and allow us to take the girl."

Matthew?

Evie's mind ran wild with questions.

The Dark Prince...

Matthew?

Nobody had ever known the true identity of The Dark Prince, yet somehow, Adeline did. But how?

"Do not call me by that name!" he bellowed. "Matthew no longer exists. He was too weak for this world, *as are you.* I am *The Dark Prince*, and you will do as I say, or you will die. Tonight, I will harness the Fae magic. I will achieve what I set out to do all those years ago, Adeline. You know it is only a matter of time..."

As The Dark Prince spoke, the sky above grew rapidly darker. The pale blue sky became dull and grey, as thick, and heavy clouds closed in, threatening Wilmington with a magical storm.

Evie could feel a silent panic rising within her as the Fae magic pulsed through her veins. Her fingers tingled as she glanced towards Adeline. Evie watched as Adeline's lips moved, uttering her own quiet spell. The wind picked up, whistling loudly as it swept through the park.

"Then we *battle*," Adeline said with a low bow, before ordering her soldiers forwards.

The Unseelies moved with a stealthy grace, stalking towards their target with bared, angry teeth.

The Dark Prince smiled and lowered his own head briefly. The demons that surrounded him buzzed with manic excitement as they too began their move forwards. Evie lifted her head, meeting the remorseful eyes of Francis as he stood watching.

Too late for regret now, she thought bitterly. Evie forced herself to the ground, rolling to the side before bending into a low crouch.

The Unseelies unleashed their magic, throwing bright sparks towards The Guardians and demons. Evie could not see The Dark Prince, but before she could spin around to look, she was hit by a sudden, sharp pain.

Evie fell to her knees, clutching her chest as Elijah stalked towards her, his face gaunt and wicked as he did so. She scrambled to her feet, keeping her eyes fixed on her brother. Anger wrapped around her, suffocating all logical thought as she threw herself towards him. Elijah growled viciously as Evie connected with his scrawny figure, forcing them both to fall to the ground. She rolled to her side, raising her hands as her palms erupted with fiery flames.

Evie manoeuvred her fingers, forcing the flames into a ball as she watched Elijah stumble backwards a fraction. For a moment neither spoke, and Evie could feel the anger fuelling her magic as each element coursed beneath her skin, buzzing with a wicked delight as she embraced the darkness of the magic.

A look of pure rage flashed across Elijah's face as Evie stalked towards him, her eyes fixed deeply with his.

Evie did not stop until she was only a few inches away from where her brother stood.

"Do you wish to harm me, dear sister?" Elijah taunted, eyeing her fiery hands. "I can see the darkness flicker in your eyes. The struggles you now face, between what is right and what is wrong. This *darkness...* it will take over. It will continue to seep through your veins until you no longer know the difference between *good* and *evil*. Between *hero* and *the villain*.

"Do it Evie," he said, his voice mocking. "You know you want to. It is who you truly are, is it not? You can stand there and continue to fool yourself. You can continue to fool those idiots who fight beside you...but you know what you really are. You don't belong in this world. Your existence is a disgrace to our people."

"You're wrong," Evie growled. "I know who I am...I'm *good*. I am a Guardian Warrior...I know who I am..."

"Are you sure?" he asked, taking a final step forward so that his face almost touched hers. "I can see the darkness in your eyes..."

Evie tried to block out the venom of his words, knowing exactly what he was trying to do, but she would not break down. She would not yield to his taunts.

She couldn't...

"I know who I am," her voice quivered slightly. "Elijah, I am your sister..."

"YOU ARE NO SISTER OF MINE!"

Elijah screamed, his dark eyes maddening as he grabbed hold of her. Evie struggled against his hold, the fiery flames vanishing as Elijah's sharp nails dug into her skin.

Elijah's strength dragged her to the ground, his impact forcing their bodies to roll down the small hill, into the depths of the glistening lake.

Elijah, though frail, was fast and his hands wound themselves around Evie's neck, tightening in a deathly grip as he dragged her deeper into the water. Evie struggled against his hold, her legs kicking hard as her fingers squeezed against his grip. Elijah stopped moving, and suddenly, his hands plunged her head beneath the water's surface.

Evie forced her eyes open, but the murky water restricted her sight. She could feel her lungs gasping for air as she fought tirelessly against Elijah's strong hold, and suddenly she was transported back to the Black Sea... to *Robyn*.

You're stronger than this!

Robyn's familiar voice was as clear as ice in her mind, and Evie felt her heart shatter at the sound. She knew it wasn't real. She knew Robyn was not truly there, yet she held onto the hope that her voice bought.

Seconds that could have been minutes passed before Elijah dragged her head back above the surface, and Evie coughed and spluttered, begging for the air to refill her lungs. She could hear Elijah's cold wicked laugh. She could feel the hatred that he felt towards her pulsating through his body. His fingers remained looped in her hair, and she knew her brother was not done.

She had to fight back.

Her magic coursed beneath her skin, reawakening at last. With Robyn's voice still clear in her mind, Evie released her grip on Elijah's hands, raising her own so that they floated above the water. She closed her eyes and felt the water spin rapidly as she gained control. Elijah fell silent. His cold laugh vanishing as his eyes fell onto the dangerous swell of the lake.

"What are you doing?" he roared.

Evie kept her focus on the water, on the magic that raged through her body. The darkness lunged, enveloping her mind as it threatened to overwhelm her.

Elijah stumbled backwards, unable to take his eyes away from his sister. Evie embraced the Fae magic, allowing it to consume every part of her body. The water rose, separating itself into watery chains, as she forced him into an unbreakable bind.

And then the images of her clouded past exploded in her mind. Evie gasped as each memory pierced her shattering heart, and slowly, the spells cast by her mother were broken.

She remembered.

The river. The poisoned milkshake. Her magic crippling her tiny body as she hurtled through the woods, desperately trying to escape.

Years of torment. Years of fighting against who she was. Against what she was. It all came back to her in a wave of terror, clutching at her thundering heart as she gasped for air. She couldn't breathe. She couldn't think.

Her life was a puzzle of lies and betrayal.

So. Many. Lies.

But now—now she understood.

"You did this, Eli," Evie cried. "*You* are the reason our parents are dead. *You* are the reason for all of this. Your heart is filled with a hatred that will never be resolved. You chose your path. You chose evil over good, and for that you must pay."

"EVIE!"

The sound of *his* voice shattered the darkness that was seeping towards her heart. Evie dropped her hands as she gasped for breath. The magic that soared through her raged viciously, the darkness too strong for her mind and body to fight. Her hands glowed as the Fae magic gained more control, coursing through her with a terrifying delight, forcing her to yield.

Her throat tightened. Evie clenched her fists as an immense amount of power rippled through her, desperate for release. She lifted her head, her dark, fathomless eyes falling onto her brother.

Yield.

Embrace it.

This is who you truly are.

Her mind screamed, piercing every inch of her aching head as her magic strengthened, filling her with a relentless amount of rage.

This was who she was. This *darkness.* This *magic...*

She was the weapon The Dark Prince sought.

A tidal wave of acceptance slammed into her, and Evie lifted her hands, staring at the ethereal glow that engulfed her palms.

She could end it.

She could end them all with this power that surged through her. The feeling was overwhelming, sucking the breath from her already aching lungs.

She felt hollow. Empty almost.

Elijah remained rooted within his watery binds, his panicked screams barely a whisper in her raging mind.

"You are the reason our parents are dead, Elijah."

Evie barely recognised the deadly voice that left her lips, and a sudden spark of heat erupted within her veins. A funnel of power stormed, and the pain she felt was unbearable. The Fae magic swirled with a maddening dance as it coursed closer to the edge, closer to the release it so desperately craved.

Evie eyed the fire that sat within her palm.

Release.

Accept who you truly are!

The voice in her head was wickedly taunting, and she felt her heart thunder dangerously beneath her chest. All she had to do, was release the magic…

"Evie. NO!"

That voice.

She could hear him. Could hear the pain and the fear that radiated as Jack screamed her name. Over and over again. She allowed his voice in, the sound shattering the darkness that seeped through her mind. As he neared, she felt her heart slowly soften, and as his warm, calloused hands gripped her shoulders, her vision became clear once more.

The watery chains that bound Elijah fell, splashing back into the lake with a deadly force as Evie gained control of her mind. Elijah fell, furiously pushing himself backwards.

"Evie. stop!" His voice was desperate now. "This isn't you—you aren't a murderer!"

Her eyes snapped to his, and she instantly drowned in the familiarity of his brilliant blue eyes.

"Jack," she rasped.

Jack pulled her against his chest, his hand holding the back of her head whilst the other wound around her waist, pulling her close to him.

"I've got you," he told her, watching as Elijah hurried out of the lake. "Evie, I've got you. Breathe. Let it go."

"I can't!" she gritted out. "It's too strong. I can still feel it. Jack they were right. They were all right. I can't be trusted... this magic... it's dangerous. I can't control it. I am dangerous..."

"No, they're not," he said firmly. "Fae is part of you, part of who you are. But you are also a witch. Your magic will only be dangerous if you allow it to be."

"I almost killed my brother," she said breathlessly. "I wanted to kill him, Jack."

"You lost control, Evie," he said, gripping her face with his hand. "But you're stronger than this. Don't allow it to consume you."

"I can't control it," she cried.

"Yes, you can!" he said urgently, lifting her head to his. "You're nothing like them. This darkness, it doesn't define who you are, Evie. You're good. You're brave. You're everything that I strive to be, and I love you. Fight this. Fight this darkness and don't allow it to consume you. Remember who you truly are."

His thumb traced her jaw, and Evie allowed herself to melt into his embrace. With each passing second, she found it easier to breathe. Easier to see, and after a few moments, she pulled her head away.

"I could have killed him Jack," she said quietly.

"You didn't," he said softly. "I trust you, Evie. I trust that you will fight this; I will be right here with you. I've got you. No matter what happens, and I will fight with you."

"Together," she pleaded.

"Through every bit of darkness that threatens your light," Jack promised, pulling her face to his and pressing his lips to her forehead. "The others need us, Evie. We need to go."

Chapter Forty-Six

Thick green slime exploded into the air as several demons vanished, leaving behind the horrid smell of burnt flesh.

Evie gagged as Jack caught up to her, and together they rushed towards the others. Tessa and Zac were furthest away, both deep in battle with two very large, and very ugly looking creatures. Cora, Hayden, and Lucas were opposite, each duelling with leaders of the New York Guardians.

Evie rushed towards the Guardian traitors, heat burning at her fingers tips as she neared.

She was good.

She would use her magic for the greater good.

She would not yield to the darkness that lurked impatiently beneath her skin.

Christian appeared from the shadow of the trees, smiling wickedly as he blocked her path.

"I was beginning to wonder when *you* would show up," he sniggered. "Ready to end this and hand yourself over?"

"Why on earth would I do that?" Evie snarled.

Before Christian could respond, Evie lifted her hand, throwing a stunning spell at his chest. He fell to the ground, eyes dazed. The other Guardians stepped back, allowing Hayden, Cora, and Lucas to hurry to Evie's side.

"Good choice," she told them. "Now if you don't want to die tonight, I suggest you leave. Now."

"Evie, I didn't want this to happen," Francis rasped, and she

could hear the remorse in his voice. "I... I was disillusioned...
I'm sorry..."

"You should have thought about that before you decided to
become a traitor," Evie growled. "Leave now. But don't think this
is over, Francis."

Francis turned to the few Guardians who stood behind him
and nodded. One by one, they vanished into the air. Evie sucked
in a deep breath as they disappeared, silently questioning whether
she would come to regret her decision to let Francis leave.

Christian remained on the ground, clutching at his chest.
Evie strolled towards him, and using her foot, she kicked him,
forcing him to roll onto his back. He smiled as their eyes met.

"I'm surprised your boyfriend isn't attached to your side,"
Christian sneered. "Do you really think a simple stunning spell
will be enough to stop me? To stop *them*?"

"Shut your mouth," Evie warned, as Cora bound his hands
together with an invisible chain.

Christian cackled, and the sound of it sent a shiver trickling
down Evie's spine.

"Bind me all you like, little witch. We both know how this is
going to end. I can taste the darkness seeping through your veins.
It's only a matter of time before you have no other choice but to
yield to it.

"I do hope Jack is strong enough to deal with what is about
to happen to you. Gods it will be such a *waste* to watch you die.
I mean you're hot, and had you been *mine*, I would have done
everything in my power to *protect* you... too bad, huh?"

"Asshole," Evie mouthed.

"Evie!"

Zac, Tessa, and Jack hurried towards The Circle.

"Gods, you guys stink!" Cora gasped, holding her nose.

"Demon blood," Tessa said in disgust. "They're retreating. The Dark Prince ordered his demons to retreat! The Unseelie's have destroyed at least fifty of his creatures. Your plan worked, Evie."

"Where are the Fae now?" Evie asked as Jack moved to stand by her side.

"They're gone," Tessa replied. "They vanished into thin air a few minutes ago."

Evie shivered, and as she twisted her head to look at Jack, she felt the colour drain from her face.

"Jack?" she said, frowning.

His entire body was as taut as a bow. His face pale and drained of colour. Jack didn't answer, and as her eyes fell onto the black menacing whirls that now snaked up his neck, she suddenly gasped.

"Gods!" she screamed, reaching for his shirt. "The blood… it's burning his skin!"

With Cora's help, Evie tugged the shirt over Jack's head as Hayden chanted a healing spell over the black whirls that were rapidly spreading over Jack's neck.

The slimy goo vanished and after a few seconds, his skin returned to its usual colour. Jack gasped as his eyes refocused.

"Can you please try not to die today?" Evie said, reaching up to kiss him. "That was a close call."

"I didn't even realise it was there," he said, rubbing his neck.

"Good job you noticed, Evie," Hayden said quietly. "We need to be more vigilant. We all know how dangerous demonic blood is to us."

"Once again, *Jack Saunders* lives to tell the tale." Christian scowled. "You're like a cat with nine lives mate."

"Shut up," Evie warned him, as Jack tensed beside her. His

naked chest rose angrily with each breath he took.

"Where are the others?" Jack asked, his eyes still fixed on Christian's bound figure.

"Gone," Evie answered, biting her lip. "We should go too. We can't stay here. My plan worked, but not as well as I hoped it would. The Fae have disappeared, and so has The Dark Prince. Adeline *knows* The Dark Prince's true identity."

"What?" Hayden said, brows furrowed.

"She called him Matthew," Evie said. "Does that name mean anything to you?"

"Matthew?" Lucas said suddenly. "The only Matthew we know is *Matthew Blaise*—you know, the witch who was murdered in the Enchanted Forest, not long after the Fae war."

"Wait, what?" Evie said. "I've never heard of a Matthew Blaise."

"It wasn't a big story," Lucas said. "I just remember my parents talking about a witch being killed in the Forest, but they never said who did it, and nobody really talked about him."

"Matthew Blaise," Evie repeated his name, but her mind gave her nothing. "Maybe it's just a coincidence that they have the same name."

"We should find a safe place," Hayden said. "We need to plan out our next move and find a way of contacting The Elders. The Dark Prince will be furious with how many demons he has lost today."

"The Fae have retreated," Evie said. "I can't feel their presence anymore. Did they lose anyone?"

Cora nodded. "A few, but not many. The Fae are strong, Evie. A lot stronger than I thought they would be, considering how long they've been in exile."

"I know," Evie replied, and twisted her head back to Hayden.

"What do *you* know about the Fae war?"

Hayden raised his eyebrow. "No more than you. Why?" he asked.

"Just something The Dark Prince said." She folded her arms across her chest as she spoke. "The Unseelie Court were the only ones to be banished. What happened to the Seelies?"

"The Seelie Court played no part in the war." Hayden shrugged.

"Adeline said the Seelie Queen remains in her Court," Evie said. "The Elders started the war. Because of me and these abilities that I have… I think there is more to it, but I can't figure out what it is. Why did the Seelie Court have nothing to do with the war?"

"Evie, don't you think we have enough to worry about right now?" Cora asked. "We have enough Fae problems to deal with without worrying about the Seelie Queen and her Court."

"I know…" Evie said, but the thoughts remained at the back of her mind. She glanced down at Christian, watching as he fought tirelessly against his binds. "What do we do with him?"

"Leave him here," Jack said coldly. "We have no time for traitors."

"Spoken like a true Guardian," said Christian. "But a true *leader* would not abandon one of his own, surely?"

"You're a traitor. You lost the Guardian title when you chose to work with The Dark Prince."

Christian laughed bitterly.

"You're all fools," he said, his voice taunting. "You have no idea of the shit storm that is about to come."

"Go to hell Christian," Evie snapped, and without another word, she tugged at Jack's arm, pulling him away.

They hurried through the park and onto the now busy streets

376

of Wilmington. Evie shuddered as they manoeuvred their way through the bustling crowd. No one paid them any attention. Had the normads heard anything at all?

Tessa and Lucas led the way, the others followed, keeping their heads down as they walked.

By the time they reached the abandoned warehouse, it was almost noon. Once inside, Tessa and Hayden cast their protection spells, whilst Cora pulled out a map of the town, spreading it across the floor.

"What's the map for?" Evie asked.

"I need to find my parents," she replied and pulled a crystal necklace from her neck. "My mum gave this to me just before we joined The Academy. It's impregnated with their blood, which means I will be able to track them."

"Oh," Evie said. "Thank God. Let me know when you've found them."

"I will. I just need to focus," she said, and fixed her eyes on the map.

Evie turned away from her, joining Tessa, Jack, and Lucas. They were deep in conversation but stopped abruptly as she neared.

"Don't stop talking on my account," she said, folding her arms across her chest.

"Are you alright?" Jack asked.

"Yes... no... I don't know." She sighed. "Something feels... off. I feel like we are missing something here, and the more I try to piece it together, the more clouded my mind becomes. Adeline knows who The Dark Prince is, Jack.

"We're missing something... something vital," she mused, her mind calculating everything that had happened. "The Elders started the war because of me. Because of what I was born with and the threat my magic posed. They forced the Fae into exile because of *me*...yet they didn't actually have real proof. All they had was a rumour. It was Elijah who told Lydia, and that was years after the war."

Evie paused, her mind reeling.

"None of it makes sense," she said. "We've all just witnessed how powerful the Fae are. How did The Guardians overpower them? They went to war based on a rumour. None of it makes sense."

"Perhaps The Guardians thought they had the upper hand by exiling the Fae," Zac suggested. "Nobody knew your parents had taken you, other than Rebecca and Tom. Your parents kept you hidden, remember."

"Hmm," Evie said. "It still makes no sense how The Guardians were able to win that war. What bothers me most is Adeline. How does she know the true identity of The Dark Prince?"

"Maybe it is just a coincidence," Jack offered. "Try not to over think it."

"Easier said than done." She sighed, then added, "we need to find a way to get this magic out of me."

"What?" Lucas exclaimed.

"It's dangerous, Lucas," Evie said. "I feel dangerous. I can feel the darkness... you didn't see what happened in the lake. I almost killed my brother. I *wanted* to kill him. This magic... these *abilities,* they aren't good."

"Evie, I'm not sure it works like that," Hayden said. "You were born with these abilities. You can't just get rid of them."

"Is that not what The Dark Prince plans to do?" she asked, frowning. "Is that not the reason for all of this? He wants this magic. He must know of a way to harness it, or else why would he bother? There has to be a way, Hayden. We need to get it out of me before either The Dark Prince or the Unseelie's manage to do so.

"I don't think The Dark Prince wants my magic just for the power he will gain," she added. "He's planning something terrible, and we can't allow it to happen."

"You can't just get rid of your magic," Jack said incredulously.

"Jack, you saw what happened at the lake," she said. "I lost control. I allowed the darkness to take over. I've already lost control with you once before…"

"What are you talking about, Evie?" Zac asked.

"Nothing," Jack growled.

"I lost control whilst we were at Cora's ranch," Evie said, ignoring Jack's seething eyes as she turned to the others. "I lost control and because of that, Jack was hurt."

"Evie…" Jack's eyes widened with silent warning.

"We have to destroy this magic," Evie said, ignoring his glaring eyes. "It is too dark. I don't trust myself… I could hurt anyone of you just by losing control."

"It will kill you," Lucas said, perplexed. "No offense Evie, but that is a pretty dumb idea. Whatever happened before, it was an accident. You will learn to control your abilities; I know you will. Destroying your magic is not the answer."

"No, it's not," she said. "Just hear me out, please. Not all Fae are born with magical abilities. I don't know why I was born with this gift, but for some reason, I was. I know I can't do anything about my Fae heritage. That is just something I will have to learn to live with. But the magic? We can remove it! Surely there must be some kind of spell…"

"It's not happening," Jack growled. "You're not doing this,

so get the idea out of your fucking head right now. It will kill you. Don't you get it? In order to harness your magic, The Dark Prince… the Unseelies… they will have to *kill you*. You can't just destroy it. Because in doing so, you will destroy everything that you are. There is a reason for you having these abilities, Evie. They are your birth right."

"Jack…"

"No, Evie," he said, and the sharpness of his voice hit her like a thousand knives.

She flinched at the harshness, aware of the other's watching them.

"It's my decision Jack," she said, trying not to let her voice crack. "We have to at least try…"

"You've lost your fucking mind," he said, his brilliant blue eyes glaring.

Evie could feel his anger and see it in the way that he looked at her, and for a moment the two of them glared at each other.

"Found them!" Cora's excited voice broke through the silence that had erupted, and Evie quickly forced her eyes away from Jack, grateful for the distraction. "They're at the university. Why on earth would they go there?"

"Perhaps they thought it would be a safe place to hide?" Tessa suggested.

Cora shrugged. "Maybe," she said. "Right, I'm going to head over there and bring them here."

"I'll go with you," Hayden offered, and hurried towards her. Tessa and Zac followed, leaving an awkward looking Lucas with Evie and Jack.

"Maybe I should go too?" Lucas said. "You guys look as though you're going to kill each other, and I really can't have that on my conscience."

He hurried after the others, and Evie felt her heart sink as the door closed behind him. If Jack was angry before, it was nothing compared to how he was now; he looked livid.

Evie crossed her arms and raised her head. She instantly regretted her decision. His ocean blue eyes echoed betrayal as they bore into her, and she felt herself shiver from the intensity of his gaze.

"Say something," she said.

"I have nothing to say to you," he said sharply. "You've made your decision, so I guess we will just roll with it, right? And if you die, then I guess we can say *at least we tried.*"

"Jack why are you being like this?" she asked, hurt by his words.

"I DON'T WANT TO LOSE YOU, EVIE!" His angry voice roared through the warehouse, making her jump. "How many times do I have to say this before it finally sinks in? You make these decisions without giving a second thought to anyone else. You think you're doing the right thing, but you're not. Destroying the Fae magic will kill you, and I won't stand around and watch you do that. I can't."

"So, what are you saying?" she asked.

"Right now, I don't know," he said. "But I won't watch you risk your life, yet again. I thought we were a team. I thought we were on the same page, but clearly I was wrong. You make these decisions, and you expect everyone to follow. You don't give a second thought to what others might think. To what *I* think."

"Jack, I don't want to fight with you," she said. "I need you to put yourself in my shoes. I have all these people who want to hurt me *because of this magic.* Every day, my life will continue to be at risk because of it.

"I know it is a huge risk. But it's a risk that I am willing to take, for the greater good. You are all risking your lives, but I am just one person Jack. I'm not worth it."

"There are not *but's,* Evie," he said, causing her to flinch at the sharpness of his voice. "I love you, and I would rip this world apart if it meant keeping you safe. Don't ever say that you're not worth it, because you are worth it. You're worth it to me."

"I just want this to be over," she said, lowering her head.

Pulling her against him, Jack wrapped his arm around her waist, lifting her chin with his other hand.

"You're not destroying your magic. You're not going to remove it," he told her. "It is your birth right… your gift. It may have come from the Fae, but it is *yours,* and you will learn to control it."

"It's dangerous Jack," she said. "Dangerous and deadly. *I am the weapon* The Dark Prince seeks; don't you see that. Whatever he plans to use my magic for, I can guarantee it won't be for anything *good.* We have seen how powerful the Fae are, yet there is a reason why they want this magic back too. We are completely clueless. Blind and clueless, Jack."

"We will figure it out," he said. "Evie…"

"I'm scared Jack," she said, feeling her voice finally break. "I am so scared, and I don't know what to do."

"I know," he said. "But you're not alone in this. I see you, Evie. I see everything that you are, and who you will be, and I am with you. These abilities don't define you. Your heritage doesn't define you. You are a good person with a true heart. And I love you."

Burying her head against his chest, Evie muffled a sob.

"I'm sorry. I thought destroying the magic would help."

"We will figure it out," he whispered, kissing the top of her head.

"I don't want to fight with you anymore," she said, lifting her head to meet with his gaze.

"Then let's stop fighting," he replied, pushing a stray piece of hair behind her ear before leaning down to kiss her. "I'd much rather kiss you than fight with you, Gray."

Evie smiled against his lips. "The feelings mutual," she said quietly. "But as much as I would love to stand here, wrapped in your arms, we have to keep our focus."

"I am focused," he teased, nibbling her ear lobe. "You're my focus."

"Jack!" She giggled, feeling the blush steal across her face. "We need to concentrate."

"Spoil sport," he said, kissing her once more before reluctantly pulling away.

Chapter Forty-Seven

The university stood ablaze with light as Cora, Tessa, Hayden, Zac, and Lucas hurried along the cobbled path.

Cora's pendant grew brighter as they entered the courtyard.

"Do you think I should have stayed with Evie and Jack?" Lucas asked, as he and Tessa walked side by side behind the others.

Tessa shook her head. "Absolutely not," she said. "They're both as stubborn as each other, but they'll work it out. They always do."

"I don't think I've ever seen Jack look that angry," he mused. "I hope you're right, and we don't go back to a blood bath."

"My money's on Evie." She laughed. "They'll be fine, come on we need to hurry and find Cora's parents so we can get the hell out of here."

They were stood outside the university's main entrance now, watching as Cora's pendent grew brighter. Cora tucked the pendent beneath her shirt and turned to look at Hayden. His face was unreadable as he pushed open the doors and led them inside. The corridors were dark and eerily quiet, but the five of them edged forwards, using the light from Cora's pendant as guidance as they searched for Rebecca and Tom.

"Are you sure they're here?" Lucas asked, after searching the fifth empty classroom.

Cora nodded. "They're here," she said. "Maybe we should split up? This place is huge. We would cover more ground."

"Okay," Hayden agreed. "Zac and Tessa, you search the east of the building. Lucas, you, and Cora take the west. I will cover upstairs."

"Do you think it is wise for you to go alone?" Tessa asked.

"I'll be fine. We all have our cell phones, right?" he asked, and everyone nodded. "Text the minute you find anything."

"Be careful," Cora said, and pressed her mouth to his.

They separated, and Cora followed Lucas towards the west side of the university. The silence made her nervous, but she pushed those nerves aside as she pulled out her pendent, holding it tightly in her hands.

"Are you alright?" Lucas asked, his voice quiet.

"I'm just worried," she answered. "This whole situation we're in, it's crazy Lucas. When Jack asked us to go to London to bring Evie home, I never once imagined that we would be in the situation we are in now. I mean, The Dark Prince was our only concern. I thought we would bring Evie home and finally put an end to him. I never thought we would have to battle against the Fae and disloyal Guardians, Lucas."

"Yeah, it is pretty messed up," he agreed. "But it is what it is, and I think it would have happened eventually anyway. The Fae were never truly banished. They would have found a way out of exile eventually. It was only a matter of time."

"Lucas, do you ever regret what we did?" she asked and lifted her head so that their eyes met. "Following Jack's orders, I mean."

"What do you mean?" he asked sharply.

"Nothing," she said quickly. "Forget I said anything."

"I thought everything was okay between you and Evie now?" he asked.

"It is," she said. "Look I didn't mean anything by what I just said, forget I said anything, please?'

Lucas sighed. "I think this would have happened anyway, Cora," he said. "Evie was bound to remove that cuff sooner or later; she couldn't have kept it on forever. The Dark Prince would have found her. I'm just glad that it played out the way it did, and Evie had us. I know that you're scared, and you're worried about your parents... Gods we all are..."

"I'm sorry. I didn't mean anything by it. Of course, I don't regret going to London. Yes, I was pissed at Evie for leaving us. I was for a long time. But I'm glad we bought her home."

"Good," he said, and pointed towards a door at the end of the corridor. "Hear that?"

The sound of muffled voices grew louder as the two of them moved towards the double doors. Cora looked down at her pendent and smiled. It was now bright orange. She turned away from Lucas, stretching her hand out until it touched the metal handle, and slowly, she pushed open the door.

"Alas," said a cold voice from within the room. "The *daughter* has arrived."

The Dark Prince smiled, his ruby red eyes burning into Cora's. Before she could react, a pair of slimy, cold, fingers slithered around her arms, forcing them behind her back. She twisted her head towards Lucas, and saw that he too, was in the same predicament.

"Do not try to fight," The Dark Prince warned. "My demons could snap you at the slightest touch, but we do not want that... not yet anyway. Where is Evie Gray?"

"Where are my parents?" Cora demanded.

"Ahh," he mused. "I am not in the mood to play games. I am running out of time, and therefore patience. The Fae are stronger than I first anticipated."

"Where. Are. My. Parents." Cora repeated.

The Dark Prince laughed coldly. "You should know, your *friends* are currently being held captive by my demons. Your

386

parents, are the *least* of your concern, girl."

Cora's eyes widened, and as she turned to look at Lucas, the doors behind them suddenly swung open. Elijah stalked into the room, his menacing black eyes filled with excitement as they fell onto Cora and Lucas.

***

"Did you find her?" The Dark Prince asked.

"No," Elijah replied, crossing the room to stand before him. "The others are keeping their mouths tightly shut too, my Prince, but if you were to allow me, I would happily torture it out of them."

"That won't be necessary," he said quietly, before lifting his head to look at his demons. "Take them away. Lock them up with the others. We will wait. It is only a matter of time before Evie Gray comes looking for them. We must ensure that we are ready. I have no doubt the Fae will be near and prepared for a second attack. We must be ready, do you understand."

"Yes," Elijah answered. "And we will be, my Prince, mark my words. The Fae magic will be yours, tonight."

"Indeed, it shall," he sneered, watching as his demons dragged Cora and Lucas away.

Elijah got to his feet. "Should I return to the main entrance?" he asked.

"No," he replied. "You are to stay with me."

"Do you not trust me?" Elijah asked, clearly scorned by the order.

"You have been most loyal to me, Elijah, therefore I cannot risk losing you," he said. "You very almost died today, at the hands of your sister. We cannot afford for that to happen again."

"Understood." Elijah smirked and seated himself next to The Dark Prince.

Chapter Forty-Eight

The day had swiftly turned to night. Evie held Jack's hand as they walked, squeezing it every now and again, and he knew it was because of the anxiety that undoubtedly overwhelmed her.

It had been over an hour and the others had still not returned to the warehouse. He was certain they were okay, but he couldn't quite shake the niggling doubts that crept into his mind. As they neared the university, Evie suddenly stopped.

"What is it?" he asked.

She turned to look at him, and he noted the watery appearance of her eyes.

"Jack," she said quietly. "I love you."

Jack frowned and pulled her against his chest.

"I know what you're trying to say," he said. "Nothing is going to happen to you. Or to me. Or to any of us. We are going to win this; do you hear me? Whatever happens, we will win. I know it because we are strong. We have been through so much already, Evie."

Evie inhaled a deep breath, breathing in Jack's familiar scent as he leant in to kiss her head.

"We have to end this," she said. "We have to stop them."

Jack nodded and tilted her head with his finger. For a moment he stared at her, and a surge of emotion hurtled through him as he pulled her mouth to his.

***

"She's here."

Morgana's voice was nothing more than a quiet whisper, yet Adeline had no trouble hearing him.

Adeline opened her eyes, and within seconds she was stood by Morgana's side, watching eagerly as Evie disappeared into the university.

"Should we follow her?" Morgana asked urgently, tilting his head sideways in order to meet Adeline's yellow gaze. "If we do not act quickly, we could very well be too late…"

"All in good time," Adeline said softly. Her voice sounded distant. "I will grant The Dark Prince his time with the girl."

Morgana looked confused. "I do not understand," he said, and as the rest of the Fae gathered closer, there was a mumble of disgruntled whispers. "My understanding was that you did not wish for The Dark Prince to go anywhere near the girl. Are we not risking everything by allowing this to happen?"

Adeline sighed. "Morgana," she said, "you are my most loyal soldier, and I would have thought you would trust me entirely. I can see from your questions and the murmurs of our people, that this is not the case."

"My loyalty has never wavered," he said fiercely. "I just worry that our plan will not work. Should The Dark Prince get his hands on the girl before we do, we will lose *everything*, Adeline."

"Morgana, trust me, our plan is set to work. The Dark Prince will not be harnessing the ancient Fae magic tonight," she told him. "I need Evie Gray to meet with The Dark Prince. There are things she must know before we make our move. It is important that this happens, Morgana. It will help us greatly."

Morgana nodded and turned to the Fae who stood behind

them. "You heard the Queen," he said. "We wait."

"This is foolish!"

Both Morgana and Adeline spun on their heels, twisting their bodies to the voice that had spoken.

A Fae male, tall and broad-shouldered, with silver white hair that flowed in waves past his shoulders, stepped forwards. His tanned oval face clearly showing he was livid.

"What troubles you, Kieran?" Morgana asked, as he looked into the deep yellow eyes of his fellow Fae. "You seem somewhat displeased by the Queen's orders."

"We have spent over twenty-years locked away, forced into isolation," Kieran spat angrily. "We come to this pitiful, dismal land of the normads. Home to those who forced us into exile and are told to wait. The girl is right within our grasp, Adeline! You are a fool to sit and wait. We must act now! We could be back in the Unseelie Court within the hour!"

"If you do not like our Queen's plan, please, feel free to leave," Morgan bellowed. "That goes for anyone else stood here. Our Queen knows what she is doing. We must trust her plan. We wait until the time is right, and then, and only then, will we make our move."

"Then you are just as foolish as she is," Kieran growled. "If King Nadia were here, he too would agree with what I say. Adeline's loyalties are to be questioned!"

Adeline barked a cold, spine chilling laugh, and Kieran fell silent. She stared at him, her yellow eyes burning into his own.

"You dare to question *my* loyalties?" she asked sharply.

"We know who she is to you, Adeline!" He grimaced. "We are not fools! A darkness is upon us, Adeline. King Naida gave you specific orders, and yet we stand here and do nothing! We are wasting precious time. Every second we spend waiting, *he*

390

grows weaker… King Naida relies on…"

"Enough," she sneered. "You forget with whom you speak, Kieran. Despite your lack of respect for me, I am still your Queen, and you will do as I say. King Naida is not here, and I shall do things my way, is that understood?"

"You're a fool." he spat. "You know she will never willingly choose *you,* Adeline. You know what he plans to do! He will not allow her to live…"

"You are treading a very fine line, Kieran," Adeline said.

"I speak the truth, Your Majesty," he spat. "Despite whom her *mother* was, Adeline, do you really think our King will let her live amongst us? He will kill her himself in order to do what must be done. You've heard the whispers amongst the leaves, Adeline. You know he is running out of time…"

"Enough, Kieran. I am tired of hearing your whining voice," Adeline ordered. Her own voice was sharper than the talons on her fingers.

She said nothing more as she closed the small gap between herself and Kieran. Slowly, she trailed her long, pale fingers along his rigid shoulder, gently caressing the nape of his neck. Adeline bought her mouth to his ear, smelling the panic that rose from his taut body.

"You are the fool, Kieran," she whispered, ignoring the barely audible whimper that left his mouth as her fingers dug into his neck, gripping tighter. "I know what I am doing. Do not forget that."

Barely a second passed, but the sound of Adeline snapping Kieran's neck was loud amongst the silent Fae who stood behind, none daring to speak. Kieran's limp body fell to the ground in a crumpled heap at Adeline's bare feet.

"The consequences of questioning my actions," she said.

Her voice held no remorse as she turned to face the others. "*Aria* was the girl's mother."

There was a sudden outburst of muffled voices, but Adeline did not falter in her stance. She continued to stare down at the Fae who stood before her.

"*Aria*?" someone gasped. "Princess Aria of the Unseelie Court is that girl's *mother*? Your Majesty, that means…"

"Evie Gray is *my* Grandchild," she said sharply. "And a Princess of the Unseelie Court by birth right. My *darling* Aria bought shame upon our Court when she fell in love with a witch, but in doing so, she gave birth to the rarest phenomenon our world has ever known.

"The magic that runs through her veins is one of the strongest known to the Fae," she said. "Her magic alone will heal our King. It will heal our people. King Naida will see the importance of allowing her to live. He will see, in time, that he will harness the ancient elements of the Fae, but Evie Gray must live. It is imperative that she *lives*."

***

The corridor of Wilmington University reeked of burning flesh. Thick green slime splattered the walls, oozing a revolting trail as it dripped onto the floors. Evie wiped her sweat-slicked hands against her trousers.

It was the fourth demon she'd killed since she and Jack had entered the university, and they were still no closer to finding the others. She swore in frustration as a loud, wraith-like screech exploded throughout the halls.

"Gods will these demons just give it a rest already," she snapped.

"The Dark Prince must know we are here," Jack said, edging her along the corridor. "Come on, we need to find the others fast…"

"I'm afraid you're too late for that," Christian's mocking voice was sharp and teasing. "We have been waiting for you."

Both lifted their heads, and Evie could not ignore the surge of fury that trickled through her body as she met with Christian's amused eyes.

"You survived then," Jack seethed through gritted teeth as Christian came into sight.

Christian laughed. "Of course," he said. "Did you really think I would be left to die? You underestimate The Dark Prince. You should join us. Save yourself all this hassle."

"I'd rather die," he barked.

"That can easily be arranged, Saunders," Christian growled.

A red spark suddenly shot through the corridor, hitting Jack's chest with a sharp thud. He fell to the ground, gasping as Evie screamed his name, but before she could reach down to him, her arms were suddenly bound behind her back.

She twisted her head, and her eyes widened as she met the empty blackness of a demon. She struggled against the creature's strong hold, but the more she fought, the tighter his scaly fingers became.

"What have you done to him?" she screamed, her eyes widening as they fell onto Jack's motionless body.

"Just a simple stunning spell. He'll live… for now," Christian mocked. He tilted his head towards the demon that held Evie, "Bring her. Leave him there."

The demon dragged Evie along the corridor, its sharp nails digging into her skin. She twisted her head, feeling her heart clench beneath her chest as she eyed Jack's unmoving body.

Please don't be dead.

Please don't be dead.

The demon continued to drag her along the corridor, following Christian through a pair of double doors that stood open at the end of the hall.

Once inside, the door slammed shut, and Evie felt the coldest of shivers trickle down the length of her spine as she met The Dark Prince's red glare.

"We meet again." The Dark Prince's voice was as sharp as glass.

"If Jack dies, I swear to the Gods, I will *kill* each and every one of you." Evie spat, fighting against the demons hold.

The Dark Prince smiled widely.

"No one else needs to die today," he said quietly. "Give me what I want, and I will release you and your friends. Allow me to harness the Fae magic. Let me take it. I will allow you to walk away…"

"Why should I trust you?" she said. "You're nothing but a liar and a murderer. All those people you killed, for what? What reason? They were innocent!"

"No one is innocent in this world, I can assure you of that," he said. "We all have dark secrets that we want to keep hidden. Your parents, for example. They kept *you* a secret for years, but they were fools. They didn't see the bigger picture."

"My parents were good people," she said. "My mother saved my life. I know she did."

"Maybe she did," he said thoughtfully. "But it wasn't her choice to make, was it?"

"Well, I couldn't have chosen, I was a baby!" she roared. "And my birth mother? Pretty sure that she didn't have a voice to make a *choice* either, because someone took that away from

394

her!"

"Your birth mother," he mused, and his expression changed as his eyes closed for the briefest of seconds. "I remember her well…"

Evie paused, contemplating his words.

"You… *you* knew who she was?" she asked.

He nodded. "Oh yes, I knew her very well," he replied. "She did not deserve to die, but Anna did what she had to do."

"What?" Evie mouthed.

"*Anna* killed the Fae who gave birth to you because she wanted *you*. Now you see, Evie, no one is innocent in this world."

"You're *lying*!" she screamed at him, pulling at the demon's grasp. "My mother was not a murderer! She would never…"

The Dark Prince rose from his seat, and as he did, Elijah stood with him. Evie's eyes fell onto her brother, and she noted a look of panic in his black eyes. She gasped as The Dark Prince placed his long, pale fingers onto the side of her face. His hand felt cold, and she grimaced at his touch.

"I am many things Evie Gray," he said, and she could hear the threat of pure evil in his voice. "Shall we begin?"

The Dark Prince closed his eyes, and his hand grew tighter against her face as he began to chant. His voice was slow as he spoke.

Evie screamed as the magic in her veins erupted.

Chapter Forty-Nine

Elijah stood with his arms folded across his chest, watching intently as The Dark Prince chanted his spell.

He listened to his sister's torturous screams and felt his heart thunder beneath his chest. He could smell and hear the fear in her voice, and a smile spread across his gaunt face.

How long had he waited for this moment? To finally stand and watch the one who had taken everything from him suffer. A wave of unrelenting hatred seared through Elijah as her screams shattered through his tormented mind.

***

Evie struggled against the demonic chains, fighting tirelessly with all her will to escape.

Darkness penetrated her mind, and after a moment, she could see nothing but a vivid blackness as her eyes became clouded by The Dark Prince's spell. Pain seared through her body, racing towards her dangerously thundering heart and a tidal wave of magic threatened to overwhelm her.

She felt her magic swimming through her veins, surging wildly as it neared the surface, eager to reach the words that called to it.

He was close, and Evie felt herself slowly drown within herself. His words were like a wicked poison. Calling for her magic to join with his. She felt weaker. Powerless to stop the inevitable.

The Dark Prince was too strong. His magic too powerful for her to even begin to contemplate. He was going to win.

And she… she was going to die…

"I thought you would have realised by now…"

Adeline's musical voice echoed throughout the small room, and Evie felt her body seize at the sound. "It isn't going to work, Matthew."

"I do not recall inviting the Fae here tonight," he growled.

The black cloud that had filled Evie's eyes suddenly began to lift as The Dark Prince removed his long, pale fingers from her temples. Slowly, her eyes refocused, but her body remained weak.

Adeline stood at the back of the room, her beautiful face, sharp and livid, but her bright, yellow eyes were full of energy and wicked intent.

"Give me the girl, and I shall leave peacefully," Adeline said quietly. "We have both suffered losses today, Matthew. Let us not lose anymore."

"Why do you call me by that name?" he hissed. "That man is no longer of this world, Adeline. He died a very long time ago."

Adeline smiled. "Our *true* selves never really die, Matthew," she said. "A part of him will always live deep within you, despite whatever dark magic you have used to tarnish your mortal soul."

The Dark Prince stood motionless for a moment as his eyes fell onto the two Fae soldiers on either side of Adeline.

"What is it you want, Adeline?"

"The girl," she said. "You know as well as I do, she belongs with us. Your spell will not work, Matthew. You are wasting your time."

"It will work," he said. "It is my destiny. The magic that runs through her veins is mine. I have spent years... *waiting*. The things I have done... the magic I have harnessed... is nothing compared to the magic that lives within this child. It belongs to me, Adeline. Now stand aside... "

Adeline sighed. "You're a fool, Matthew," she told him. "King Naida is still *very* angry with you. I should summon him here and allow him to enact his revenge for the pain and suffering you caused to my people. To my Court. But first, I think Evie should be enlightened with the tale, don't you?"

"What are you talking about?" Evie gasped.

Her voice barely a whisper as she tried to gain control over her body. The burnout was excruciating.

"I'm talking about *Aria*," Adeline said, mournfully. "My beautiful Aria. She was my daughter. So full of life and adventure, but she was a rebellious little Fae. She was never quite *content* with the life we lived. When she turned of age, she took it upon herself to leave the Land of Wonder... an *adventure* she called it, but she ended up in the one place that was forbidden to the Fae... The Enchanted Forest. Even to this day, I do not know *how* she managed to step foot in that wretched land.

"But she was forever breaking the rules and finding ways of displeasing her father. *You* remind me of her, Evie. Aria was stubborn, just like you."

"Why are you telling me this?" Evie asked.

"Because you must know the truth," she replied. "Aria fell in love with a man who promised to protect her. Promised to keep her safe amongst his people, and with his protection she could live the life she'd always dreamed of. But she was a fool. She believed the lie and fell under the wicked spell. She disgraced our court by spilling our secrets. Precious Aria..."

"I don't understand..."

"Aria was the princess who broke all the rules, Evie,"

398

Adeline snarled. "She fell in love with a monster, yet in doing so, she gave birth to the rarest phenomenon...*you*. You are the child born of Fae and witch. The most powerful combination to ever walk this earth, and the rarest. You have *no idea* how important you are."

"No..." Evie stammered, fighting back the surge of angry tears that threatened her eyes. "No... no... no..."

"*Matthew* was the witch who impregnated Aria."

There was no amusement in her voice now.

Only anger. Pure, relentless, anger.

"He promised her the world in order to get what he wanted, but his plan failed, didn't it Matthew? So blinded by the idea of harnessing the ancient magic of the Fae, you did not see that Aria was already on to your plan. She knew exactly what would happen once the child was born. She entrusted her secret with the Seelie Queen, and together they cast a spell to protect the child from *you*. So, you see Matthew, you will never harness the Fae magic, because *this* girl remains under the *protection* of the Seelie Queen."

"No!" Evie screamed. "NO! It can't be... THAT MONSTER IS NOT MY FATHER!"

"The Fae do not lie," Adeline said. "Everything I have told you; it is the truth. Aria was your mother. I am your grandmother, and *you* are a princess of the Unseelie Court..."

"Stop! Stop it!" Evie cried, anger burning in her throat. "This isn't happening. You're lying!"

"Fae cannot lie you foolish girl!" Morgana spat bitterly and tilted his head to Adeline. "My Queen, we must summon the King, immediately!"

"Quiet, Morgana," Adeline ordered. "Evie, you must come with me, back to the Land of Wonder. It is the only place you will ever be safe. I will protect you, you have my word, but you must *choose* to come with us."

"No." Evie growled, biting back the tears that threatened to consume her.

The magic within her veins began to rage, burning every inch of her skin with great intensity. Her eyes widened, and the creatures that held onto her suddenly released their long, scaly fingers, shrieking as their demonic flesh melted to the floor.

Her body tingled as adrenaline surged, heating her entire core. She bought her hands forwards, feeling the dark wells of her magic as it caressed her fingers, thrashing wildly as it searched for its release. The darkness pushed at her core as she fought to control the magic that raged within her.

But she was losing control.

The windows suddenly shattered with a loud explosion, and a gust of wind rushed through the room. Manoeuvring her hands, Evie called to her wind element, forcing her magic to bind the Fae. She lifted her hands, and the Fae were lifted into the air before her.

For a moment, they were motionless, and Adeline's yellow eyes exploded with fury.

"Don't do this," Adeline warned.

Time seemed to stand still as the two locked gaze. The only sound audible, was that of her magic, singing its wicked melody beneath the veil of her mind.

Evie smiled, titling her head to the side.

"You killed my best friend," she said, her voice barely recognisable.

"I had no choice… " Adeline pleaded.

"Everyone has a choice," Evie snarled.

She raised her hands once more, ignoring the words that left Adeline's mouth as her power surged once more, blasting the Fae into the starless night.

Evie turned towards The Dark Prince, and shuddered as she met his menacing stare.

"I am sorry that it must end like this," he said quietly. "I was a fool to underestimate the Princess. I should have realised a mother's love is stronger than any kind of magic. We could have made the perfect team, you, and I..."

"You're a *monster*." Evie sobbed, as a ball of fire appeared in her trembling palm.

"Are you going to kill me, Evie?" he taunted. "Your own father? You're much too weak..."

The fireball blasted through the air, hitting The Dark Prince square in the chest. He fell to the floor as Elijah screamed, throwing himself down beside him.

Evie didn't wait. She turned on her heel, and ran out of the room, running as fast as she could along the silent corridors. She stopped as she neared the canteen, clutching her chest as a searing pain ran through her.

She could hardly breathe as she lifted her head. She saw her reflection in the glass pane of a classroom door and screamed at her reflection. The Dark Prince's cold face stared back at her, and without another thought, she punched her fist through the glass, cursing as it shattered. Evie pulled her hand back, squirming as fresh blood trickled over her fingers, and clenched her fist.

"Poor little Evie Gray."

Lydia's voice was sharp and taunting as she and Julias stalked forwards. Evie lifted her head, feeling her body freeze. They weren't alone. Several other Guardians followed closely behind Lydia and Julias.

"Come any closer, and I swear on the Guard, I will kill you!" Evie warned.

Lydia laughed coldly. "Kill me?" she smiled. "You don't have it in you."

"You underestimate me," Evie seethed. "I just blasted your precious Prince with my flames, and I would be extremely happy to do the same to you assholes too."

"What did you say?" Lydia's voice stammered as she turned to look at Julias.

"You heard me," she growled.

"Julias, take the others and find The Dark Prince," Lydia ordered. "I will watch over the brat."

Julias nodded and signalled for the Guardian's to follow him. Lydia tilted her head back to Evie and pursed her lips.

"Your hand looks very painful, but I am sure it's nothing compared to the pain you will feel when The Dark Prince finally gets his hands on you."

"I guess you were too late for *that* party," she scowled.

"What are you talking about?" Lydia said.

"The Dark Prince has already tried… and failed… to harness the Fae magic," Evie said.

"You are a lying little bitch," Lydia hissed.

"Get the hell out of my way, Lydia."

"I don't think so," Lydia said, raising her hand forwards.

Evie darted to the floor, rolling onto her side as Lydia's spell blasted along the corridor. She raised her own hand, gasping as roots erupted from the ground, snaking their way towards Lydia. Her earth element moved at a deathly pace towards its target.

Lydia screamed as the roots engulfed her, wrapping around her body like a vice.

Evie did not hang around a second longer as she hurtled past Lydia's struggling figure.

Chapter Fifty

The sound of muffled voices penetrated her ears as Evie turned yet another corner, and as panic filled her, she slowed her pace, panting.

Her hand throbbed, oozing with fresh blood. She needed to heal the wound. The smell of blood made her stomach violently churn. Evie stepped forwards, and noticed a familiar golden glow, emitting from a set of double doors at the end of the corridor.

Relief rushed through her, and she found herself running towards the door. The second she neared it, the doors burst open, and Evie hurtled herself inside.

She fell to the floor, gasping as the doors slammed shut behind her. Several voices screamed her name, but her mind blocked them out, focusing on the one voice that she was so desperate to hear.

"Evie." Jack fell to the floor beside her, gripping each side of her face with his hands.

"You're alive." She sobbed, gripping him. "I thought…"

"Ssh," he said, forcing her eyes to his. "We're safe. You're safe."

Jack pulled her towards him, and Evie winced as he caught her hand.

"My hand," she cried.

"Rebecca!" Jack shouted, turning his head behind him.

Several figures hurried forwards, some of which Evie

recognised, but there were also six unfamiliar faces who now stood around them. Rebecca knelt down, lifting Evie's hand into her own.

"How on earth did you escape?" she asked as she held her other hand over the wound. A bright, white pearly glow erupted from her palm, and Evie felt an instant relief as the blood began to disappear.

"I…" Evie began but couldn't find the words. She felt weak and disorientated, and her head throbbed. She wanted to lie down, to forget the world and everything that had just happened.

"What happened?" Jack asked. "When they took you? Tell us everything. Where is The Dark Prince now?"

"He's… he's…" she stammered. "Jack, I can't…"

"Ssh, it's all right," he said as Rebecca moved aside. "Just take your time. We have enchanted this room. Only we can enter. We are safe here, for now. You are safe, I promise."

Evie nodded and turned her head towards the others in the room. A man with chestnut brown hair, and a pair of familiar, piercingly blue eyes stared at her with great intensity, and after a few moments, his face broke out into a friendly smile.

"Hello, Evie," he said.

"Evie," Jack said, "I'd like you to meet my dad, Marc."

"Your dad?" Evie said, confused. "I thought your parents were in Australia?"

"We were," said the woman who stood next to Marc.

She had a soft face, and her hair had been scraped into a tight bun behind her head. She smiled as she took hold of Marc's hand.

"We came back the minute we discovered what was happening back home. I am just so sorry we didn't get to you sooner. Unfortunately, we could not trust The Guardians with our travel arrangements. By the time we arrived at the safe haven, it

404

had already been destroyed. I'm Penny by the way. Jack's mom."

"It's nice to meet you both," Evie said, and slowly, with Jack's help, she stood.

Tessa, Cora, Lucas, and Zac stepped forwards, and Cora threw her arms around her. They took it in turns to hug each other, and when they were done, Evie felt the panic within her begin to ease a little. They were in the sports hall, and as she glanced around, she noticed the same golden glow that she had seen outside the hall.

"Come sit down," Tessa said softly. "You look exhausted."

"Story of my life," Evie replied. She felt drained after using so much of her magic. "When did everyone get here? How did *you* guys escape?"

"The demons who captured us weren't exactly the smartest," Tessa said. "Lucas stunned them, and we made our way here. Rebecca and Tom were already here, with Jack's family... that's his sister over there."

Evie followed her gaze, and her eyes fell onto a girl who was stood at the back of the room, talking rapidly into her cell phone. She was tall, and like Jack, she too had chestnut brown hair. Her slim figure was dressed in black fighting gear, and her posture oozed the same confidence as Cora.

"Are your parents here?" Evie asked, turning her head away from Jack's sister.

"Yeah, they're here," Tessa replied. "My dad is real pissed at The Guardians. I've never seen him so angry!"

"The Guardians betrayed us all. He has every right to be pissed off."

"Not all of us."

Evie looked up and was surprised to see four people standing in front of them. Three of the faces she recognised; Lucille

Bartholomew, Gideon Hobbs, and Hugo Peterson, but the fourth, a man, with a silvery grey beard, and an elderly, but sharp face, she did not.

"Evie Gray," he said. "I am Barnabas Elsmere. You may know me as Barny."

"You're The Elders,' she said, feeling a burst of angst explode within her.

"I am deeply sorry for the betrayal you have experienced," he said. "Mark my words, those involved will face severe punishment. Myself and my fellow Elders are here to provide protection and assistance. We want to help you."

"Okay," she said. "But you might change your mind after you hear what I have to tell you."

"What are you talking about?" Jack asked.

Inhaling a deep breath, Evie sighed.

"Jack, can you gather everyone? I need to tell you all something."

***

"This is impossible!"

The Elders stood grouped together, watching intently as Tom paced back and forth. Evie stood beside Jack, her head throbbing as she replayed the conversation in her mind.

As expected, there had been an uproar of shock and horror as Evie told the others the tale, and she now stood with her back against the wall, desperately trying to forget the horrified faces of her friends.

She felt sick to her stomach.

"Thomas will you please calm down!" Rebecca almost yelled. "This isn't helping anyone. *Especially* Evie."

"Rebecca, you don't understand, this changes everything!" he said. "Matthew Blaise is The Dark Prince! He was terrible as a mortal."

"Who *is* Matthew Blaise?" Zac asked.

"A Guardian who went rogue," Marc answered. "He was part of *our* Circle, back in our day. We always knew he was trouble, but we didn't expect him to do what he did. We all thought Blaise was dead. He disappeared after the Fae war."

"He was part *of your* Circle?" Tessa mouthed. "The Dark Prince was a Guardian Warrior, like us?"

Marc nodded.

"He was, and he was a good warrior, until he started meddling with dark magic," he said. "This is bad. Evie, what else did the Queen tell you."

"I've told you everything I know," she said quietly. "I'm sorry, I know how terrible this is. Believe me, nobody feels as disgusted as I do right now... I..."

"Evie," Tessa began.

"Don't Tessa," she said. "Nothing you say will make this any better."

"Evie, you didn't choose your parents."

Jack's sister stalked towards her and reached for her hand. "*You* saved my brother's life. You risked your own life to ensure that his was protected, and for that my family and I will be forever grateful. I see how much you mean to him, and he to you. It doesn't matter who's blood runs through your veins, Evie. What matters is that *we* know who you are. You are a part of The Circle and a Guardian Warrior. A true Guardian, always remember that."

"Molly is right," Jack said. "This doesn't change anything, Evie."

"It changes everything, Jack," she said.

"It changes *nothing*," he pressed. "We will all fight to protect you, do you understand. Everyone in this room is on our side. We will fight, and we will win."

"I'm sorry," Tom said suddenly. "Evie, I am sorry, please forgive me. What you have just told us… it was a lot to comprehend. Please, do not think for one second that this changes anything. I just… Matthew Blaise…"

"Is a monster. I know," she said. "We might have an advantage on our side. When Matthew tried to harness the magic, it was painful, but nothing happened because I am protected by the Seelie Queen."

"The Seelie Queen?" Tom gasped. "What does the Seelie Queen have to do with this?"

"This is where it gets complicated," Evie said. "The Fae who gave birth to me, her name was Aria. She was *Adeline's* daughter, that is why I have a connection with Adeline. When Aria found out about Matthew's plan, she went to the Seelie Queen for help. She *wanted* to protect me, and she did. The Dark Prince can't harness my magic."

"Why would the Seelie Queen help a Princess of the Unseelie Court?" Zac asked.

"I don't know," Evie said quietly. "But I have to find out. It could help us."

"What good will that do?" Jack asked.

"Aria was my birth mother Jack," she said. "She knew what Matthew… The Dark Prince, whatever you want to call him, was up to. She knew what he truly wanted, and she *went* to the Seelie Queen for help. Aria *wanted* to protect me. I have to know why. Why didn't she go to Adeline? She purposely chose to go against her own people and sought help from their enemy. That has to mean something."

"Maybe she thought the Unseelie King would kill her if he knew about you?" Lucas said. "King Naida is cruel; he would never have allowed her to keep the child of a witch."

Evie shook her head. "No," she said. "He already knew she was pregnant, and he knew the father was a witch. Adeline said so, anyway. I don't understand why Aria would ask the Seelie Queen for help."

"This *is* complicated." Tom blew out a frustrated sigh. "Let us start from the beginning. We all knew Blaise was meddling with dark magic, but when the Fae war broke out, he slipped from our radar, and the next thing we knew he was dead. Or so we thought. Aria must have been a pawn in his plan, but it didn't work. He underestimated her. Whatever spell she and the Seelie Queen cast upon you clearly worked."

"But why did he want the Fae magic in the first place?" Lucas asked. "If he was already meddling with dark magic?"

"That is the worrying question," Tom said. "Blaise is already powerful. The elemental magic of the Fae is ancient and is the strongest to ever exist. It dates back thousands of years, Lucas, and as far as I am aware it hasn't been seen until now.

"I don't know what The Dark Prince plans, but I assure you, it won't be good," Tom said.

"We need to visit the Seelie Court," Evie said promptly.

"WHAT?" Jack exploded.

"Jack, we have to," she said. "The Seelie Queen helped Aria. I have to know why. Maybe she could help us too…"

"No, it's not happening," his voice was thunderous.

"Jack, we have to!" Evie protested. "This is just another piece of the puzzle, to my very fucked up life, that I have to solve. We have to see the Seelie Queen. She could have the answers to the questions we have. I need to know *why* she cast a protection spell over me. Why would the Seelie Queen help a Princess of the Unseelie Court, Jack? It makes no sense!"

"Evie is right," Molly said, edging forwards to stand beside her brother. "You said so yourself, Jack, this whole situation is crazy. Evie deserves to know the truth. We all do. And if that means we have to pay a little visit to the Seelie Court, then that is what we need to do."

"Don't encourage her, Molly," Jack warned fiercely. "We have enough to worry about *here* without planning a trip to the Land of Wonder. It's just another disaster waiting to happen."

"Well, our current *situation* isn't exactly perfect," Evie said hurriedly. "I thought *you* of all people would understand. I've just learnt that the monster who you've all been trying so desperately hard to capture is actually my father. Do you know how sickening it is to hear that? Do you know how that makes me feel? No, you don't, because it's not your reality. It's mine."

"Evie," Jack began.

"Don't," she said, lowering her head as her eyes began to burn with angry tears "You have no idea how any of this feels Jack."

"It changes nothing," he said.

"Maybe we should all take a breather." Penny's voice was soft beside Evie, and she wrapped her arm around her shoulders, squeezing her slightly. "We can talk about this when our heads are a little clearer."

"There is nothing to talk about," Jack said sharply. "We aren't going to the Seelie Court."

He stormed away, stalking to the furthest side of the hall. Evie sighed, pulling out of Penny's grasp.

"He will come round," Molly said. "He's just worried, that's all."

"The last thing I wanted was *another* fight with him," Evie said, folding her arms across her chest.

"Come sit down," Molly said.

She reached for Evie's arm but before Molly's hand reached her, Evie suddenly jerked away. A mouth curdling scream followed as she gripped the purple pendant that hung loosely around her neck.

Chapter Fifty-One

Jack darted across the hall as Evie fell to the floor. Her hands clutching the side of her head. Her body shook rigorously as more screams escaped her mouth.

"Stand back!"

Barnabas stepped forwards, followed closely by the rest of The Elders.

"Jack, stand back," he repeated. "We must wait for her to return to us."

"What are you talking about?" Jack yelled over Evie's deafening screams.

"There is nothing we can do," he said. "This is Fae magic, Jack, we cannot meddle with what we do not know. Whatever, or whoever, is inside her head, we must wait until they leave. We cannot interfere."

"So, we just stand and watch?" he barked, and ignoring The Elders protests, knelt down placing himself in front of Evie.

He lifted his hand to her face, conscious of the many sets of eyes that watched.

"Fight it," he told her. "*You* control the magic not the other way round. Get them out of your head, you're stronger than this Evie!"

"It's horrible… Jack." She sobbed uncontrollably. "She didn't deserve… why? WHY?"

"Evie, fight it!" he demanded, forcing her eyes to look at his. "Please, Evie, you have to fight! You are in control!"

"Jack, what's happening to her?" Cora gasped, clutching at her own chest. "Do something! She's hurting so much; I can't stand it!"

"Evie, look at me!" Jack thundered. "Look at me! Only *you* can stop this!"

Evie closed her eyes, clenching her eyelids shut. She felt the warmth of Jack's hands against her own and shuddered slightly as his lips brushed against her ear. She could hear his voice, soft and familiar, grounding her.

"Jack," Evie rasped, and as her body weakened, she fell against him. "It's over."

Jack held her for a moment, pulling her tightly against his chest as the others stood around them. For a while, the room was silent, and the only audible sound was Evie's muffled sobs.

"Is she going to be okay?" Tessa asked.

"I..." Barny started but paused as his fellow Elders stepped forwards.

"The Fae magic that lives within her is very strong," Lucille said quietly.

"It wasn't the Fae," Evie said, and everyone turned to look at her.

"What do you mean?" Jack asked.

"It wasn't the Fae," she repeated.

"Evie what exactly did you see?" Rebecca asked.

"Aria," Evie said, and lifted her head. "I saw her die."

"What?" Jack exclaimed. "Evie you're making no sense!"

"He lied," she seethed. "The Dark Prince lied. He told me my mother killed Aria so that she could take me. But it wasn't her. Adeline killed Aria."

"Queen Adeline?" Barny said.

Evie nodded, feeling the anger rise within her.

"Adeline killed her daughter. *My birth mother.* Then she tried to kill me," she said. "The protection spell stopped her."

"Okay, this is really starting to get confusing," Cora said, eyes widening. "Are you sure what you saw was *real?*"

"Why wouldn't it be real?" she asked. "Adeline wanted me to see the memory in the Land of Wonder because she wanted to gain my trust, and for a second it almost worked, didn't it?"

"So how did this happen tonight?" Cora asked. "How can we even believe it is true? I'm sorry, Evie, I'm just being cautious…"

"I understand," Evie said. "I don't know why I saw what I saw, and I don't know *who* wanted me to see it… I just know it happened when I touched my necklace."

"Your necklace?" Lucille repeated. "May I see it?"

Evie nodded and watched as the Elder stalked towards her. Lucille stood before her, tilting her head slightly as her eyes examined the purple pendant that hung around Evie's neck.

"Where did you get this?" Lucille asked.

"It was a gift," Evie said. "From my parents. I've had it for as long as I can remember. Why?"

"And has anything like this ever happened before?"

"No," Evie said.

"The necklace you wear is enchanted," Lucille said.

"Enchanted?" Evie repeated. "Enchanted by who? What do you mean?"

"The pendant is not of this world," she said. "To be honest, I've never seen anything like it other than in the descriptions of old texts. I believe the stone was a gift given to the first Queen of the Fae, many centuries ago. It is blessed with magic that allows the stone to hold memories."

"Memories?" Evie said. "I don't understand…"

"Aria," Tessa said. "Evie, of course! The Fae you saw in the

414

Land of Wonder… that was *Aria*! It had to be! Your necklace… perhaps it belonged to her!"

"And she entrapped her final memory within the stone?" Evie said.

Tessa nodded. "It would make sense," she said. "For all we know, she could have left the necklace with you before your mum took you."

"We need to go to the Seelie Court," Evie said sharply, regaining her strength as she looked at the others. "It's the only place we are going to get answers."

"And what about The Dark Prince? What about Adeline?" Jack snarled. "Have you forgotten about them? Do you not remember what happened the last time we were in the Land of Wonder? We could be walking straight into a trap…"

"Always *Mr Negative*." Molly rolled her eyes. "Have *you* considered the idea that the Seelie Queen *might* want to be on our side? She helped Aria, who was an Unseelie Princess."

"Molly, you're really not helping," he said, and there was a razor-sharp bite to his tone. "Look, we have enough to deal with here. Our mission is to stop The Dark Prince and send the Unseelies back to the hell hole they came from. We can't afford to venture off into the Fae realm on the basis that the Seelie Queen *might* want to help. It isn't worth the risk. We need to stay here and figure out a way to stop what is happening."

"I need answers, Jack," Evie said. "My life is a puzzle and most of the pieces are missing. The Dark Prince wants my magic for reasons only the Gods can imagine. He *started* this. He knew what would happen if a child was to be born of witch and Fae heritage. He *knew* that I would have these abilities.

"We aren't going to find out *why* by staying here, Jack," she said. "We need to go to the Seelie Court and speak with the

Queen. There is *a reason* why she helped Aria."

"I don't like this, Evie," he said.

"None of us *like* it, Jack," she cried. "None of us like the shit storm that our life has become. Look at us! We are Guardians, and we are *hiding*. Adeline murdered her own daughter. She tried to kill me, Jack. The Dark Prince is a monster, and we are blinded. Whatever he plans to do with my magic won't be good. You know that. I know that. He won't stop until he gets it. This magic is dangerous, Jack, and we need help."

Jack sighed, and she could see the struggle in his eyes.

"We will have to go back to The Academy," he said after a few moments.

"I know," she said, and glanced at Hayden. "We used the portal when we were looking for you."

Jack nodded. "We will go at sunrise," he said. "There will be too much demonic activity tonight."

"Thank you," she said.

Jack said nothing and turned away from her.

Evie watched as he joined Hayden, Lucas, and Zac, and she felt a bile of anxiety rush through her.

He was angry with her, that much was obvious. The thought of going back to the Land of Wonder terrified her, but the idea of discovering more about her past, about *Aria*, fuelled her with a strength she did not know existed.

The Dark Prince was injured, and she did not know *where* Adeline and the rest of the Fae had gone, but she did know they would be back, and soon.

The Seelie Queen had gone against everything by helping a Princess of the Unseelie Court, but why?

Why was her magic so dangerous? And what did The Dark Prince have planned?

So many questions and so few answers. Evie sighed, stretching her legs out in front of her. Every inch of her body ached, and her stomach roared with hunger. She looked down at her hand, and although Rebecca had done well healing it, the wound still felt sore.

"Hey, you home?"

Evie lifted her head, surprised to see Molly and Penny both staring down at her.

"I'm sorry?" she said.

"I said we have somewhere to sleep, thanks to Tessa and Lucas," Molly said, and twisted round to point to the back of the hall. Several sleeping bags were dotted across the floor, and the smell of hot cocoa drifted through the air. Evie felt her stomach rumble.

"I don't think I could, even if I tried." She sighed, lowering her head.

"We are safe in here, take advantage of it and try to get some rest. We will need our strength." Molly smiled.

Evie nodded briefly; her eyes focused on Jack. He stood on the far side of the room, talking in depth with his father and Hayden.

"I should speak to Jack," she said, biting her lip.

Evie stood up and after a quiet goodbye, she walked across the hall.

Jack twisted his head as she approached, but he quickly returned his attention back to Hayden and his father. Evie stood with her arms by her side, and for a moment she felt awkward. She could feel his anger radiating from his rigid posture.

"Are you alright?" Marc asked.

"I think so," she said, and with a heavy breath, she added, "Do you mind if I steal Jack from you for a moment?"

"Go ahead," Marc replied, and she saw Jack's posture stiffen even more. "We'll give you both some privacy."

Hayden nodded his head to her, and quickly followed Marc.

"I feel as though we have had this conversation a hundred times already," she said after a few moments. "I know you're angry. I know you don't agree with my plan, but for once, could you just see it from my point of view? So much has happened since I came back from London. My whole life has been turned upside down not once, but twice, and I have no idea who I am anymore.

"I need you to understand, Jack, because I can't do this without you. I am sorry if I have put you in a position that you don't want to be in. I'm sorry that we have yet another puzzle to solve, but I have to do this. I need to find out the truth about my magic... about who I really am. Everything about my life is a lie, Jack. My parents lied to me. I don't know who I am anymore, and it is killing me. I have the blood of a monster running through my veins and it disgusts me. It disgusts everyone in this room. I can see it in their faces, despite what they say."

She paused, willing him to say something, but he remained silent.

"I know we are taking a huge risk by going back to the Land of Wonder," she said. "I don't know what we will find there. The Seelie Queen could refuse to talk to us, let alone help us. But I have to go. I have to, because of Aria. She knowingly went against her own people and sought help from an enemy, to protect *me*. That has to mean something. Will you just say something, please?"

"You've made your decision," was all he said.

Stung, Evie flinched as he walked away. His body was tense as he pulled a sleeping bag to the other side of the room, and she

418

watched as he kicked off his boots before pulling his shirt over his head. She wanted nothing more than to run over to him and wrap herself in his arms, but the look she had seen in his eyes stopped her.

Instead, she walked over to Tessa and Cora, and pulled her own sleeping bag towards her.

"He will calm down," Cora whispered.

"I doubt it," Evie said. "He's furious. I just wish he would understand."

"He does understand, which is exactly why he's reacting the way he is," she replied. "Our first trip to the Land of Wonder wasn't exactly plain sailing, was it? He's afraid. We all are. He loves you, Evie. You have to understand how hard this is for him, too. None of us can predict what the Seelie Queen will do or say. We are about to step into unknown territory, and the uncertainty is frightening.

"Everyone in this room is on your side, Evie, and we all want to do the right thing, but you need to understand, it's difficult. Jack is struggling right now, but he won't tell you that, because he knows how much you want to discover the truth, and deep down, he wants that for you too. He just doesn't want to see you get hurt."

"Maybe this whole idea is a mistake," she said. "I am so desperate to find answers. I haven't even thought about the risk we are about to take."

Cora shook her head. "No," she said. "I don't think we are making a mistake. The Seelie Court is where we will find answers, Evie. I know it."

"Do you really think so?"

"Yes. I do. Go and speak to Jack," she ordered. "Cast a silencing spell over you both, and you can talk in private. None of us will hear or see you."

"And if we end up killing each other?" Evie said, and Cora rolled her eyes. "I don't think he wants to talk to me right now, Cora," Evie added.

"Well, I don't care what *he* wants. Go and *make* him talk to you," she ordered.

***

Evie stood up, and with an encouraging smile from Cora, she made her way across the hall towards Jack. As she neared him, she drew in a deep breath and whispered the silencing spell, watching anxiously as a silvery glimmer encircled the two of them.

Jack looked up as the enchantment settled around them, but his face showed no emotion as their eyes finally locked. Evie paused for a moment, her mind reeling with unspoken words.

"You should get some sleep," he said quietly.

"How do you expect me to sleep?" she asked. "We need to talk, Jack, but you won't even look at me for longer than a second."

"Don't be ridiculous," he said.

"Talk to me then," she said. "Tell me everything that is on your mind. I need to know what you're thinking."

"I can't stop you from going back to the Land of Wonder, and I won't stop you," he said. "I understand you wanting to know the truth. The Seelie Queen might have helped Aria, but you have to remember, *she* is just as dangerous as Adeline and the others. I don't know what tomorrow will bring, but the thought of losing you is tearing me apart. I want you to learn the truth about who you are, Evie, really, I do, but I don't want...

420

I've already lost you once."

"Jack." She sighed and moved closer to him.

Her hands reached for his face, and he tilted his head against her palms.

"I love you, Jack. You are the most important person in my life, and I don't want to hurt you, which is exactly what I am doing, and I am sorry. It was never my intention to hurt you."

Sighing, Jack closed his eyes, and after a few moments, Evie saw the tension in his shoulders begin to fade. He opened his eyes as he wrapped his arm around her lower back, tugging her against his chest.

"I'm sorry," Evie cried.

His other hand reached for her chin, and his calloused fingers slowly tilted her head upwards forcing her eyes onto his own.

"Don't cry," he whispered against her ear.

"I'm sorry," she said.

Jack smiled. "Are you apologising for crying?" he said.

"I don't know. Maybe," she replied. "Jack, we don't have to go back to the Land of Wonder. Our mission is to stop The Dark Prince, and that is what we should be focusing on. It was a stupid idea…"

"No, it wasn't," Jack said. "Evie, I act the way I do because I care about you, and I don't want to see you hurt. These past few weeks have been a nightmare for all of us, and we have all watched your life literally turn upside down. You deserve answers, and you deserve to know the truth about your birth mother and your past. I want you to find your answers, and if that means we go back to the Land of Wonder, then that is what we will do."

"The Seelie Queen could refuse to help me," she said. "Then it would have all been for nothing."

"None of us know what the Seelie Queen will do," he said.

"The Seelie Court has not been seen since the Fae war, Evie. We don't know how the Queen will react to us. The Guardians gave the Seelies their freedom, but we don't know what deal *they* had to make in order to gain that freedom.

"The Queen has already used her magic to protect *you* from the Unseelie Court and The Dark Prince. I won't stand here and tell you that I'm happy about us going back to the Land of Wonder, but I also won't stand in your way."

"Do you think it's supposed to happen this way?" Evie asked. "Us going back there, I mean. All this started in the Land of Wonder. Maybe it's supposed to end there too."

"I don't know," he answered honestly. "Maybe."

Evie nodded and pulled away from him slightly as she wiped her eyes. "Jack, can I ask you something?"

"Sure," he said.

"Do you trust me?"

"Of course I trust you," he said fiercely. "Why would you even ask a question like that?"

"Because we just found out that I am the daughter of a monster," she said, and stepped further away from him. "My blood is tainted with darkness Jack, and I don't know how to deal with it. You saw what happened by the lake… I lost control. I could *feel* the darkness spreading through my body. I almost killed my brother…"

"He was going to kill you, Evie," Jack said. "The only reason I stopped you was because I didn't want you to have that on your conscience. The blood in your veins does not define who you are. *I* know who you are, and I trust you with my life. You have a pure heart. You are *nothing* like them, do you hear me?"

"I don't think you get it," she said. "I *wanted* to kill him, Jack. Every inch of my body felt so much hatred towards him. I have never felt anything like it before, but it all makes sense now. I'm scared Jack."

Jack moved towards her, pulling her back into his arms. At first, Evie resisted, but after a few moments she stopped fighting.

"I know who you are," he told her. "You're Evie Alyssa Gray, and you are the bravest person I know. You are a true Guardian, Evie. I don't care whose blood you share. It doesn't define you. I love you, and I will love you until the day I die, and nothing will ever change that. Everyone in this hall is here because they want to be here. We will figure this out, I promise you."

"Jack," she whispered. Her tired eyes filled with more tears as Jack rested his hand against her cheek, wiping an escaped tear with his thumb.

"I trust you, Evie," he said. "You are nothing like them."

"How can you be so sure?" she cried.

"Because I have never been surer of anything in my life," he said, wiping away the tears that fell with his thumb. "We are going to get through this. Today, tomorrow, and the many days that lay ahead of us. I promise I will always be by your side. Your heritage…it changes nothing. I love you, Evie. We will figure this out. Together."

Evie smiled weakly, her mind absorbing the words he spoke. His brilliant blue eyes bore into her own, and she treasured the glistening sight as he pressed his lips to her forehead.

"Together," she repeated, holding on to his words as she rested her head against his chest.

Together.

Always together.

Her magic stirred within her, a wicked melody reminding her of its presence as Jack wound his arms tighter around her trembling body. Evie closed her eyes, breathing in his intoxicating scent.

She would find out the truth. She would find the missing pieces to her puzzle.

Every. Last. One.

She'd learn how to control her magic. How to live with the darkness that now sung to her soul.

And when she did, she would use it to end them all.

Epilogue

The smell of lavender and warm honey filled the late morning air as she strolled across the spongy, moss-covered path.

Music, and a gentle pouring of excited laughter echoed throughout the court, and she could not help but smile as a group of Seelie children danced merrily beside her. The children giggled and waved before they hurried away into the luscious green fields that surrounded the path she walked.

She could see the White Castle in the distance, looming magnificently into view, its turrets sparkling beneath the blisteringly hot sun. Her heart raced as she walked along a cobbled path, leaving behind the spongy moss as she sauntered into the grounds.

Seelie soldiers stood either side of the path. They wore tunics of deep purple that were embroidered with a delicate gold thread, and each radiated with pure Fae elegance.

She brushed off her sudden feeling of unease and walked through the golden gates that would take her to the Queen of the Seelie Court.

Inside, the castle bellowed with deep richness. Its white-washed walls were covered with portraits of previous Seelie Kings and Queens, each protected by solid oak frames. The stone floor was masked by a luxuriously thick velvet rug, silencing her footsteps as she stepped further in.

The Seelie Queen clearly had an appreciation for the finer things in life. Her home was nothing like that of the Twisted

Castle. She shuddered at the thought of the wicked castle.

Of the Fae who walked its many halls.

A grand staircase welcomed her, and the sound of muffled voices told her where she needed to go. She climbed the stairs, taking her time as she made her way to the first floor.

The voices grew clearer as she reached the first-floor landing, and she followed the dimly lit corridor as far as it went. A large oak door stood at the end, guarded by a handsome Seelie guard. He was tall, and strongly built, with thick broad shoulders and a head of silver coloured hair. His amethyst-like eyes studied her carefully.

The guard grunted as she approached him, but said nothing as he pushed open the doors to allow her in.

A golden throne dominated the oval shaped room, and upon the throne sat the Queen of the Seelie Court.

The Queen radiated utter beauty, and had an elegant grace known only to the Fae. Her taut face echoed with youth despite the years she had dominated the throne. Like everyone else who resided within the Seelie Court, the Queen's eyes were a deep shade of purple, glowing as brightly as the pendent that hung loosely around her neck.

She wore a satin green dress that hung tightly to her delicate figure, falling gently to her ankles, and revealing a pair of tanned, bare feet. The Queen smiled, beckoning her forwards with a long, pointy finger. She did so, not quite aware of her feet moving at all. She stood a few feet in front of the throne, keeping her eyes fixed on the Seelie Queen.

"Well, isn't this a pleasant surprise. I did not expect to see *you*, daughter of the Unseelie Court," her lips pursed into a tight line. "You are either very brave, or very foolish, to come to the Seelie Court."

"Please," She said, finding the courage to speak. "I need

your help."

"I am not in the mood to help *anyone* today," she mused.

"Please… I came all this way…"

"Your own foolish choice." She pursed her lips once more, and for a brief moment, the Queen became lost in thought. "You have caused *quite* the stir, haven't you."

"Please help us…" she cried, clutching the bundle that lay in her arms.

The Queen frowned and sat forward in her throne.

"Why do you seek help from me?" she asked curiously, placing her hand beneath her bony chin. "Most would not dare to ask for help from the Seelie Queen, but then again, I suppose you are not most, are you."

"So I've been told," She said, casting a nervous glance around the room.

"Fear not. We are alone." The Queen smiled. "You are safe here. For now."

"I am not leaving without your help, Your Majesty."

"Is that so?" she mused.

"Yes." Her voice was defiant, despite the nerves that filled her.

"Unfortunately, I do not wish to involve myself in something which has nothing to do with me or my court…"

"It has everything to do with you, Arabella."

"You dare to speak my name?" the Queen's voice rose angrily. "You really must be a fool child…"

"I am *begging* you…"

The Queen released a heavy sigh before rolling her eyes.

"I must be going senile in my old age." The Queen's voice was as sharp as knives. "Very well. I will agree to help you… Under one condition."

"I will do *anything*," she cried.

The Queen smiled tauntingly, the sight sending a nervous shiver down Aria Thornewyre's spine, chilling her to the core, as the Queen rose to her feet and slowly stalked towards her, and the sleeping bundle that lay tucked against her chest.

The Story Continues...